The True Purpose of Vines

"A headstrong Portuguese winemaker meets her match in an arrogant Englishman who threatens her beloved vineyards. Dive deep into Portugal's rich culture in this intoxicating story about wine and love."

Giovanna Siniscalchi

ISBN 978-65-997410-9-8 (ebook)

Contents

I'm eternally grateful to my husband for his immense support in every tiny step of this delicious journey and my kid's patience and understanding. I must also thank my mentors, Lindsey Alexander and Jack Smith, for their gentle guidance and my lovely editor, Ceara Nobles.

Let's connect! Join my Wine and Love Club
for updates on The Winemaker's series.
https://giovannasiniscalchi.com

Click here to claim my gift for you, The Wedding
Surprise, book two in the Winemaker Series:
https://dl.bookfunnel.com/khuba4lsda

Once, a proud people lived on a frosty island where no grapevines grew. They found delicious wine in a sun-drenched land beyond the ocean and settled there to send this nectar to their homeland. These merchants built their lives on foreign soil and created a prosperous community separate from the native winemakers. For centuries, they shared this passionate livelihood but little else.

Until a boar and a tiny cicada invited them to share much more . . .

Chapter 1

Oporto, Portugal - June 1870

A gust of wind blew in from the sea. Members flocked inside the British Factory House, holding their top hats and flapping coats. They lived outside the motherland but could still enjoy a gentlemen's club as luxurious as White's in London.

Griffin left his hat and coat in the vestibule and entered the foyer. Light from two horse-sized chandeliers flashed on the arched ceiling. Voices and clinking glasses mingled with the pianist playing a sonata in the corner. All the British port-trading gentlemen were here. Some stood near the tall colonnades while others talked in groups, their black and white finery stark against the blue walls. Friends, passing acquaintances, competitors — all would give their left foot to be in Griffin's position. After courting Croft for a year, he would extract a yes from the wily fox.

Nothing could go wrong. Their partnership was a *fait accompli.*

Griffin's pulse hammered a staccato rhythm on the veins of his neck. He rolled his shoulders to release the tension as he scanned the crowd. Coat straining over his stomach, Croft chatted with Fladgate and Taylor. He looked like a benevolent sea lion with the points of his mustache curving down like ivory tusks. His appearance masked his ruthlessness in business. The man knew the value of things, be it wine, horses, or properties, and could bargain a fellow out of his trousers and sell it back to him for double the price.

They made eye contact, and Croft waved. Waiting to speak with him until after lunch would be as pleasant as shaving himself with a barbed wire. Griffin wrestled a place on the leather couch and hoisted the Times, scanning the London news.

He usually enjoyed the newspaper, as it arrived in Oporto only once a week, but today the headlines blurred. Failure crept into his thoughts, listing everything that could go wrong. Griffin shut his eyes, dispelling the unusual pessimism. Croft neared retirement. With no sons to assume his business, he had reason to value a partnership.

The upholstery dipped. "You know what would be grand? If my dear friend lent me the phaeton and his flashy team tomorrow."

Griffin lowered the paper a few inches and raised a brow. Charles Whitaker eyed him expectantly, his hair in disarray, sporting a bright yellow vest that clashed with his striped trousers. No doubt he had sailed from a night of debauchery straight into the Factory House.

Griffin lowered the paper. "Another race? After last time—"

"No, no! Not that. Your blacks put to shame any horseflesh in Oporto, and I mean to impress—"

"The *baroneza's* husband will kill you if the races won't."

Charles' affair had ended in a very public and embarrassing duel. Griffin abhorred expressions of passionate liaisons, be it drunken serenades or pistols at dawn. His mistresses needed to be desirable, but discreet. Let the Portuguese rant and rave about love. His life would never be ruled by such animal instincts.

Charles extracted a cigar from his pocket. "This isn't about Carmen. I promised Anita an outing to Sintra. You know her. The ballet dancer. Come with me tonight." He brightened. "She has this blonde roommate that does a marvelous *rond de jamb*." He licked his lips as if he meant a dessert and not a dance step.

Griffin grimaced at the alcohol fumes his friend exhaled, strong enough to burn his nose. "I'm taking Anne to the opera." His little sister had pestered him all week to see the reopening of *Nabucco*. The brat had a way of sweet-talking him into doing her bidding. "Why don't you try a respectable outing for a change? You may even like it."

"You sound like my father. But I must warn you, I have a hell of a time understanding his speeches when

I'm soused." Charles perked up and spoke in a plummy imitation of Mr. Whitaker, the senior. "What a man does in private, he repents in private, but what he does in public, he regrets in his privates."

Griffin hid his laughter under a stern façade. "A little decorum, for heaven's sake. This is the Factory House, not some shady tavern."

The two gentlemen across from them glowered, whispering behind their hands as they moved to the whist table.

Charles narrowed his eyes. The devil-may-care attitude seeped from his features to reveal an unusually thoughtful expression. "You are just like them, are you not? The best sportsman in Oporto, a really capital fellow, locked in this... this paddock like sheep." He gave the company of gentlemen a contemptuous look. "There is a whole of Portugal you ignore, waiting beyond these walls."

Not caring for Charles' unflinching stare, Griffin crossed his arms, forcing a blank expression. If he had embraced Portuguese temptations, he wouldn't have transformed his uncle's small trading firm into the fastest growing port company in the city. "I'm taking the coach to the countryside tomorrow."

Charles gaped, the unlit cigar slipping from his lips. "You? Leaving town?"

Griffin shrugged. "A few weeks. I'm going to the high Douro. My late uncle's Quinta is leaking more money than a drainpipe, and I will set it to rights."

"You know there are no English people up there, don't you?"

The Douro River was Portuguese territory—home to the Quintas that produced port wine. It was a wild, unruly corner of the world that held no interest for Griffin. Still, the business required his attention. "I'm perfectly aware the Queen won't be there to greet me."

"Will you sell the place?"

"I don't know yet."

The bell sounded, and Charles staggered to his feet. "It will do you good to spend some time outside this paddock."

Griffin watched him swagger to the dining room. Had Griffin ever been carefree like Charles? Of course not. His mother and sister had been under his care since he was seventeen years old. If this partnership went well—no, not if, but when—he would restore his family to the former status they'd had in London.

The hours dragged by as Griffin endured lunch and stilted conversation. His watch pulsed inside his pocket as if counting the seconds until he could speak with Croft, a countdown to his future. On a sidebar, servers lined up port decanters.

Croft grabbed a bottle, chest puffed. "I raided the cellar for this gem. I dare you to guess the year and the producer."

Members applauded while the footmen distributed chalices. Griffin ignored the bets. When his glass arrived, he took it by the stem and twirled the amber liquid. Why this fuss? There was good wine and bad wine. Obsessing about terroir, vintage, and bouquet fell in the same category of Portuguese romantic notions he avoided. When Croft declared the winner, Griffin didn't raise his eyes.

Finally, members left in pairs and trios, some unsteady on their legs.

Griffin strode inside the treasurer's office, taking in the battle paintings, the stale tobacco smell, and the tray filled with port and whiskey decanters. The anxiety that had plagued him all day left in waves, leaving in its place the cold-headed focus that guided him in daily life. Croft sank behind his Georgian desk and invited Griffin to sit.

"Great lunch," Griffin said, wondering how much small talk was needed before he could speak about the partnership.

"Glad you enjoyed it, Maxwell." Croft lit a cigar and puffed a steady stream of smoke. "Do you know a wine property named Quinta do Vesuvio?"

If he'd never heard about the best wine producer in the Douro, he wouldn't have a long life in this business. Griffin pulled the flap of his coat to sit. "I believe they neighbor my uncle's plantation."

"Two years ago, I lent money to Mr. Bernardo Ferreira so he could increase wine production. But the man died, and I'm worried—"

"You want me to see if they complied?"

"I would consider it a great favor." Slightly out of breath, Croft flattened a yellowed map over the desk. Vesuvio stood to the Douro River's right side, closer to Griffin's property than he had expected. "These are the current plantings. Call it an old man's intuition, but I think they hide something there, and it's not codfish."

Griffin pocketed the map, dismissing Croft's fears. In his few dealings with the Portuguese, he found them to be many things, but not dishonest. "I will let you know."

"I've sent Mrs. Costa a letter. I told her it would be a personal favor to me if her estate manager gave you guidance in winemaking."

Griffin needed no help from this widow. How hard could it be to make a Quinta profitable? If the Portuguese could do it, so could the English, with better results. A few weeks in the countryside would be enough to succeed in this now dual-task—check if Vesuvio had increased production and make his property thrive.

Croft stood and faced his battle paintings, cigarette smoke cascading from his mouth. "We won Portugal back to them. I was a lad, but my father helped Wellington's forces scourge the frogs out of Oporto."

If Croft started talking about Napoleon's peninsular battles, Griffin would never hear the end of it. It was time.

Griffin rose and moved behind the chair. "I examined your firm's client list. If you agree with the partnership, the overlap will be small. Your clients are based in London, while mine are spread over Scotland, New York, and Russia. Together, we'll have a major market share."

Heart pounding in his ears, he counted the rise and fall of the older man's chest. One, two, three.

"I don't want you as a partner," Croft said, staring at the redcoats.

Griffin gripped the back of the chair, his stomach lurching as if he was inside that clipper again. Croft knew. A vision flashed of his family's retreat to Oporto twelve years ago—the cramped third-class cabin, his sister's gray pallor, his mother's constant weeping.

Croft turned, his skin flushed, and laid a chilly hand on Griffin's shoulder. "I want you as a son."

Griffin sucked in a breath, thoughts scattering like pickpockets after a police raid. Speech deserted him, and he focused on Croft's red-rimmed eyes.

"Cheer, boy, cheer! You look as if you saw a ghost. I am not getting any younger, you know." Croft chuckled, exposing yellowed teeth. "I fear for my business, but also for Beth's security."

Griffin staggered away. What a wallop in the gut. Had he heard correctly? Could he be proposing marriage? "Your daughter wants this?"

"What is there not to want?" Croft followed him around the room like an insistent salesman. "She is probably in love with you already. Half the girls here are. Anyway, she is a dutiful English lady." He extinguished the cigar in the crystal ashtray. "Go fix Quinta da Boa Vista. When you come back, we will sign the papers."

***

Griffin´s leather soles echoed over the long warehouse's cement floor. His lodge at Gaia's wharf housed port wine barrels from low in the ground to the high beamed ceiling. He traced the letters written in chalk. The next delivery was destined for Petersburg, residence of Vladimir Pavlovich, Grand Duke—one of the new markets Griffin had opened last year.

Exhaling, he plodded to his office. The curtain-less window invited the brackish fishery odor from the river. The boiling mass of water churned below. After a squall, the Douro turned unpredictable, as the giant oak floating in the depths could testify.

Griffin shut his eyes, fisting his hands on the windowsill. After this partnership, no one could ever uproot his family again. His mother and sister would be sought after in Oporto's British community, no scandals hovering over their prospects like clouds before a storm. They could shove the past behind them—his father's bankruptcy in London, the risk of debtors' prison, and losing every single asset they owned.

But marriage? He did not expect the partnership to come with those strings attached—cunning old Croft had gotten the upper hand, after all. Griffin envisioned the girl's youthful face, cornflower blue eyes, and blond ringlets. Elizabeth Croft was eighteen at most. The thought made him feel ancient, but he must marry at some point. He was thirty-one. The girl would make a good wife, dutiful, proper. A man could do much worse.

"Sir, you wanted to see me?" Edmond, his secretary, placed a ledger atop his desk. The fresh-faced lad from Liverpool had been living in Oporto for only two years, but he'd proved to be exceedingly competent in the short period.

"Have you studied the new purchases arriving on today's steamboat?"

"Of course."

Griffin grunted. "Wine deliveries are booked until the year's end. I will deal with vintage acquisitions when I come back." He stared at the boy. "Anything amiss—and I mean anything—you know where to find me."

"If it's urgent, I will telegraph the Concelho at Vila Nova. Otherwise, I will send you weekly reports by mail coach." Edmond sported his most confident grin, no doubt anxious to test his corporate muscles. "I have everything under control. You can travel with ease."

Nodding once, twice, Griffin strode to the door. On the way out, he halted in front of the framed newspaper decorating the otherwise bare wall—an index of the largest port traders. In 1869, Maxwell Co. had made it to the prestigious ten.

"Next year, we will be in the first place, Edmond." The frame leaned to the left, and Griffin adjusted it. "Mark my words."

***

"I don't need a new house. This one is perfect for our needs. Soon Anne will marry, and it will be just an enormous empty house." Griffin's mother served herself a sherry and sat behind the piano.

"Nonsense. It's the best in Oporto, and you deserve the best." Griffin clutched the stem of his glass with more force than necessary.

He faulted the excessive colors for his temper. Flowery wallpaper wrapped the parlor, the design enough to give any man a migraine. A rug imported from the Orient completed the elaborate decoration, and so many knickknacks poised above every surface that he had trouble finding a landing place for his glass. The walls, though, sported only two paintings. Both Faustino's landscapes, which Griffin had purchased here in Oporto.

Their former house in Repton had hundreds of portraits by local painters and renowned artists, including a square William Fowler, his mother's pride and joy. She and Father had taken great delight in them. But not here. This house could fit inside their former family estate.

"If you added some grandchildren, it would not be so lonely," his mother said, spearing him with a hopeful glance.

Griffin paced to the window. The wind had stopped, and the street was filled with couples taking a night stroll, the gas lamps casting round yellow pools on the paved sidewalk.

"You'll have your wishes granted, after all." He turned and held her gaze. "Croft offered a marriage between our families."

"Marriage?" She furrowed her brow. Her blue eyes were a softer shade than his, but sharp as a needle. "You can't mean little Beth."

He shrugged, his jaws locking against his will. "Beth is his only child."

"But she is exactly that—a child. You need a woman, one who puts you in your place from time to time."

"What the family needs is this partnership." His voice sounded harsher than intended, and he forced a leash around his anger. Why must he be the only person in this family who worried about their future?

She flinched, raising her palms. "All I want is your happiness."

"I assure you that as soon as I get back from the Douro—"

"I don't mean money." She touched his face with her soft, chilly hands.

Griffin looked into her eyes, the emotions brimming there, unsure what she expected from him. He patted her slim shoulder blade, but she continued to stare.

Anne floated down the stairs in a cloud of blue silk, white-blonde hair shimmering in the candlelight.

"About time," Griffin grunted, thankful for the timely interruption.

Anne gave him a pretty moue. "Must you always frown so?"

"I never frown."

"Stop teasing your brother. We will be late."

Anne shrugged a dainty shoulder and blew him a kiss. "But it's always so fun to tease him. Griffin doesn't know what the word means."

Griffin gave the girl a warning look and closed his cufflinks.

She grinned. "Can we go, then? I've waited the entire week for the reopening of *Nabucco*, the tragic tale of love and loss."

"Imagine that." He rolled his eyes. To live in Portugal was to be besieged by sentimental music. The natives would hear only Italian opera and sing only love songs.

She sighed dramatically. "Must you be so . . . *insensível*, Griff?"

Narrowing his eyes, Griffin ushered the ladies to the front door. His sister was too peninsular, mixing Portuguese words with English, caring too much for her local friendships, not to mention her irrational romantic ideas. It was his fault. If he had prevented them from moving to Portugal, she would be a proper English lady. When he returned from the Douro, he would send her to a finishing school—a British one.

Chapter 2

"Plant no tree sooner than the vine."
Alcaeus, 580 BC

Julia brought her glass to the gas lamp. The port's color sparkled, deep russet with a ring of amber crowning the top. "What do you think of the bouquet?"

Abelardo's shoulders slumped. With thick spectacles and a suit too large for his lanky frame, he resembled a scholar from Coimbra University, not a Quinta estate manager. "I guess… grapes?"

Julia smiled reassuringly. "Try closing your eyes."

He inhaled, nostrils flaring, and sneezed. "My nose is blind, Mrs. Costa."

She chuckled, bringing the chalice of Tawny closer. The aroma rose in delicate waves. "Ripe berries, caramel, and Vesuvio's mineral stamp. Wood also, but just a hint."

He tugged his cravat, his forehead damp with perspiration. "This is really necessary? I need to mark the barrels for tomorrow's shipment."

"You need the practice." She raised the glass to her lips. "To Vesuvio." The body caressed her tongue, silky and smooth. She coated her mouth with the rich taste, enjoying the notes of almond and roasted nuts, figs, and plums. "Do you see how this port is ready?"

Abelardo gulped. "If you say so."

"What about the finish?"

"I beg your pardon?"

Julia exhaled, pinching the bridge of her nose. "The sensation in your mouth after you swallow the wine."

Another blank face. Somehow, she would instill the love of winemaking in him. It wasn't his fault. She'd hired him for his expertise in numbers, not his nose. While he handled the dreaded accounting, she focused on what she did best—wine. Still, it would be nice to have someone to share her opinions.

"For me, the persistence is mild, with the ripe fruit staying like an afterthought."

"Is that good?"

"I suppose so. It's like making a new acquaintance. Some people are pleasant enough, but after they leave, nothing of their presence remains. Others linger, their nuances and flavors persisting in their wake." It crossed her mind to explain about Mr. Ferreira's mystical soul wine, the one with the impossibly long finish, but Abelardo had a lot to learn, and it wouldn't do to fill his thoughts with romantic notions.

He swirled the wine in his glass and cleared his throat. "The stone wall is four feet tall already."

"I went there yesterday with Tony." A smile crept to her lips at her son's enthusiasm. He had climbed the construction, watching the workers fit the rocks with fascination. To her seven-year-old son, the fence was a giant toy, not her well devised shield against curious eyes. "A few more days and no one traveling from the village will see our secret valley."

Most port traders clung to Oporto, never venturing far from their cricket clubs, separate churches, and bathing spots at the beach. Still, she would not risk it. The source of their higher production had to stay concealed for two more years.

"Can I proceed now?" Abelardo removed his notebook and shuffled through the pages. "The *rabelo* boat arrives tomorrow. The shipment is for fifteen barrels."

Another sale to Oporto in unmarked pipes. Julia sighed, her shoulders drooping, and jerked her chin to the twenty years port. "You can mark the 1850 Tawny for delivery."

"*Carpe vinum* as you *carpe diem*." Ignoring her displeasure, Abelardo scribbled away.

Scratching filled the humid silence of the cellar, and soon the barrels flashed with his neat chalk markings. Julia drifted to the Ruby vats. The giants stood fifteen feet tall, dutiful sentinels protecting Vesuvio's treasures. She splayed her hand over the ancient wood, the bristly surface cool under her palms. "Don't you think it's a shame to sell it in bulk, like corn or wheat?"

He nudged the spectacles up his nose and stared at her with his bright, matter-of-fact eyes. “Isn’t port exactly that? A commodity?”

Julia couldn’t suppress an unladylike snort. “Vesuvio wine is different. To compare it with the other Quintas is unfair, if not insulting. Some of our neighbors add elderberries to improve color. Some don’t even prune their grapevines. It’s all quantity for them.”

“There’s certainly too much effort applied to a drink,” he said under his breath, averting his eyes.

Julia discarded his dismissive attitude as inexperience. His loyalty compensated for his difficulty understanding the truth about wine. Plus, he deferred to her opinions on all things, especially her new methods. It was a world of improvement from her late husband’s estate manager, who had fought her will at every turn.

“Wine is not just a drink. Can you think of a better combination of sun, soil, rain, and work?”

“I can name countless mankind achievements that aren’t related to grapevines,” Abelardo said, staring at the granite floor.

“Wines are better than men.” Julia lifted her chin, warming to the discussion. “They smell better, taste better, and age better, and one can always separate the good from the bad with a well-trained nose.” Wine never broke a woman’s heart, either, but she kept that thought to herself.

He crossed his arms, a look of impatient tolerance on his face. "As a philosopher, you are a great winemaker, Mrs. Costa."

She laughed, shaking her head. Abelardo was like a young red wine. The potential was there, but he needed a lot of maturing to round his tannins. If only she could put him in a French oak barrel to speed the process a bit.

He dusted his hands on his trousers, leaving white smudges on the wrinkled fabric. "If you are all finished here, Mrs. Costa..."

"Go ahead. I'll be right up."

Abelardo's footsteps vanished up the stairs. She closed her eyes and inhaled the scent of wood and wine. Grapevines had a meaning. What better purpose than to produce wine? If her father-in-law had heard Abelardo's lack of respect for winemaking, he would have gripped him by the lapel and launched into a sermon about how wine was Portugal's most cherished treasure.

But Mr. Ferreira wasn't here, was he? Since he had died, no one else understood. The family and the Quinta workers hardly cared, and her neighbors, who were winemakers themselves, frowned upon her unnatural interests. Shame on her for wanting to cross into their male universe.

Hugging herself against the chill of the underground cellar, she crossed the cavernous space to the table. Her bottle stood there, the black glass reflecting the gas lamp's golden hue. She traced its contours, the glass cool under her fingertips, and inspected the flawless design. The flat bottom allowed it to stay upright, and the cylindrical shape could be stacked on a ship for safe transportation. Another British invention, forged in their furnaces, with their black coal. Strong enough for the wine to travel far and age within.

While the vats and barrels held the past and the present, the bottle would hold Vesuvio's future. Her greatest dream, just two years away. After settling the contract with Croft, Vesuvio wouldn't sell wine in unmarked barrels like other producers, but by the bottle. Kings and statesmen, bureaucrats, and professional men would know the port they drank came from this land. Her land.

She was alone in her endeavor, but she would not be lonely. Her son would be there.

It would be enough.

***

Late for tea again, Julia emerged from the cellar. A soft breeze settled over her cheeks, carrying moisture from the river, and the sweetness of thousands of tiny grape flowers. Julia halted her steps, inhaling their fragrance. A shaft of brilliance pierced her eyes. It was Vesuvio manor. The sun's rays glinted off its whitewashed facade, sparkling against its gilded ornaments.

The house looked like a crystal perched elegantly on the hill. A magnificent, breakable crystal.

The weight of it descended on her shoulders, and a mixture of pride and dread rolled in her stomach. What if she failed to deflect the stones aimed at their roof? How would they collect the broken pieces? Her hands curled into fists, broken nails biting into her palms. Curse Bernardo and his recklessness. The sudden bitterness appalled her. A stronger person wouldn't complain, wouldn't nurture unkind thoughts about her late husband. But how could she not? The contract, his ultimate betrayal, hovered over her head, a giant boulder aiming to shatter her son's future.

Cackling sounded in the garden, and Julia resumed her stride, shooing away the gloominess. Her secret valley would bear fruit, and in less than two years, she would build a new roof, this one made of steel.

The squawking, shrill sound grew louder as she neared the front door. Zezé lifted his plumage high, shimmering his tail. The crowd of D'Angola hens ignored the peacock's plucky attempt to call their attention and pecked their way among the hydrangeas, oblivious to the self-proclaimed king.

Chuckling, Julia shook her head at his antics. "Males."

She had reached the palm trees' shade when Tony pounced, flinging himself on her chest like a mountain lion. Grunting, she stumbled back a step, then circled her arms around his sturdy body, breathing the outdoors in his chestnut hair.

After two heartbeats, he wiggled free. "Tea is ready."

"Have you finished your lessons?"

Tony shuffled his weight from side to side, chin glued on his chest. "Amelia is not a good teacher, *mamã*."

"Why do you say so?"

"She is a girl." He scrunched his face, sticking out his tongue. "And why can't she just tell me how to write the words? She makes me guess."

Julia concealed her amusement behind narrowed eyes. Tony wished to be Vasco da Gama, the Portuguese hero, and to find a new route to the Indies. Like Vasco, he fancied to learn everything of sword fighting and sailing, but nothing of reading and praying.

"She wants you to know your letters, that's why. Promise you will try harder tomorrow?"

He nodded, his hazel eyes lowered in a sweet but not so believable repentance.

Julia clasped his tiny hand, and they went inside. The scent of cinnamon and pastries mingled with the breeze from the veranda, and the vines printed on the wallpaper danced in the gas lamp light. Tony hurried to the tea cart, a wheeled wonder filled with candied fruits, iced cakes, *pasteis de Belem*, *toucinho do ceu*, and every other pastry one could invent by combining sugar and egg yolks.

Upon seeing her, Aunt Rosario bounced a little on the brocade upholstery and patted the place by her side. "Julia dear, you forgot your bonnet again. Why, if you keep exposing your lovely face to the sun and refusing to use the cosmetic powder I've brought you from Oporto, you will have wrinkles before your time. Every lady of fashion must take care of her complexion. It's a woman's most valuable asset."

"Is it? I guessed it to be the mind, but of course, the skin is much more important." Julia pecked her aunt's powdered cheek.

Aunt Rosario huffed. "Cheeky girl."

Julia's coloring was typical Portuguese—black hair and even blacker eyes. All the world's obnoxious zinc-filled cosmetics wouldn't make her olive skin turn alabaster like fashion dictated. To her, only drinking preference mattered. As long as port remained the wine of choice worldwide, she was content.

Julia sat and served herself some tea. Cousin Amelia greeted her with an angelic smile and produced an envelope from her basket. "Oh, how silly of me. I almost forgot. This arrived for you with the mail coach."

Julia turned the letter in her hands, frowning. Croft's seal, a crown with prickly spikes, glared up at her. She had never met the Englishman, but she would bet her best vintage he was like a too-aged red wine—bitter, heavy, and hard to swallow. What could he possibly want? She still had two years to deliver the higher production.

"Good tidings, dear?"

Julia swallowed and lowered the envelope. "Just business from Oporto."

Aunt Rosario huffed. "You exhaust me with all your business. If you followed my advice and found a husband, you would not need to work so hard. It's unladylike."

Of course, Aunt Rosario's answer to all women's troubles was an advantageous marriage. But Julia had already done that and had the invisible scars to prove it. Now she had something no married woman could boast—the freedom to lead her future and Tony's.

Aunt Rosario sipped her tea. "The duchess of Beira gave me some exciting news."

When they didn't respond, she lifted her brows and cleared her throat dramatically. Amelia stopped embroidering and Julia folded the letter on her lap, both giving Aunt Rosario her requested attention.

She patted her fluffy curls and puffed her chest, straining the silk of her scooped neck gown. "You'll never guess who the new president of Vila Nova's Concelho will be. The Count of Almoster!"

Julia startled, perching in her seat. "Pedro Daun?" Her childhood friend had been groomed for greatness. Why would he want the administrative position here, so far from the court in Lisbon?

"The one and only." Aunt Rosario leaned back, smiling like a well-fed cat.

How was he, after all these years? Pedro could bring progress to the region, including the railroad expansion. Vesuvio's wine would have a much smoother way by train than by the tortuous boat route. Hopefully, he would not frown upon her manly concerns like the last president.

"Forgive me for being so outspoken, but wasn't he living in Paris?" Amelia lifted her eyes from her embroidery.

"He resigned his diplomatic post in Napoleon III's court. You must be prepared, dear. We should order a few dresses from Oporto. Imagine catching his attention." Aunt Rosario winked.

"Whatever you wish, Mother." Amelia blushed and went back to her precise, neat stitches.

Julia's smile wobbled. More dresses! Their finances were strained. She had to employ their resources to increase production. Inhaling for courage, she raised her palms. "Aunt Rosario?"

Both ladies glanced at her, their faces expectant and utterly unaware of their troubles.

The words died in Julia's throat. How could she tell them about their change in circumstances? The family was her responsibility. She should be able to provide for them, just like her father-in-law had. He would never have burdened them with financial matters.

Aunt Rosario leaned forward, squinting at Julia's palms. "Goodness, what in heaven did you do with your hands? Don't tell me you have been working with the peasants again." She rose from the couch in a cloud of indignant amber silk and left the sitting room.

Julia caught her cousin's eyes and chuckled. Amelia stifled a laugh and went back to her embroidery. Aunt Rosario never failed to rant about Julia working in the vineyards, but her displeasure never lasted more than a few huffs and puffs. Would Aunt Rosario's husband ever send for them? It had been at least three years since he went to Brazil, and still no news. By now, Julia couldn't imagine life here without them—her aunt's fussing and Amelia's comforting presence.

Julia lowered her eyes to the letter again. Foreboding made her stomach queasy, and she ripped open the envelope. In scratchy handwriting, Croft explained that an esteemed friend had inherited Quinta da Boa Vista and desired to make the property profitable. She snorted. If the English port traders learned how to earn money producing wine, the Douro would have only a handful of Portuguese winemakers.

The following lines made the blood drain from her face.

Mr. Croft requested a personal favor—Vesuvio's help to this Mr. Maxwell person. A stranger here, sent by Croft. What if he discovered the valley? How could she keep her secrets with a pompous, overfed Englishman residing at Quinta da Boa Vista?

She crumpled the letter in her lap.

He would be their ruin.

Chapter 3

"Wine makes a man more pleased with himself; I do not say it makes him more pleasing to others." Samuel Johnson

Dull and endless, the three days traveling over Portugal's corrugated roads only stoked Griffin's conviction to be back at Oporto as soon as possible. The nights—spent at inns whose quality was inversely proportional to the distance traveled—were uncomfortable and even longer.

Griffin shut the coach's window, keeping the scent of new leather and polished wood uncontaminated by the dust outside. The steady clip-clop of the matching blacks filtered through the lacquered panels. Griffin craned his neck to see Thunder's elegant gait hitched behind the coach. The horse had cost him a king's ransom, but the thoroughbred imported from Weatherby's, with his well-chiseled head, lean body, and bold spirit, was a prize. If anything, Griffin's stay in the country would be an excellent opportunity to stretch its legs and test the horse's speed.

Coachman Roberto, a tenacious Portuguese of undetermined age, gave the horses free rein. At least Jako, his jack of all trades, had preceded him to the Quinta last week. Otherwise, the servants' constant chatter would follow him all the way to the Alto Douro.

The carriage jostled forward, sending Griffin's briefcase to the floor and scattering his carefully organized papers. Sitting back in the leather squabs, he closed his eyes and tugged at his neckcloth. His legs were too large for the confined space. Restlessness started in his stomach and traveled to his feet, making them twitch. Why was it such a bother to travel? He forced his jaw to unclench—the prize dangling after this blasted trip, the status Maxwell and Croft Port Shippers would amass, was worth it.

Exhaling, he collected his envelopes and greeting cards, then the book on financial futures he meant to read. Next came the useless "Guide for the Englishman Gentleman traveling up the Douro" with its queer illustrations.

One paper lodged below the back-facing seat—the map of Quinta do Vesuvio. He flicked his eyes over the poor rendering of the property. It certainly wasn't a work of Baron Forrester's precise cartography. Croft had asked him to check the property's production, but Griffin was in no hurry to visit this Quinta.

Vesuvio. He scoffed. Didn't they know it was spelled Vesuvius? Only after he set his own property to rights would he go meet this paragon. His mind conjured an image for the widow—a hirsute crone with codfish breath—and he flinched. Better to deal directly with the estate manager.

The carriage lurched and came to a sudden stop. Muffled sounds of shouting and laughter came from outside. Through the window, Griffin saw only tall shrubberies and wild vegetation.

"Move!" the coachman yelled.

Griffin rapped on the roof. "What is it, Roberto?"

"It's the diligence, sir."

Just his luck to meet the Portuguese mail coach on this rutted road. Griffin unlatched the door and alighted, landing in a lake-sized mud puddle. He lifted a foot, glaring at his dripping boot. Damn, his new Hessians were ruined.

An urchin raced by, splotching foul-smelling muck all over Griffin's tailored coat.

Cursing under his breath, he followed a trail of laughter, cheers, and hollered profanities. Blocking the narrow road, at least a dozen people crowded around some sort of vehicle. He took a few steps closer and rubbed his eyes against the harsh sunlight. "What is going on?"

"Nothing much, sir. Their harness broke," Roberto said.

Wild vegetation flanked the path on one side, and the fence of a pasture stood to the left, trapping them behind the swarming peasants. Griffin took his handkerchief and failed to clean the drying splotches of mud peppering his silk cravat and vest. His watch showed half-past twelve. They were running forty-five minutes late.

"How long will it take?"

His coachman cleaned sweat from his brow. "Not long, sir."

The diligence driver, a bow-legged man shaggier than the beasts, wrapped a stout rope around the animals as if trying to tie them together to prevent them from falling. At least three kinds of quadruplets were hitched—two bedraggled horses in the front row, a mismatched pair of mules next, and the last two could either be jackasses or oversized terriers.

Finished with the rope, the shaggy coachman climbed on his perch atop the wooden coach. Howling obscenities, he flared his long whip, showing without grace it was time to leave.

Meanwhile, the passengers hooted with laughter and took part in the bizarre spectacle by pushing the pathetic Noah's Ark on wheels. Blessedly, the animals understood they needed to go forward, and the vehicle took off. Peasants dashed after it, climbing the box, and many hands appeared to help.

Griffin scoffed, shaking his head. The bloody diligence was a unified effort to be ridiculous.

The stragglers ran after the diligence, and Griffin fought the urge to run in the other direction. To escape this unruly corner of the world filled with sawdust pillows, sleepless nights, old flycatchers, and toothless grins, and go back to his orderly townhouse.

Eye on the prize, Griffin.

With great strength of will, he pushed inside the Brougham for the last stretch of road.

Chapter 4

"From wine what sudden friendship springs!"
John Gay

Griffin submerged himself in Boa Vista's study, assembling every single ledger, note, and receipt, trying to make sense of the property's bookkeeping. The Lusitanian logic, or lack thereof, was incomprehensible. And worse, without the previous estate manager, who had apparently left to try his luck below the Equator, Griffin's progress crawled like a snail traversing hot pavement.

Shouts outside alerted him to another match between Jako and the housekeeper. He closed his eyes and rested his face in his hands. When would this constant bickering end? He was drowning in heaps of paper and poorly cooked food. How hard could it be to make proper potatoes and beef?

Griffin slammed a receipt on the desk and marched outside. A challenging ride around the countryside would do him and Thunder a world of good. He closed the distance to the stables in a few angry strides. The farm shed door hung open, one hinge shredded. Inside, the scrawny stable lad swept the floor. The slabs were yellow, strewn with corn kernels and oats. Two sacks lay ripped in the corner.

"What happened here?"

The lad dropped the broom and removed his hat. "It came from the woods, gray, with white tusks and this big—" The boy raised a hand waist-high to illustrate.

"A boar?"

The boy nodded several times, which Griffin assumed to be an affirmative. Just as well; a hunt would suit him fine. This evening, the dinner would be roasted boar. He only hoped the cook could not bungle that.

While the lad saddled Thunder, he darted inside the house. He grabbed his Henry rifle from its perch behind the bedroom door, checked for ammunition, and left. The sun stung his eyes and he cursed the thick layer of clothing smothering his back. He reached for the horse's reins, instructing the lad to have a wheeled cart at the ready to carry the felled beast.

He took off galloping between the rows of vines. The foliage came to his knees, emerald leaves rippling like a lake. Thunder breathed in measured bursts, powerful legs thumping the rocky ground and lifting shale pieces. The wind cooled the sweat from Griffin's forehead, and he filled his lungs with the fresh air, a significant improvement from the moldy accounting books.

Following the corn kernels trail led him to the property's edge, where the plantation ended in a line of tall trees. The thoroughbred nickered and danced to the side as they crossed between the trunks of cork oaks.

Whistling, Griffin patted the horse's neck. Its muscles quivered under his palms. Sunbeams filtered through the vegetation and pooled on the golden hay covering the ground. He touched his heels to Thunder's flanks, letting the horse stretch his legs among the trunks, sounds muffled by the soft undergrowth. The oaks, denuded of cork bark, guarded the forest like armored soldiers.

Grunts and twigs snapped to his right.

Griffin dismounted and looped Thunder's reins around an olive tree. Silently, he adjusted his rifle's leather strap and stepped around a prickly shrub. There, fifty feet before him, the beast drank at a stream. He brought the gun to his shoulder. The surrounding forest vanished, his world reduced to the target and his finger touching the metal arc. He pulled the trigger, and the recoil jerked his arm. The blast echoed in the ravine. Wings flapped over his head, upsetting the silence.

Instead of an animal grunting in pain, a scream pierced the forest.

What the hell? Heart thundering against his ribs, Griffin rushed in the sound's direction, vaulting over a fallen trunk, the sounds of his steps echoing in the wake of that very human screech.

He reached a clearing. There, by a circle of rocks, a body sprawled on the dirt—a woman. He dropped to her side, sending up plumes of dust, and reached for her neck. The steady drum of a heartbeat greeted his fingers. Thank God. His heart moved from his throat back to his chest, and he huffed out a breath. Her clothes were intact, free of gaping wounds or bloodstains.

Hands quivering, Griffin cradled her head, upsetting her straw hat and freeing a lush black mane. The soft strands tangled around his fingers and covered part of her face. He passed his hand over her smooth brow and prominent cheeks.

A pair of wide eyes appeared from behind curling lashes. Her forehead creased, and she tensed to rise from his lap.

"You are hurt. Try not to move." Griffin put a hand to her shoulder blade, trying again in his poor Portuguese. "*Fica deitada.*"

She shifted her face from side to side as if getting her bearings, and then her eyes glazed over. A heartbeat later, they fluttered shut. Had she fainted?

Griffin brought a trembling hand to her cheek. Her skin warmed his fingertips, satiny and dewy and soft. Too soft. "What is your name?"

"Julia," she croaked.

"Julia, look at me. Where are you wounded?"

"I . . . I think . . . my head hurts." She tried to stand, and Griffin helped her, careful she did not topple down again. She brushed dirt from her clothes, and her lips curled upward. That smile was quite remarkable, white teeth bright against her olive skin. "Thank you."

"Don't thank me yet." He averted his eyes. "I shot you."

"Shot? No, I fell from... from that megalith." She turned to the line of rocks behind them. "The gunshot startled me. I must have lost my footing."

"Are you sure?"

She raised her arms and spun in a slow circle. "There, satisfied? No wounds."

Griffin nodded, and the muscles of his shoulders released their grip on his spine. He hadn't harmed her, thank God. He wiped his hands on his trousers and inspected their surroundings. They were in the middle of a flat patch of land, a valley encircled by vine-planted hills. Beyond the rocks, dry hay covered the ground, a few olive trees rising like green islands in a straw-colored sea.

The woman arched a black brow. "Why were you shooting? Is something wrong?"

She was young, mid-twenties, but she was no simpering miss. There was an air of authority in her posture, in her clear voice, and she looked straight into his eyes.

He cleaned a speck from his coat. "A boar."

"Boar?" She scoffed. "There is no boar here."

He narrowed his eyes and straightened. "You are mistaken. I saw the boar in the oak forest."

Mischief twinkled in her eyes. "It was a pig."

He eyed the impudent Portuguese woman, positive he'd never beheld an English lady dressed like that, a coal-gray vest over a white shirt and a narrow skirt. The garments could be called masculine if not for how they outlined her trim torso and flaring hips. A few buttons of the skirt must have ripped during her fall, giving him a glimpse of thighs clad in scandalous black breeches. He could not object to those, at least.

He shook his head and squared his shoulders. "It was gray and furry. Definitely not a pig."

"A black pig. The herds roam the oaks, eating acorns. Have you not tasted the *presunto*? The smoked ham?" Laughter bubbled out of her in loud, unapologetic bursts, making her body bend. He caught his breath at the sultry sound, unladylike and free. "Well, Englishman, you are far away from home." A small tear left her uplifted eye and caressed her cheeks. He tracked the path down to the corner of her lips.

A grunting noise intruded on her laugh. Griffin turned. A gray boar, white tusks and all, lumbered between the oaks not ten feet from where they stood.

"*Javali*," she whispered, face blanched.

He grabbed her hand. "Listen, when I count to three, we run for that boulder. Do you hear me?"

Julia nodded without taking her eyes from the menacing figure. The boar eyed them, head dipped and shoulders tensed.

"One, two—"

She took off running.

Stunned, Griffin followed, leather soles slipping on the loose dirt. He turned his head in time to see the beast stampeding, hooves eating the ground.

Julia reached the boulder first and stuck half-way up. He gave her a mighty shove from behind. The beast's breath warmed his heels, and he vaulted up. She landed on her stomach, and he on top of her. They were a tangle of limbs and black hair. Her back pushed up and down with her heavy breaths, his own ruffling her mane, and her lush curves cradled his hips. Her softness and warmth fired his blood, and Griffin crouched as far away as the boulder's flat surface allowed.

"Do Portuguese women learn to count?" he panted.

She pushed to a sitting position, knees close to her chest. "We do. We just lack the patience."

"Or common sense," he said under his breath.

She chuckled between gasps, the sound strained but mystifying. He tried to picture a single woman of his acquaintance who would laugh in a moment like this but could not think of any.

Below, the boar pawed the ground. Its eyes were threatening black orbs in its rectangular face, and it breathed the dirt through its shiny nose as it peered up at them.

Griffin reached for the leather straps of his rifle and winced. His gun lay forgotten on the ground, out of reach. "Seems we can't leave this boulder."

"It's a megalith."

"Mega-what?" He adjusted his position, sitting on the hard surface and looping an arm around his raised knee.

"Megalith." She removed a few strands of hair from her brow. "You have one in England. Stonehenge." She pointed to the cylindrical rocks. "Abelardo believes the Celts placed them here. Five thousand years ago." Her English topped many Portuguese he knew. She belonged to the higher classes, for sure. Still, there was something else, something about the way words left her mouth. An exotic quality that made everything she said seem exciting.

"Your husband is a scholar, then?"

"He is not my husband." She looked away, resting her cheek on bent knees.

"Are you studying these mega boulders, then?" he asked, but he already knew the answer. She did not look like a scholar. She had the air of a professional woman, but not a bluestocking.

"You will not get it right, will you?" The corners of her lips lifted. "And no, I am more of a grower type."

"Wine?"

She raised her chin. "What else?"

A thin blood rivulet fell from the line of her hair—crimson against the warm olive of her skin.

"You are bleeding." He took his handkerchief and brought his face close to hers. Her eyes fluttered shut. She smelled like earth, and clean skin, and some exotic flower he could not name but wished he could.

A few dabs and the blood faded. She opened her eyes. The sun chose that moment to appear from behind a cloud, and the rays illuminated her irises. He could swear they blazed with a golden light. It was irrational, but he doubted others had ever witnessed their true color.

A blast of gunfire brought them swiftly apart.

The boar darted into the forest.

Griffin sheltered her body as much as possible from incoming bullets while scouting for the owner of the discharge.

A man carrying an ancient-looking musket came out from behind the boulders, ambling in their direction. He wore a shirt and trousers, but no coat, and a red sash tied around his barrel-sized waist. A haphazard beard covered most of his face.

Griffin's heart hammered in his chest as he looked between the shooter and Julia. The gunman might turn on them. Who knew what passed in the heads of these people?

Julia peeked from behind his torso and waved at the stranger. "*Obrigada*, Carlo. Thank you."

"Do you know this man?"

"Yes."

Griffin grunted. So typical of the Portuguese to answer a question with only a literal yes or no, when it was perfectly clear it required more explanation. With a shove, he slid from the rock and came around the other side, hands eager to span Julia's waist and help her down.

She was already on the ground, talking in Portuguese with the burly stranger. She turned from the man and looked at him, hands on her hips. "Do you need assistance, Mister Englishman?"

"Why would I need—?"

Her eyes twinkled, and her lips twitched. "I think we established you are far from home."

He caught his breath. She was teasing him. It was his turn to laugh; the sound was foreign and rusty. "My horse is just beyond that line of trees." He passed a hand over his hair and affected his most charming smile. "Listen, I—"

"Well, then. It was a pleasure."

Before he could do so much as complete the thought, she walked away, hips swaying and posture erect as if she owned the world, the burly stranger by her side.

At some point, he remembered to close his mouth. No woman had ever walked away from him. This was to be a day of firsts, then. The first time he missed a quarry, the first time he shot a woman, the first time—

She climbed atop an odd carriage and took off, gaining speed, and a perilous curve later, raced out of his sight.

***

"Sorry, sir!"

Griffin knocked Jako on his way inside the house. Shaking his head, he eyed the servant's surprised face. "What?"

"If I may be so bold, sir." Jako dipped his chin, fingering the pearl on his elaborate neckcloth, and a smile spread across his tanned face. "You are grinning, sir."

"Cheeky wretch." Griffin's lips tugged up. "I'll have my dinner on the veranda today." He crossed the parlor's open space and paused. "Inform the cook I'll have Portuguese ham."

Jako's eyes bulged in an incredulous stare. "Portuguese ham, sir?"

"I believe the natives call it *presunto*."

Jako bowed. "Right away, sir."

Griffin's boots left mud splatters on the marble. He dropped into an iron chair facing the river and propped his feet on the red-painted railing. He rolled his neck on the upholstery, the white cotton thick and comfortable, and inhaled the fresh-scented breeze from the river. A charming cricket and the chirping of fussing birds mingled in a sonorous melody.

To his right, a bridge spanned the Douro River, the gray stones reflected in the water below. He could as well have been looking at another bridge, a lifetime away. Warmth seeped into his body like the Douro's gentle current. The resemblance to his father's estate in Repton was remarkable. He hadn't thought about the place in years, not since leaving London more than a decade ago. But now it all came back—the summers spent fishing in the River Trent, balancing in the small skiff, his mother laughing with the other ladies, Anne still in a pram. An ocean away from here, but so similar.

He closed his eyes. Repton faded from his thoughts, and Julia's onyx eyes and pert nose flashed inside his skull. Her olive skin, soft and inviting, had imprinted on his fingertips. Her trim figure and those black breeches. Who was she? She had given only her first name. Of course, proper introductions during the boar attack had proven impossible. Still, the scent of her skin, that exotic flower, lingered on his clothes. Was she someone's wife?

His gut tightened at the thought of her belonging to another. But what could he do? He had too much on his hands to chase skirts this far from Oporto. He had to focus on his goals. Tomorrow, he would finish the property accounts. A few weeks more and everything would be settled. He would return to the city.

The maid came in, balancing a tray. After delivering her goods, she bowed and left. Atop the side table, Griffin's meal awaited. The ham taunted him with its smoky scent and blood-red color. Bowls with olives, almonds, bread, and a jug completed his first native meal.

He served himself a glass of port and cut the bread. He smelled the olive oil and drizzled it, then topped it off with a slice of the odd ham. Though his stomach rumbled, Griffin lowered the bread back to the plate and pushed it away. To give in to the peninsular way was to lose his English roots, shallow as they were. He needed to stay firm, to have his goals clear in his mind—no distractions.

Temptation beckoned with ebony eyes, but tasting it would only distract him from his aim. Or would it? He was so far from the British community—days away, in fact. Who could fault him for indulging himself?

Griffin reached for the *presunto*, bringing it closer to his mouth. This changed nothing. The first bite brought salt and smoke, perfectly blended with the rye bread. He finished in quick bites.

Damn, it tasted good.

Chapter 5

"[I]t is the wine that leads me on, the wild wine that sets the wisest man to sing at the top of his lungs, laugh like a fool—it drives the man to dancing... it even tempts him to blurt out stories better never told."
Homer

The Saint John's party sizzled with excitement, bright colors flashing in the night. Tony played tag around the bandstand, his pale coat illuminated by the bonfire. Paper lanterns swung from the cottages, sprinkling the whitewashed walls with an amber and green glow.

Tourists mingled in Vila Nova's square, purchasing sweets and enjoying the quadrille. Julia inspected their groups, watching for a tall figure with a chiseled profile. Would that stray hunter from the megaliths be in the village tonight, or had he already returned to the city?

Why had that ridiculous thought sprouted now? Instead of that too handsome Englishman, she should worry about Croft's obnoxious friend. The cursed letter had arrived two weeks ago, but he had not appeared to ask for help with winemaking or poke his nose where he shouldn't. Though he had yet to show his face, it did not mean he desisted. They were still at risk.

Aunt Rosario waved goodbye to their neighbors and rejoined their small group, a tired smile on her face. Perhaps the Albuquerques knew about Croft's friend.

"Did they chat about Quinta da Boa Vista?" Julia tried to keep her voice level. It wouldn't do to make her aunt worry.

"Why would they? Pedro Daun's arrival is all everyone talks about." Aunt Rosario yawned and fluffed her blond ringlets. "That and our little gathering to welcome him, of course."

At the mention of Aunt Rosario's welcoming party, Flor raised her brows to her widow's peak. Julia's maid had the vocal and annoying belief that Julia should explain the contract to her family. Still, acting as Vila Nova's hostess gave Aunt Rosario so much pleasure. How could Julia deny her? At least they would not have to buy wine.

Aunt Rosario squeezed Julia's hand affectionately. "I'll be returning now. My joints are paining me."

"I'll take you home. It's past Tony's bedtime—"

"Absolutely not. You young people should stay for the fireworks. Tony will return with me in the Albuquerques' carriage, and you can chaperone Amelia."

Julia nodded, watching them depart. An unseasonably chilly breeze ruffled her cotton skirts, and she hugged herself.

Flor tweaked her shoulder. "Why are you so tense? Let loose a bit. It's Saint John's party, for heaven's sake." Her maid and friend twirled her saffron skirt in tune with the accordion, her long braids swinging.

"Forgive me for being so outspoken, cousin, but I think what Flor said has merit. You work too much." Amelia glanced down, a blush covering her angelic cheeks.

Flor had a penchant for drama, but if even shy Amelia had the same opinion, then they must be right.

Abelardo straightened the carnation on his lapel and bowed deeply, asking Amelia to dance. A group of chattering tourists cut in front of Julia, and when she could finally pass through them, the young couple had vanished.

"I'll chaperone them. You enjoy the party," Flor yelled as she too blurred in the sea of people.

Julia inhaled to protest, but they were gone. She clutched her skirts and tried to follow, squeezing herself between starry-eyed couples, but she made no progress.

In the center of the square, she halted. The music continued, oblivious to her plight. Lively, the quadrille twirled a few paces from her; there, but too far. Surrounded by people she'd known all her life, she had never felt more alone. Her throat burned, and ridiculous tears sprang to her eyes.

"Found you."

The words breathed near her ear stirred goosebumps on her arms. She turned slowly and her breath caught—the Englishman from the megaliths. The bonfire's glow made his chiseled lines softer, almost inviting. A thick beard shadowed his straight jaw and chin, and his skin had been kissed by the sun, now the color of light caramel.

"I thought you went home." She raised her voice above the music.

"You don't want me around?"

Julia crossed her arms. "I did not take you for the country type, that's all."

"I'm not."

"Enjoying the party?"

"I haven't formed an opinion. Yet." He cleaned a speck from his black coat. The suit outlined his broad shoulders and lean frame. How had he gotten here without a single wrinkle in the crisp cloth?

Julia shrugged. "I guess it differs greatly from the city."

"If I had a kind soul to show me around..." The words dangled between them, and he stood with his body slightly forward and hands in his pockets.

Where were Flor and Amelia? To converse with strangers was immodest, even for a widow. She swept her eyes over the crowd, watching for judging villagers, but people seemed distracted by the quadrille. "I don't think it would be proper—"

"You owe me. I saved you, remember?"

"I don't even know your name," Julia blurted, more to convince herself it was a bad idea than because she wanted an answer.

"Call me Griffin."

The name suited him, sharp and arrogant. Griffin. She rolled the two syllables in her mouth, savoring it like a vintage port.

He tsked. "I've never thought Portuguese were inhospitable."

She puffed her chest. "I'll have you know, sir, that we Portuguese are gentle, hospitable people."

"Prove me wrong." He presented his arm, a lopsided grin on his face.

"Fine." She tucked her hand into his arm with more force than necessary and regretted her carelessness. Now she had wrinkled his superfine coat, more suited for a ballroom than a Saint John's party.

They started down the promenade—he nonchalantly, as if escorting women was his expertise; she battling an idiotic flutter in her stomach as if she had caught the attention of the most sought-after boy. Who was she fooling? Everything about him—his height, the way he carried himself, his confident speech—was the opposite of the familiar, long-bearded, brown-clothed men from Vila Nova.

She started the tour at the church. Whitewashed and with a matter-of-fact square design, its only decoration was an ornate belfry. "It's no cathedral, but it was built after the great earthquake in Lisbon. I guess the stonemason cut the frivolities."

"No dangling parts to threaten the lives of unsuspecting pedestrians. I appreciate the logic."

"I think so, too." She studied his face but found no evidence he mocked her. "Father Cosme's sermons are a bit tedious, but when his digestion is not bothering him, he can be quite inspiring." Julia squeezed his arm. "I'm sorry. You are not a Catholic, are you?"

Had she offended him by asking? She had no experience with other faiths, as all her acquaintances attended mass on Sundays. Much as the sun controlled the seasons for crops, the church set the seasons of their lives, tolling their hours, celebrating their rites, organizing their traditional parties, absolving their sins.

"I was baptized, but I'm not a religious man."

She frowned. "I thought Englishmen were Protestants."

"My mother is Catholic." He paused. "Would you look at that?"

Julia followed his gaze. The full moon, shining from behind a smoky cloud, cruised the sky in silvery brilliance. "I love summer. Grapes growing on the vines, longer days, nights begging for moonlit strolls. Everything turning riper, sweeter, unique."

"Indeed."

Their gazes met, and for a heartbeat, she could not move, entranced by his cobalt-blue eyes.

He cleared his throat and pointed at the stucco building with tiles lining the windows. "Is that the tavern?"

"Yes. Mrs. Manoela, the owner, is a splendid cook. You shouldn't leave Vila Nova without tasting her *açorda*. She lets the stew simmer for a full day. The lamb meat gets so soft it melts. It's really famous." She gave him a sideways glance. "Oh, and never accept her green wine."

"Why not?"

"Tourists don't like it. It's too *riscante*." She steepled her fingers. "What's the word in English? For tastes that leave your mouth watering?"

He stared at her lips. "Tart?"

"Yes, tart." She resumed walking, hoping the shadows disguised her flaming cheeks. "But her husband is a talented blacksmith. He can mend anything for you."

He chuckled. "I'll keep that in mind."

"There is a marina south of here in Barca D'alva. The Douro in summer is a lake, excellent for fishing and cruises."

"Do you perform guided tours on the river, too?"

She narrowed her eyes. "No." They had circled to the long line of makeshift stalls parallel to the main street. "I'll be right back."

She hurried to the booth selling traditional Portuguese treats, vibrant with red and green flags. The baker's daughter bent over the counter to give the Englishman an accessing glance. Julia should have left him out of sight. "Good evening, Luiza. Two *pasteis, por favor*."

"My, who is that?"

"An acquaintance from Oporto. A tourist."

"With the fancy clothes? He looks like a *Fidalgo* to me." She handed Julia a paper sack with the sweets. "Introduce me?"

"Maybe later." Julia gave her three *reis* and turned away.

When he saw her coming, he offered his arm. "You live here in the village?"

"Up north."

She led him to her favorite place in Vila Nova, tucked between the Assembly building and a stone wall. The Sorrow Fountain. Water spouted in a gentle arc, spilling into the shallow pond. A statue of a slender girl perched in the middle, a basket on her lap. Julia loved how the torchlight reflected on the Portuguese tiles behind the pool, the teal arabesque dancing as if underwater.

She made a sweeping gesture with her hand. "The last stop of your tour."

Except for a few stragglers passing along the walkway, the place was empty. Julia released his arm and touched the water. Coins twinkled on the bottom, thousands of wishes thrown over the years, proof she wasn't the only one with dreams.

He came closer. "What are you thinking?"

"I have a story to tell. It's about this fountain. Tourists love to hear the legend of the maiden and the moor—"

"It's fine, really." Raising his palms, he shook his head dismissively.

"As you wish." Julia sat on the marble steps. Dribbling sounds echoed in the secluded corner, and she hugged herself, the cold of the stone seeping through her thin skirt. What had produced the change in him? A moment ago, he was enjoying himself, appreciating the village's sights. Maybe it was the guide he found lacking.

He exhaled audibly. "Go on, then. Tell away."

"Some other time." The air by her side shifted, and she lowered her gaze, studying her palms.

He bumped her with his shoulder. "Please?"

"Now you wish to know?"

"Perhaps I want to listen to your voice. Indulge me?"

His own voice, low and smoky, made her cheeks warm. If he mocked her, she would stand and leave. She chanced a peek. He had crouched on the same step, hips only an inch from hers. While his posture was nonchalant, his stare enthralled her. His blue eyes flickered in tune with the torchlight, the intensity invading her defenses. She caught her breath as a thrill raced down her spine. Fear or excitement? She couldn't tell. A faint note of freshness rose on the breeze, no doubt a trace of his cologne, evaporating like a decanting wine.

Julia smoothed her skirts, studying the tiny vines painted on the hem. "It happened centuries ago when the Moors invaded the Douro. The Portuguese had never accepted the Sultan's rule." She smiled. "By now, you must know we are a stubborn lot."

He leaned on the fountain's rim and crossed his ankles. "Some more than others."

Their knees touched, and a languid sensation flooded her legs, pulsing through her veins, making her lightheaded.

Shaking her head to dispel the effect, she scooted a few inches to the right. "A local girl, beautiful and kind, used to come here and sit on these steps, singing and weaving vine baskets for her father. The dashing Sultan's son, returning from Gibraltar, heard her, and her gentle melody enchanted him."

His eyes were crystalline in the fire's glow. "And then?"

"He came every day. At first, he was content to listen to her melodies, and then they fell in love. Neither her family nor the Sultan blessed the romance."

"Typical."

Julia glared at him. "You want me to stop?"

"Go on."

"Secretly, they planned to run away, to live their passion where differences didn't matter. On their escape day, the King's army invaded the city, expelling the Moors to the south. The Sultan's son gave up his riches and came back for her. Before they could reunite, the soldiers killed him. Afterwards, the girl sat here, pouring out her tears. Legend says her sorrow created the fountain." Julia sighed. No matter how many times she told the story, a drop of sorrow still found its way inside her chest.

He stood and brushed his trousers. "Is there such a place?"

Without him seated on the step, the stone chilled her. "I beg your pardon?"

"A place where differences don't matter?"

"I guess their differences brought them together. Do you like it?" She cringed at the hopeful note in her voice.

"Do you? I didn't take you for the romantic sort."

Julia rose and shook her skirts. "I'm not. But you can't dismiss these things, you know. The tales, the myths, the idioms, the food. They are as much a part of Vila Nova as the people are."

"Charming." He leaned over the fountain. "But why the coins?"

"The town folk believe it works like a wishing well, granting any heartfelt request made on Saint John's Day. Some say it helps to find a spouse."

"That's how you got him?"

"Who?"

He tilted his head to the side. "Your husband."

She averted her face. If she was married, she wouldn't be here with him, would she? "I don't have one."

He reached inside his coat and held a coin between his elegant fingers—fingers that had probably never seen a single day of manual labor. With the copper reflecting the torchlight, it looked like he had caught a firefly. "Tell me what you wish, Julia, and maybe it will come true."

"I don't believe in folktales." She hid her calloused hands behind her back, creasing the paper bag with the pastries. "And that's not how it works. You have to wish for yourself."

He shrugged and aimed. When he flipped the coin, it went flying and landed in the pond's center.

"Your marksmanship has improved. Have you been practicing?"

It started as a groan, but then it changed his entire face, softening the stern lines and making his eyes twinkle. He laughed. Warmth tingled on her insides, and she felt like the wittiest of mortals.

A memory caught her by surprise. She was ten, trudging the vineyards while her guardian separated grapevines by variety. He had noticed she could tell a *Touriga* from a *Tinta Roriz* and a *Tinta* from a *Franca*. The smile brightening his face had been so marvelous that she had wracked her brain for other ways to catch his elusive attention again.

The pastry. Tourists loved Portuguese sweets. Reaching inside the paper sack, she proudly offered Griffin one.

He eyed it as if it was a nasty bug. "What is that?"

"A *Pastel de Belem*. See all this crumbly dough?" She pointed at the perfect golden crust on top. "It's filled with cream. Will you try it? I promise it's better than it looks."

He frowned. "I'm thinking about it."

"And?"

"The answer is no."

"Why?" Julia bit into the pastry. "See? It is not poisonous."

She offered him the second sweet, but he balked. One more step and he would plunge into the fountain. He frowned, and his spine bent a few degrees backward as if prepared to fend off ominous, bloodthirsty foes and not a dainty *pastel*.

Laughter bubbled out of her. "This is a surprise. A big Englishman afraid of pastries."

He glared. "Are all Portuguese women impudent like you?"

"I don't know... are all Englishmen scared of sweets?"

"You never let go, do you?"

"Certainly not. In fact, I'll dare you." Smiling smugly, she gave a hearty bite, exaggerating the "hmm" when the cream burst inside her mouth.

"Challenge accepted."

When she realized the change in him, it was too late. Eyes burning, he grabbed her wrist with his right hand and took the pastry with his left, keeping it out of her reach. She watched as he dropped the perfectly fine *pastel* on the ground.

"Release me now, you—"

He pulled her close. The sudden movement tilted her balance, and she tripped, landing on his chest. Before she could protest, the Englishman snaked his arms around her back. His scent of leather and bergamot made her head spin. She stilled, frozen on the outside, while inside, waves of heat traveled up and down her chest. Undaunted, he brought his face within an inch of hers. And then closer.

And then he kissed her.

Her eyes fluttered shut. His lips were firm and warm, with a faint trace of spirits. Sounds faded into hearts thumping, hers and his.

When his tongue traced the seam of her lower lip, Julia sputtered.

Had he just tasted her?

Leaning away as much as she could with his arms still circling her back, she stared at his face. He frowned, his eyes intent on her lips.

"Release me, sir."

"Only if you tell me where you live."

"Absolutely not."

An explosion surprised them both. The midnight fireworks sparked colorful arcs in the sky. Splaying her hands on his chest, Julia pushed. He stepped back, losing his hold on her torso. Cheeks flaming, legs unsteady as if she had imbibed too much port, she spun. He caught her wrist, but she tugged, and her arm slipped from his grip, leaving him grasping only the half-eaten pastry. Heart beating in her throat, she raced away, boots clattering on the cobblestones.

When she reached Main Street, she weaved among families and larger groups, stopping only when she arrived at the bandstand. She still held the paper sack, and she crammed the evidence of her inappropriate behavior in her skirt pocket.

Panting, she touched her lips. Her chest shook with a rush of giddy laughter, and she covered her cheeks with her palms. This was crazy. She should not have provoked him into kissing her. What if someone had seen? The tales would titillate the whole parish. She straightened her skirts, trying to regain her composure. Englishmen were oblivious about most things, but by Saint John, how they kissed.

Griffin.

She tasted his name one last time. When would he leave the village? Tourists usually left after the party. It was better this way, and under no circumstances could she moon after him.

She chanced another glance over her shoulder. Flor had told her to enjoy herself, hadn't she? She only had one regret—she would never know if he had liked the pastry.

Chapter 6

"Age appears to be best in four things - old wood best to burn, old wine to drink, old friends to trust, and old authors to read." Francis Bacon

Julia curled in her favorite chair, the upholstery enveloping her in a comfortable leather scent. The afternoon sun filtered through the floor-to-ceiling windows and pooled over the sheepskin rug, forgetting her side of the study. Gazing at the door to assure herself she was alone, she retrieved the paper sack from her drawer and placed it atop the scarred surface of her desk. Brushing it with her palms, she smoothed the creases. All night, she had avoided picturing his chiseled face, had valiantly ignored memories of the kiss during breakfast, nipping those images much as she dropped grape clusters the vines wouldn't sustain.

She rubbed her lips. Even after all the pruning, a faint tingle remained. What kind of Englishman would kiss a woman like that? As hard as she tried, she couldn't place him with the others. He didn't look down on her like a few she had met at the English country club. Still, he wasn't like the coarse wine dealers who came before vintage, carrying their leather valises and horsewhips and speaking poor Portuguese. He neither resembled the pompous men bustling about *Rua do Ingleses* with their top hats sitting like black towers atop their heads.

The mantel clock struck the hour. In came Wentworth. The butler was punctual as always, carrying the silver tray with two chalices of port on top. Julia pushed the sack back inside the drawer and jumped to her feet. Glass in hand, she dropped onto the armchair, tucking her bare feet by her side, ready for their daily ritual.

Wentworth perched on the twin chair by her left, back straight and chin high. Julia smiled, eying him askance. She had known him since she was ten, and one would think he would have dropped the British formality, but like an aged Madeira, his stiffness hid a sweet core.

They watched the view in silence, the river glittering down the ravine, the mountains cradling its exuberance.

Julia twirled the wine in her glass. Wentworth had chosen a ruby for today's tasting, but the color struck her as murky, not bright and clear as expected from this style. The producer must have waited too long to harvest the grapes. The scent was rich, though, with a lot of fruit and a hint of roses. She took a sip, swirled it around in her mouth, and caught the jammy, flat flavor from overripe grapes. No finish, though. The taste vanished swiftly after swallowing it.

"Not this one, Wentworth. I am sorry."

He grunted.

"At some point, you will need to give up this quest. Not that I don't appreciate this..." Julia waved a hand between them, unsure what to call these daily meetings where they tasted port and talked. Well, mostly she spoke, and he listened. When he had appeared for the first time after her husband's funeral, she had been surprised, but now she treasured his arrival every day at six sharp.

"I must ignore your skeptical remarks, Mrs. Costa. I won't be dissuaded from the promise I made to Mr. Ferreira."

She missed her father-in-law—his passion for wine, his kindness, and his infinite patience. In life, he had searched high and low for this mystical *Vinho D'alma*, the Soul Wine. A once-in-a-lifetime wine with a long finish, one that stays with you, lingering, moving you with its complexity, its flavors, its nuances. He had never found this Holy Grail of winemakers, and neither would Wentworth.

She exhaled, a dull ache blooming in her chest. They turned back to the windows in time to see the sun's final dip behind the western mountains. A lonesome boat appeared by the river bend, white sails bowed, floating in the river's golden waters.

Wentworth cleared his throat, tugging at his silver cravat. "If I may be so bold as to impart some advice."

Julia leaned forward in her chair. "Be as bold as you please."

"Mr. Ferreira had firm beliefs about how each person needs to find their own soul wine. Perhaps it's time you started looking." Face flaming, his voice sounded strained. "He would not want you to stay alone forever."

Julia stifled a gasp. Was she doing such a terrible job that she needed a husband to take her place? "I don't know what you mean."

Pushing the chair back, she went to the painting of her father-in-law. Dressed in a black suit, a hand over his heart, the patriarch overlooked his domain. He made it seem so easy. Under his rule, Vesuvio had thrived. Even before she had married his son, when she lived here as his ward, the estate had worked with minimum friction.

Julia closed her eyes. "Your dear friend worried I would muddle everything?"

"You misunderstand. Vesuvio was his dream." Wentworth followed her to the portrait. "You breathed life back to it. Mr. Ferreira made you his son's bride, but he chose you for the Quinta."

She pushed the tears back with a long swallow of port. She had been only seventeen, with no say in any of the choices made for her. At least she had gotten Tony. Her son was worthy of any sacrifice.

"He wouldn't want you to be lonely. I remember his last words, his guilt about how things turned out with Bernardo—"

"Please, Wentworth, no more."

A heavy silence fell on the study, the clock booming the minutes. Julia kept her eyes on the painting, the colors blurring together into a gray splotch.

"If you will excuse me, I have to oversee the dinner preparations." Wentworth bowed stiffly and left.

As if she needed some foolish, romantic notion. Julia opened the drawer and grabbed the paper sack. With brisk, efficient gestures, she crumpled it into a ball and flung it in the trash.

Chapter 7

"It has become quite a common proverb that in wine there is truth (In Vino Veritas)." Pliny the Elder

Vesuvio's formal parlor glittered with countless candles. Footmen carried drinks back and forth while Wentworth intoned guests' names from the massive oak portal. The Count of Almoster, the guest of honor, had not arrived yet, and the other guests mingled in the spacious sitting areas.

Surrounded by the wives and daughters of neighboring Quintas, Julia tried to avoid calculating the cost of all that beeswax and food by paying attention to the ladies' conversations. Sporting yards of frilly cloth, the women perched on the settee like hens on a branch so their long trains, a must fashion for ladies of style, would not wrinkle.

The conversation flirted with the same subjects: how to suffer their husbands' many grievances, and how to get husbands for their unmarried daughters.

Pedro Daun's promised presence added a glow of excitement to their matchmaking efforts.

Julia gazed at the porcelain vase, counting the roses' petals for the second time, when the buzz of the women's voices became lower, more secretive.

Mrs. Albuquerque covered her mouth. "No one has ever laid eyes on him."

"My cook is friends with the housekeeper from Boa Vista. She told me he does not eat our food."

Julia straightened. They must be talking about the Boa Vista owner. Mr. Croft's friend.

"My maid told me he is unmarried." A girl, Amelia's age, fidgeted with her skirts. "Do you think he is here to stay?"

"You better cast your sights elsewhere. They keep to their own society," Mrs. Albuquerque said.

"They are Protestants, all of them," a matron whispered as if it was a sin.

"But if they have good hearts, St. Peter will open heaven's gate for them, won't he?" The girl pouted, looking forlorn.

Julia rose and excused herself, making her way to the balcony doors. The odors of cologne and food warred with the flowery scent, making her stomach roll. They must be wrong. Surely, if Croft's friend was in Vila Nova, he would have appeared on her doorstep.

Unless he had spied on her lands already.

Dizzy, Julia leaned on the buffet.

That's when she saw him. Julia squinted her eyes at a broad back, tailored in formal black. The cropped chocolate hair, curling slightly at the starched collar, struck her as familiar. No, it could not be her Englishman. A warm flush covered her cheeks, and she covered them with the silk of her gloves.

While Mr. Brotero talked animatedly, flapping his arms, the stranger listened nonchalantly, one hand on the back of the armchair, the other holding a glass of port.

Aunt Rosario, her peacock dress shimmering in the candlelight, approached him. Julia couldn't hear them over the glasses clinking and loud chattering. Still, when her aunt linked arms with the man and tilted her head in Julia's direction, she held her breath. It could not be him.

They turned.

It was.

His mouth froze mid-sentence. Recognition flashed in his cobalt eyes, there and gone. A few strides brought him too close.

Aunt Rosario's smile lit up her face. "This is my dear niece, Mrs. Julia Costa-Ferreira."

His brows furrowed, and his mouth pressed into a forbidden line.

Julia braced herself not to take a step back. Why the anger?

He recovered quickly and bowed. When he kissed the air above her silk-clad hand, she felt his lips as if he had touched her naked fingers.

Aunt Rosario cleared her throat. "Julia, this gallant gentleman is our recluse new neighbor, Mr. Griffin Maxwell."

Chapter 8

"Wine brings to light the hidden secrets of the soul."
Horace

Julia's steps echoed over the empty veranda. Her Englishman was Croft's envoy? Fate couldn't be so cruel. The waning moon escaped behind black clouds, plunging her into darkness. Julia gripped the railings with clammy hands. Below the porch, the river murmured softly, so different from the turmoil inside her mind threatening to drag her under.

Panic or wallowing in self-pity wouldn't help. She had to understand what he wanted. But how could she face him? The mere thought of their last encounter turned her insides into pulp. Best to plead a migraine and go to her room. Tony slept next door. Safe.

But would the safety be real? The contract had taught her the perils of trusting men. Unless she kept the Englishman away from her secrets, safety would be an illusion.

"Why are you lurking in the shadows?" The smoky voice intruded on the silence.

Julia's breath hitched, and she spun, colliding with a tall frame. She stumbled back a step and lifted her gaze. The dappled moonlight shied away from his face, but she caught the relief of a prominent jaw and a straight nose. "Pedro?"

"You expected someone else?"

She stepped forward, lifting her arms to hug her childhood friend, but remembered her manners and curtsied. "Welcome to Vesuvio, Your Excellency."

"Pedro will do." He pulled her up with a leather-covered hand, his mouth lingering above her silk glove. "I looked for you inside."

"I came for some air."

He steered her away from the balustrade into the murky expanse of the veranda, his soles striking the checkered marble. His scent, sandalwood and tobacco, wrinkled her nose. Not that it was unpleasant, but that it was so different from the smell of horses and worn books he had carried when they were children. Every summer, he had visited—a boy with solemn eyes and too many tutors. He had spent his free time seated at a jagged rock between his father's Quinta and Vesuvio, watching the other kids splashing in the Douro.

They neared the gas lamp on the wall, and she tried to glimpse his face, but he twirled her around, leading her below the glaring light. The brightness blinded her, and the burner stung the side of her face. When his fingers held her chin, she took a step back.

He exhaled. "You haven't changed."

Hadn't she? Perhaps not on the outside. "We best return. The guests came to see you."

Julia went inside, and Pedro trailed close, a step away from the train of her dress. Indistinct voices and clinking glasses granted a respite from the silent balcony, diffusing the knot in her stomach. Why this foolishness now? She'd known Pedro Daun forever. Mr. Maxwell was the stranger and the one to blame for her frayed nerves.

She held her skirts and turned. The candlelight flickered over Pedro's military uniform, the epaulets accenting his strength and shoulders. He wore his hair longer, tied at the nape, the rich burnished gold a shade darker than Julia remembered. His face had the same classical lines, but now a close-clipped goatee gave his princely façade a roguish flair.

"You are quite different. How was Paris?"

"Too far."

"Congratulations on your appointment."

He pierced her with an unwavering stare. "I wanted to come sooner when I heard of Bernardo's—"

"As you said, France was too far. You wouldn't have arrived in time for his funeral."

"You were never far from my thoughts." He leaned forward. "I am here now, and you can depend upon it."

"Thank you." She didn't need his help or anyone's, but hoping to show appreciation for his kindness, she smiled.

"Excuse me." The Englishman put himself between them. "I wished for a minute with you, Mrs. Costa."

Pedro changed before her eyes, his intensity turning into aristocratic superiority. "Do you know him?"

A sardonic smile appeared at the Englishman's mouth. "Why, we are—"

"Neighbors," Julia interrupted, sucking in a breath. "Mr. Maxwell is Quinta da Boa Vista's owner. Right, Mr. Maxwell?" The smile plastered on her face made her cheeks hurt. Would the madman expose her?

Hoping her voice came out steady, Julia made the introductions. The men shook hands as amicably as generals on opposite sides of the battlefield.

"Oh, there you are." Aunt Rosario approached, peacock feathers bouncing in her hair.

Julia thanked the timely interruption. Apparently, her articulation and Mr. Maxwell couldn't abide each other.

"Dinner is served." Aunt Rosario caught Pedro's arm. "Would you escort an old lady, Your Excellency?"

"Old lady?" Pedro glanced around, frowning. "I see no old lady here." After a gallant bow, he proceeded to the dining room with a preening Aunt Rosario.

The Englishman presented his arm like a gauntlet. "Shall we?"

Julia poised her hand on his forearm, curbing the impulse to wrinkle his formal black and white wear like she had on Saint John's Day.

His eyes narrowed, as if daring her to do it, and he led her after the guests. "We meet again, Julia," he said close to her ear.

Her neck prickled, and she flinched. "It's Mrs. Costa, please."

"You gave me leave to use your given name."

"You should have offered your surname. Imagine my surprise today."

"You never asked." He shrugged, an unrepentant smile on his face, and jerked his chin in Pedro's direction. "Charming fellow."

"Portuguese men learn good manners."

"Touché."

She entered the dining room by his side, hoping her outside appearance resembled that of a cordial neighbor, while ripples of heat and cold battled inside her chest.

They stopped near the open windows, a soft breeze making the gauzy curtains flutter.

"Why are you here, Mr. Maxwell?"

He tilted his head, a frown creasing his brow. "I thought to enjoy the evening."

Julia cringed. What was she, a sullen child? "I didn't mean to be discourteous. After Croft's letter, I expected a visit from you sooner."

"Are you so eager to help me?" He took an improper step closer.

She lifted her chin. "I don't like riddles. You know I am obliged to Croft."

"I prefer to leave the business to daytime."

Julia inhaled to reply, but the guests had long since seated themselves. After a strained nod, she took her place on the Count's right, as befitted her position.

Mr. Maxwell sprawled two seats to the left, facing her. Any misstep and she found herself looking straight at his inquisitive blue eyes.

Julia twisted the linen napkin on her lap. He was too cunning. If she wanted to learn his intentions and hide her secrets, she must prepare herself better.

Mr. Nogueira drank deeply of his green wine. "Are you enjoying our village, Mr. Maxwell?"

"The estate's accounts have kept me inside most of the time, but I'm surprised by a few sights." He turned his stare to Julia.

"What a shame. The Douro has many secret places to be explored."

"I'm sure he won't have time for all that," Julia said under her breath.

"And what about our cuisine?" Aunt Rosario took a suggestive bite of her celebrated codfish recipe.

"I confess I never stray too far from my homeland food, but I particularly enjoyed the Portuguese *presunto*."

Julia choked on an olive, covering her mouth with the napkin. When the subject shifted to the railroad construction, she said a prayer of thanks. All the while, Mr. Maxwell kept a sardonic smile on his face, eyes twinkling, no doubt enjoying flustering her. Would this dinner never end?

Mr. Nogueira leaned forward. "Begging your pardon, but I don't want the steam horse here. Ruin the landscape, it would. Bringing throngs of unsavory people right up to our doors."

Julia straightened. "Gentlemen, with the tracks here, transporting wine to Oporto will be much more efficient."

Both her neighbors gaped, and Aunt Rosario widened her eyes reprovingly.

Julia leaned back in her chair. By their reactions, one would think she had sprouted a second head, not merely offered her opinion on a manly matter.

Mr. Maxwell leaned forward. "I think Mrs. Costa's argument has merit. The Royal Company brings progress. It's the future."

Julia's cheeks grew warm with his show of support. She must not allow him too close.

Pedro lifted his palms. "The prime minister is evaluating the issue with care. I am sure my father will take everyone's interests into consideration. My opinion, as a military man, is favorable. The railroad won the war for Prussia last year. Their army assembled in less than three days because of the train, while Austria took over two weeks to bring their soldiers to the front."

Mr. Albuquerque crossed his arms, a deep frown appearing above his bulbous nose. "Your Excellency, what about the wine plague in France?"

Pedro's expression turned somber. "A terrible affair, for sure. Whole vineyards decimated. Bordeaux is no more. The *nouvelle maladie* has reduced the French to drinking wine from Anatolia."

A shiver crept up Julia's spine. She had heard about phylloxera after harvesting last year, but the barrel merchant from La Rochelle had believed it to be contained to the north of Bordeaux and no worse than a mildew outbreak. "Do you think we are free from it?"

"The French can't agree on what is causing the plague. Some say it is a bug. Some say it is a vine weakness." Pedro squeezed her hand. "I didn't mean to scare you."

He withdrew his hand, and she stared at the empty space, wondering about its meaning. When she glanced up, she found the Englishman watching them intently.

"Do you believe the physiology theory, Your Excellency?" Mr. Maxwell raised a brow, drawling the honorific.

Pedro glowered back. "Many years of a single culture and unmerciful pruning can lead to the vines' weakness. Would you not agree?"

Aunt Rosario clicked her tongue. "Enough with these depressing subjects. What about the entertainment in Paris?"

"Call me nostalgic, but I missed our own social gatherings." Pedro turned twinkling eyes on her aunt, and she blushed, fanning herself. "What better entertainment than the *modinhas* played by our talented ladies?"

The table was cleared, and the footmen brought the vintage port Julia had chosen from the cellar. Before it could be served, Aunt Rosario stood and suggested they all sojourn to the music room, where they could enjoy Vesuvio's port.

While Amelia's notes drifted from the piano, Julia tried to guard her own frustration. The party was almost over, and not only had she not gleaned Mr. Maxwell's intentions, but she had practically invited him to come back.

Chapter 9

"Wine is wont to show the mind of man."
Theognis

Sprawled on a Louis XV chair facing the piano, Griffin stared at his quarry—a perfect lady sitting with her back stiff, a faraway look on her face.

Mrs. Costa-Ferreira.

The name tasted like ash, and he rubbed a hand over his face, remembering to shut his gaping mouth. Of all the women, did she have to be the one indebted to his future father-in-law? Couldn't she remain Julia, no surname required, an impulsive Portuguese with a penchant for stories and for haunting his nights?

Surname or not, she didn't belong with this boring company, all of them too polite to do anything but offer platitudes.

When she glanced away from the singer, their gazes clashed. Her dark eyes called to him, hypnotizing. She lifted her chin regally, an exotic princess recently escaped from a man's fantasies. Silk certainly suited her, embracing her lush curves like a lover's caress, but he preferred her in breeches.

Griffin forced his gaze away. Like the rest of the house, the music room had wealth and good taste written all over it. Heavy moss-green curtains hung behind the piano and a mirror spanned the sidewall, framed by blue Portuguese tiles. Not a single sign of financial strain. Why had she signed the contract with Croft?

The count grabbed a Portuguese guitar from a peg close to the piano. "Julia, would you sing *Rosas Flores*?"

Griffin stifled a growl and the desire to kick his aristocratic ass.

Her expression turned inward, and she rubbed her chest. "I'm sorry, Your Excellency, but I must decline."

Griffin took pleasure in how the count's face fell, like a cat denied cream. Still, he would like to hear her sing and would bet Thunder's hind legs it would be just like her laugh—loud, pure, and unapologetic.

Another girl, puppy-eyed and staring at the *Fidalgo*, offered to sing. Almoster obliged the audience and strummed the guitar, accompanying the blonde girl at the piano, puppy-eyes contributing to the mellow notes with a saccharine voice.

This kind of song, the *modinha*, combined Italian opera with salon music. The new fashion, shipped straight from the Brazilian Imperial Court, infected dinner parties from Lisbon to Oporto. It was sentimental nonsense.

Griffin caught a glass of tawny from a passing footman. Julia refused the sherry served for the ladies and accepted the port instead. Why was he not surprised? She wore breeches; of course she drank port.

As she sipped the wine, her entire face changed, a glimpse of the megalith smile lighting up her eyes.

Griffin released a pent-up breath and drank his own port. The wine was superb, a vintage tawny for sure, old but just so. He stood and moved closer, a desire to ruffle her feathers making his hands tingle. She ignored him, attention fixed on the piano. Griffin chuckled and dropped his weight by her side, dipping the couch on purpose. Even sitting askew, she kept her gaze straight ahead.

"Is this one of Vesuvio's wines?"

She deigned to look at him, brows raised. "It is one of mine, yes."

Hers? How odd that a lady was so possessive of a Quinta's wine. Most would prefer other drinks. Port scared females, small children, and the feeble of heart.

"I think it's corked."

"What?" she sputtered, straightening. Her outburst startled the singing girl, and her aunt frowned.

Griffin stifled a laugh.

She flayed him with eyes glittering black fire. "You are mistaken, sir," she whispered furiously. "Where do you smell cork here? This is an 1857 vintage, one of the best there ever was. Can't you taste the prune and ripe berries? Here, take my glass. The nutty and smoky aromas are quite strong. Even an Englishman will scent it."

When he took the glass from her hand, he stroked her fingers on purpose, intending to fluster her. The contact with her hand, cool and clad in silk, brought memories of their kiss. How he missed her taste!

Adopting the betting face earned during his short Cambridge stay, he brought the glass close to his nose. After a long inhale, he shrugged. "Prunes? I can't find any."

She bristled, cheeks flushed. "You have a poor nose, Mr. Maxwell."

Griffin leaned back in the chair, narrowing his eyes. There was much he did not know about her. Yet. But unless he had completely misread her, the winemaker here—the one behind the best in all the Douro region—wore skirts. At least part of the time.

He inhaled her exotic floral scent and whispered close to her ear, "Touché."

***

Thwack. The dart hit the target with a satisfying thud. Griffin pushed the papers and books to the side of the desk to take better aim. He positioned the dart again, about to shoot it, but the rooster outside cackled loudly, celebrating the new bloody day as if it owned it.

Griffin exhaled, eyes gritty from doing sums for half the night. Images of Julia, not in last night's fancy silk but in tantalizing breeches, plagued him. Damn it, as Croft's debtor, she might as well hang with the stars—out of his reach.

Straightening, he retook aim. Thwack. Another bullseye.

At least he had finished the property accounts. He closed Boa Vista's ledger and tapped the worn leather of the cover. Five years of accounts set to rights.

Instead of money leaking through excessive expenses or embezzlement from the runaway estate manager, he had discovered a terrible truth—the Quinta was not productive enough. The vines yielded too few grapes. Where was the sensational return, reputedly four times higher than any other crop, the pride of the British community?

He dropped his head to the back of the chair. This was not his expertise. Give him a financial problem of any kind, a price to negotiate, a deal to improve, or a contract to settle. But farming? Not a chance.

He retook aim. This time, he pictured the face of the Count of Almoster.

Jako entered the study, crossing in front of the target.

Thwack. The dart lodged an inch away from his servant's head. Thank God.

Jako eyed him quizzically, wearing a bloody rose-shaped neckcloth with his signature pearl pin in the middle, and skimmed a stack of letters in his direction.

Griffin scanned Edmond's missive, satisfied that his business in Oporto still thrived. The second, from his sister Anne, he put inside his breast pocket. The last was from Croft. With brisk movements, he ripped the envelope open and ignored the pleasantries. Two sentences resumed the content of two pages. Croft was still waiting for news about Vesuvio, and Beth had begun shopping for the wedding.

He crumpled the paper. "A bloody trousseau."

"Congratulations in order, sir?"

Griffin raised his eyes from the cursed letter. "Listening to private conversations now, Jako?"

Jako looked offended. "Oh, I keep forgetting Your Excellency doesn't like to be interrupted when speaking with such important personage—himself."

Griffin ignored the jibe and pinched the bridge of his nose. "Elisabeth Croft is buying a trousseau."

Damn Croft and his manipulative ways.

"Will you do it? Marry the girl, sir?"

Griffin tore the letter into pieces. "It's a simple equation. Marry the girl, earn Croft's firm."

Jako stopped dusting the shelves and gave him a look of abject horror.

"What? She has all her teeth, is young, and English."

Griffin could tell Jako did not understand, though. People in Goa must marry for romantic reasons. He blocked Julia from his mind and stood. He couldn't do much about the trousseau. Still, he could tackle both problems with a single move—instruct himself about farming the vines and appease Croft's curiosity about Vesuvio. Perhaps he could unearth why the property had accepted Croft's financing.

Jako dusted the shelves, looking dignified in his immaculate clothes and with the ever-present pearl on his cravat.

Griffin scanned the books. Almeida Garrett, Alexandre Herculano, Camilo Castelo Branco. All romantic garbage. "Don't waste time cleaning those. Use them for kindling."

"What a pity. What if you decide to read a few someday?"

"Why would I do that?"

"To better understand the Portuguese?"

"Nonsense. I know them. They make great wine, they have a bloody complicated language, they love weird food and romantic nonsense, and they like to respond to reasonable questions with monosyllabic nonsensical answers." Griffin ignored the servant's scoff and retrieved Vesuvio's sketch from a niche below the books. "Can you read maps?"

"'Jako, can you read and write?' 'Jako, can you do sums?' 'Jako, can you do stitches?' 'Jako, can you hire servants?'" The servant, with a sullen expression on his face, peeked at the paper. "Yes, Jako can read maps. Thanks for asking."

Griffin pointed at the circular lines. "These lines mark Quinta do Vesuvio's original terraces. I want you to check if they increased the planted area." He smoothed the crinkles on the yellowed paper. The rendering of the property was poor, the scales off. Something was wrong, but he couldn't point his finger at precisely what. Yet. He rolled the paper. "Do you think you can walk around, talk with a few peasants without attracting too much attention?"

Jako rolled his eyes, accepting the paper. "I wonder when my job will stop gaining new attributions."

"Keep a low profile. Nobody likes foreigners nosing around their business."

Jako raised his bushy eyebrows. "Don't they all?"

Time to pay Vesuvio a call. They had an idiom in Portugal: at night, all cats were black. Griffin looked at the sun shining through the window—broad daylight.

Well, Mrs. Costa, time to learn your true colors.

Chapter 10

"Let us have wine and woman, mirth and laughter, Sermons and soda-water the day after." Byron

"Do you know who Aunt Rosario invited to yesterday's gathering?" Julia crumbled the bread, her stomach tied in knots.

"Let me guess. That old groping goat from Quinta da Saudade?"

Julia wrinkled her nose. "Worse. A friend of Mr. Croft, the old goat I owe money to."

Flor's brown eyes widened, and she stopped arranging the linen napkins on the breakfast table. "What did you do?"

Stared at his chiseled features for most of the night? Attempted a few questions, most of which he turned down at her face? "Stood my ground, of course."

"Good."

"But he is on to something. Like a dog with a new bone."

With that teasing voice, the whispers close to her neck... She needed to keep her wits to form a plan.

Flor peeked right and left and dropped into a chair beside Julia. "What now?"

"I don't know, but I can't allow him to find out about the secret valley. He can advise Mr. Croft to foreclosure." The word ruined her appetite.

Voices down the hallway alerted them of the family's arrival. Flor sprang to her feet, taking her toast, and returned to the kitchen.

Tony pounced on Julia's lap, the light from the stained-glass windows painting his eyes with green flecks. "*Mamã*, I want to go swimming."

Brushing hair from his forehead, she kissed his cheek. "Not today. I'm sorry." She had to choose oak samples for new wine barrels.

"Good morning, dears." Aunt Rosario dragged her feet to a chair, yawning. "Did you notice how the count plays the guitar? He is a perfect match for my sweet Amelia."

"Where's my cousin?" No rest for Aunt Rosario until she arranged a favorable marriage for Amelia.

"She is still asleep. Resting, naturally."

Poor dear. With her shyness, she must be exhausted after performing for strangers. Julia would check on her after breakfast.

Tony tugged on her hand. "Please?"

"Tell you what. Tomorrow, I will take you fishing."

He pursed his lips. "But you are a girl."

Julia tried to raise a single brow to convey her displeasure but ended up frowning instead.

He crossed his arms and pouted. "Fine."

After gobbling his bread, he left in his usual whirlwind, Nanny struggling behind.

Wentworth came in, salve in hand, followed by Abelardo. Both looked pale.

Julia straightened, eyes narrowing at the salve on the butler's hands. The white calling card glared at her. With shaking fingers, she read the bold letters.

Griffin Maxwell, from Maxwell Co.

The blood drained from her face, and Julia bounded from the chair. He was here? So soon? What would she do?

Aunt Rosario stood, seeming to forget her tiredness. "Oh, the charming neighbor is here. I must wake Amelia posthaste!"

At the ruckus, Flor came back from the kitchen, eyes wide. "What's wrong?"

"Mr. Griffin Maxwell is here to learn about winemaking." Abelardo gulped. "Do you want me to talk to him?"

Julia hugged herself. "No, it's better if I go. I'll—"

"Let Abelardo go. What will this Englishman think when he learns you run Vesuvio? A mere woman?" Flor opened her arms wide. "Remember that time with the last Concelho president?"

She'd rather forget. The man had refused to speak with her about buying pesticides for the smaller properties.

"If I may be of assistance." Wentworth glared at Flor. "I hate to mention this, but Florinda is right. As a British myself, I daresay the gentleman sitting in the receiving room will be more comfortable talking about business with another male."

Julia peered at Abelardo. With his gray suit more creased than normal, spectacles sliding down his straight nose, he looked the opposite of an estate manager.

Flor produced a comb from inside her apron. "Abe, let me fix your hair."

Wentworth rearranged the boy's neckcloth with precise movements. "Head high, straighten your back. There. Keep this position. Remember, posture defines a man."

What a crew, ranting about the best ways to deceive the Englishman. A maid with a penchant for drama, an unflappable butler, and a young scholar. Julia had never served in the army, but she would bet that before a battle, comrades felt this mixture of chest-puffing pride and gut-wrenching fear.

"Stop."

They turned to Julia, and the fussing halted.

She wrung her hands, eyes turning liquid. "I cannot let Abelardo go. This is my fight."

Flor touched her shoulder, and she welcomed her friend's warmth. "Let us help you. When you took me from that employment agency, no one would have a fallen woman from Lisbon." Her chin wobbled, and she used the tip of her apron to wipe her tears.

Wentworth nodded. "You gave us all assistance at one time or another."

Julia took a deep breath and eyed her friends. Their faces were expectant, seeming more secure than she felt about tutting the Englishman about the vineyards. What if they were right? Her judgment had proven faulty where it concerned that man.

"Take Mr. Maxwell to the school vineyard, then the *lagares*, but end the tour in the cellar. Englishmen love the cellar." She bit her lip. "Whatever you do, don't go anywhere near the valley."

Abelardo rubbed his neck. "But... what if he finds out I'm not really—"

"Keep your mouth closed. Only answer direct questions," Wentworth said.

"Yes, but play the part." Flor rolled her shoulders and flapped her arms. "Loosen up a bit."

Abelardo's expression shifted from fear to determination. "I can do this."

Flor followed him to the edge of the room. "Break a leg."

Chapter 11

"Of all things known to mortals, wine is the most powerful and effectual for exciting and inflaming the passions of mankind, being common fuel to them all." Francis Bacon

The day turned from hot to scorching, and the sun extracted a ripe smell from the black grapes growing around them. Griffin's pocket watch revealed it was noon. When he had left Boa Vista this morning, he had expected to see Vesuvio through Julia's eyes. He had been eager to ride by her side and watch that black hair flowing in the wind like a sail. Yet while he rode Thunder, she hid inside the house.

Griffin eyed Vesuvio's so-called estate manager, at least three feet below his line of sight, riding a mule of all things. "Do you sell the wine directly to the shippers or at Regua's Market?"

At his question, the boy looked up, eyes confident for the first time since they'd left the house. "We sell just for the one."

"One what?"

"One port shipper." He adjusted his glasses. "Croft Shippers."

Griffin hid his surprise. A property this size, selling for just Croft? The largest Quintas kept several selling partners. Another incongruity he would add to Julia's list. Once again, he had to wonder why she had signed the contract. So far, he had seen no newly planted hills, only matured vineyards, and the boy seemed unable to differentiate between the two.

A faint whirring turned stronger as they trotted along the edge of a crest. When a windmill appeared, white blades revolving, the mule planted sturdy legs on the schist and halted abruptly. With a groan and a thud, the boy capsized like a half-empty potato sack.

Griffin chuckled. "All right there?"

The boy straightened, cheeks aflame, and returned to his dubious steed. He grabbed the reins and tugged. One had to admire his perseverance, but the beast refused to move. The wind picked up speed, turning the blades faster, and the mule's eyes rolled, its back quivering.

Griffin eyed the cause of their troubles. The stone mill glowered back, its white blades circling menacingly. He snorted. The irony struck home. They certainly looked the part—he, a Don Quixote riding a mighty steed, and the boy, his underfed Sancho Panza.

He supposed he could dismount and help. With a sigh, he alighted the horse and approached the boy and mule. The beast—a sturdy animal with gray wool pelt, big rabbit ears, and a surly face—eyed him skeptically.

Abelardo brushed off his suit. "Sorry, Mr. Maxwell. I don't know what is wrong."

He seemed like a good boy. Honest and open, with the innocence of a man whose life had treated him kindly. Griffin tried but could not fault him for Julia's deception. After the party last night, he had a pretty good idea who managed Vesuvio's estate.

"You've never ridden this animal before?"

"I have no cause to. I usually walk."

Griffin looked at the unobstructed view stretching for miles around them. Every hill they passed had rows organized so precisely they seemed to have been measured with a ruler. While Boa Vista's vines fought with other plants for territory, Julia's grapevines ruled supreme, weed-free. Invisible lines stretched among the stakes and perfectly displayed clusters of grapes like amethysts on green baize.

"Sometimes Miss Julia drives me around on her buggy."

Griffin gritted his teeth. Did she think him stupid? If this boy was the estate manager of a Quinta like Vesuvio, cows would fly around the sky.

Well, for the job at hand. The mule smelled like wet shoes and dust. Griffin grabbed the beast's leather reins and pulled. Nothing. He planted his legs and flexed his knees, applying all his strength. Still nothing. When sweat moistened his brow and his shirt glued to his back, he knew it was time for another strategy.

Griffin crossed his arms, catching his breath. "It's simple mechanics. She has her feet and legs locked tight. We must disturb her balance. When she shifts her weight, we will move the ornery ass." He removed his coat and put it atop Thunder's saddle. "Hold the reins and pull with all your might. I will push her forward."

"Like a stuck wheel?"

"You got it."

Abelardo nodded twice. "*Divide et Impera*?"

"Save the Latin for the ladies, boy." Griffin chuckled, shaking his head. If ever there was a wrong situation to quote Julius Caesar, this was it. "But you are right. We will divide her attention and conquer the beast."

Griffin placed his hands on the mule's flanks, the coarse pelt quivering under his palms. "One, two, three."

While the boy pulled the reins, he gave a mighty shove. The mule's hooves lost their lockdown hold on the ground, and he felt the moment the beast shifted. He knew it. The mule bowed to human intelligence.

Instead of stepping forward, the animal lifted her hind leg and kicked.

He sucked in a breath as pain exploded in his thigh. "Hellish beast!"

The mule jumped and screamed as if a demon were atop it, emitting nasal hees and hohhhs and careening downhill like a banshee.

"Are you all right, sir?" The boy approached him at his own peril.

Griffin's muscles contracted. Ignoring the cursed bruise on his leg, he limped back to Thunder's side. In his black mood, he would be wise to go home and think this through. "Come. We are going back to Vesuvio."

Chapter 12

"Wine cheers the sad, revives the old, inspires the young, makes weariness forget his toil." Byron

"Do they teach deception in Portuguese schoolrooms?"

Julia stilled, dropping her cup. Who had allowed him inside her glass house? Heart accelerating, she rose from her chair and turned. "Most Portuguese girls don't go to school. They learn to be perfect brides right from their drawing rooms. It is after marrying that they learn other tricks to survive."

"Tricks?" The Englishman leaned on the shelves, the sun reflecting on his white coat and ricocheting off the glass walls.

What arrogance! Julia fisted her hands, rummaging through her brain for the perfect set down. Advancing inside her private workplace as if he owned it, he gazed at her with anger and defiance, as if daring her to utter a word. Mud peppered his trousers and caked near his temples, and his gait favored the right leg. What had happened in the vineyards? Had he found her secret?

"What do you want?" Her voice sounded like two rocks grating together.

His shoulders shadowed her vision. "Why did you send the boy?"

"You wanted to speak with Vesuvio's estate manager. Abelardo is—"

"The boy is no more an estate manager than mules can fly."

Julia's breath caught. "Will you tell Mr. Croft that—"

"That's why you buried yourself here?" He tilted his head to the side, his brows furrowed. "Afraid I am going to tell Croft who runs the property?"

Julia's heart pounded in her ears, and she gripped the silk of her skirts. "I don't know in which world you live, Mr. Maxwell, but here a woman—"

He raised his hands. "You can breathe easily. He won't believe the best wine property of the region is run by a woman."

Her shoulders relaxed a notch, and she forced her hands to unclench.

"Why did you sign it?" His voice dropped an octave.

"Do Englishmen learn to talk with ghosts? If so, please ask my husband. I bet he would be pleased to tell you all the details."

Glowering, he gritted his teeth. "No more games. My temper took a bruising today."

She swallowed, her throat dry as wood bark. "What do you wish to know?"

"Start at the beginning."

Growing up with men had taught her when to push and when to give in to their moods. She lifted her brows and exhaled, as if preparing for a long story. "From the beginning? All right. I was born on June 23, 1844. The year *Nabucco* made its debut in Theater São Carlos. My father loved it so much he wanted to call me Fenena. I am glad my mother did not allow it."

His mouth gaped, and then he chuckled. The anger hardening his features faded like alcohol decanting from wine. With his eyes crinkling at the corners, he looked like her stray Englishman from the megaliths.

Julia bit her cheek not to join his humor. She couldn't forget his identity and his purpose here.

He looked at her with narrowed eyes, as if reassessing his strategy, then turned away to prowl around the greenhouse. His boots clattered on the granite slabs and his huge hands hovered over her herb pots and dried flowers.

When he reached for the first vine Julia had grafted, her heart tottered around her chest. Oblivious to her distress, he plucked an emerald leaf and fingered the link connecting the foreign rootstock to the Portuguese grapevine. What if he asked about it? Could her secret stand a direct hit?

A heartbeat passed, then two, and he moved on.

Julia sagged against her worktable, releasing a pent-up breath.

He circled the room and faced her, his gaze landing on the new samplings atop the desk. "Wood shavings?"

"Pieces of oak for wine barrels."

He invaded her side of the table. "I thought they were all the same."

She pushed the first porcelain cup in his direction. "Smell them. See if they are the same."

He brought the cup to his straight nose. "Wood?"

"This is French oak. It adds notes of vanilla and smoke to the wine."

"And this?" He pointed to the second cup.

He seemed genuinely interested. What should she make of such behavior? Most would be yawning and mooning at the door, looking for a way out. Still, it could be a ruse to make her lower her guard.

"This one is American. It is smoked but adds an assertive note, more powerful but less delicate than the French."

"But why do you need them?" A lock of chocolate-colored hair fell on his brow, giving him a boyish appearance.

"Tawny Port, like the human male, is expected to evolve with age, becoming more complex, adding notes of spice, smoke, and nuts. The barrels are crucial to flavor this change."

He raised a single brow, a smile lurking at the corner of his lips. "And women?"

She fidgeted with the wood shavings, teasing the vanilla scent from the cup. "Women are expected to do the impossible. Stay the same, maintain the same color and sweetness and fruit, like Ruby Port. To achieve that, the Ruby doesn't need wood. It ages inside huge, ancient vats where oxidation is minimum."

He advanced one more step, his gaze caressing her face. "Impossible indeed. Are there tawny women?"

Julia had to glance away, crossing her arms over her chest. "Perhaps."

He raised his firefly-catching finger and guided her chin up, capturing her more effectively than if he had used chains. "Why did you sign it?"

He loomed too close. She lost her thoughts in his starched collar, her fingers itching to feel the bristles of his beard above the white linen.

"Julia?"

His gravelly voice threaded her insides into grape pulp. Her secrets stirred inside her chest, ripening, growing branches, wanting out. Could she unburden herself, make him understand? He didn't seem scandalized by the fact she ran the Quinta. What would he think about her experiments? About her advancements in Botanic?

A breeze whispered inside the glass panes, shuffling the leaves of the grafted vine. The foreign root fed water to the Portuguese scion, and in turn, the scion produced grapes. They were stronger together despite their different nationalities. If it worked so well with plants...

Tentatively, breathlessly, she met his eyes again. "Mr. Croft's lawyer came two months after my husband passed away."

Against her will, her body leaned closer to him, searching for his warmth. Not a lamp's dry feverish heat, but fragrant and comforting like the heat of a steaming bath.

"Go on."

The words rushed to escape her chest, and Julia inhaled to speak.

Wentworth cleared his throat. The butler, stoic expression restored, intoned from the threshold, "I'm sorry to interrupt, but the Count of Almoster is here."

"Take him to the drawing-room, please," Julia said, trying to control her racing heart.

Griffin's mellow expression soured into vinegar. "I see why you would not give me a tour of the property today. Someone else is sampling your tricks."

She flinched, and shame flooded her chest, her throat, her face until it choked her. "Since you showed yourself in, you can show yourself out. Good day, Mr. Maxwell."

***

Julia's silk dress dragged on the pebbled path, catching as many leaves on the hem as a rake. How dare he?

Invading her home and insulting her reputation. What was wrong with receiving a visitor? Pedro was a friend of the family. The arrogant, hypocritical Englishman—she stumbled and would have fallen on her face if not for her grip on Pedro's arm.

"You are distracted." His voice sounded amused.

"I am sorry." Julia shook her head. Mr. Maxwell didn't deserve her consideration, and she wouldn't give him an ounce of attention.

Pedro smiled. His expression was relaxed as they walked along the path, gazing at the river and pointing at places they had explored as children. "I've missed it here."

"Surely you've seen amazing sceneries in the eight years you've been away."

He halted. "Seven years and four months."

The sun filtering through the elm trees glinted off his epaulets and golden hair, emphasizing his classical beauty. He stared at her, the intensity of his brown eyes a tad unsettling.

Julia glanced away, resuming their stroll. "Did you see Phylloxera in the *Comercio do Porto* today? The newspaper reported the wine plague is a louse, barely visible, attacking the roots—"

"You should not concern yourself with such matters."

"But if it gets here—"

"Allow me to take care of it. Soon, you won't have to occupy your beautiful head with these matters."

Julia frowned. What did he mean by that? As the new Concelho president, perhaps he would deal with the situation. Or was it something else? Whatever the case, she didn't like the implications.

They reached the dovecote. The tall tower reached for the sky, a few thrushes flying around the triangular-shaped roof. Pedro steered her inside. It was empty now, but thousands of pigeons used to make their nests on the checkered walls.

Julia rubbed her arms, wrinkling her nose at the moldy odor. "I am surprised you remembered this place."

"How could I forget? When I arrived that day, you were holding up the ceiling's beams. Almost killed yourself to get to that hurt house martin." His gaze turned thoughtful, a single line between his golden brows. "Always trying to save broken things."

"The other children laughed and pointed at me, but you climbed all the way in there to save me." Julia turned, searching for the broken brick she had used that day. "It was the last month you spent here."

"My father took a treasure from me that summer." The tone of his voice was low, and his smile turned brittle. "Now I'll have it back."

"Surely the duke didn't know its worth, otherwise—"

"Do you know there used to be rules for building dovecotes?" He turned away and touched the crumbling mortar.

Julia dropped the subject, remembering his father's violence. "What rules?"

"Only *Fidalgos* could build them. They are a reminder of when things worked, of when our people were fed and housed and protected. Now they are scattered, going hungry, prey for foreigners, forced to leave the country."

What was better? To be locked inside the dovecote or to be free? The circular walls housed thousands of safe nesting places, built one on top of the other. Just looking at them made her stomach lurch. Freedom easily trumped safety.

A shadow passed above their heads, followed by some eerie cooing and the flapping of wings. The hairs on her arms and neck lifted, and she strode out of the confined tower. Outside, she blinked to adjust her eyes to the bright daylight. The breeze, fragrant with junipers, was a welcome respite.

In under a heartbeat the count was by her side, reaching for her hand. He brought it to his cool lips, eyes burning. "Julia, I want you to be my wife."

Words failed her, and she stared at the Count's hopeful expression. No doubt he saw the carefree girl who saved house martins and sang with abandon. A free vine spreading in all directions. But she was not that girl anymore. Her branches had been clipped several times, trained to the lines, growing close to the stakes.

"I surprised you." He pressed his lips into a thin line.

"Certainly, this is unexpected. I . . . I don't know what to say. You may choose any girl, younger, richer..."

"I've wanted this for a long time."

When his eyes locked with hers, his expression softened. Julia's throat turned dry, her skin prickling. What if he kissed her? She opened her mouth to argue this was madness, but he closed it with his fingertips.

"Don't answer me now. You need time to consider the advantages of this match." He kept his voice low, but a tendon stood out on his neck. "But don't make me wait too long. I'm not a patient man."

Chapter 13

"Good wine ruins the purse; bad wine ruins the stomach," Spanish saying

Griffin pushed inside the Vila Nova Tavern, banging the door on the wall. Quaint lanterns decorated the salon's ceiling and the walls sported bright Portuguese tiles. The place had a nice, upbeat atmosphere. In his current mood, he had hoped for a dimly lit tavern with cutthroats and gin.

He nodded at Mr. Albuquerque, one of Julia's neighbors. The man stood and politely introduced the two other occupants of his table.

He did not invite Griffin to sit. Griffin did not ask to. Moved on.

For several moments, he stared at the wooden counter. The waitress looked back, waiting for his order. A knot formed in his stomach, but he could not blame the kitchen's greasy smell. What had possessed him to insult Julia like that?

"If it's ale you want, you came to the wrong place. They don't drink beer."

"Boyd?" Griffin clasped the large Scotsman's hand. "What the devil are you doing here?"

Boyd tapped at his dusty knee-length leather boots with a horsewhip and ran his hand through his russet hair. A beard of several days darkened his tanned skin. "Just passing through. I'm returning from Jerez."

Like him, Boyd had come to Portugal as a lad. Now he owned a wine property in Spain and the loft in Gaia, selling port to the husbands and sherry to the wives.

Well, except for Julia. She drank port.

"Why the long detour?"

"I'm headed to the hunting lodge in Regua. Come, let's sit." Boyd inclined his head to an empty table and pushed a few *Reis* to the serving lady. "Two *Verdes, por favor.*"

The scarred surface soon bore two earthenware cups. Griffin gulped the pale green liquid. The green wine made his mouth water, stinging his throat, acidic in the extreme. Too late, he remembered Julia's advice about the tavern's *Verde*. He grimaced and lowered the cup. "How's the vintage market?

"Swelled like the Douro in spring."

"Prices down, then?"

"Not by much. People are nervous about phylloxera. I don't know about you, but I am buying all the wine I can stock."

Griffin frowned. "All this because of the plague in Bordeaux?"

"Have you not heard? They believe a few vineyards near the beach in Viana do Castelo have been stricken."

Griffin leaned back in the chair, mouth suddenly dry. How would Julia take this news?

Boyd took a swig of the acid stuff and coughed. "When will you return home?"

Was his townhouse in Oporto home? Of course it was. Griffin cleared his throat, gazing at his hands. "I must find an estate manager first."

"I know a fellow in Regua. Name is Silva. On my way back, I can ask him to come to your Quinta."

"Thanks."

Boyd pushed the cup away. "Christ. This place shouldn't be called a tavern. Give me the three Bs instead of this vapid stuff." He counted on his blunted fingertips. "Beer, brawling, and buxom maids."

Griffin stiffened. "What's wrong with Portuguese maids?"

There was nothing wrong with his particular Portuguese maid. The way she had flinched from him today brought a heaviness to his chest, and he drowned it with a long swallow of the *Verde*.

Boyd leaned forward, lowering his voice. "If you are leering at some *rapariga* here, you better forget her. Portuguese and English people don't mix. Take our good old king Charles II. He could not get a son out of that Portuguese woman, Catherine of Braganza. Went to his cold grave without an heir. No mixing, I tell you."

Did Griffin know of a marriage between these two countries? British families in Oporto often sent prospective brides and grooms to England for a season or two. Otherwise, inbreeding would have diluted them to a bunch of idiots. But he could not remember a single occurrence of marriage between a Portuguese and a Briton.

"At least the marriage brought Tangiers and Bombay," Griffin said absentmindedly.

Boyd's theory was utter rubbish, but it had merit. A proper explanation for why this stubborn strip of land had stayed separate from Spain, repelled the Moors, and ousted two French invasions. They didn't mix.

Julia's eyes flashed inside his mind, and he took a long swig of the biting stuff.

Better they did not mix.

Chapter 14

Men are like wine—some turn to vinegar,
but the best improve with age.
Pope John XXIII

Griffin guided Thunder on a path winding from Vesuvio's manor to the river. He shaded his eyes but couldn't see anything beyond it. That old groom was delusional. It was too early for a woman to be about—fishing, for Christ's sake. Griffin tugged at his cravat. He had treated her abominably yesterday, and as a gentleman, he owed her an apology.

The slope turned steeper, and down there, flanked by grapevines, he spotted her. She wore breeches again—arms bare to the elements, hair tied back, a few ebony strands resting on her shoulder. The sun lent her a halo of light that both blinded and branded his eyes. Mouth dry, thoughts more scrambled than the pancakes the cook had served him for breakfast, he touched his heels to Thunder's flanks.

He alighted from the horse and faced her.

She glared at him, shoulders and neck tense, lips pursed—the petite Portuguese ready for battle.

Griffin raised his palms, bracing himself. "I've come to—"

"Wow, I've never seen a silver horse!" An urchin, only four feet tall, appeared from behind her legs.

Griffin backed away, mouth agape. "Who are you?"

The boy ignored him, petting Thunder's nose. The horse blew on his chubby hands, and the lad giggled.

Julia crossed her arms, eyebrows raised. "Mr. Maxwell, meet Antonio, my son."

Griffin sucked in a breath, gaze shifting from Julia to the boy. "You have a son?"

Could it be true? The lad's hair and eye color didn't match, but he would bite his own foot if the pert nose and proud chin were not Julia's. What else would he uncover about her? First, she owed money to his future father-in-law, and now this—a four-foot fence with shining eyes and a too-eager disposition. As if there were not enough obstacles between them.

Griffin exhaled, shaking his head. He should beat a hasty retreat to Boa Vista.

"This must be the mightiest horse in the world." Antonio pushed to his toes, tangling chubby hands in Thunder's mane.

Well, at least the boy had a good eye for horseflesh.

"Can I ride him?" Without waiting for an answer, he grabbed the stirrup and tried to propel his weight up.

Griffin flung his sturdy body atop the horse, grunting at his unexpected weight. The lad hooted; delighted, it seemed.

"Hold here." Griffin pointed to the saddle's pommel.

The boy was clearly thrilled by the horse. Would it be too objectionable if he proposed a trade? Send the lad to enjoy a ride along the countryside, while Griffin stayed to enjoy the lad's mother?

"Are you certain it is safe?" Julia's eyes darted from Griffin to her son, as if he had mounted a dragon. "He doesn't know how to ride."

No trade, then. Griffin raised an eyebrow. "It's just a horse, and I am holding it."

Her shoulders lowered a quarter inch. "What brings you to Vesuvio, Mr. Maxwell?"

"I just wanted a word, but I can come back another time. I don't want to interrupt your fishing expedition."

"Come with us? Mommy doesn't know how to bait the worm."

Griffin winked. "Girls never do."

Julia glared, a flushed glower that would no doubt scare wayward children. "I am sure Mr. Maxwell has other obligations, Tony."

"It would be my pleasure." He accepted just to see her disgruntlement and lifted the lad down from Thunder.

She inclined her head regally and led the way, carrying the fishing equipment. He followed, trying not to focus on the sway of her hips enveloped in those tight breeches.

The narrow path gave way to a garden, an idyllic place with flower beds and benches facing the Douro. They had barely stopped when Antonio scampered toward a pier shaded by willows.

Griffin rubbed his neck. "Julia, I came to—"

"The count is a friend of the family. No matter what you think, I am a respectable widow."

He exhaled and looked away. "I'd hoped forgiveness to be among Portuguese women's many virtues."

"I don't know. Do all Englishmen insult women in their homes?"

"No, just this boar of an Englishman, it seems."

"Boar? Don't you mean pig?" She tossed her hair and left him gaping to run after the boy. "Tony, be careful."

What an impertinent mother hen. Why toss a perfectly acceptable apology back at his face? Befuddled, he closed his mouth and followed, boots clanking over the pier's wooden planks, then squatted near her. She shifted, crouching as far as away as possible without falling in the Douro. The boy had no such reservations and dropped by his side, scooting closer. How did one deal with overeager kids? Griffin gave him a stern look, but Antonio's grin seemed painted on his face.

While the boy fidgeted with his implements, Griffin extended his legs, his gaze trailing to the river. The sun's rays reflected on the water, glinting off Julia's olive skin and lighting her black eyes from within. Even frowning like a Portuguese Boadicea, she was too enticing for his peace of mind.

Antonio pushed a can at his face. "The worms."

Griffin startled and shook himself from her thrall. Right. Worm baiter, his job. He picked one of the slimy creatures and the fishhook. "This is how you do it."

Antonio followed his movements like an eager soldier preparing for battle, eyes huge, brows raised. If only his sister Anne paid attention to his instructions with the same enthusiasm.

"The secret is to push until the tip of the hook is clear. This way, the fish won't be able to bite the worm without being caught." Griffin passed him the implements. "Now, you try it."

Julia inclined forward. "Careful you do not poke your hand."

Griffin pitied the lad. He had grown up with an overprotective mother too, and it had been a nuisance. After a few missed shots, Antonio got a smile on his face and a passable worm on his hook. The fishing began, their long bamboo rods reaching a few feet over the river.

"Oh!" Antonio squealed and rose, about to topple headfirst into the water.

Julia vaulted up, but Griffin stopped her. "Let me handle this."

Griffin held the boy's scrawny arm and guided him a step back. The line stretched, tensing and pulling.

"Keep both hands on the rod."

The lad wrestled with the fish, a frown creasing his forehead. "It won't come out."

"Steady. Just pull and release. It will tire soon." Tentatively, Griffin patted his back. "That's it. Look at its fins."

The lad yelped. Sputtering and twitching, the pint-sized brown bass emerged from the water, and Tony grabbed him with both hands, pride puffing his chest. He shared a look of triumph with Griffin.

Griffin ruffled the boy's hair. "Nice work, kid."

The crease left Julia's brows, softening her eyes, and she mouthed a thank you that warmed him from the inside out. While Tony crouched again, intent on the river, Griffin stared as she arched her spine, cupped water, and splashed her face. Her skin glittered as if adorned with diamonds.

A thirst for those drops gripped him with such force, Griffin had to look away, clearing his throat. "Why is it called Douro?"

"Some say there used to be gold here. Not the kind you have to dig to find, but the gilded pebbles that lie in the riverbed, waiting to be caught."

Her voice, the river lapping under the pier, and the willows whispering in the breeze brought a foreign peace to Griffin's chest, releasing the tension from his shoulders. He leaned back on the wooden planks, crossing his ankles. "Do you believe in this theory?"

"I believe there is still gold here. Another type of gold, more precious. One that is not yellow nor metal. While gold can be found worldwide, this can only come from here."

"Port." Griffin cringed at the huskiness of his voice.

Nodding, she smiled, the kind of smile that turned a man inside out. He felt absurdly pleased to have answered her question correctly, like a schoolboy angling for his teacher's attention.

This was just a passing attraction. He was too long without a woman, she was a widow with a small son, and he would soon be engaged.

Still, his resolve wavered like the willows on the riverbank.

***

Julia spread a checkered cloth over the grass, keeping her gaze on the fishermen. Tony and Mr. Maxwell were still at the pier, heads bent together in a conversation she couldn't hear. Occasionally, either or both laughed. The Englishman had made a good impression on her fatherless boy, and Tony was too small to stay detached. Saint George knew she was having a hard time trying. Handsome and charming, he certainly was, but he could yet cause their ruin.

Girding her determination, she arranged the food for the picnic. After this morning, she would cut their interactions. Mr. Croft had asked for a favor, and she could simply say no. First thing tomorrow, she would place a guard on the valley, protecting it from curious eyes. That would do the trick.

The fishermen arrived to eat. Tony grabbed an apple and kneeled by the bucket, examining the fish. Mr. Maxwell sprawled atop the cloth, his interminable legs touching the sun outside the trellis shade. Framed by magenta blossoms, his bisque coat splattered with mud, he didn't look threatening—not to the vineyards, at least.

Squeezing onto her allotted fraction of the picnic cloth, Julia offered him bread topped with white cheese and slices of ripe fig. Shaking his head, he pushed it back to her. A tug of war followed, with the insufferable man moving the morsel to her and she forcing it back to him.

"Try it." She laughed. "It tastes better than it looks. You have my word."

"You are overly fond of that line, are you not?"

"I use it to cajole children."

With a ferocious glare on his face, he finally placed his teeth on the bread and took a bite. He closed his eyes, expression softening, and a moan escaped his lips. Staring at his chiseled jaw, Julia imagined him tasting the creaminess of the goat cheese and the figs' flowery taste, the flavors exploding inside his mouth. When he opened his eyes, their gazes met. Warmth spread to her limbs, making her dizzy.

A movement beyond the trellis shook the bougainvillea, raining down magenta blossoms on the grass. Her son had flung himself atop the Englishman's horse, perching precariously on the saddle.

Julia shot to her feet and grabbed Mr. Maxwell's arm. "Oh, my God."

Grinning, Tony slapped the horse's rump, and they took off with a swoosh. Terror rooted Julia's legs to the spot, but Mr. Maxwell bolted in pursuit.

The stallion galloped toward the main house. She watched, paralyzed, as the Englishman cut through the grapevines, racing uphill, his path perpendicular to the rows of the vineyard.

Breathless, she forced herself to move, following the walkway leading to the house in an unsteady run. The horse cantered with Tony still wrapped around his neck like a flagging scarf. Her heart pounded in her throat, and she increased her pace.

Please, God, keep him safe. If Tony reached the road, the horse would run unfettered. Miles of hard ground stretched all the way to the village. They would certainly find his body trampled along the way.

Images from a different accident intruded on her mind, and she clenched her teeth, keeping her eyes wide open. Not him. Not her son. The schist soil crumbled under her feet as she climbed the path, her thighs burning with the effort. Horse and rider vanished from sight. Lungs about to burst, praying for her boy's safety, she reached the crest in time to see them cantering away.

The horse veered to the left, in the road's direction. Hand covering her mouth, Julia stifled a scream. Just when her legs had turned to mush, Mr. Maxwell flung himself from the row of vines, catching the horse's bridle.

"Whoa, Thunder, stop!"

Julia half-raced, half-stumbled the last few steps, her throat so dry it seemed she had swallowed sand. Mr. Maxwell patted the horse's neck, murmuring in his hoarse voice. The beast panted, eyes wild, muscles quivering under the Englishman's soothing palms. Tony hid face in the horse's neck, his brown hair mingling with the grayish mane.

"Shh. It's over now." Griffin peeled Tony from Thunder's back.

Her son latched onto his neck. Mr. Maxwell patted her boy's back, chest heaving with the force of his breaths. Winded, half-blind by the sun, Julia drank in the sight. Tony alive, saved by the Englishman.

"Thank you. Thank you so much." Her voice shook, and she buried her face in Tony's downy hair, inhaling deeply, infusing her body with his scent—still alive, still warm, still the same.

Mr. Maxwell grunted and pulled away from her.

Had she just embraced him? Julia wrung her hands, her cheeks flaming.

"Here. It's over now," he said gruffly, and passed Tony to her.

Julia shifted Tony to her hip and stared into his wide eyes. "What were you thinking? You could've been killed."

Tony touched her face. "Please don't cry, *Mamã*. I hate it when you cry."

"He needs riding lessons," Mr. Maxwell said.

Julia lifted her face. "What?"

"He needs to learn how to ride."

"I appreciate your concern, but he is too small—"

"He is what, seven?"

"I will be seven in December," Tony said.

Hands splayed on his knees, Griffin addressed Tony. "Tell you what, tomorrow I will come and teach you."

Tony squeaked, a grin illuminating his face.

Julia rubbed her eyes, her legs still unsteady. "It is a kind offer, but you are a busy man—"

"If it makes you feel better, we could trade. Tony needs riding lessons, and I need wine lessons, so to speak." Gazing into her eyes, he lowered his voice. "But I want the expert's help. If she is available."

Warmth spread in her chest, and she bit her lip. "I don't know . . . I must inspect the fields. Harvest will start soon. I can't spare the time."

"Take me along then. An *in loco* lesson. Even better."

Spending time with him was a risk to Vesuvio, if not her heart—and Tony's. But after what he had just done, how could she deny his request?

The Englishman stared at her, his hands tucked nonchalantly in his pockets. His brows were lifted, but not in challenge. "Deal?"

"Deal." She smiled and shook his hand.

Chapter 15

"The priest instructs, and so our life exhales,
A little breath, love, wine, ambition, fame,
Fighting, devotion, dust—
perhaps a name." Byron

Julia kneeled, and stood, and sat, and sang, but she couldn't pay attention to Father Cosme's sermon. Would the Englishman really come today? It seemed like a lot of trouble to teach a boy how to ride. Her distraction attracted raised brows from Aunt Rosario. Body alternating between cold and heat, she tried to read the mass book, only to realize it was upside down.

When she glanced right, she met Pedro's eyes again. Hunkering on the men's side, his stare lifted the hairs on her nape. On the women's side, the excitement was thicker than the incense leaving Father Cosme's thurible. It wasn't every Sunday a *Fidalgo* graced the mass. For once, the separation by gender had a use. At least it saved her from Pedro's insistence. Why did he have to change their relationship? Couldn't they be friends as before?

After finishing the Holy Father, she hastily said goodbye to Aunt Rosario and Amelia. While a well-dressed gentleman talked with Pedro, she collected Tony and left. If she hurried, she could reach the carriage without having to answer Pedro's absurd proposition.

Outside, she maneuvered through families and couples talking under the shade of acacias. Just a few yards more, and they would reach her buggy. She helped Tony atop the carriage and circled to the other side.

Pedro's sudden appearance made her catch her breath. "Is he Bernardo's son?"

Panting, Julia placed a hand on her chest. "Yes. Mine, too."

He leaned close. "Ride with me? I've planned a—"

"I don't think it's a good idea. During the growing season, I'm hard-pressed to—"

"I insist." He squared his shoulders, his expression hardening. "I trust tomorrow is acceptable for you."

Pursing her lips, she inclined her head. "As you wish, Your Excellency."

Seated on the buggy, she exhaled and shook the reins. Besides a childhood infatuation, what could explain this sudden interest? Perhaps he wanted Vesuvio, hoping to increase his power in the region. She must make him desist without giving offense.

As they left the Vila Nova's Main Street, villagers waved and children raced behind the carriage, laughing. Tony shot to his feet, balancing with his legs splayed to wave back. On the road, near home, her heartbeat started a crescendo rhythm. Would the Englishman be waiting for them?

By the time they crossed Vesuvio's iron gate, her heart stomped louder than the horse's hooves. Tony gripped the seat, knuckles white, searching the courtyard. But the place was empty—no tall, imposing figure to be seen. Turning on the driveway, she stopped near the stable door. Jose hurried to secure the buggy and help Tony alight.

With a heavy sigh, Julia went down on her haunches. "Dear, don't be sad, but I believe Mr. Maxwell—"

"Good morning." He stepped into her shadow, the sky reflecting on his well-polished boots.

Tony jumped, a huge grin on his face. Julia sprang to her feet, praying her expression didn't show the same excitement as her son's. In the same breath, Tony abandoned her side, racing to the Englishman.

"Traitor," she muttered.

Mr. Maxwell ruffled his hair. "Ready, lad?"

They went to the paddock behind the stables, Tony skipping to catch up with the Englishman's longer strides. Uninvited, Julia followed and leaned on the wooden fence. Thunder's height made her jittery, but his eyes seemed docile. When the Englishman flung Tony on the horse's back, he accepted the weight without flicking his ears.

After several brow-furrowed instructions, Mr. Maxwell tied the horse to a long rein, leading it around the paddock like a clock hand. While Tony swayed from side to side, Julia shuffled from foot to foot, biting her nails. When Mr. Maxwell clicked his tongue and the horse trotted, she clutched the folds of her dress with enough force to bend the crinoline. But Tony had a grin on his face, and she couldn't ruin this for him.

Nanny Maria joined her by the fence. "How is the lesson?"

"Wait for it to end here, please. When it's over, take Tony inside." With a shaking breath, Julia took refuge in the stables.

Chapter 16

"All our knowledge begins with the senses, proceeds then to the understanding, and ends with reason. There is nothing higher than reason." Immanuel Kant

Griffin paused at the entrance to the stables. He should have left after Tony's lesson, but her voice had beckoned him in. The building looked old but well-tended, with unpolished granite floors and exposed beam ceilings. Most of the stalls were empty, with a few housing grains and other farm supplies. He found her inside one halfway down the line, her back to him as she brushed a champagne-colored horse.

Julia gazed at him above her dainty shoulder, lifting her brows as if challenging his right to be there. Griffin strolled inside anyway. A pale light glinted off her fetching plum dress, making her ebony hair shine.

"How did it go?" she asked nonchalantly, but her eyes were expectant. What was her problem with horses?

"Fine. He fell just once."

She dropped the brush. “What?”

Chuckling, he picked it up for her. “He is a fine kid. Ever considered trying not to control him so much?”

“Since when do you know how to raise children?”

“If you cannot deduce by yourself, I was a boy once.”

“Really? I could not tell.”

“I am positive Tony is part English. The boy is a natural.” Griffin moved closer.

Julia raised a delectable shoulder. “Portuguese men are skillful riders.”

“And the women?”

She frowned, gaze intent on the horse. “Some are good.”

Griffin glided his hands across her horse’s neck, admiring the lines. “What’s his name?”

“Diuro.”

How had she managed so many vowels? “Deeourou?”

She shrugged. “I could tell you the River God’s legend, but you don’t care for my stories.”

Griffin glanced away, lest she saw exactly how little he cared for her stories. “You will allow an Englishman to stop your patriotic ramblings? I thought you Portuguese were made of sterner stuff.”

When she exhaled audibly, blowing the hair from her forehead, he knew she had taken his bait. “After all the rivers were created, Diuro slept and missed the call to reach the ocean. When he woke up, the other rivers were already on their way. Impetuous, Diuro raced them, wishing to reach the Atlantic first. He used a shortcut, spanning ravines, plunging in canyons, crossing steep scarps. That's why the Douro has such a torturous path."

His eyes turned heavy-lidded. "And he won?"

She grinned. "Of course."

"Andalusian?"

"Surely you jest, sir. This horse is not Spanish. Can't you see the lines? It's a Lusitano."

"What's the difference?"

"The Lusitano is a noble breed. Legend says they inspired the Greeks' centaurs. They were bred for war, brave and strong, but they are also gentle, always trying to please their owner."

He winked. "That certainly is useful."

She blushed to the roots of her hair.

Griffin advanced one more step. "I heard Lusitano horses need to be exercised faithfully. Otherwise, they become hot and difficult to handle." He wanted to see her ride this majestic animal. He wanted to gallop these hills side by side with her.

"I don't ride him anymore." Light flickered in her eyes like a flame left in the breeze.

Griffin shoved his hands in his pockets to keep from reaching for her. "Why?"

"Are all Englishmen inquisitive like you?"

"We are a curious lot." Her silence was unacceptable. Tenderly, he held her chin. "Tell me."

Her eyes turned liquid. "My husband died in a horse accident."

Griffin released her, taking a step back. "I'm sorry. If you are afraid, I can assure you it's perfectly safe—"

"I am not afraid."

If not fear, then what? Had she loved her husband so much that she avoided riding in his memory? His gut tightened. Did she still love him?

"You paid your part of the bargain." She stored the brush, pausing at the stall's door. "Tomorrow, I need to inspect the fields. Would you care to join me? For lesson purposes?"

The change of subject startled him, and he crossed his arms over his chest. Tomorrow would suit him well enough, as he had scheduled to meet Boyd's estate manager later this week. Her instructions would help him judge the man's competence, and afterward, he could return to Oporto. Mouth dry, he followed the gentle sway of her hips in the long corridor until the trail of plum taffeta vanished.

A shuffling sound made him turn. Jose emptied a bucket of corn into Diuro's feeder. With a checkered cap covering his eyes, the old groom was gnarled and sturdy like an olive tree.

Griffin patted the horse's neck. "He is a thing of beauty."

"That he is."

"Shame your mistress doesn't ride him. Do you know why?"

The man's face was stuck in a perpetual scold. "If it's tales you want, sir, save your breath."

Griffin turned to leave when Jose touched his shoulder.

"That horse of yours is well-treated. I can always tell a good gent from a bad just by looking at his mount." Jose took a handful of kernels and put a few in his mouth. "The little miss used to ride him every day. If you think Diuro looks fine here, you should see her putting him through his paces. A thing of beauty indeed." He grinned, revealing a distressing glimpse of chewed corn and missing teeth.

"And why did she stop?"

"All I know is what this eye sees." He removed the cap, pointing to his single good eye. "The mister went out one night. The horse came back alone, mind you, with a gash on either side of its belly."

"Spurs." Griffin abhorred men who compensated for their lack of riding skills by using spurs, especially the barbed ones that cut the horse's coat.

"Drunk as a skunk and riding hell-bent, if you ask me. The word is he broke the neck."

Could Julia be in love with such a fellow? She seemed too sensible a woman to fall for that type. Still, love often eliminated a person's judgment.

"After the accident, the miss sold all the horses but this fancy piece, the plow horse, and the mule." Jose pointed to the last stall.

Griffin recognized his asinine nemesis. The beast munched corn, oblong face as surly as ever.

Jose spat corn on the floor. "You better steer clear of her."

"The mule? I don't mean to go anywhere near that cantankerous beast."

"I mean the little miss."

Griffin squared his shoulders. "You can mind your own business."

Jose gave him a one-eyed glare. "I saw the way you look at her, sir, and she is not that kind of woman."

Chapter 17

"Wine is sunlight, held together by water." Galileo Galilei

The new riding habit's velvet felt heavenly on Julia's palms, and she closed her eyes. Would the Englishman like the flattering amber color? What did it matter if he liked it or not? This was business, nothing else. She flung away the fancy dress. Briskly, she donned her functional clothing and marched outside, instructing Jose to ready her buggy.

The morning sun painted the courtyard in a harsh, blazing light. Julia wrung her hands, planning their trajectory. She would take him to see the hills, keeping a safe distance from the secret valley. Hopefully, by the end of this outing, the Englishman would issue a favorable report to Mr. Croft. Everything would be all right if she could secure time for the special vines to produce.

Mr. Maxwell crossed Vesuvio's iron gates astride Thunder, and she sucked in a breath. Perfectly groomed in impractical white breeches and a chestnut tailored coat, the man seemed impervious to the sun.

He halted before her. "Where is your horse?"

Had he forgotten their conversation? "Jose is readying the buggy. If you could please take your mount to the stables, we can proceed."

"What? I saw you driving that thing. I prefer to ride my stallion, thank you very much."

Jose brought her carriage, and Zeus shook his neck, jingling the harness.

"You can follow me on your horse, then." She climbed atop the bench, securing the leather reins. Feigning great interest in a flock of swallows flying around the orchard, she waited.

"Jose, take good care of Thunder."

She released a pent-up breath, and what seemed like ages after, the buggy dipped as the Englishman dropped his weight by her side.

"Stubborn woman."

Unable to hide her smile, she clicked her tongue, and the horse took off. The buggy picked up speed outside the gates, trotting along the path shaded by giant elm trees.

Mr. Maxwell held the bench with both hands. "This is the first time I've been driven by a woman."

"Oh? I would advise you to lie back and enjoy the privilege, then."

"Humph." He crossed his arms. "Why not ride your horse instead of bumping around in this poorly constructed pile of wood, pulled by this craggy bag of bones?"

"His name is Zeus, and he is a fine—"

"Zeus?" He laughed, eyes crinkling at the corners. "You must be joking. I'll name him Shaggy."

Julia stared ahead, ignoring his outburst.

When they entered the vineyards, he quieted. Julia peeked at him curiously. Relaxed, an arm flung behind her back, he gazed at the view. Perhaps in admiration? The vines rolling on both sides were heavy with grapes, and she savored the berry-scented wind as she lazed on the bench, enjoying the ride and his silent company. How many times had she passed here, hoping to share the beauty of her lands?

Too soon, they arrived at the vineyard she had chosen for his lesson.

They climbed the path leading to the terraces, and Julia stopped near a well-developed vine. Sprouting from the schist soil, the ash-colored trunk supported new twigs, emerald pentagon-shaped leaves, and many pounds of grapes.

Griffin removed a notebook from his coat and stared at her, eyes alert, frowning in concentration. Was he really interested in winemaking? Either way, the attention flattered her more than she cared to admit.

"The vine has a single goal in life. Do you know what that is?"

"To annoy unsuspecting males?"

Julia rolled her eyes. "To make wine grapes. As vine-growers, we need to force them to focus on that, only that."

He tapped the notebook with his pencil. "What do you mean?"

"Pruning." She took a pair of gardening scissors from her satchel. "While we cannot control the weather, we can control the vine. We must prune every branch except the main one after harvesting, and then the unproductive ones after the spring sprouts come out."

She aimed the scissors at a branch growing free from the staked line. It gave way with a satisfying thud. Next, she slashed the barren sprouts rising from the main stem. If unnecessary, it needed to go. She turned to twigs that carried crippled clusters, the grapes either too small or shriveled, and dropped those too. The scissors opened and closed with oiled efficiency, slashing everything that kept the vine from its purpose. The distractions, the vanities, the frivolities—the blades sliced them with precision. She positioned the twin blades again, tensing to shut them.

He touched her shoulder. "Are you all right?"

Julia halted and stared at the hand holding the scissors as if it belonged to someone else. Her fingers were numb. Chest heavy with lead, she removed the blades a moment before slicing a portly purple cluster.

"Must you be so thorough?" Mr. Maxwell's gaze shifted from her face to the leaves and twigs scattered on the ground.

Panting, she stored the scissors in her satchel. "Yes. All energy must go to the wine."

The droning of insects filled the heavy silence. Mr. Maxwell frowned. His chocolate brown hair hung over eyes that saw too much. Thankfully, he let the matter drop and pointed his pencil at the other plants. "Are all these vines from the same variety?"

"No. Here I have *Tinta Barroca, Tinta Roriz,* and *Touriga Nacional.*"

"*Gesundheit.*"

Julia offered him a black grape. "Try this."

He brushed it on his sleeve and eyed it at arm's length. Perhaps he feared the fruit would bite him. She hid her laughter behind a cough. His skittishness with food was an unexpected aroma in a complex wine, rounding the edges of his intense personality.

"Winemakers must constantly taste their grapes. Otherwise, how would we know when to harvest?"

Grunting, he pressed white teeth into the skin, and the fruit exploded, splattering juice on his chin.

Julia chuckled.

With a handkerchief, he cleaned his face. "You enjoy this, don't you?"

"A bit." She shrugged. "You just tasted a *Touriga.*"

"Much sweeter than table grapes, are they not?"

"Yes. The three grape varieties are blended to make port. *Touriga Nacional* is the port's body, adding the heaviness on the tongue, the structure, the great tannins, and the acidity. *Touriga Franca* and *Tinta Roriz* are flimsy and aromatic. From them comes the aroma of ripe berries, violet, and wild roses." She sighed. "To me, they are port's soul."

"You really love this, don't you?"

The words touched her skin like the sun's first rays after a long winter. Her father-in-law had pride in her abilities too, always boasting that she knew every grape variety by look and taste. How, even blindfolded, she could name the wines in the cellar just by scenting their aromas. Pride had been a heady feeling for a young girl, but Julia wasn't a girl anymore. The wine interested the Englishman, not her.

"It's all I know...to make wine," she blurted, and then cringed at the words spoken without thought.

"Beg your pardon?"

"Come, there is much to see."

She turned to leave, but he grabbed her arm. "You could not possibly believe that."

"My beliefs are my own, Mr. Maxwell."

After a breathless silence, he let go. She proceeded down the hill. Close to the last terrace, she stopped. His breath fanned her neck, making her shiver.

"The grapes are ripe enough. I will harvest tomorrow." Julia stared at a branch growing free of the stakes, the tendrils forming a sweeping arabesque. The scissors cooled in her palms, but she was loath to cut such a beautiful design. "You can come, if you wish."

"Why the rush to harvest?"

"The grapes could rot, which would spoil the wine. Think about an apple. If you eat it too soon, the taste will be tart and have herbal flavors. If you delay too long, it will be overripe, and it will taste flat and old. It is the same with wine. The winemaker's greatest dilemma is to find the exact time to pick the grapes."

"Like a bet, then?"

"I suppose." She had never thought about it that way.

"Are you a betting woman, Julia?"

Julia shook her head; the Englishman did not know how much of her life she gambled just by allowing him here.

***

Griffin gripped the seat of the infernal conveyance. Julia bungled another turn, pushing the left rein when she needed to hold it steady. It was a wonder she hadn't capsized the buggy. His fetching teacher was a poor driver. The shaggy plow horse—he refused to call it Zeus—slugged along the steep road, winding through the circular track. The sun hung beyond its zenith, sometimes hurting their eyes, other times hiding from sight. He craned his neck to see the view, but it played with him, always veiled by olive branches or cork oaks.

They had made tremendous progress. Julia had shown him the east-facing vineyards and the west, explaining the difference between them. Climate, terroir, how the vines needed to be pruned in winter and again in spring, how the schist soil had to be dug in January to allow the roots to receive water and then covered again in summer to avoid burning the roots—she knew it all. The science and financial concepts behind vine growing were fascinating. He was eager to apply the concepts to Boa Vista.

She had made him taste different grape varieties, but he had trouble focusing on sugar content and acidity when he couldn't take his eyes from her mouth. More than anything, he was curious about Julia's bittersweet relation to it all.

He eyed her petite form, concentrating on the sharp turns. At times, she gushed passionately about the subject, eyes glittering and chin up; others she turned introspective, her lips a downward arc out of place on her luminous face. Either way, these hours together had revealed glimpses of her personality, and he craved more.

The wind ruffled her hair, the strands teasing her eyelashes and the corner of her mouth. When it reached Griffin's face, he stole a long lock and inhaled its flowery scent. The name lurked in his mind, but he couldn't grasp it. Still, he couldn't say it was foreign anymore.

They arrived at the crest of the hill in one piece.

"Meet First Light." She stopped the buggy close to a grass patch. "Care to see the ruins?" Without help, she alighted and looped the reins around a scrawny tree.

"Why Julia Costa and not Julia Ferreira?"

"Must I teach you everything?"

Griffin eyed her, pushing up an eyebrow.

"Portuguese women keep their family names."

"Even after you marry?"

"Even after that." Her face took on that faraway look he despised.

"I would like my wife to wear my name," he blurted.

His words got lost in the breeze.

They entered the stone structure that persevered as a relic from the Middle Ages. Damp, chilly air greeted them inside and shadows played on the rugged walls. She navigated the spiraling stairs with precision, the wind blowing her hair, a black flag guiding him.

They emerged onto the roof, a circular space surrounded by a gaping crenelation, the russet stones warm to the touch. A lamp and a faded blanket peeked from below a bench. His imagination conjured midnight clandestine meetings, her skin uncovered to the star-studded sky.

"Care to explain?"

She pointed to the east. "Sometimes, I cannot sleep, and I come here to see the sunrise."

Following the direction of her hand, Griffin gaped at the view rolling for miles in every direction, the sky meeting the mountains' crests on the horizon. He absorbed the gently rolling hills carved in terraces, the olive trees, the oak forest where they had first met until his eyes blurred around the coppers and greens.

True to Julia's story, the Douro dashed through terrains mild and rough, a mirror reflecting willows and vines, seething down canyons and ravines, white foam scraping to show rocks beneath. Near the horizon, caught in sunset's spell, the water turned liquid gold. He saw its beginning, and he saw its end, and it was stunning.

Inhaling the crisp mountain air, he had the sensation of being suspended in time and place, of at once knowing all directions. It was overwhelming.

Griffin turned to the woman by his side. Her ebony eyes glittered in the afternoon sun, hard-working hands pointing at her favorite spots on Vesuvio's land. It was impossible not to admire it. To share her enthusiasm. Up here, their differences shrunk, like the houses lining the main street of Vila Nova, irrelevant specks in the distance.

"This served as a watchtower during the Aviz dynasty."

"Were they not the ones who started the great navigations?"

"You know our history well . . . for an Englishman." She looked at him sideways and turned to the horizon. "They posted sentries here to watch for the Spanish invading from the north and the Moors returning from the south. From here, you can see the first rays of the sun at dawn and the last at twilight."

"First Light." He exhaled, picturing the sun rising and sinking, the way the colors would change, the shadows dancing on the ground, the temperature increasing and decreasing.

She went on with tales of battles and old kings, but he ignored the words. The sound of her vowels lifting and falling enthralled him. He closed his eyes, her voice lulling him to a calm he had not felt in years. A lightness of spirit he could not explain—the fleeting sensation of being where he wanted to be.

"Do you like it?"

"What?"

"The view." She peeked at him, weight shifting from heels to toes, eyes huge in her oval face.

He shrugged, trying hard not to grin. "It's passable."

An artist should paint her face. While he forced his lips to stop twitching, her forehead creased, nostrils flaring, until she burst with a firm swat on his arm.

"Ouch." He laughed, raising both palms. "It's breathtaking."

"More than London and Oporto?" She tucked hair under a perfectly shaped ear.

"Infinitely more."

They stared at each other. The wind blew Julia's hair around them, weaving them together. A heartbeat passed, two, and neither of them moved.

A groan escaped his throat, words vanishing from his mouth. He looked at the two inches separating them but saw no obstacles, just air and attraction. Leaning forward, arms drawing her in, he closed the distance between them until she touched him everywhere he craved.

Her tongue came out to wet her lips, and that was all the invitation he required to meld their lips together. God, how he'd missed her taste. He was like a seafarer reaching home port, an explorer returning to his country.

He caressed the supple muscles of her back, her arms, her nape, trailing fingers over the bumpy ridges of her ribcage. She arched to accommodate him, her skin warm, fragrant with her scent, the exotic aroma that eluded and chased him. He deepened the kiss, his tongue coaxing an entry, plundering, exploring her mouth's moist crevices.

Quivering, she poised her hands above his shoulders.

Griffin teetered precariously on the edge of reason. He sifted his fingers through her hair, pinning her closer. The world revolved around their embrace, a pinwheel atop the First Light ruins, spinning.

She splayed her palms over his chest and pushed. "Mr. Maxwell, please."

"Say my name."

He pressed his fingers to her waist, holding his breath, willing her to say it. An eagle screeched above their heads. The wind rustled her shirt and the lapels of his coat.

"Griffin."

His name on her lips sent a wave of heat through his chest, stunning him. The intensity was so powerful that he backed away, and she seized the moment to spin for the stairs.

Breathing heavily, Griffin leaned on the crenelation for support, watching her slight frame disappear inside the ruins, his heart galloping like an untried colt. Their relationship had spun out of control. He must use the seemingly useless appendage between his shoulders. He had been one step away from ravishing her on a crumbling ceiling. And that wasn't the most dangerous thing.

Try as he might, he could not summon an ounce of regret.

Chapter 18

"For when the wine is in, the wit it out." Thomas Bacon

Julia crept inside the house, cheeks flaming, her breathing unstable. Griffin's kiss had been different this time. In comparison, the peck he had given her at Saint John's party seemed chaste. What was she doing? Taking him up to the ruins, inviting his advances like a shameless hussy. She needed to keep her eyes on him, not her hands! She must resist his allure, ignore the interest he paid to her stories, the attention he gave to her when she spoke about wine.

These emotions needed to be pruned before they took root, stealing all her energy, all her focus.

She touched the corner of her mouth where the faint taste of the Englishman lingered. Feeling this much wasn't part of her purpose.

A metallic voice pierced the parlor's silence. "Where were you?"

Julia halted, scanning the room. Pedro sprawled on the couch, ankles crossed, while her aunt perched on the chaise, a smile plastered on her face. The windows were closed, making the air thick. Over the center table, a tea service laid untouched. If only she could pretend not to have seen them, she could escape to the safety of her room.

"Would you excuse us, madam?" Pedro stood and thumped the floor with his cane.

Aunt Rosario left, her cheeks and frills bobbing in her haste to reach the door.

The Count strolled in Julia's direction, dressed in a suit the color of a dark winter sky, golden hair tied at his nape, handsome face forbidden in its aloofness.

"Where were you?" he repeated, his voice low and ominous.

Julia cringed at the dangerous spark in his eyes. How could he have changed so much from the boy, a friend, she used to play with?

"At the vineyards, checking the grapes." She glanced away, heat rising to her cheeks.

"You promised to ride with me today." He thumped his cane on the ground. "That was two hours ago."

She gasped. "I am sorry. I completely forgot."

"You will take a chaperone when you leave the house."

Arms straight and hands curling into fists, she stared back at him. "You are not my keeper, Pedro."

"You are my future bride, and I take care of what is mine."

This man was not the friend from her childhood. How could she make this stop without incurring his wrath? Vesuvio couldn't afford an enemy this powerful. If he understood their financial problems, he would drop his suit. But could she share her burdens with him? What if he told others? Still, either she revealed the contract or endured his constant advances.

She took a deep breath. "I must tell you something."

He came closer, his mouth softening. "Anything."

Unable to face him, she turned to the portrait of her father-in-law, his confident face giving her some courage. "Before the accident, Bernardo promised an enormous increase in wine production to an Englishman. The money vanished. And as of today, I still don't know if we will deliver."

"What is this Englishman's name?"

She felt the air stir behind her neck with the menace in his words. What would he do with the knowledge? "It's not important. Vesuvio could change hands in the future, and—"

"You think I am after your property?" Tendons tensed in his neck above his white cravat. "You don't know me at all."

She had hurt him. The words died in her throat. He was right; she did not recognize him, and the reverse was also true, despite what he thought. Julia was about to apologize when his expression changed before her eyes. All emotion disappeared, replaced by gelid determination.

"You should have come to me sooner, but I am glad you did now." He brought a gloved hand close to her face. The whisper of leather on her cheek brought only coldness instead of the warmth she felt with Griffin.

"Pedro, I am sorry, but I can't marry you." She closed her eyes. "I'm not what you need."

"What do you know about my needs, Julia?" he whispered, dropping his hand. He bowed stiffly and left.

A chill raced up her spine with the certainty this wasn't over.

Chapter 19

Love is the same as wine (...) both are intoxicating." Julio Dinis.

Pedro pursued Cristiano around the gilded room, their soles leaving dark tracks on the marble floor. He cornered his brother near the piano, their fencing clothes ghosting the lacquered surface. "Julia will change her mind."

"I must be turning deaf." Cristiano pushed forward and parried Pedro's upward lunge, his voice strained. "But did the lady not deny the lofty Count of Almoster today?"

At the reminder of Julia's refusal, Pedro's vision blurred. Only his iron self-control stopped him from cleaving his brother in two. He took a step back, shaking his head to clear the anger haze.

Cris panted, sweaty black hair plastered to his brow, and studied him with his head tilted to the side. "Why do you want a widow? You could have any girl in the realm. Better yet, why rush to marry? You are only twenty-eight, for Christ's sake."

Cris couldn't understand Pedro's connection to Julia. But he hadn't grown up in the duke's dark lair, had he? Pedro had endured his father's corrections alone. Except for her.

That summer afternoon, Julia had flitted into his life like a water sprite. A flimsy girl, all black hair and luminous eyes. When she had spotted him with her liquid eyes, she could have fled. But she had stayed. Faced his bruises with Colossus' courage. Dabbed at the blood with a grape-stained handkerchief, her tenderness cleaning more than the shallow wound. She had written their fates that day. Pedro just had to make her realize it.

"Why we want what we want... it's puzzling. You, for instance. When will you give up trying to catch the duke's interest?"

Cris's face lit up, and he let the sword point drop. "Did he tell you about the letter?"

By God, when would he rise above this groveling? Sometimes Pedro had difficulty believing they shared blood. "Do you think the lofty prime minister writes missives? For your own good, cease. The Duke of Titano is equal parts manipulative and cruel. He has nothing to give in lieu of fatherly affections. I thought you would have realized that by now."

The duke had never recognized Cris, forcing his brother to live with the double shame of bastardy and scorn. Pedro circled around him, searching for weaknesses. His brother relied on brute strength and his intimidating size in battle, but today the cavalry sword seemed to weight Cris's arm, his high guard inching lower.

Pedro feinted left and attacked from the right. Cris made a puny effort to lift his sword, not even pretending to defend himself, and Pedro poised the point of his sword above his brother's neck.

Cris stilled, his eyes ever so trustful. A flick of Pedro's wrist and his carotid would gape open.

"Afraid?"

A grin split Cris's tanned face. "You wouldn't hurt me."

"Never lower your guard." Pedro held the saber a second longer, then dropped it and stepped back. His brother's ignorance about human nature persevered despite all they've been through in Mozambique. One day, it would get him killed. "Julia gave me the door to her heart this afternoon."

"Beg your pardon?"

"Vesuvio is the door to her heart. You are turning deaf after all."

Pedro forwarded another attack at Cris from his right, effectively disarming him, and his bastard brother raised both palms. His saber clanked against the cream marble twice and lay forgotten between them. His black hair, so different from Predo's, was disheveled. For once, he seemed defeated. "Are you sure you should use this door?"

Pedro gripped the sword handle, the edges biting into his palms. How could Julia claim he wanted her property? The world had reason to expect the worst from him; she was the only one who shouldn't. Her denial pierced him again, the pain spreading to his chest, and he let the sword fall from his hands.

There was no other door. She had made that clear today.

Chapter 20

"Where there is no wine there is no love."
Euripides, Greek playwright

"I want every basket inside before the sky opens, Carlo!" Julia shouted above the gale.

The day turned to night, all light vanishing behind black clouds. A pungent scent of green pepper and damp earth weighted the air, no doubt from rain falling south of here, where the horizon collided with the mountains and painted the sky a charcoal gray.

The vineyard came alive. Men and women gathered the last grapes, red scarves, and threadbare clothes flying like pennants. Thunder rumbled, adding more urgency than any demand of speed she could make.

Julia's fingers were numb and stained purple from picking grapes all morning. Still, she grabbed a basket on the path by a row of vines and ushered a few women who kept talking while the wind tangled their skirts around the green vine branches. "Take those inside the *lagares* now. I won't have watered down wine this year."

The weather would not interfere. She wouldn't allow it. This vintage would be perfect.

The workers stormed to the building like ants to the anthill. Abelardo relieved her of the basket, coat-tails flapping, and sprinted inside. A crack sounded in the semi-darkness, and Julia whirled in time to see lightning flaring behind First Light. The ruins turned bright yellow in a glorious momentary brilliance, only to vanish again, hidden behind bruise-colored clouds.

The sky opened, showering her face and plastering her hair to her head. She raised her arms, joy bubbling out as the water gushed down in fat drops. She had beaten nature. The harvest was secure.

A smiled on her lips, she entered the *lagares*, admiring the sparkling clean windows and spotless white-washed walls. Griffin would be pleased to know she applied the Viscount of Penafiel's guidance, Portugal's authority on winemaking techniques. No doubt he would take notes and tease her for her fastidiousness.

Julia ambled around the ten rectangular tanks, passing her hands over the granite, now filled with grape clusters, an entire year's worth of work.

Flor embraced her. "You did it."

She took strength from her friend's smile. "Another year."

Carlos, her foreman, ordered the threaders to hike their clothes and wash their feet. Julia tied a knot on the side of her skirt, two inches above her knees. The men politely averted their eyes so the women could climb the steps. Laughing, she raised her leg above the railing. Aunt Rosario would pout for a week, but Julia preferred purple feet. She plunged inside the tank, the liquid welcoming her like an old friend, deliciously cool on her heated skin, bathing her legs in dark nectar. A thousand bubbles massaged the bottom of her feet and between her toes. She closed her eyes, absorbing the ripe, sweet scent.

When the men joined them—fathers, brothers, and sweethearts—they formed two lines facing each other. Julia glanced at the portal. No sign of Griffin. What did she expect, really? She should be happy he hadn't appeared.

Carlo counted in his bass voice. One, two. One, two. One foot after the other, they moved forward until they met the other line and then returned to the edge of the tank. They matched the rhythm, lifting their knees and stepping down. The grape skins gave way to the pressure, exploding in heaps of juice, moisture, and pulp.

After two hours of organized threading, her foreman ceased counting. A loud cheer ensued, and the musicians began an upbeat folk song. Couples formed, dancing inside the tanks, the juice twirling in tune with the notes.

As if she had grapes inside herself, tiny bursts of delight and pride ignited in Julia's chest at the pure wonder of winemaking. If he were here, would the Englishman feel it too?

***

"Sir, you will be pleased with my findings."

Griffin adjusted his coat, inspecting his reflection in the bedroom's mirror. "I'm on my way out, Jako. Don't hold your breath waiting for me."

Julia expected him for the harvest, and he expected much more from his teacher. In fact, a sleepless night had given him the sweetest of plans. He would find a private place, and then he would conduct a private tasting.

Jako brandished a rolled paper. "But sir, you took me out of my duties for this, remember? I've spent two days slaving under the sun. My back is more scorched than the housekeeper's mutton."

Vesuvio's map. Griffin had forgotten about the bloody thing. Pulling his fob, he checked the hour. Half-past two.

"Fine, give me that." Griffin flattened the map on the desk. "What are these markings here?"

"Oh, it's where they planted the new vineyard. A valley so large you don't see its end."

Griffin raised his palms. "Valley? What in heaven's name are you talking about?"

"It's what I saw."

"Are you sure it was grapevines, not corn or flax?"

Jako frowned, his bushy brows connecting in the middle.

"Speak up, man. This is important."

Jako cringed. Eyes fixed on his shoes, he started a long litany of justifications. Now that he realized the news had displeased Griffin, questioning the servant would be useless. Something about the karma of bad news.

Stomach knotted, Griffin saddled Thunder and rode the path between Boa Vista and Vesuvio. Pushing to a gallop, he tracked the place Jako had indicated on the map, the fields and terraces blurring into a gray-green mass. Soon, the hills vanished to expose a vast expanse of land, stretching between mountains.

Rubbing his eyes, he stared agape at the newly planted vineyard. An entire valley, soil still revolved, pierced by row upon row of vines. The staked lines resembled a camp of fences running side by side.

Griffin dismounted and crouched by a vine. Close to the ground, a strip of cloth patched the branch. On closer inspection, every vine sported the same bandaging, just like the plant in her greenhouse. Griffin unrolled it. The branch had been cut and glued back together. What was the meaning of this?

He stood, shaking his head. It did not matter. She had arranged all these plantings outside the demarcated area. Port wine could only come from the terraces. Was this how she expected to repay Croft? By deceiving his future partner with some rogue production?

The ride back to Boa Vista lasted only half an hour. Griffin slouched in his chair, piecing together the facts—her fright at the Count's reception, the way she had bristled like a scalded cat when he surprised her at the greenhouse, not to mention Abelardo's unwillingness to talk.

The memory of their kiss atop the ruins came unbidden, and he rubbed his chest. Had that been real, or had she decided it would be best to lure him to her side?

It was his fault. He knew better than to get involved with people in this country.

Unclenching his fists, Griffin grabbed a sheet of paper. He would denounce her. That Portuguese woman was nothing to him.

A thunderclap shook the glass panes, and long shadows formed inside the study, where just a few minutes before the sun had poured over the sturdy furniture.

He stared at the pristine vellum, knuckles white from clutching the fountain pen. No words came out.

Damnation, why was it so hard?

Grinding his jaw, he hurled the pen across the room.

He pushed from the desk and ordered the carriage ready. The Brougham's interior was as dark as his mood, rain pelting the windows without mercy. He spent the short ride to Vesuvio staring outside, watching the wheels hurl mud.

When he arrived at her property, Jose indicated the way to the *lagares*. Griffin crept closer but didn't enter the rectangular building, choosing to stay outside, watching. The Bacchus theater held lively music and cheerful dancing over juice-filled tanks.

While he waited in the shadows, they celebrated. Julia frolicked in a purple and red checkered blouse, skirts raised to her knees, a vine entwined around hair that shone onyx-black over her shoulders. Envious of the grape pulp caressing her skin, he wanted to go inside and shake her. And then taste her over the fragrant juice.

Hours or mere minutes had passed when the music stopped and Griffin stepped forward.

Julia noticed him at once, like a magnet finding metal. She had berry bits decorating her cheeks and forearms, and he followed their design greedily. People around them moved, using cloths to remove the purple matter from their limbs, faceless peasants wading away. The macerated grapes steeped the air like a violet mist.

They stood facing each other, she with smiling eyes, perhaps with pleasure to see him, he with a foolish quickening pulse, clenching his fists. The rest of the building faded to a hazy blur. When the last peasant had left, he crossed to the side of the tank and she came forward to sit on the edge.

Their heavy breathing mingled with the rain punishing the windows. Julia smelled like grapes, overpowering her fragrance—earthier, heady even. Her eyes, glittering by the torches' light, concealed shades Griffin wanted to understand.

"Allow me." He went down on one knee and grabbed a cloth.

She startled but acquiesced. Slowly, deliberately, he brought the cotton to her hands, caressing her wrists, sweeping the fabric over her palms and between her fingers. A blush made her skin glow.

Griffin stared at the purple lines drawn on her skin. "It seems I caught you dirty-handed."

She tilted her head, revealing the side of her neck, and he forced his jaw to unclench. Frowning, she tried to pull her hand back, but he clasped it.

Determined, he applied pressure on her wrist and brought her hand close to his face. "Do you think it tastes better than it looks?"

Her breath caught. He kept a tight leash on himself until he took one of her trembling fingers inside his mouth. She sought to resist, but he would not be denied. When he swirled his tongue on her skin, the juice went to his head, his heart bursting to consume more, to consume it all.

Griffin exhaled and strived to be objective. Julia should appall him, but instead she intoxicated him. He needed to confront her, but he wanted to consume her. He had to stay apart, but he could not stay away.

He tried to remember his partnership, his status, his family, but everything blurred at his tongue's first contact with her syrupy palm. Her taste of grapevines went to his head immediately, his skin tightening until he neared combustion. If this was madness, call him insane because he wanted more. This was why he strove to keep separated from this country. She disturbed his mind.

He dropped her hand and pushed away with an oath. "I saw your secret valley."

Her eyes widened, and her olive skin turned gray.

"Miss Julia, there you are." Abelardo came running inside. "Mr. Borges is here. He is frantic, wanting to talk to you. Part of his vineyard died without cause. He thinks it is the plague."

Chapter 21

"We observe what we are prepared to observe." Louis Pasteur

A depressive silence soaked Mr. Maxwell's carriage. She should have denied his request and drove to Mr. Borges' estate by herself. Under the Englishman's stare, being led to her neighbor's property stripped off her control. Throat dry, she shifted on the polished burgundy seat. Her corset dug into her waist. Mr. Borges wasn't faring any better. The poor man's shoulders were hunched, and his face was as crumpled as his brown suit.

The Englishman stared outside, brows drawn together, lips pressed into a grim line. She wanted to shout why she had planted the valley, that it had been the only course left open to her, but his expression was prohibitive. Would he alert Croft?

She closed her eyes and pressed her temples. No use thinking about Croft now.

What did Griffin Maxwell stand to lose? Julia knew what she had on the line—everything. A vision of Vesuvio's valleys and hills blackened by invisible lice eating the vines' roots flashed through her mind, and she clutched the magnifying glass until the edges pierced her palms.

The coach stopped at Mr. Borges' property. Her heart wanted to escape the confines of her ribcage, and she took a deep breath. It was September. This could be just another outbreak of mildew.

A slab of wood above the gate spelled *Quinta da Felicidade*. Julia alighted, the schist soil warm under her boots, and shielded her eyes against the afternoon sun. The storm had blown away as swiftly as it had appeared. Only the yellowed walls of the main house could be seen among the sea of jade-green leaves, and the long shadows cast by the vines looked like ghosts trembling in the wind.

"Mr. Borges, please show us the way," Mr. Maxwell said.

The farmer bobbed his head and started on a trail. They walked single file between the three-foot-tall trellis system, thick foliage heavy with black grape clusters. Julia stumbled, and Mr. Maxwell gripped her upper arm. For a second, they locked eyes. Her breath caught, searching for a flicker of emotion, but his stoic expression remained unchanged. With a sinking heart, she straightened and continued forward.

Mr. Borges pointed with his crunched cap. "It's here."

There were ten, fifteen vines with brown foliage in the affected area. Julia sucked in her breath. It looked as if winter had struck this stretch of land. Below the dry leaves, the clusters were still attached, a feast for flies and ants. The rotten fruit stench made her stomach turn.

Julia bent a cane. It split easily. The plant was dead.

Perspiration dampened her back and forehead, and she tried to control her breathing. This wasn't mildew or any disease she knew. She searched for Mr. Maxwell's imposing figure and found him a few steps away, examining a pentagon-shaped leaf.

Mr. Borges waited, hat in hand, browbeaten.

Julia clutched the magnifying lens. "Let's dig it up."

Mr. Borges grabbed the trunk. It came loose easily, exposing the root system.

Dread swirling in her stomach, Julia bent and examined the tendrils through the lens. "Clean."

Her shoulders sagged. She massaged her neck, able to fill her lungs for the first time since Mr. Borges had arrived at Vesuvio. Maybe this was not phylloxera.

She brushed dirt from her skirts, but her smile faded when she saw Mr. Maxwell's expression. Brows deeply furrowed and eyes narrowed, he seemed the opposite of relieved. The wind rustled her hair, bringing an unexpected chill.

He left the circle of dead plants and reached for a green leaf of a healthy vine. "We need to dig a living one."

"This plant is not sick." Mr. Borges shook his head. "Look at the grapes—almost ripe."

"We need to be sure."

Julia's stomach tightened, and she clenched her hands. The Englishman had no authority here. Light speckled the leaves, making the vine glow. Could the appearance of health be deceiving? Beyond their differences, Griffin had wisdom to spare. What if he was right? If they walked away not knowing, wouldn't it be worse?

Julia chose a vine with only three developed clusters. "I know you are close to vintage, but it will be just this one."

Both men were needed to yank the living plant from the earth. It came out breaking the soil, exposing brown, worm-like roots.

Heart beating madly, Julia kneeled by the exposed roots. A powder stuck to the tendrils. The magnifying glass revealed not one, not a hundred, but thousands of bile-colored insects. They were everywhere, on the shallow and the deepest roots, sucking the life from the vines.

***

All that remained of the First Light guardhouse was the ancient circular tower, but it was as dear to her as if it was the King's Queluz Palace. Julia placed her lamp on the floor and sat at the granite bench, adjusting her legs beneath the folds of her heavy skirts. The night sounds were faint, locusts calling and owls hooting, the cry of a wolf -- distant, poignant, lonely.

She inhaled the scent of grass and breakfast cooking fires, but the stench of dried leaves and rotten fruit was imprinted on her nostrils. She tried opening her eyes wide, first at the sky, the thousands of stars blinking like luminous grains of sand, then at the river, the deep currents drifting between the mountains, but only saw thousands of plant lice choking the life from her vineyards.

It had been useless leaving her bedroom. The nightmare had followed her all the way to her sanctuary. She hugged herself, trying to dispel the horrid images.

Footsteps clattered on the stairs, and she shot to her feet. “Who is there?”

Light spilled from a lantern, illuminating a tall frame. “Isn’t it a little late for Portuguese women to gallivant around rooftops?”

She sucked in a breath. Was she to have no respite? “How did you find me here?”

“I remembered that evidence.” He pointed to the quilt, forgotten by the alcove. “I figured rest would elude you tonight.”

She stiffened. “Are you here to confront me? About the valley?”

Mr. Maxwell exhaled and came closer. His hands were fisted by his sides, mouth pressed in a hard line, but his voice was low and tentative when he said, "Not today."

Julia closed her eyes, chin falling to her chest. She could not deal with those secrets now, her misdeeds and shortcomings. She had taken a beating today, and she had no fight left.

Breathing white plumes of condensation, he placed the lamp atop the bench and stepped closer, long legs eating the distance between them. Julia stood her ground, not knowing what to expect but unwilling to turn away. The air shimmered between them, alive with crickets and fireflies. She opened her mouth, ready to ask his intentions, but the words died in a gasp as his arms enveloped her in a tender embrace. The scent at his collar, the clear, fresh bergamot, ousted the pungent smell of rotting fruit.

She straightened, bumping his chin. "Are you here to kiss me, then?"

He chuckled, the sound like warm caramel. "Are all Portuguese women this blunt?"

"I fear I would do a disservice to other Portuguese women if I kept linking myself to them."

"Ever the patriot." He shook his head, stubbled chin rubbing against her forehead. "I thought to check on you, ensure that my teacher had not broken a limb or been eaten by wolves. Who would help me with Boa Vista then?"

She settled against his chest, the strength underneath a heady, rugged comfort. "Do you think the guards who stood here centuries ago felt fear? Wanted to run away during the long, sleepless nights?"

He grunted, still holding her close.

"Probably not. They were men, sturdy, bred for war." She closed her eyes, longing to rub her cheek on his chest, to absorb his warmth.

"Even men fear from time to time." His gruff voice ruffled her hair.

"Have you?"

"I was afraid today."

"Of phylloxera?"

He inhaled and opened his mouth as if intending to speak, but then he stiffened. "You shouldn't come here alone. It's not safe."

Griffin removed his arms from around her, and the cold seeped into her skin. She watched, puzzled, as he spread her quilt over the stone floor and sprawled out, resting his back against the granite bench, his legs touching the crenelation. He extended a hand and tugged her down beside him, adjusting her weight and pillowing her head over his left arm.

A modest woman would protest his familiarity, but she needed this solace, just for now. This illusion of being protected, of a burden shared, was headier than any port she could blend. They turned to the view with its black hills and the last traces of moonlight glinting off the river.

"Did you see the vines? Their canes were dry as ash." She took a shaky breath. "They are powerless to fight this."

"They are strong. They will survive. Vines have existed for what? Thousands of years? The ancient Greeks had wine, and the Romans."

"But not like this—"

"Not by themselves." He stared into her eyes.

She sighed, willing this moment to memory, this contentment chasing the darkness away. The sky brightened in the distance and the hills emerged from the shadows. Shooting from the eastern horizon, the first beams of light conquered the night, the sky a canvas of oranges and navy blues. Then the sun surged from behind the mountains, painting the landscape in golden tones, from copper to rose to russet.

"What happens now?" she whispered.

"I'm taking you back to Vesuvio."

***

Juniper trees secluded the orchard, and Julia pointed to a round table with two iron chairs shaded by a mulberry bush. Her eyes lacked their usual fire, but the despair he'd glimpsed after they had discovered the phylloxera had faded. Still, the tightness in his chest wouldn't go away. Daylight hadn't helped, only shedding light on the strained silence.

Griffin sat as she unpacked a breakfast basket, removing bread, cheese, peaches, and a linen-wrapped volume. The lines of her palms and under her nails were purple. She tried to hide it when she caught him staring, but he grabbed her wrists and forced her hands open. He used his thumbs to trace her callouses, massaging her palms in circular motions.

She inhaled sharply and her cheeks flushed, ebony eyes following his every move.

Could she feign that?

The smell of coffee permeated their secluded breakfast spot, so mundane and yet carrying a spark of intimacy. A *rabelo* boat, its hull filled with wine barrels, sailed downstream, bound to the wine lodges on Gaia's wharf. That was where his life used to be, his own lodge, his own townhouse in Oporto. A world away from here.

"They make the journey early in the morning." She shielded her eyes, following the boat's progress. "The heat can be harmful to wine only days old."

"Will Vesuvio's pipes do the same?"

"No. My father-in-law built a large cellar underground. It's always cool there, even during high summer."

"Are you one of those winemakers who hates to add spirits to your wine, to taint it with brandy? Do you despise all Englishmen who enjoy it?" Griffin released her and fisted his hands. Did she despise him?

She traced the spiraling mosaics on the table. "Port is a style and a tradition. The British love drinking it, and we love making it. Our countries have shared it for hundreds of years." She lifted her eyes to him, her voice soft. "I realize now it should bring our people closer, not push them apart."

Griffin shut his eyes. "Why did you do it?"

She shook her head and ambled to the riverbank, her long braid reaching her hips, fine hairs flying with the breeze.

Pulse speeding up, he followed her. "I need to know."

She picked a mulberry, gaze transfixed on the black fruit. "I couldn't lose Vesuvio, not without trying everything first."

"Even being dishonest?"

She sucked in a breath but did not move, as if awaiting his onslaught. "The hills were not enough."

Griffin shook his head, pinching the bridge of his nose. What could she hope to gain? "Grapevines don't survive the clay soil of the valleys, and planting outside the demarcated area is forbidden." The Marquis of Pombal had erected three hundred and thirty-five pillars to mark the boundaries of port production to shun wine of questionable precedence.

"That is why I grafted the Portuguese vines with American rootstock."

"American grapevines are not fit to make table wine."

"Grafting doesn't change the grape's acidity or sugar content. It just makes the vines stronger. I planned to prove the wine's quality and then deliver it to Croft. It would harm no one if I succeeded."

Griffin tilted his head, working to absorb the overload of information. If she succeeded, it would mean a significant advance in winemaking. The entire thing exuded ingenuity and impetuosity—like Julia herself.

"After Bernardo died and I discovered the contract, I knew our terraces weren't enough to yield that enormous amount. It wasn't my wish to deceive anyone, but I couldn't lose my son's heritage without trying everything first. I just couldn't."

Griffin exhaled, pushing hair away from his brow. He'd been seeing the situation through Croft´s perspective, ignoring hers. Julia fought alone—a widow with a small boy defending her lands. What sort of bastard would leave his wife and son in this situation? "Can I see the contract? And Vesuvio's books?"

She lifted her palms, her eyes wild. "Please, if you tell Croft before I can prove the wine is good—"

"Croft and I will be partners." He tucked a lock of hair behind her ear. "You don't have to be afraid of him. He is a tough businessman, but a fair one."

He failed to mention Croft would also become his father-in-law, and the omission burned inside his stomach.

She crossed her arms over her front, her gaze pleading. "But what will you do?"

"Wine is your expertise. Numbers are mine. I might see some detail you overlooked."

She stared at him, searching his eyes. "Thank you."

He held his breath, his chest squeezing painfully. "Was the rest a lie? Us?"

"No, I..." She placed her palms over his cheeks. "How can you think such a thing of me?"

Her eyes weren't guarded for a change. They brimmed with tears and something else, something he could not name, but sparkled more delicate and precious than her flowery scent.

Griffin released a pent-up breath and, cradling her face, brushed her tears away. She kept still, face tilted up, eyes heavy-lidded, and Griffin touched his lips to hers. Fusing their lips, Griffin deepened the kiss, and she pressed closer, the warmth of her skin dispelling the heaviness in his chest.

Chapter 22

"In water you see your face's reflection; in wine you see others'." Portuguese saying

The half-opened window allowed some air inside, diffusing the musty smell and rippling the curtains' gauzy material. A ray of sun crept over her pale curves, half-hidden beneath red satin sheets, exposing the whore's reddened wrists and ankles. The rope lay coiled on the floor, now forgotten.

Turning from the sight, Pedro scrubbed his nails and fingers, the small brush hurting his skin. Efficiently, he put on the leather gloves, each finger covered in black, and closed his cufflinks.

The whore stretched her arms above her head, exposing a creamy breast. "Going so soon?"

His body demanded attention again, and Pedro jerked his head, disgusted. After marrying Julia, he would be free of these animal desires. He crossed the vulgar room, ambling as far away from the bed as the bare wall allowed, and made his way outside.

When he descended the steps of the madam's house, Hemera, white coat out of place among the wilted flowerbeds, lifted her head. He gave the groom a warning glance and caressed the mare's mane.

"I did not expect to find you here." Cris came rushing down the stairs, hair messy and wet, jacket partially open. "Again."

Pedro wiped his face of all expression. He could not stay away from the whorehouse for an entire week, and his perfect brother knew it. "Do you have it?"

"It arrived yesterday via telegraph."

Pedro scanned the letter. "John Croft. Four years. Three hundred pipes of port."

At last, a strategic lead. Closing his eyes, Pedro crumpled the paper in his palms. That's why she'd been acting differently than he remembered. But after he paid her debts, she would be grateful. Julia would be his.

"Where are you going?" Cris held the mare's rein as he adjusted his weight over the Spanish saddle.

"To pay my bride a call."

"Is she expecting you?"

"You are getting soft. Why should I relinquish the element of surprise?"

"I wasn't under the impression this was a battle, big brother."

"One more instruction for you, then." Pedro touched his heels to the mare's flanks. "It always is."

Hemera obeyed his commands, extending and contracting her front legs, the impact of the brisk gallop absorbed by the hay-covered ground, the cadence winding along high crests and shallow rises. Pedro's heart throbbed, anticipating the gratitude in Julia's eyes. Her final submission.

Pedro cantered inside Vesuvio's courtyard and reined in the mare as Julia left the *lagares* building, her petite figure hallowed by the sun. He vaulted from the saddle, his boots sinking into the crushed stones, and tossed the reins to the old stableman. Julia smiled her artless smile, and Pedro's chest felt lighter, cleansing some of the night's corruption.

A man emerged from the same door behind Julia.

Pedro's hand went to the hilt of his saber and he stilled, watching. That Englishman from Vesuvio's party walked by Julia's side, eyes shining with intent, his body too close to hers as he spoke near her ear. Pedro kept his position, waiting to be noticed, bridling the impulse to purge her from the bastard's grasp.

Julia's gaze connected with his, and she stopped. As the Englishman's look was fixed on her face, he took a second longer to notice Pedro's stance below the palm trees.

"Oh, Pedro. Good morning." Her voice sounded strained. "This is Mr. Griffin Maxwell, from Quinta da Boa Vista."

Pedro caressed the hilt of his sword. "I remember him."

The Englishman squared his shoulders and took a step closer to Julia.

With practiced detachment, Pedro unclenched his hand from the sword. Before he acted, he needed to understand this man's intentions.

"It is fortunate you came. Can I offer you some tea? There's an urgent matter to discuss. Mr. Maxwell was just leaving, right?"

The Englishman looked straight into Pedro's eyes. "On the contrary, I think I may add to this discussion."

Julia released her grip on her skirts and indicated the oak portal. "Then, by all means, let's enter the house."

Cutting the Englishman off, Pedro offered his arm, and Julia's hand fluttered above his forearm. He escorted her inside and to the couch, lowering himself by her side, and kept his tone mild as he asked, "Why are you here, Maxwell?"

The Englishman sprawled on an armchair, but his jaw was locked, eyes alert. "It's none of your—"

"He came to see Vesuvio's winemaking process." Julia stopped pouring the tea.

"Are you interested in making wine, then? I thought your kind only traded it."

Pedro accepted a cup of tea, careful not to touch Julia with his black hands. She glided her fingers over the rough cloth of her skirts, nails stained purple. After the marriage, he would clothe her in silk, and she wouldn't labor for as long as he lived.

Maxwell shrugged. "We have all kinds of interests nowadays."

"And when do you plan to leave the region? I imagine you must miss your beloved British community."

The Englishman shrugged. "I haven't decided yet. I find the countryside quite entertaining."

Julia splotched tea on the saucer. Her nervousness was evident, and Maxwell seemed too sure of himself. Pedro touched the telegraph in his pocket. Could the Englishman be an envoy from Croft, pressing her to repay?

The child raced inside the room. His disturbing resemblance to Julia was a breathing reminder of what Pedro had lost.

The boy went straight to the Englishman. "Did you bring Thunder?"

"Tony, please greet our guest before accosting Mr. Maxwell." Julia took the child's hand.

After a hasty good morning, the boy raced outside.

Pedro leaned back on the couch, his stomach hardening. The Englishman had been here before, gaining the child's trust. Only years of training under the duke's fists allowed him to leash his aggression and keep a stoic facade. Growing up, whenever Pedro had shown a response, his father had strived to wipe it out. If it was a delight in food, he snatched away. If it was something he feared, the duke placed it in his bedchamber until he learned indifference. If it was a girl he wanted . . .

Pedro gazed at Julia's gentle face. Well, a few lessons were harder to digest. Why couldn't she see the bastard was nothing more than a foreign poacher?

"I have some distressing news. We found signs of phylloxera at Quinta da Felicidade."

"We?"

She flushed and looked at the Englishman. "Griff—Mr. Maxwell accompanied me there. Mr. Borges asked for my help."

"The affected area is contained to a single vineyard." The Englishman leaned forward. "I've heard they blockaded affected areas in Bourdeaux, helping to contain the plague. The same should be done here."

Pedro ignored the man's attempt to order him like a lackey. Phylloxera here changed the scenario, and he would need to consider all implications. "The government of Portugal will act for the benefit of all parties involved."

The country's best interests would prevail above foreigners this time. Mr. Maxwell had impinged himself on this household, much as the British had entered this country. Ever ready to help but never ready to leave, bringing in their rags and salted fish, involving the country in their wars, offering dubious military protection, swamping them with industrialized products and draining Portugal's reserves, all for their precious port. But phylloxera had the power to inflict change, painful but necessary—no vineyards, no port, no British port traders.

The plan had merit, but it would take time. Maxwell needed to leave now.

Julia yawned, the purple circles around her eyes pronounced against her pale skin.

The Englishman stood. "We should leave Mrs. Costa to her rest. Phylloxera must have kept her awake for most of the night, I am sure."

Pedro rose and kissed her hand. "Be at ease. I will take care of everything."

Chapter 23

"Go, little book, and wish to all
Flowers in the garden, meat in the hall,
A bin of wine, a spice of wit,
A house with lawns enclosing it,
A living river by the door,
A nightingale in the sycamore!"
Robert Louis Stevenson

Griffin half-listened as Mr. Silva, the state manager Border had sent, conveyed his references. His mind kept straying to his secretary's letter. In his weekly report, Edmond had asked if Griffin would return in time to approve the season's wine purchases.

Before coming here, his goal had been to set the accounts to rights, hire a competent estate manager, and be back to Oporto as soon as possible. The Quinta's books couldn't be more ordered and a qualified estate manager was within his reach. His mother would have returned from Algarve by now.

A weight settled on his chest. His time at the Douro had ended too fast.

Mr. Silva cleared his throat. "The vines are well over twenty-five years, explaining the grapes' low yield. You could replant it in stages to avoid production breaks."

"Right."

Mr. Silva talked about the virtues of constructing a *lagar* in Boa Vista instead of selling the grapes to other wineries. He was competent enough. After Julia's lessons, Griffin had the knowledge to say so. The sensible course was to hire the man and be done with it. But when they finished the tour, Griffin couldn't say the words.

He shook hands with Mr. Silva. "I will let you know of my decision."

"Thank you, Mr. Maxwell."

Instead of waiting for the estate manager to leave, Griffin strolled to the front colonnade of Quinta da Boa Vista. Courtesy of the Douro, the air had a slight breeze to it, sweet and earthy. Up in the elderberry tree, chickadees fussed around, preparing for the coming evening.

Feet braced apart, Griffin looked at his house, really looked. The white walls and red-framed windows complemented the surrounding green vines, and bougainvillea adorned every corner. The vine-covered trellis concealed a perfect place to steal kisses from Julia, sheltered from the house's view. Her face would be colored by a gorgeous blush, asking him if all Englishmen were shameless.

The realization came in clear droplets. Business transactions and hasty meals fit poorly in Boa Vista.

His uncle had built this house to spend time within, sitting on the veranda, enjoying the river breeze, and sharing a port with friends. For children to play while mothers strolled around the shaded paths. Tony would go crazy exploring the alcoves and the small pier.

Griffin strolled on a path paved by cream-colored stones. It led to the orchard. Planted in a spiral pattern, apples, plums, and cherry trees still bore summer fruit. The trail of stones continued beyond, leading to a wall. Ivy covered the barrier, and one side ended close to the river, the other perpendicular to the hill. A hidden door peeked from the blanket of tiny paw-shaped leaves. He tried opening it, but the lock did not give way.

"Lost something, sir?"

Griffin glanced over his shoulder. "Do you know where this door leads to, Jako?"

"A door? I've failed to notice it before."

"Find out where the key is."

He caught a whiff of Julia's fragrance and followed it to a medium-sized tree. Tiny white buds peppered the thick foliage. Griffin picked one flower, the petals like marzipan sweets, and brought it close to his nose. One pull of the sugary, jasmine-like scent, and he floated back to the First Light ruins, her eyes flashing with the afternoon sun, lips glistening from their first true kiss. His hands tingled to span her waist and bring her closer, eliminating the distance between them.

"What kind of tree is this?"

"This one?" The servant tore a leaf from the dense foliage. "Smell it, sir. You will recognize it."

Unmistakable citrus fragrance wafted from the crushed leaf—a common lemon tree. Laughing, Griffin clapped Jako's shoulder. Julia's scent wasn't exotic after all.

He couldn't leave now. He needed a few more weeks to help Julia with Vesuvio's accounts and to see how autumn would change the region's colors.

The weight he had carried the entire day lifted from his shoulders, and he filled his lungs with her fragrance one more time. Griffin would invite his mother to visit. She would appreciate the climate, and it would be good for her health. As for his business, he could take a brief trip to Regua and handle this year's Maxwell's Lodge wine purchases from there, halfway between here and Oporto.

Back in his study, he penned a short missive to Julia explaining his trip to Regua and asking her to send Vesuvio's ledgers. The letter to John Croft couldn't wait. He began by stating Mrs. Costa did her best to comply with the contract. An absolute truth. He then wrote about phylloxera's appearance but reassured him the local authorities would act before it spread.

His hand tingled to write further—about the engagement.

Griffin's eyes strayed to the wall. A painting of a bridge over a silver stream in sunset colors hung slightly askew. Not a single portrait, not here and not in

Oporto's townhouse. After his father's death, the creditor envoy had ceased his mother's portrait collection.

Griffin hardened his resolve. He couldn't forget his obligations to the family. His decision to stay had to be temporary.

He took the pen, his handwriting wavier than usual, and explained to Croft he would extend his presence here for longer than expected. He tried to picture Beth's face, but when only onyx eyes flashed inside his mind, the pen made a black blotch on the paper.

He finished the letter stating he hoped to continue partnership negotiations upon returning to Oporto. No need to mention the marriage, as it would be implied. He folded the paper and put it inside the envelope with jerky movements, then stared at the wax seal until his eyeballs hurt. The crest seemed soiled.

Chapter 24

"A man cannot make him laugh–but that's no marvel; he drinks no wine."
Shakespeare

The smell of macerated grapes permeated the Quinta, calling Julia to the *lagares* building. She sped through the courtyard, boots crunching the rocks underfoot, the gray clouds so close she feared they would fall upon her head.

Inside, the warmth created by the fermentation clouded around her skin, moist and fragrant.

"Good morning, Carlo."

The foreman's greeting was strained. Deep lines carved around his eyes and his body hunched in exhaustion. No doubt he counted the hours until he could rest. Four workers stirred the grape must with long spoon-like tools, sloshing rhythmically, making sure the juice kept in contact with the skins.

After three days of fermenting, the liquid inside the shallow tanks was neither juice nor port—just a whiff of warm alcohol and flashes of deep violet whirled by wispy spoons. The Englishman would call her whimsical, but vintage after vintage, wine never failed to wonder her. For as long as men crushed grapes with their feet, they worshipped the Gods for whipping grapes into wine. Science said the precious liquid wasn't a divine gift but the work of wild yeasts. For Julia, it was magic—the grape, threaded by feet into pulpy black must; the must, fermented by yeast into wine; the wine, now ready to receive brandy and change into port. Port continued to evolve inside the oak barrels, attaining balance, body, and soul.

She dipped a vessel in the *lagar* and brought it to her nose. The alcohol bloomed in an intoxicating mist, spreading the aroma of red fruit. The sugar burned her tongue, and the harsh tannins and acidity made her mouth water. If she didn't add brandy, the fermentation would continue and produce an ordinary red wine. Mixing the spirits would kill the yeast and leave the wine sweet, as required by the port-style so appreciated by the British.

"It's done."

Grunting, Carlo opened the first tank, removing the cork with a pop. The young wine drained, leaving skins, seeds, and a few stems forgotten on the bottom. The ducts would lead straight to the cellar's wooden vats below through a series of pipes engineered by her father-in-law.

Abelardo approached, nose wrinkled, a small notebook under his arm. "Good morning, Ms. Julia."

"The brandy is ready?"

"Of course."

Julia clapped her hands, calling the others' attention. "Work awaits in the cellar, gentlemen."

She left the *lagares*, blinking to adjust her eyes to the brightness of the white sky. The harvest changed Vesuvio. Flanked by grapevines, dressed in white gilded ornaments sparkling here and there, the house looked like an exacting mistress demanding every drop of sweat the workers offered.

Color flashed in the vineyard to the right of the house, and Julia rubbed her eyes. Six rows above the path, out of place in the sea of green vines, a red spot mocked her. For long heartbeats, she could not move as the crimson blurred her vision. Then she raced, slipping over the graveled rocks, gaining speed on the downward slope, her lungs laboring to keep up with the urgency she felt within.

She climbed the steep terraces, not bothering with the lines, hurling over the stakes, tumbling down over loose stones, rising again, the red taking shape just ahead. Struggling for breath, Julia fell on her knees, splaying her hands over the rocky ground. The vines trembled, feeble branches whispering in the wind, roots confined in the schist soil, bound to the land, imperiled, vulnerable.

The leaves—the leaves were the color of blood.

"No." She dug, her breath escaping in painful bursts.

When two shadows appeared from behind her, the tips of her fingers were bleeding, but she felt no pain. Could it be Griffin? Heart pounding, she glanced over her shoulder to see Abelardo and Carlo staring at the affected vine. What had she expected? She was alone in this, as ever.

"What is this, Miss Julia?"

Julia stood, her knees burning, unable to meet their eyes. What would become of these people? Her people?

"This is phylloxera."

Chapter 25

"Poetry is devil's wine." St. Augustine

Griffin ordered coachman Roberto to give the blacks free rein on the trip back from Regua. Romulo and Remo delivered fast speed on the dusty roads, and they arrived at Boa Vista in record time. The journey had been a success. The Douro vintage had been bountiful, flooding the market with enough barrels to keep prices close to last year's, even with the phylloxera threat. He had bought enough port to fill his lodge at Gaia.

Whistling, he entered the house and threw his hat at Jako. In less than thirty minutes, he paced the front steps, waiting for the stable lad to bring Thunder. His heart sped at the prospect of seeing Julia again after four days away.

The sound of hooves alerted him of an intruder. Almoster rode a supreme specimen of Lusitano, milky-white mane reaching a palm below its neck, elegant legs raising a trail of dust.

Griffin raised his palm. "Don't bother dismounting. I am on my way out."

The *fidalgo* flung himself from the saddle. "It could be profitable for you."

Griffin stared down at the Count, satisfied that his extra two inches gave him the advantage. The cad was dressed in a military uniform, his customary saber strapped at the waist, his woman-like hair tied at the nape. What the hell did he want here?

A blast of thunder sounded to their right and drops of rain splattered the pavement. The mare whined and pranced, frightened by the worsening weather.

"You won't leave a peer to drown in the storm, will you?"

Griffin saw no peer in his courtyard, but he narrowed his eyes and handed the mare's reins to the stable lad. The creature had no fault of her owner. "Be grateful I'm considerate to horses."

Griffin indicated the house's main door, mounting the steps without waiting to see if the count had followed him. All windows in the parlor were open to the elements, and the wind came up in waves from the river, carrying an odd, sulfurous smell.

Griffin crossed his arms and leaned on the back of the couch. "I'm listening."

Almoster prowled inside, touching Griffin's belongings with uninvited familiarity. Frowning, he removed a tome from the shelf and flicked through the pages. "You have great taste in literature. I didn't expect an Englishman to own Camões."

"Those are not mine, and I don't have the entire afternoon."

"I like his love poems, much better than your bard. I enjoy this—"

"Keep the book. I'm leaving." Griffin pushed away from the couch.

Almoster chuckled unpleasantly. "Aren't you to the point? I want to buy Quinta da Boa Vista."

Damn aristocrats and their damn feudal beliefs of entitlement. Griffin gritted his teeth. "The house is not for sale."

"I was under the impression you wanted to make this Quinta profitable. Might I add that with phylloxera biting our heels here, there is little chance of you succeeding?"

The wind whistled inside, banging the shutters. Griffin sealed the window, mooring the room against the storm. "The answer is no."

Almoster released the book and rolled the fountain pen over the desk, black-gloved fingers like a scorpion enveloping it in his leather grasp. "Won't you at least hear the price I will pay? I meant it as a marriage gift."

Griffin's stomach rolled, and he swallowed the sour taste in his mouth. "Who is the lucky bride?"

Eyes flashing, the count smiled, his lips tugging up in a secretive sneer. "You did not know? Mrs. Costa, of course. She is soon to be my countess."

Coldness gripped Griffin's spine, his legs weak as if he faced a precipice. That's why he had come, then.

Hands fisted at his sides, Griffin wiped all expression from his face.

"Congratulations. I will think about your proposition." He pointed to the exit and dropped his hands, controlling the flames that threatened to consume his civility.

The count released the fountain pen. It rolled away from his claws and clattered on the floor, splattering ink on the Persian carpet. Watching him swagger through the front door, Griffin locked his jaw, his nails digging into his palms.

For a long moment, he stared at the set of books lining the shelves. It all made perfect sense. The *fidalgo's* visits, the way Julia had wanted to remain alone with the other man. How gullible he'd been. Mechanically, he grabbed the Luiz Camões volume the count had toyed with and scanned the first stanza.

> *"Love is a fire that burns unseen,*
> *a wound that aches yet isn't felt,*
> *an always discontent contentment,*
> *a pain that rages without hurting,"*

Not hurting, indeed. Griffin ripped the page from the leather-bound volume, enjoying the sound of the paper disconnecting from the binder. Crunching their outstanding achievement in poetry into a ball—a tiny, insignificant ball—he hurled it at the fireplace. The matchstick combusted greedily, and Griffin crouched near the floor, lighting the crumpled page and watching with grim satisfaction as it consumed the hated lines. The fire flared up in bright yellow and orange flames, but the momentary brilliance soon curled into black ashes.

He ambled to the liquor cabinet. Shoving the port away, he reached for the whiskey.

"Are you all right, sir?" Jako sauntered close. "I've just seen the Count of Almoster out."

"Not now."

"What is the matter—"

"Leave!"

Griffin removed the cap with his teeth and spat it on the floor. The first mouthful trailed a fiery path, the alcohol fumes scorching his nose and eyes, but the second swallow rolled down smoothly, reaching burning tentacles in his stomach and dulling the pain.

Chapter 26

"Despite these repeated warnings, the population of this rich département does not want to believe that the scourge which menaces their vineyards could lead... to the almost complete destruction of their vines." Le Messager Agricole du Midi of Montpellier in 1870

The *concelho* at Vila Nova loomed two stories high. From the sidewalk, Julia gazed inside its dusty windows. Brimming with black, brown, and gray coats, the vision wasn't encouraging in the least. She had every right to be here, same as the other landholders. Like them, she needed to understand the government's response to phylloxera.

Julia took a fortifying breath and pushed inside. When she greeted Mr. Albuquerque and Mr. Nogueira, her neighbors ogled her as if she balanced a plate of fruits on her head. Some faces she did not recognize. Some were British. She scanned the masses for a tall, imposing figure, but she would know if he was here.

The atmosphere felt dull, empty in his absence. She took a shaky breath. Griffin had probably returned from Regua, but he hadn't sent a note or come to Vesuvio. Maybe he had forgotten about his promise.

The secretary cleared his throat and raised wiry arms. "Quiet, please. All will be explained in a few minutes. The commission leader is on his way."

Commission leader? Someone elbowed her in the ribs, and she inched closer to a side door, the blue of her clothes standing out against the somber-colored coats and withdrawn hats. The men whispered among themselves, giving her arched glances. She looked straight ahead, lips tight. Her paid taxes entitled her to whatever help could come from the king's government.

A voice boomed from the center of the room. "Gentlemen! Silence, please."

The men leaned forward—a bulk of limbs and heads taller than she. Julia rose on tiptoes, glimpsing the speaker's bald head and gray suit. Voices started again, dread and excitement gushing forth like waves rippling the sea.

"What should we do with the affected vines?" someone asked.

"Will there be a blockage?" someone else shouted.

"Gentlemen, I understand everyone's concern. My name is Joao Lero, and I have been appointed by His Excellency the Count of Almoster as the commission's leader for the study of the phylloxera. Over the next weeks, I will contact representatives from each citizen class and politicians from Oporto. With the approval of His Excellency the Count, this commission will focus solely on ridding this region of the hateful plague."

One by one, the voices quieted. The wave of dread subsided as the men accepted this bureaucratic commission as if it would solve all their problems.

How could they be so blind? The man offered only empty promises. If Griffin was here, he would protest their inertia and demand immediate action.

Julia barreled from her corner, pushing her way to the front. "Sir. Hey, sir! Begging your pardon, but what are we supposed to do meanwhile?"

The bald Mr. Lero eyed her up and down from his hawkish nose as if she belonged to a different species. "This is no place for a lady."

The crowd parted, a sea of reproving black coats and somber faces watching her being set down. Her ears burned, and she sucked in a gush of air. Before she could think of a proper reply, the man had whirled on his high heels, already moving to the exit. Julia prepared to follow when a hand clamped around her arm.

"Mrs. Costa, right?" The stranger pointed to a side door.

Covering her burning cheeks, Julia followed him inside a better-kept room with two couches and a side table. He brushed away a rakish slip of black hair that covered his forehead and looked at her with striking, intelligent green eyes. "Allow me to introduce myself. I am Cristiano Queiroz, Pedro's brother."

"I thought Pedro was an only child."

"He is." He shrugged. "I'm sorry for what just happened. With phylloxera, the moods are a little high. I don't think my brother would approve of your coming here by yourself."

As if she needed anyone's approval. "Well, Pedro is not the one with a blood-red vine, is he?"

He smiled crookedly. "She has spirit. One would never guess from how Pedro speaks about you."

She inclined her head. "Well, Mr. Queiroz, where is the count then? I need answers."

"His father summoned him. He will not be back until the end of next week. Can I offer you a conveyance? Pedro would have my neck if I didn't see you safely back to Vesuvio."

Safety. A fleeting concept giving the circumstances. Julia ignored his offer and left the building, her feet dragging along the cobbled stones of Vila Nova's main street. People strolled up and down the square, smiling, enjoying the cooling autumn air as if tomorrow was a given. What blind normalcy. This city lived because of port wine, and they were ignorant of what had infested their soil.

Julia's throat constricted, making it hard to swallow, hard to breathe. If phylloxera fed on their vineyards, it meant nobody else would.

***

Julia's eyes were glued to the glass panes of her study. The floor-to-ceiling windows that had once been a door to her daydreams became like a theater box presenting the best view of her vineyard's demise. The first blood-red vine, now dull brown, trembled in the epicenter of two circles, a festering wound spreading its poison. The malady had grown, forming concentric rings like ripples disturbing the calm surface of a green lake. Phylloxera colors were painfully beautiful, an explosion of deep burgundy and orange tones, but soon the leaves would turn brown and perish.

She ached for Griffin's comfort, cradling her face, brushing her tears away, kissing her so tenderly. She covered her cheeks with her palms, but her hands were cold and raspy, not scalding and engulfing like his. The memory of his citric scent, so vivid, had faded.

A knock on the door brought Wentworth, face solemn.

She perked up in the chair. Maybe it was him.

"Mr. Borges and his family are here."

Julia's shoulders deflated. "Take them to the parlor, please."

Mr. and Mrs. Borges perched on the love seat while their children stood, all submerged in the cool light filtering through the curtains. The oldest neared manhood, and his hand rested on a small boy's shoulder. Madalena, a rosy-cheeked girl with a scarf tied around her chestnut hair, fidgeted with her pinafore.

Mr. Borges, his eyes sunken and forlorn, clasped his hands. "Miss Julia, we came to say goodbye."

"Goodbye?"

He rubbed his neck. "We are leaving for Brazil—"

Mrs. Borges perked up, her dress sagging over her diminutive size. "I wanted to go to America, but he is so stubborn, Miss Julia. I said, let's go to America; they have vines there, but no. He wanted Brazil. What will we do in such a faraway place?"

Mr. Borges groaned. "Woman, do you speak English? You don't, and neither do I. It's better to go to Brazil. At least we will be understood."

Flor sailed into the parlor, placed a tray on the table, and after casting an inquisitive eye over the whole family tableau, sashayed away.

Mrs. Borges hugged herself. "What use is plain old Portuguese if we have to fend off aborigines?"

At the ominous remark, young Madalena flinched, her eyes downcast. The oldest boy, Antero, named after her father-in-law, stared straight ahead while the youngest, Francisco, had eyes so wide they looked about to bulge from his face.

Julia raised her palms. "What about Quinta da Felicidade?"

"Sold it." His chest caved in. "A man came with a three-piece suit and fancy tie and bought the land. I was grateful. I can't imagine what he will do with it now that the vines are dead."

Her lungs flooded in turbid water. Had it been a month since the phylloxera had appeared? Was that the future awaiting her?

Mrs. Borges sobbed but quickly controlled herself, dabbing at her tears with a handkerchief. Julia could hardly muse about her own problems when phylloxera had flung this family in the wind.

Lifting the plate of pastries, Julia kneeled on the floor. She tapped the carpet, beckoning the children to sit. Madalena and Antero looked unsure, but Francisco dropped by her side, eyes shifting from her to his parents.

She offered the sweets, but his hands were closed around a secret volume.

"Don't you want some, Chico?"

He shook his head without taking his eyes from the pastry.

"I see you are carrying a precious thing there, am I right?"

He nodded, his curly hair floating around his chubby face.

"Can I hold it for you while you eat? I promise to take good care of it."

He looked shaky in his little man clothes and frowning rusty-colored brows.

Julia gave him an encouraging smile. When he opened his hand, it drifted from his fingers, and the slight weight skimmed her palm. The toy had yellow walls and small carved doors and green shutters—a wooden house.

Her chest constricted painfully, and she tried to convince them to stay, but they were adamant. Mr. Borges would not hear of receiving money from her, and they left to a fate as fluid as the ocean they would cross.

After they had gone, Julia flew from the parlor. She crossed Vesuvio's courtyard in a run and didn't stop until she'd reached the Roman bridge. Her steps resonated over the gray stones and the rocks were damp and mossy as she braced her arms along the rail.

A sigh gushed out of her lungs, her shoulders sagging with the force of it. She leaned over the rail, watching her distorted reflection in the water below. Would she need to follow in her neighbor's wake? Leave winemaking, her son's heritage, and her people?

She closed her eyes, listening to the rustling of the leaves and the vague drone of insects. If she was true to herself, she listened for something else too—powerful hooves arriving from the south, a teasing voice.

An unseasonably icy wind rose from the river. The flamboyant trees trembled, crying down petals, and painted the water red. Foliage long gone, the naked gray branches stretched above the water, reaching for a solace that would never come. A yearning to go there, to Boa Vista, gripped Julia's limbs, making her shake. She clutched the stone railing with a white-knuckled grip. Go there? Why? Had she not experienced enough humiliation during her marriage?

Chapter 27

"The best use of bad wine is to drive away poor relations."
French proverb

For once, the secretary was not guarding his father's study, and Pedro burst in. "You wanted to see me?"

Father froze, hands caught inside his private safe, the one Pedro shouldn't know about.

Pedro masked his grin behind a polite façade. Perhaps the duke had lost his edge. As if Pedro would reside here without uncovering the Quinta's secrets. From the two safes to the peepholes to the hidden exit, nothing has escaped his scrutiny.

"I taught you better than to creep up unannounced." The duke's shoulders lifted for a telltale second. When he closed the heavy iron door, the combination's clicks sounded like elephants stomping on the marble floor.

So his father kept secrets even this far from Lisbon. But what? It would be pointless to ask. Pedro would have to find out later.

"Why, I am ever your dutiful son. You asked for me." Pedro cleaned an imaginary speck from his velvet coat. "Here I am, eager to be of service."

With strained movements, the duke bent and took the portrait resting near the desk. He covered the vault with his own conniving face, this one painted after the civil war some thirty years ago.

Satisfied with his work, the duke enthroned himself behind his desk, assuming a business-like facade. "I will receive important guests, and I want them entertained. A little *panem et circenses* to facilitate their agreement to my intentions."

Pedro touched one of his father's sabers. His weapons were honed as if he prepared to go to war between four and six o'clock political appointments. "What kind of entertainment?"

The duke sneered. "Not the salacious kind you are so fond of."

Pedro kept a blank expression and raised a brow. At least his women were willing. "Would the *coudelaria* be 'bread and circus' enough for your . . . interests?"

"Yes. The property is removed enough to allow for privacy and grand enough to impress them. The railroad president will certainly appreciate the comforts." He flapped his hand dismissively.

So typical of Father to cut Pedro out of his machinations. Not this time. The Douro region belonged to him. Instead of leaving, Pedro squared his shoulders and planted his feet wide. "I believe the government should add more incentives to the train company. Exempt them from taxes."

The old man narrowed his eyes, a gaze that could pierce metal. "Do you know the Duke of Chagas is ready to make a political alliance with the Titano family? His daughter turned eighteen."

Pedro stilled. "Aren't you old for another wife, Father?"

"Don't play coy. I am talking about you."

"The answer is no."

"I thought you were brighter than that. The political connections and the dowry alone—"

"I already made other arrangements." Pedro's hands turned into fists, but he kept his expression bland.

"That worthless widow?"

Pedro raised his chin and took a step closer to the desk, blood pounding in his ears. "Yes."

"I wonder when you will learn the lesson, boy."

Boy. Father thought him still a child, taking his beatings in silence, but not this time. He would marry Julia, and his father's machinations would fail.

Pedro forced his muscles to unclench and strolled to the door. "The *coudelaria* will be ready to receive your guests by the end of the week."

"I will have to instruct you again."

Chapter 28

"The phylloxera cause or effect is no longer a debatable issue. M. de Serres at Orange has put the insect on healthy vines and it has killed them. M. Faucon at Graveson, on the contrary, has cleared away all the aphids from vines severely attacked by means of a prolonged submersion, and it has saved them. Destroy the phylloxera and you save the vines, it is an established fact." De Ceris 1870

Julia's bedroom received plenty of sunshine in the mornings. She hadn't noticed it before. Shadows formed through the white canvas, tiny beings with leafy bodies and scrawny legs. They danced and shook in tune with the wind blowing the trees outside. It was a pagan celebration, with vigorous shaking of limbs and odd-shaped faces and butterfly wings. When the draft quieted and the fairies stilled, the shadow became a face peeping at her, mouth agape.

Flor entered her bedchamber. "Why are you still abed?"

"Hm?"

Flor opened the curtains. The sun invaded Julia's room, uninvited and harsh. Her eyes hurt, but not as much as the dull pain throbbing in her head.

"Up with you!"

"I am not well."

The maid set a breakfast tray on the bed near her face. The smell of coffee and yeast made her stomach queasy. "Why so gloomy?"

"Don't you see? Vesuvio is in great peril. Without the vineyards, what will we do?"

"A woman always has choices." The maid turned and swayed to the vanity. "You could accept the count's offer."

Could she? After struggling so hard to lead her future and Tony's? Was it time to admit defeat, then? But how could she marry him when her thoughts belonged to another man? It would not be fair to Pedro, and her soul wouldn't survive.

Tony raced inside and jumped on the bed, bouncing the mattress and splashing coffee over the tray. "Mamã?"

She forced a smile for his sake. "Come and share breakfast with me."

While she held the cup, not caring that her palms were red from the scalding heat, she gave Tony the crusty bread and he ate it with gusto.

Flor had left the newspaper on the side of the tray. Julia cleaned the spilled coffee with a napkin, scanning the "*Journal do Comercio.*" The comings and goings from Oporto to Brazil and England, who died and who married, and myriad selling offers. How could life seem so ordinary in the printed letter?

A name caught her attention—the Viscount of Penafiel. She had both his books on grape cultivation and optimal practices. In bold letters, the headline stated the *fidalgo* had been visiting Montpellier University and had returned to his Braganza Estate.

After attending a conference by J. E. Planchon, the famous biologist responsible for studying phylloxera in France, the viscount is preparing a dossier on the plague to be presented to King Luis I.

She vaulted to her feet, knocking against the tray. Braganza was what? Three, four days' travel from here? She hugged Tony with such enthusiasm that the boy groaned. Her chest felt lighter for the first time in days. She would go there. Why wait for a bureaucratic commission when she could find out the latest treatments? The viscount must have learned how to fight phylloxera.

"Flor, prepare a valise and clothes for a week, please."

"Where are you going?"

"To the Viscount of Penafiel's estate in Braganza."

"What kind should I pack?" The maid winked. "A gown for night entertainment?"

Julia had not been precisely invited. The memory of Mr. Lero looking down on her made her deflate like a burned paper lantern. If a province lawyer declined to talk to her, what would the King's peer do?

The leafy shadows changed again, traveling all the way to the wallpaper, resembling soldiers carrying spears. She stiffened her spine. Perhaps . . . if she had a gentleman to accompany her, someone assertive and arrogant and an Englishman to boot, the *fidalgo* would be obliged to receive them. Her heart bounced, warmth spreading in her chest at the mere thought of seeing him again. Could she go there and ask for his help?

He wouldn't agree. Would he ask if other Portuguese women were as crazy as she? Surely even he could be convinced of the situation's gravity. Without a cure to phylloxera, he too would lose his business. They could be partners in this—she with her knowledge of vines, he with his influence and wits.

***

Julia climbed the three steps leading to Boa Vista's front door. A woman with striking eyebrows and a conservative dress asked her to wait. After a few minutes, she came back. The master would receive Julia in the study. She followed the woman's gray skirts around a long corridor, heart stomping louder than the woman's soles on the wooden planks.

Before entering the room, she paused. Would he be pleased to see her?

She blinked a few times, blinded by the brightness. He sat behind a somber oak desk, beard clipped, hair tamed, concentrating on a sheaf of papers. Julia checked the impulse to get closer and trace the creases on his forehead.

The maid left, closing the door with a soft click.

He never looked up.

Julia smoothed her skirts, the plum silk crinkled by her clammy palms. “Hello.”

“You requested to see me?” Griffin gazed at her, eyebrows raised and lips set in a flat line.

Warmth flooded her cheeks, her throat dry. He must be busy, that was all. But time was crucial to the vineyards, and he had offered his support. How hard could it be to ask him?

“Phylloxera appeared at one of Vesuvio’s vineyards. The vines are too vulnerable. Mr. Borges’s vines were dead after only a month.” She wrung her hands, biting her lip. “I have three weeks to find a cure. I—”

“Are you sure the vines are weak? More like deceitful creepers, casting their vise with no scruples.” He returned to his precious papers.

Frowning, she stared at the chiseled edges of his face. “Mr. Borges is gone. He went to Brazil.”

“Good for him. As for Vesuvio, the government of Vila Nova must have the plague in hand.”

"What? I went to the *concelho*. They created a commission—"

"See, you have no reason to fret." He pointed to the exit.

"No reason?" Could he be this naïve, or was he just goading her? "Let me tell you a story."

Leaning away from her, Griffin shut his eyes and rested his head on the high-backed chair.

She took a fortifying breath, hoping for his scent but inhaling only dust and contempt. "Once, a rich man lived in Sintra with a fortune built in the colonies. He brought many exotic animals from India. One morning, a hut-sized elephant escaped from his menagerie. For days it roamed free, stomping on wheat, raiding the orchards, terrorizing the villagers. Do you know what the government did? They created a commission to apprehend the elephant, employing men for this unusual hunt. Do you know what the commission did?"

He pinched the bridge of his nose. "I am sure I am about to find out."

"They pretended to chase the beast from sunup to sundown, but they actually never found it, you see? If they ever caught it, there wouldn't be a need for a commission in the first place, would there? They would lose their wages."

How could she make him understand? He was so distant. The man colonizing the Georgian chair had closed himself into another continent while she awaited on Portuguese soil, open and vulnerable.

He pierced her with unwavering blue eyes. "Mrs. Costa, I am a busy man. What do you want?"

"I need help." Her voice broke. "The government won't act. I found someone who may, but he wouldn't receive a mere woman. I want you to come with me to speak with the Viscount of Penafiel."

He glared at her, jaw locked so tight she could swear his muscles pained him.

She braced herself and spoke before she lost courage. "I must go tomorrow at dawn if I am to speak with the viscount before he leaves his property. Braganza is four days away from here, and the *fidalgo* is expected in Lisbon by the end of September."

His expression became thunderous. What had she said to offend him? Unable to face his rage, she looked away. Two boxes sat near an empty bookshelf, their lids closed. A white cloth covered the couch.

The truth curdled her stomach. "You are leaving."

Throat clogged and dry, tears threatening her composure, she started for the door, needing out of here, away from his presence. By God, she had never humiliated herself like this.

He closed his hand around her forearm. "Why don't you go ask for the count's help? Go tell your spellbinding tales to His Excellency."

"What?"

His face contorted in a sneer. “Is he not your fiancé?”

“Who told you that?”

“The mighty Count of Almoster in the flesh—”

“No, he isn’t. I’m sworn off from all males.” She twisted her shoulder and pulled her arm with all her strength. His grip loosened, and she stumbled. Heart pounding, she spun on her heels and hastened to the door.

Chapter 29

"Wine is sunlight, held together by water." Galileo Galilei

Julia was not getting married.

The words flashed in his head like a ballad's refrain as Griffin stumbled across Boa Vista's parlor and exited to the veranda. The sun caught him straight in the chest, dazzling him. After blinking several times, the colors sprang to life—pale-greens, lime-greens, and yellow leaves rustling by the riverbank, the golden-green water, a profusion of tawny, rusty-reds, and crimson terebinth blossoms.

Griffin tugged at his cravat. The river below the railing twinkled invitingly. Without considering the sanity of the action, he did what he'd wanted to do since setting foot in this place. He removed his boots and jumped.

For a breathtaking second, he hovered neither earthbound nor immersed, traveling the ten feet drop in a moment of weightless suspension. Then he plunged headfirst.

The sweet water refreshed his skin and his thoughts, and he kicked the sandy bottom, pushing his head above the surface. Griffin inhaled the river's fresh, herbal scent, filling his lungs for the first time since the count had delivered his lies. A tortoise, vexed by his lack of restraint, jumped from an island of mossy trunks. Griffin laughed, and the sound startled a few mallards conveying at the closest olive tree.

That slick bastard had tricked him, and he had fallen for it like a goose.

Floating, eyes closed, the tension of the past few days diluted, washed away by the crisp water. Griffin swam to the small pier just to the right of the house. A skiff should be roped to that post. The Douro lazed for at least a mile in both directions, a feast for boating and fishing. He would ask it made right away at the marina in Barca D'alva. Two oars and seats for three.

Jako awaited with a towel flung over one arm, a silver salver on the other. "I assume this bath has to do with a young lady I've met, the one rushing away as if Kali bit her heels?"

Griffin raised himself to the pier, shaking water from his hair, and grinned. "As a matter of fact, it does."

Jako shook his head, a mischievous glint in his eyes. "It's not good for my karma. To work for a master who enjoys scaring young women into running for their lives."

Griffin chuckled. "Impudent Indian."

Jako stepped away from the puddle left by Griffin's clothes. "This just arrived with the mail coach."

His servant prattled on about the sudden decision to swim, and if he could please use a bathing suit next time, and how the water would ruin the silk of his cravat and vest. Griffin stopped listening and, drying himself with brisk strokes, grabbed the envelope.

Jako looked at him, waiting for an answer.

"I don't wear bathing suits," he said absentmindedly and opened the envelope.

In only three lines of economic handwriting, Edmond stated he had befriended a clerk from Croft's office. Symington, the senior, had visited Croft two times in the past week, and the office jittered with rumors that the old gentlemen had negotiated a partnership.

Griffin lowered the letter and stared forward. A confusion of plants crowded the other side of the riverbank, perching precariously over the naked rocks. Willows and wild shrubberies, a few with their roots exposed, reached for the water as if content inhabiting not here nor there, undecided.

"Sir, the luggage is ready. Roberto is asking when we leave for Oporto. He wants to check the blacks' horseshoes."

"Oporto?" The word slurred as if he spoke underwater.

If this letter had arrived last month, Griffin would have jumped inside the coach, only alighting at Croft's

Victorian two-storied office. His partnership and reputation were at risk. Still, his top concerns were that Julia would not marry and that tomorrow she would kill herself in a lunatic scheme to reach Braganza.

Eyes shut, vertigo consumed him as if he stood atop the First Light ruins. At noon, the sun favored all parts at once, making it impossible to tell north from south, west from east. He would not be lost. No, not that, because he could see all directions at once, all the pathways there at his feet. But he felt suspended, the choices overwhelming.

When he had believed Julia was another man's bride, he had known his north—back to his life in Oporto. Last night, he had bottled up his feelings and emptied the whiskey, convincing himself it had been for the best.

Why had Julia stumbled into his life? Before, everything had been so orderly and predictable. His days had been planned; his nights, too. He'd known what he wanted and what he needed to do to get there—his firm figuring first place, the partnership with Croft, the beachfront mansion in Oporto. The latter had been so vivid. He tried to visualize his family's needs, but this passion threatened to control his life.

"Are you all right, sir? You seem so different." Jako glanced down, his face reddening. "I only say so because I hold you in the highest regard."

Griffin shoved a hand through his wet hair. "I do not know what you are talking about."

What had he become? A romantic fool, like the ones he used to mock, a guitar-strumming, serenading Portuguese? His orderly life seemed far away, impossibly so. His stomach dropped. Could he fit into that life again?

These impossible emotions were to blame, growing inside him, twisting around his limbs, climbing near his heart like one of Julia's vines. Passion made logic hazy; without logic, a man became a fool, and only a fool would let his goals slip through his fingers.

There was only one solution. He must nip the thoughts in the bud. Onyx eyes reflecting the sun. Lemon flower-scented hair. Sultry laughter. Soul-stirring stories. And most dangerous of all, that elusive, perplexing sensation that only with her could he feel at home.

Unable to stand still, he strode to the house. He must set his priorities straight. He couldn't risk his hard-won business, his uncle's heritage, and his life goals. A life suspended, borrowing time, was not for him and not for Julia. He would take her on this trip, but as soon as they returned from Braganza, he would go back to where he belonged, and in time to salvage his partnership.

Chapter 30

"If maid or widow you would win,
And wear your wished-for treasure,
You'll find it best to fill your skin
With just the proper measure.
With less than that to feed your flame,
You'll prove too cold a lover:
While more might overshoot your aim;
So woo her-half-seas over."
John Herman Merivale

Griffin arrived before dawn to see Shaggy being held by Jose, already hitched to the rickety buggy. Did the madwoman intend to go all the way to Braganza on that? He alighted and advised his coachman to push the Brougham forward and block the exit. The courtyard swarmed with preparations, but Griffin found her at once. Framed by the imposing house, she looked too young.

She startled like a scalded cat and glared, the condensation fogging in front of her face resembling rage fumes. "What are you doing here?"

Jose speared him with his one-eyed glare, and the turncoat butler puffed his chest like a silver-haired rooster. Griffin took her arm and steered her from the carriageway, separating her from the crew of fateful servants. "I came to put some sense in your thick head."

She raised herself to her full diminutive height, eyes glittering black fire. "Save your breath."

He exhaled and rubbed his forehead. "Have you planned this trip?"

"Yes." She jutted her chin and looked at him defiantly.

The one-syllable reply made him grit his teeth. Invading her space, he bent his torso until he stared at her eyes. "Elaborate."

She bit her lip. "Jose will drive me to Vila Nova, where I will catch the diligence to Braganza. Four days will take me there and to phylloxera's cure."

"This is not a plan. This is your goal."

"I won't over-plan like an Englishman. What are you doing here, anyway? I thought you'd be back in your beloved city by now. I've been dealing with my own problems long before you graced us with your presence."

He looked to the sky, pleading some heavenly force to gift her, if not with wisdom, at least some common sense. "You cannot take this journey by yourself."

"Flor is accompanying me."

"Who?"

She looked sideways. "My maid."

He squared his shoulders and advanced one step, but she shrugged and circled around him, walking toward her buggy. Griffin's lips tugged up—his Brougham blocked the way out.

"Remove your carriage, sir!" Her chin trembled. "I don't know what you mean here, Mr. Maxwell, but you are too late. I am losing precious time, so you better move your—"

"Listen to me." He took a long, well-deserved breath. "I will take you to Braganza."

"I won't go anywhere with you."

"This is the second time you have intruded on my sleep, and I had to leave my bed at this wretched hour to save your pretty little neck. So help me God, you will enter the carriage and you will do so gracefully."

She gaped at him, then raised her chin, her body so tense he feared it would snap. His chest tightened, and he shoved his hands inside his pockets to keep them from drawing her close and rubbing the tension away from her shoulders.

"Having my escort is the best alternative. I know you are an intelligent woman, Julia."

Circling around them, the butler tried to come near, but Griffin's expression must have alerted everyone to keep their distance. Even her shy cousin, nightcap still on her head, swelled the numbers of the glowering faces in the courtyard.

Julia's shoulders deflated, and her chin dropped to her chest. She looked up, her mouth a grim line so unlike her that he fought the urge to shake her sorrow away. Was it so difficult to accept his help?

"Can you take me today?"

Griffin's shoulders relaxed. At least he had avoided her going by herself. Of course, his first intention to change her mind had been as feasible as making his asinine nemesis drink tea with the queen. "As soon as you are ready."

She nodded and took her time with her goodbyes. They flocked close to the palm trees, out of Griffin's hearing range. He glimpsed some angry hand gestures, heads shaking, and occasionally a chin lifted in his direction. With her usual matter-of-fact authority, she placated everyone and turned to the boy. His chest ached at the sight of mother and son clasped together so tenderly. Only then did Julia allow him to steer her inside the carriage.

A tug on his coat made him look down. Tony rocked back and forth, his ivory pajamas bright against the murky courtyard. Excellent. Griffin needed to set a few things straight with the urchin. He could not run amok, causing havoc and getting himself hurt.

Griffin flung Tony atop a wooden crate and stared into his eyes. Today, they lacked their usual sparkle. With shoulders drooping and fists curled by the sides, the kid looked on the verge of crying.

Griffin cleared his throat, preparing a string of threats. "Tony—"

"Will you bring *mamã* back?" His chin trembled. "Walking on two legs, not lying on a cart?"

Griffin's breath caught, and he nodded once, twice. "I will."

"Do you promise?" Tony's eyes shimmered with repressed tears.

Griffin managed a grunt before Tony pushed his chubby hand forward, and they shook hands. Brushing his arm over red-rimmed eyes, the boy blinked, a smile spreading on his face like the sun breaking the predawn shadows. Griffin exhaled, the weight that had just left the boy's shoulders settling like an anchor on his chest.

Griffin pushed a strand of the boy's hair off his smooth forehead. "Tony, you need to keep away from trouble. Let your nanny breathe from time to time, eh? You are the man of the house now. Are you up to it?"

The boy nodded, bouncing from heels to toes.

"If you behave, I will take you for a ride on Thunder when I come back. Can I have your word as a gentleman?"

"I promise." Tony kissed his crossed fingers.

Griffin reached forward to put him down, but the boy flung himself around his neck with such force he stumbled back a step. He patted the boy's small back and tried to push him away, but the kid persisted, his arms holding him in tender shackles. Griffin took a shaky breath and gave up, enfolding the little body with his arms, inhaling his vanilla scent. As he pressed him closer, it felt . . . good.

Before he could compose himself, Tony jumped to the ground, running in the house's direction with his nanny scurrying after him. Griffin cleared his throat and looked around. Thankfully, nobody had witnessed the exchange. Taking a few unsteady steps, he entered the Brougham and settled on the front-facing bench.

Julia glanced at him and averted her eyes, clutching rosary beads, a black mantilla covering her silhouette like a shield. That's when Griffin noticed the third occupant of the limited space—the maid. Griffin had spent the entire night awake, girding his resolve to keep his hands to himself, but his sleepless night had been unnecessary. She had brought a bloody chaperone.

The carriage took off. By the roadside, Vesuvio's vineyards were touched by fall, leaves turning a bright yellow. The sun was rising when they crossed the old Roman bridge linking their side of the Douro with the road to Braganza, near the northern frontier with Spain. The river, his close neighbor these past few weeks, reflected the vines in calm contemplation. Soon, the rainy season would begin and the Douro would turn wild and unpredictable.

They passed along phylloxera-stricken vineyards in the early stages of the disease.

Julia clutched the beads, her lips moving in a fervent prayer. Griffin hoped she was right, for her sake and for his. Without grapevines, the wine market would cease to exist.

Chapter 31

"I like best the wine drunk at the cost of others." Diogenes the Cynic

The Almoster *coudelaria* had baroque stables more imposing than many aristocratic homes. Pedro tried to see his horse breeding property through the guests' eyes—rolling green pastures, a lake surrounded by juniper trees, the sprawling mansion flanked by manicured hedges. No wonder the two John Bulls were in awe, sitting at the edge of their seats, smiles plastered on their faces. The rectangular table faced the turf arena. Near the Grecian colonnades, a duo of violinists played Mozart's *Concertone in C Major*, a favorite of His Highness the Duke. In seconds, Erebus would enter and provide the entertainment.

"His Majesty is interested in the railroad development." Pedro's father lazed at the head of the table, flaunting his marshal's uniform. At least fifteen medals, including the envied Order of the Sword, adorned his chest. His advanced years hardly showed on his tanned complexion, blond hair mixed with white, the long mustache a testament to his authority.

Pedro turned to the pair of Englishmen. John Bull number one, a Mr. Ashwood, was tall and reed-thin, with a ruddy nose he enjoyed making ruddier with periodic pinches of snuff. The other, lesser in the railroad company's hierarchy, strained his poorly fitted clothes, a perpetual sheen of sweat coating his upper lip.

For the tenth time this afternoon, Pedro wondered why the Duke of Titano had left Lisbon and his matters as Prime Minister to settle a railway up the Douro River. He could not fault the two Englishmen, though. Even Pedro had his ears open, searching for the meaning behind the duke's sudden interest in the completion of the steam train.

The horse master entered the arena atop Erebus, Pedro's most prized steed. The stallion, black flanks shining under the afternoon sun, sheer size and lines a testament to the Lusitanian superiority, passaged perfectly, long legs pulling and pushing in cadence to the music. When the pair stopped perpendicular to the table, the rider lifted his hat, and the horse extended the front leg in a perfect salute. While the two Englishmen were enraptured, his father's expression remained blank, looking beyond the field as if the presentation was beneath his notice.

"Your Excellency, it's in the Company's best interest to reach the border with Spain in Salamanca. I'm sure it's also so for the government of Portugal." Mr. Ashwood spoke over a mouthful of caviar.

"Of course, of course, how intelligent and expedient you are. I must recommend you to Gladstone. Your Majesty's chancellor must hear of such an expedient young man. Don't you agree, Almoster?" The duke raised his glass of Chateau La Tour and leaned closer, voice a soft murmur. "Because I care for the Company's interests, I'll offer my most humble advice."

The men widened their eyes, at risk of stumbling face-first on the table, more pliant than Erebus and his well-rehearsed *piaffe* performed in the arena.

"The high Douro region has a sparse population and only a few wine properties. You would lose money to increase the railroad this far. I only say so because I care about the interests of the Railroad Company, of course."

That was low, even for his father—pulling their strings like that. The Company would increase profitability by extending the line, as port led the country's exports. Pedro could not help admiring his father's political finesse. But why did he want to avoid railroads here?

When Erebus performed a flawless pirouette—back legs rooted on the turf and front legs trotting in a circle—John Bull number one leaned forward. "Tell us how you make them do that. Heated whips, I presume?"

The duke removed an imaginary speck from his navy blue coat. "I couldn't tell. Dressage is Almoster's sport, not mine."

Pedro's jaw locked, and he forced it to unclench. "This is not a circus. The Lusitano is a treasure among horses, obeying the rider, striving to cooperate, to accept its domination."

The man sneered, his nose swelling further. "Do you teach women, too?"

Pedro drained his wine, hiding his disgust at the crude remark. When he lowered his glass, movement near the Grecian columns caught his attention. Cris stared at the duke. Curse his brother's insistence. Had Pedro not ordered him to stay close to Vesuvio, watching Julia?

The duke gave him a scornful look. "Almoster, you may leave us to attend to your personal business."

Pedro rose without excusing himself. Cris followed him from the arena into the stable entrance. "He doesn't want to see you. How many times must you hear this?"

Cris grimaced. "I'm sorry—"

"You and your *bourgeois* notions of a happy family. When will you let go? The duke is not worth it."

Cris cleaned sweat from his brow. "I'm not here for him, all right?"

"What then?"

"Mrs. Costa left for Braganza. With that Englishman."

Pedro sucked in a breath, hands closing into fists. "What do you mean, they left?"

Cris raised his palms, taking a step back. "The maid is with her. She has been chaperoned at all times."

He caught his brother by the scruff of his lapel. "You will go there, and you will use whatever means necessary to stop this trip, do you hear me?" He pressed his brother against the wall. "You will bring her back, unharmed."

Heart slamming against his ribs, Pedro adjusted his cuff links and returned to the arena. A folded vellum awaited atop his plate. His father's precise handwriting glared at him.

Whoever walks with the wise will become wise, but the companion of fools...

Lifting his eyes from the paper, he met his father's sharp gaze. The other occupants of the table vanished. The arena turned into a charged void, steel gray. Behind the Duke's slate eyes were Pedro's childhood companions—a disgusting combination of superiority and violence.

Violins increased the tempo. Erebus cantered in place, performing another beautifully orchestrated pirouette. The music swelled, a crescendo, notes rising until they exploded with Erebus leaping four feet into the air, kicking viciously with its back legs—a perfect cabriole. If a man's chest had received the impact, it would have pulverized bones and lungs.

Chapter 32

"Where there is no wine there is no love." Euripides

The bell tolled the hours. Beyond the inn's bedroom window, the city of Moncorvo prepared for the night. Shop owners closed their doors while a stooped figure reached high on the posts to light the gas lamps. The square combined houses in the Swiss chalet style as well as typical whitewashed Portuguese cottages. The union of cultures may seem crazy for some, but to Julia it was lovely.

Thoughts of other nationality combinations crept into her mind, and Julia closed the shutters with more force than necessary. Several hours jostling in the carriage had left her body a mass of cramps and muscle aches. The two beds, with their ragged but clean bedclothes, beckoned. She would forego dinner and retire now.

Griffin's voice carried through the room's thin wall, and Julia tried to decipher the muffled conversation. Was he speaking with his manservant, or a maid eager to help him with his bath or worse?

"You should forget him," Flor whispered. "He is a handsome devil, for sure. But he is not the man for you."

Julia turned away, face flaming, and opened her bag. The maid must think her a fool, pining for a man like him. Her steps shuffled near, and Julia tensed. Her feelings for Griffin were too private and sore for Flor to rummage through them as if searching for clothes in a cramped valise.

Flor placed a hand on her shoulder. "Have you thought about the count's offer? At least he will make you a bride."

Fisting her hands, Julia moved to the other side of the bed. Of all people, Flor should understand her reticence.

A soft knock on the door made them turn.

"I asked for water for your bath."

It wasn't a blushing maid but a tall Englishman, a hand on the threshold, glaring at Flor as if prepared to do battle. "Care for a stroll outside, Mrs. Costa?"

Ignoring Flor's admonishing expression, Julia took a fortifying breath and grabbed her shawl. She exited to the inn's hallway, closing the door on the maid's gaping face.

The crescent moon hovered above the thatched rooftops, adding a silvery hue to Moncorvo's public garden. They strolled, following a path lined by flowerbeds and statues. His hand brushed hers, and she crossed her arms.

"What is this smell?"

Julia inhaled the alluring, sweet scent. "Jessamines—*dama da noite.*"

"Jessamines?" He tilted his head, cobalt eyes twinkling in tune with the gas lamps.

"A flower. It blooms only at night, not more than four times a year. Unpredictable, but not when it rains. I think it helps to have a clear sky." Julia gazed at the brilliant stars. "Are you sure you don't know it?"

"Positive."

She sighed. "If moonlight had a scent, it would be this."

He came closer, and her heart sped up. Leaning forward, his face an inch from her hair, he inhaled. "I doubt it."

Ignoring the shivers on the back of her arms, she strolled along the path of terra cotta stones. The walkway led to a marble fountain, the drizzling water a mirror to the silvery light. Sure as spring, the jessamine bush grew behind the spray, near the city's wall.

"There."

He closed his eyes. "Hmm, the scent is..."

"Beautiful, isn't it?"

Shadows played over his face and on the planes of his broad shoulders. Griffin caught her stare, holding her captive for long seconds. He cleared his throat. "Are you comfortable? The inn was full, and—"

"The room is fine, thank you." She drifted to the jessamine bush. "I am much indebted to you, Mr. Maxwell."

"Back to Mr. Maxwell? I thought we had dropped the formality, at least when we were alone."

He touched her chin, and she pulled away. His hand, elegant and powerful, stood raised for a heartbeat, then fell by his side. She was glad he did not press her further. She truly was. His breath brushed her brows just before he reached for one of the moonlight-painted blooms. Before he could make contact, she caught his wrist.

"They are more delicate than they appear. Look." With the tip of her finger, she skimmed one. They both stared as the bud floated down in a haze of perfume.

He pinched the bridge of his nose. "Listen, I am sorry for the way I treated you at Boa Vista."

"It's better if we keep our distance. At some point, you will leave, and I..." She swallowed, her throat dry as chalk. "The night blossoms are not the only ones that bruise easily."

Griffin extended his hand again. While she held her breath, expecting him to reach for the jessamine and prove her wrong, he whispered a caress on her cheek, soft and dreamlike and evanescent, like the kiss of butterfly wings. Water dripped on the fountain. The breeze sighed around them. Julia willed him to deny her, to pledge his intentions to stay. He didn't, and though his touch barely stirred the downy hairs on her skin, the foolish hope she had nurtured during their brief acquaintance wilted just the same.

She'd better remember that.

***

Griffin crossed the too-quiet inn's courtyard after breakfast. Where was the coachman? They were losing precious daytime. Julia wore the hated mantilla again, covering her upper body so efficiently she might as well use it as a shield. He pushed his hands inside his pockets and kicked a stone lying unsuspectedly near his feet. Another day with the maid looming between them. The stifling silence inside the carriage was enough to make a man want to kick himself.

Jako came out from the shabby stable, shoulders hunched, muttering to himself. When Griffin caught the servant's eyes and he turned them hastily to the floor, he knew at once. Bad news. Jako and his quirks would be comical if they weren't directed at him.

"Out with it."

"It's the carriage, sir." He fidgeted with the blasted pearl on his neckcloth. "The axle is broken."

"How can that be possible?"

Jako shuffled his feet. "I'm sorry, sir."

Griffin stalked inside the moldy, dusty shed. True to Jako's words, his Brougham lay defeated, the gleaming lacquered coach dull with dust and mud after two days on the road. Roberto crouched near the left wheel.

"Is it true?"

The coachman stood and cleaned his hands on his trousers. "I'm afraid so, sir. It was in perfect condition before we left, I swear it."

"What do you think happened?"

"It could have worn out, but I doubt it." He scratched his head. "Someone did it on purpose."

"What? Who would profit from such action?"

Griffin glanced at the room. The space had no tools or vestiges of sabotage, only worn wood and corn sacks, a stray chicken or two. He raked his mind for whoever would want to hold them here. Of course, the count. A ruse to keep them from reaching their destination? But why?

The innkeeper came puffing, a look of confusion and abject misery on his rotund face. "*Senhor*, I don't understand. My son went out with some wanton woman and left his room at the hayloft. A brigand must have come and—"

"Just arrange for its repair. If you please," Griffin snapped.

"I will send my son to Amarante right away. In four days, he will be back with the repairman."

"We can't wait that long," Julia said.

Griffin had not noticed her presence. Jako must have shared their predicament, then.

She wrung her hands. "The king expects the viscount in Lisbon by the beginning of September. We would lose him."

"Is there no one closer?" Griffin addressed the innkeeper. "A place where we can rent another conveyance?"

The man scratched his shaggy mane and clucked his tongue. "I am sorry, sir."

Griffin took Julia by the arm and led her to the side. "After we fix the Brougham, it will be too late."

Her gaze darted from him to the carriage. "Can we proceed on foot?"

"For fifty miles? Impossible."

"But we came this far. It is just another day until we get to Braganza." She threw her arms up, and the mantilla fell, her hair emerging in a glorious tangle of shining tresses. He took a step closer, inhaling the scent of lemon flowers he craved more than air.

Silently, she gazed at the stalls, forehead furrowed. "What about your coach horses?"

"What about them?"

"Can we continue to Braganza on horseback?"

His heart sped up. "But you don't ride."

"I know, but I can't let this stop us from finding the viscount. There is too much at stake."

Griffin took her chin and searched her eyes. "Are you sure?"

"Yes."

"Fine. But I won't take you if you can't control the impulse to act on your own."

She gasped. "Beg your pardon?"

One would expect she had not a single impulsive bone in that delectable body.

Griffin raised a brow. “Remember the boar? When we agreed to count to three, but you left me on the two?”

She tilted her head, smiling. “You remember that?”

“I remember everything,” Griffin said, his voice hoarse.

“You have my word.” She kissed her crossed fingers.

Griffin stared at her lips. He talked about her impulsivity, but he fought urges himself. To seize her wrist, bring her palms to his mouth and kiss her fingers as she just did, and then her forearms, climbing to her shoulders and neck until finally arriving at her lips. God, how would he hold to his restraint?

While Julia left to arrange a valise, Griffin saddled Romulo for her. Of the two Yorkshire trotters, it was the more sure-footed, never flinching from anything. Jako came from the kitchen with two saddlebags.

“Stop. Let me see what you put inside.”

When Griffin was satisfied it carried enough provisions, he allowed Jako to adjust them over the saddles. Coachman Roberto held both horses by the bridle, and the sun filtering over the inn’s yard made their ebony coats gleam. Griffin opened the region’s crude map and studied the roads crossing over hills and rivers. After conferring with Roberto, he decided on the safest path to reach Braganza.

Preparations had been completed, and the horses were ready. Where was Julia?

Griffin could hardly believe they were going to ride in this beautiful countryside. Actually, only a few things would make him happier, and all of them involved fewer clothes and zero horses. Or zero clothes and . . . he sweated under the white flannel coat, a feat in this chilly morning. Damn it, he must remember his resolutions.

A hush fell on the courtyard, and he turned. Julia came forth, a long raven braid flowing down her shoulders, the mantilla nowhere to be seen—an Amazon queen in tight breeches and knee-length boots.

Griffin's heart took on a perilous rhythm at the sight of how the man's clothes outlined her shapely legs. He would revise his latter thought. Zero horses and those delicious breeches would make him a very, very happy man.

***

Julia inhaled the courtyard's dry, chilly air. She would do this. With unsteady legs, she came closer to the horses. "What is his name?"

"Romulo."

The horse's glassy eyes watched her, intelligent but friendly.

Julia patted his neck. "*Cuida de mim, por favor.*"

“He doesn’t understand Portuguese,” Griffin whispered near her ear.

Closing her eyes, she ignored the shivers his voice brought to her back and nape. They didn’t have time for this. Dawn was long gone, and if they did not get to Braga in time, they risked traveling all the way there for nothing. She used to mount Diuro without help. Could she do it with this giant beast? She grabbed the thick mane and applied many forgotten muscles to push her body up, up, up until she was astride him. The first glimpse of the courtyard atop the foreign animal was dizzying.

Griffin gaped at her, brows furrowed.

She raised her chin with a bravado she did not feel. “Are we going or not?”

Griffin mounted his horse in a practiced, elegant movement without upsetting his white coat or the position of his hat.

They trotted over the cobbled pavement of Moncorvo, the mustard-colored buildings cramming in on her as they traversed the narrow streets of the medieval city. The cathedral’s bell rang, a warning of a penitence not fulfilled, and Julia crossed herself. Would God punish her for disobeying the promise she’d made at her husband’s funeral? Two years without riding, depriving herself of the freedom to come and go, to feel the wind on her cheeks, the connection only horse and rider shared.

The impact of the metallic horseshoes over the stones jarred her bones. She strove to control her movements, holding tight to the reins and grinding her legs to the sides of the saddle.

They crossed the gates of the walled city. Outside, the landscape spread in front of them, the chalky road winding over immense flat fields planted with flax and cherry-colored blossoms.

Griffin led them to the right. "We won't get to Braga if we keep this rhythm." He eyed her atop the giant horse and shook his head. "I thought Portuguese women were better riders."

Heat climbed her cheeks up to the tip of her ears. She straightened her posture and pushed her heels over the mammoth horse's flanks. It responded with a jump forward, and she held on for life as it went for an ungainly canter. She bounced on her saddle as she watched Griffin gallop away, back shaking with mirth.

She gulped air and raised her eyes from the horse's ears to the green grass and the windswept willows touching the glassy lake by the roadside. Energy radiated through her body, splitting her face into a grin. She brushed her leathery whip on Romulo's neck. Instead of bumping as if she churned butter, she let her body take control. Memories of racing over the beaches of Viana do Castelo, sailing on Diuro's back, returned to her. She let go, all her weight on her knees, her bottom lifted from the saddle, and pushed her torso forward, close to Romulo's neck. The view blurred in tones of emerald and saffron. The horse soared over the vast landscape, sweeping along the road, the vegetation billowing in time with the wind blowing her hair and swelling her shirt. Like a captive peregrine testing its wings over the plains, she soared.

Julia gained on the Englishman. Griffin's tall frame moved in tandem with Remo's powerful gait, a statement to his perfect horsemanship. He blocked the road, so she touched her heels to the black's flanks and twisted the reins to the left, leaving the chalk and stepping over the pasture by the roadside. Heart racing, she galloped over the soft undergrowth, gaining speed and whooshing back on the path in front of him. She glimpsed his befuddled expression.

Too soon, a narrow bridge appeared ahead, mossy stones and thick foliage covering most of the riverbank. She reined in a few feet before the crossing, the horse's hooves lifting a plume of white dust as they came to a stop. Warmth radiated through her chest as she waited for Griffin to catch up.

She had ridden a horse, and it had been marvelous. The sky had not fallen on her head, and her guilt lessened as if blown away by the wind. She wouldn't keep herself from this pleasure again.

Griffin reached her side, panting. "Where did you learn to ride like—?"

"A man?" She raised her brows, feeling awake for the first time in years.

"A lunatic wanting to break her neck!"

She batted her eyelashes at him. "Why, Mister Griffin, proper Englishwomen don't ride at breakneck speed?"

He looked heavenward as if deeply grieved, but then laughter burst out of him. Julia laughed too. Scolding and arrogant, the Englishman was dangerous to a woman's heart, but with a grin crinkling the side of his eyes, he was devastating.

***

Griffin spotted the three-storied stucco building—the Hotel Mourisco—and released a constricted breath. A grinning boy accepted a coin to stable the blacks. Julia passed her leg over her horse's back and alighted. She looked windswept and gorgeous—a carefree smile, hair in disarray, cheeks glowing. Cooing in Portuguese, she caressed Romulo's black muzzle and the lucky bastard nickered, nuzzling her waist.

A full day slobbering over her thighs encased in tight breeches and he could neigh himself, or better yet, howl like a rangy wolf. God, he needed a bath, preferably cold, and a drink, preferably strong. Soon. But first he must settle Julia in her own room. Better yet, advise her to lock her door and only open it tomorrow at dawn.

Griffin grabbed her arm with more force than necessary and propelled her to the hotel's front entrance. A couple passed them on the way out. The woman, her crinoline as large as a horse's rump, stared down her haughty nose at Julia. Griffin glared back. Dusty from the road and wearing man's clothes, Julia topped any freshly minted, obnoxious society lady.

The well-appointed common room had two large sofas, a coffee table, and a patron smoking an offensive cigar. A mustached man called them from behind a granite counter.

"Do you have vacancies?" Griffin asked.

The innkeeper, dressed in a too-tight coat and a yellowed cravat that swallowed his neck, looked from Griffin to Julia, his eyes measuring her.

Face flaming, she took a step back.

"This is not the kind of establishment you are looking for, sir. You should take her to the inn beyond the city walls."

Jaw locked, Griffin pulled her to his side and passed an arm around her hunched shoulders. "This is my wife, and you will treat her with respect." Griffin slammed a note on the counter with enough force to shake it. "I require your best room. Now."

The clerk gulped and stumbled in his haste to reach for the key hanging on a cork display. "Of course, sir. I beg your pardon, sir."

Chapter 33

"The great evil of wine is that it first seizes the feet, it is a crafty wrestler."
Titus Maccius

Nothing would happen. A night slept, coincidently, under the same roof. Julia paced around the bedroom. Spacious and uncluttered, the room had white sheets, gauzy white curtains, and whitewashed walls. The sterile feel emphasized Griffin's caged energy, prowling about like a panther. His colors, tanned skin, fierce blue eyes, and chocolate hair stood in sharp relief.

She gulped. "Hum . . . there is only one bed."

"We are a married couple," he said dryly.

"Except that we are not. How will we manage with—"

"That man had no respect. What would you have me do?"

She lifted her palms. "Thank you, but was it wise to—"

"I will sleep on the floor."

"No, I don't want you to be—"

"Just leave it."

Why was he so cross?

He inspected the window; she flicked through a Bible; he rummaged through his valise; she straightened the counterpane; he scrubbed his hands. When he settled, unpacking clean clothes, Julia hastened to the small water closet hidden behind a silkscreen. She washed and donned a fresh shirt and a lavender skirt she had stowed in the saddlebag. She had brought a nightgown too, but how could she wear the transparent linen with him here?

Peeking over the partition, she assured herself he was decent before returning to the bedroom. She neared the bed when she spotted them. His feet spread over the oak planks, long toes shamelessly poking out from his trousers. Her breath caught, and for all the white expanse of the room, she could not move her gaze from that spot on the floor.

A knock startled them both.

"The dinner."

"I'll get it." She reached for the doorknob, and their hands met. Scalded, she retreated, brushing her arms.

The maid set the table below the window—a vase of daffodils, a jug of wine, bread, and—Julia crinkled her nose—some plain potatoes and beef. They sat face to face. While Julia nibbled the bland food, Griffin devoured his without the slightest measure of caution. His enjoyment warmed her heart.

"When you finish, we should make plans for the morrow. I've brought the map—"

"What's with this English obsession for arranging everything ahead?" Julia yawned, stretching her arms. "Can't we keep an open mind? Our plan didn't include a horseback ride, did it? And it turned out well enough."

Griffin shook his head. "Are you not straining reality just a little? Planning is not an English exclusivity, for Christ's sake. Do you think your ancestors accomplished the Great Navigations by leaving their destiny to fate?"

"Not at all. When Cabral left Lisbon, he sailed for India, but when the wind switched and blew them west, he did not fight it. He went with it. And *voila*! They discovered Brazil." She tapped her forehead. "See? Open mind."

"I rest my case." Laughter boomed out of his chest, crinkling his eyes at the corners and softening the harsh lines of his jaw. He cleaned his mouth with a napkin. "Is everything to your liking?"

"I haven't drunk the wine yet."

He served her from the crystal decanter. The aroma rose in a heavy cloud of cherries and plums.

He raised the glass to his lips. "A claret?"

"You think so?"

He shrugged. "I suppose, but not a regular Bordeaux, though."

"Bordeaux wine has lighter bodies, and the aromas are not quite so intense. More elegant, like a French lady."

Griffin inclined his head. "Portuguese?"

"Cheers to your sagacity." She rolled the wine in her mouth, coating it with the powerful tannins, the sweetness balanced by fruit and acidity, the finish pleasant but not persistent. "When you don't add brandy to Douro reds, this is what you get."

"Your land makes delicious wine, Julia." His eyes caught hers and held them captive. "Why do you suppose they started adding brandy to the wine?"

"I think Napoleon is to blame. After the British banned French wine, they imported it from Portugal. But our reds could not make the sailing trip without getting spoiled. Adding brandy fortified the wine to bounce around the ship."

He furrowed his brows, staring at his empty plate. "Crossing the English Channel is certainly easier than six interminable days on a clipper."

Was he longing for England? She forced a smile, kicking him playfully under the table. "Can you imagine how the world would be if your island produced drinkable wine?"

With his bare toes, he pressed the arch of her foot. She stilled, missing the thread of conversation, a sudden heat invading her limbs. Slowly, Julia retrieved her feet, anchoring them below her chair.

"Or if we didn't like wine so much." He chuckled. "I bet one day the world will be ready for Douro's unfortified reds."

"Can I tell you a secret?"

He leaned forward, his eyes intent. "Is it a plan to unravel the wine market?"

Julia drank more and rested the glass on the table. "Perhaps. After I settle the contract with Croft, I want to sell Vesuvio's wine by the bottle. I've dreamed about the label. A fancy French paper sporting Vesuvio's crest."

"Will you allow me to market your dream bottles?"

"Are you any good?"

He winked. "The very best."

His offer felt like a wine with a pleasant aroma but too many tannins, making her throat ache. Should she be flattered? She gazed beyond the windows, to the fast-approaching dusk. She wanted him in her future, except not as a business partner. But beyond that, what kind of relationship could they have?

He lifted the decanter to fill her glass.

She held his wrist. "Please, I'm not used to more than one cup."

"Why?"

"I make the wine. I don't—"

He lifted his brows. "Enjoy it?"

He was right. Why couldn't she drink like everyone else? She released his wrist, and the ruby liquid splashed into her glass.

"You are different. Lighter somehow, smiling more often."

"I guess it was the riding. I don't know how to explain."

"Try."

She drank deeply, the wine bolstering her courage. "You will call me crazy, but all this time, it's like I've been pruning a part of myself. All the branches and ripe grapes. But this trip, galloping in the countryside..." She sighed. "It was liberating."

Perhaps Griffin understood. The wine blossomed in her chest, warming her from the inside out. Night fell, covering the sterile whiteness of the room in cozy shadows, the edges of their private space now set by the orange glow of the candle flame.

"I'm glad." He made lazy circles on the back of her hand, touching only an inch of skin, but the caress resonated all over.

She cleared her throat and sipped again. "This is not a soul wine, though."

"Soul wine?"

"Never heard about them?"

"Should I?"

"Mr. Ferreira spoke so much about it. I assumed everybody knows what it is."

"Indulge me." He smiled crookedly. "By now, you must have realized I don't particularly hate your stories."

Warmth swirled inside her chest faster than the wine in the crystal glass.

"If a wine pleases your palate, surprising you with its complexity. If the finish is so long and so delicious you want to keep tasting it forever, then you found a soul wine. A *Vinho D'alma.*"

His eyes burned, making her breathless. A breeze blew from outside, kissing her cheeks and raising goosebumps on her arms. The candle flames danced, and one of them blacked out, reducing the space between them to a flickering copper glow. She closed her eyes, waiting.

He smirked and sprawled on the chair. "There you go again with your romantic notions."

"The concept isn't romantic, sir! It's actually quite scientific." She bit her cheek at the shameless lie, her voice slurring just a little.

"Soul wine? Scientific?"

Julia winked, or maybe she just blinked crookedly. "I don't have a single romantic bone in my body."

"Are you sure?" He swept her with twinkling blue eyes. "I must check. For scientific purposes, of course."

Julia's cheeks flamed, and she gulped more wine. She'd better change the subject, or he would realize the idea had not appalled her in the least. "Cheers to your blacks. Romulo and Remo. The finest, gentlest brutes this side of the Atlantic."

He raised his glass. "Cheers to you, the Portuguese Amazon."

She laughed. "Don't mock me. Was I so terrible then?"

His eyes were tender, but then his lips tugged up in a devilish grin. "Not entirely disastrous. I can give you a few lessons on riding astride."

She sipped again, ignoring her flushing cheeks. Who knew that wine could be medicinal, releasing the tight muscles on her neck, the soreness from her calves and thighs? Melting without the tension, her feet slid from beneath her chair, resting over his, searching his warmth. How odd that his naked feet had shocked her senseless before, but now barefoot wine tasting with the Englishman felt as natural as Friday tea. Even more so.

The cheers continued for a while. Minutes or hours—she lost the notion. The Englishman came up with brilliant ones. In fact, she had stopped listening to his actual words, fascinated by a tantalizing strand of hair teasing the side of his left eye.

She fluttered her eyelashes at him. "Do you know the joke of the Portuguese priest and the English pirate?"

"No."

The anecdote poured out from her with mixed languages, and she laughed so hard a few tears sprang to her eyes. Someone snorted. Griffin laughed too, the sound making strange things happen to her innards.

"I love hearing you laugh." She blinked. Had she said that out loud?

She reached for the wine, but he caught her hand first.

"You've had enough." He pushed the decanter away.

"Certainly not."

"Julia, you are drunk."

She huffed. "Why do men always wish to decide what is best for us?"

Accepting the burden of defending her sex to this arrogant Englishman, she stood, finger raised. A bout of dizziness caught her unaware, and she held the edge of the table to straighten herself. The room tilted to the side and balancing on two feet proved too hard. She certainly wasn't tipsy. Only her legs were.

***

Before she could tumble face-first, Griffin circled her midriff, steadying her petite form against his chest. Skin glowing, lips purple from the wine, she enchanted him with her colors. Heart beating in double measure, he tried to pry her away and steer her to the bed, but she looped her arms around his neck. When had she sprouted so many limbs?

He should put her to bed to sleep this off. Her arms traveled from his nape to the base of his spine, each agonizing inch a hammer to his restraint. She laughed, just like when she had raced him.

He rested his forehead against hers. "You drive me insane, Julia."

"Kiss me, then."

All restraint forgotten, he descended on her mouth. When her lips touched his, a groan escaped his chest. An eternity had passed since he had last tasted her. She kissed him with abandon, slanting her face, exploring him, her hands coming up to sift through his hair. He verged on the precipice of his control. Damn it, she was drunk. He had to do the honorable thing, but his conscience took a trouncing, waterloo style.

He forced their lips apart.

She moaned in protest, and Griffin caught her wrists to stop further assaults. He lifted her, ignoring how good her weight felt against his chest, how breathing became effortless, and brought her to the bed. He picked up a glass of water from the tallboy and brought it closer to her plump lips.

"Drink it all."

She drained it in big gulps and slumped against the pillows, patting the place by her side. Griffin had to admit, he enjoyed this version of her tremendously. He untangled her legs from the covers. She had beautifully arched feet, and he could not resist massaging her soles and her instep.

Soon she snored, an unladylike sound so like her it struck a chord inside his chest. Sitting close to her hips, he kissed her eyelids and the tip of her nose. She murmured but kept her eyes closed, turning on her side, hands cradling her cheeks, a contented smile on her wine-stained lips.

Griffin pushed away from the bed, cursing under his breath, and splashed water over his face. Not frigid enough.

He removed his shirt and lowered his body over the covers, his back to her, staring at the fading roses on the wallpaper until the cursed stems stirred.

With a groan, he turned. Faced her. Sleeping, her brow smooth, tiny blue veins crossing her eyelids, she looked too young. This force that animated her stubbornness made her inches taller. Without it, she seemed smaller, fragile. What should he do with her? She rested right by his side and yet so far away.

To hell with the distance, at least for tonight. He reached for her slight frame and pulled her tight against him. She sighed and snuggled closer, her cheek resting against his chest. Griffin filled his lungs with the flowery scent of her hair and smiled in the dark. There. No distance.

***

The vegetation thickened, trees shading most of the sun, and the air changed, heavy with wet earth and grass. Abruptly, the path they'd followed all morning ended, and a river took its place. The other bank couldn't be more than a hundred feet away, but the current raced faster than the Douro.

"I thought the road led to a bridge." Julia rose in the stirrups, searching the river's expanse.

"Portuguese don't know how to give directions."

"English people need to learn how to ask for them." Julia shaded her eyes, pointing to the other bank. "Over there. It looks like a ferry of sorts." She dropped her hands. "Perhaps this is how we are supposed to cross?"

"Let's hope so." Griffin dismounted.

Patting Romulo's neck, Julia kicked her left leg from the stirrup. When she slid from the horse's impressive height, his hand circled her waist. He brushed her against him before allowing her boots to touch the undergrowth. A wet kiss on her nape made her shiver.

"Griffin, I don't think—"

He turned her around and smashed his lips to hers in a voracious kiss that left her reeling. As suddenly as it began, it stopped, and she stood planted on the tall grass, eyes closed, her body alive, waiting for more.

"I will water the horses."

She opened one eye.

Grinning wickedly, Griffin swaggered away, taking Romulo and Remo by the reins.

"Rogue!"

When the ferry arrived at the wooden platform, Julia's shoulders slumped. The watercraft was no bigger than Vesuvio's skiff. How could they fit two giant horses on that? The oarsman, a broad-shouldered, middle-aged man, threw a long rope and a lad jumped off the boat and tied it to a post.

Griffin took a step forward. "Good afternoon. Is this the river Tua?"

"Yes, sir." The oarsman removed his straw hat.

Griffin opened his map. "We were supposed to cross to Braganza here."

The oarsman clucked his tongue. "That bridge is no more, *senhor*. Crumbled in the rainy season."

"And they have not rebuilt in an entire year?"

The boy grinned. "That was three years ago."

Griffin shook his head. "And where, pray tell, is the next bridge?"

"Gimonde." He scratched his hair. "Fifty, sixty miles north."

Griffin turned to Julia, frowning. "This will add another two days—"

"We can't afford to lose that much time." Julia's stomach sank. There must be another way. "Do you accept passengers on your boat, sir?"

"If you'll excuse us." Griffin steered her to a secluded grove of pines. By the creases in his forehead and the tight jaw, he hated her idea.

Julia braced herself.

"What do you think you are doing?"

"We must cross the river, must we not? It is only fifty feet long. If we hurry, we can walk to Braganza and reach the city by nightfall. It is the only option."

"Walk? On a strange road? Consider the danger. You cannot be this irresponsible."

"I won't lose this chance to address the viscount." She crossed her arms. "I won't."

"What do you suggest we do with the horses? Send them flying over our heads?"

She bit her lip. "The oarsman can take them back to Moncorvo."

"We will cross the bridge in the next city. And if we lose Penafiel, so be it." He squared his shoulders, using that arrogant tone she hated.

She held the reins of her life, not him. She shook away from his hold and stomped her feet. "I will do no such thing."

"If you had any sense in your mulish head—"

"I will cross here. You can return with the horses."

He flinched as if struck, and Julia immediately regretted her words.

"Fine." He strode to the wooden pier, shoulders stiff, hands planted on his waist.

What had she done? The air left her lungs in a rush.

She watched him stride back to the pier, stunned into complete silence. He'd left. Of course he would go. She'd insulted his male pride. Her independence had finally shoved him away. It surprised her he'd come this far.

It was better this way. It really was. Griffin distracted Julia from saving her lands, her livelihood, her winemaking. She brushed dusty tears from her face, repeating the words over and over. They wrung false.

Julia wrestled her gaze from his retreating back. On the other side of the riverbank, a lonely path meandered between wild shrubs and forlorn pine trees. The crossing, so simple minutes ago, seemed impossibly wide. She needed to reach Braganza, but she wanted to do it with Griffin.

The thought washed away her denials, leaving no place to hide. She wanted him in her life, on this trip, in her vineyards, in her future, and she had scared him away. Perhaps forever.

Julia walked on wooden legs back to the pier, her throat dry. His expression forbade the apology locked in her chest.

Griffin passed a few coins to the oarsman and made a sweeping gesture without meeting her gaze. "Your boat awaits."

Julia nodded once, twice. With a heavy sigh, she adjusted the strap of her satchel. About to climb on the skiff, she paused. The plea tasted salty on her tongue, but she swallowed it back. Perhaps he needed an excuse to leave. Her late husband had found plenty of those. Why would he want to stay?

Avoiding his stare, she dropped onto the backward-facing bench. She kept her eyes on the water as the oarsman assumed his position, unwelcome tears clogging her throat. If she but looked at him, her resolve would falter, and she couldn't afford to falter now. She had to remember her goal.

The boat rocked from side to side, and she gripped the crude bench with both hands to avoid toppling into the river. Julia lifted her eyes. Griffin had embarked and stood with his feet spread wide, several pounds of angry male blocking the sun. Julia sucked in the sweet-scented air, her mouth gaping. His scowl could scare a wolf, but she couldn't care less. Griffin had chosen to stay with her.

Chapter 34

"There is no such thing as being lost in a vineyard. You are always at the right place." Portuguese saying

The old Roman road snaked through a forest, its pavement oscillating between stones aged into smooth, slippery danger or blanketed by dirt so thin it resembled chalk powder rising in clouds to stick in a man's throat. He'd bet the ancient Romans had been the last to trudge along the five-foot-wide trail. They pursued it for ages, climbing the hills under the shade of oaks and elms. Julia never complained, never faltered in her steps. If she were gracious enough to nag, Griffin could lash out at her, purging this bitterness, but no, she breezed on like a mountain goat.

Each step that brought no sign of civilization caused a fresh dent in his temper. She would have come by herself, the stubborn creature, worse than his asinine nemesis back on Vesuvio. Shadows approached inexorably. The sun dangled only an inch above the cliff tops. Too close, damn it. He increased the pressure on her wrist and the speed of his strides, staring ahead to avoid looking at her.

They needed to arrive soon. Tony's red-rimmed eyes flashed in his mind, pleading to bring his mother back walking on two feet, and Griffin's gut twisted. His promise had become a herculean job—protecting her against her will, miles away from civilization.

To avoid helping her cross a fallen branch, he gritted his teeth and crossed his arms. They made slow progress, and after one more hour tracking the mountains, the sun approached the hilltops, light seeping away like the sands of an hourglass. No sign of a city, a village, a hamlet, or a single hut. They were lost.

"Should we stop?"

He looked at her over his shoulder. "Are you so keen on sleeping outdoors?"

She shrugged. "It seems to be the only alternative."

Griffin grunted and pushed forward, his boots kicking the earth of the infinite desert and cumbersome path. They circled around fallen logs, stepped over snaking roots waiting to trip an unsuspecting traveler, and climbed until he thought they would reach the gates of heaven.

His toes were numb from walking all day, and the saddlebag flung over his shoulder weighed like a dead body. Still, he kept the rhythm, unwilling to give up the hope of finding some sign of civilization.

The sun had vanished, the light scurrying away beyond the dense vegetation, just black outlines now against a dark blue sky. A scent of wet earth came first, then the foliage opened into a clearing flanked by pines and thick shrubbery. If they must spend the night, this was the least wrong place to do it.

He didn't wait for her opinion, as she relished not listening to him, and dropped the bag on the ground. "We will make camp here."

Over the edge, veiled by thick holly bushes, boulders sprouted from the soil. He climbed on top of a large horizontal slab. Between naked rocks stood a pool, lazy heat plumes drifting up from the water. Through the translucent surface, he saw a clear stone bottom. A vision flashed of Julia bathing, her practical shirt turning wet, revealing tempting breasts and—nothing would happen. She would rather he had stayed behind.

"What a beautiful place."

Ignoring how her swaying hips affected his resolve, he stooped down, collecting dry branches and twigs. Soon they had a fire crackling and a meager meal spread on the checkered quilt.

"You are good at this." Julia sat too close, a tentative smile on her lips.

Griffin grunted and accepted the food from her hands. The stale bread and hard cheese tasted like sawdust. His shoulders and neck were stiffer than the rocky ground, and the scurrying and snapping sounds from the woods only made it worse. He was to blame. A man that a woman could sway? His peers in the British community would scoff at his predicament. Tomorrow first thing, they needed a way out of here.

Without notice, Julia laid her palm over his forearm, and he flinched.

"I'm sorry for what I said earlier." She exhaled and removed her hand. "I did not mean it."

He looked away.

She threw a pebble into the fire. "You will keep brooding."

"Better to brood than be reckless like you. Someday, you will get killed. Hopefully, I'll not be there to watch."

"What are you talking about?"

"You will pretend ignorance? Let me refresh your memory. Our encounter with the boar, going to the ruins at dawn, driving the buggy without knowing how, planting outside the demarcated area, having an inexperienced boy for an estate manager, jumping headfirst in this cursed trip." He sucked in a breath. "Deciding to cross the river without asking for my opinion!" He stressed the last words with a thump on his chest. "Do you wish me to continue?"

"I've told you to go back."

A howl, too close, made him grit his teeth.

He leaned forward, eyes unflinching. "I should. But unlike you, I have more than wine in my brain. I reflect before I act. You are wrong if you think you can do it all by yourself." He spat the last words like a curse.

Silence descended over their camp. Only the creeping fire and an owl hooting over their heads punctuated the tension. The smoke, with no wind to dissipate it, stood trapped between them, making his throat sting.

Griffin chanced a look at her. Curtained by flowing black hair, the orange flames accentuated the shadows beneath her eyes. She looked so tired and somehow ethereal.

A dull ache spread inside his chest, and he failed to brush it away. "Listen, I am—"

"I'm sorry for the way I treated you. I truly am." She lifted her shoulders, and when she dropped them, the last of her spirit faded. "It will be pointless, will it not? I'm swimming against the river current. No matter how much I swing my arms and kick my feet, I stay in the same place."

"Julia, if anyone can fight this plague, it is you."

She shook her head, her chin down. "If not for port, what else do I have to offer?"

Her voice dragged, low and monotonic, not the exciting way she talked about wine, about her land, her country. Griffin had the impulse to shut his ears. He grabbed her hand instead. "You said that once, and I let it pass, but I will not allow you to repeat it."

She pulled her hand away. "It is true. Without Vesuvio—without the wine—I am nothing."

"What kind of nonsense did your late husband say to you?"

"Bernardo hated wine. He hated Vesuvio. I was an intruder, stealing his father's affection." She laughed bitterly. "As if I had another choice. After my parents died, I had no one else." She stared at the fire, her eyes glazing. "I remember crossing Vesuvio's portal, dropping my valise, and gaping at the parlor. Mr. Ferreira smiled and showed me Vesuvio's vineyards. Pride colored every word he spoke about wine. He loved the place so much. You would sense it, too, if you had the chance to meet him."

He didn't need to meet her father-in-law. Her pride and love sparkled like thousands of diamonds. Griffin would always carry it with him.

She inhaled. "He taught me about grapevines, about winemaking. Bernardo went to England for college. When he came back, Antero wished us to be married, and I complied."

"Did you love him?"

"In Portuguese, we have a word for how I felt then. *Apaixonada*. The dashing boy who traveled the world thought me a gauche tomboy whose only interest was winemaking."

Griffin clenched his fist. The bastard. Why belittle her?

"The entire time Mr. Ferreira was alive, he resided in Oporto."

Tears coursed down her cheeks and pooled at the corner of her mouth. She was not a pretty crier, his Julia.

"You see? That is why Mr. Ferreira wished me to marry his son. He feared Bernardo wouldn't carry on his dream to make Vesuvio grow and prosper. He entrusted that responsibility to me." She placed her palm over her chest. "And I'm failing him."

For all his apparent virtue, Vesuvio must have obsessed Mr. Ferreira to the point of shunning his son. An attention-starved Julia would do all in her power to impress and earn such a man's love, and what better way than through her guardian's passion? No wonder she believed wine was her only worth. If Mr. Ferreira loved her so much, why sacrifice her happiness?

What a hypocrite he had become. Julia's marriage resembled his arrangement with Croft—continuing the family business at all costs. Until this summer, Griffin could vouch for it as a logical and beneficial arrangement.

"And when your father-in-law passed away?"

"Then Bernardo moved to Vesuvio, and it worsened. Everything in me that delighted his father only increased his despise. In the end, I think he hated me."

"I don't believe it." He cradled her face, engulfing her wet cheeks. "And if he failed to love you, he was an ass."

She fought his hold, her eyes wild and her hair lashing against his chest. "You should not say that. He is not here because of me. That night he died, I drove him to it. He wanted us to move with him to the city, and I refused."

He tried to pull her closer, but she kept her palms up as a shield. How could he show her the truth? She needed to stop living this lie.

“Jose told me about his accident. He fell because he rode while drunk. You are not to blame.”

***

Julia stared at the fire, hoping for the feverish heat to dry the tears, but they wouldn’t stop.

Griffin gathered her close to his chest. “I forbid you to be guilty about his death. I mean it.”

She exhaled in a shaky burst. He was so arrogant, this Englishman, but also the most intelligent person of her acquaintance, and if he believed in her innocence, perhaps . . . perhaps she could let go of this burden. “I will try.”

“Forgive me for lashing out.” He rested his chin on top of her head and rubbed—God, how she missed this tender caress.

“Here, with you . . . I never felt more protected in my life.”

He kissed her head. “You certainly don’t make it easy on a chap.”

She stared at his mouth. “Am I always impulsive?”

“We are in this together. Would you mind discussing with me before rushing headlong into decisions?”

“Are we?”

“Hmm?” He dried her tears with his palms.

"In this together?"

"I am here with you, am I not?"

"Yes, but . . ." Concentrating with him kissing her eyelids proved difficult. "It is so hard to trust another, after—I know so little about you." She studied his blunt nails and long fingers and turned his hands, tracing the lines of his palms. If only she could divine answers from the sinuous marks.

"You know more than most." He shifted away from her and flung a hand over his knee. "Everything that matters."

Julia counted the rise and fall of his breaths. Without his touch, the night's temperature decreased. Griffin's gaze remained lost in the forest. His past disturbed him. Some wines took longer to decant, and in time, he would open. A breeze shook the black outlines of the foliage, swiping over the schist and flickering the fire. When the wind reached Julia's cheeks, she hugged herself, brushing her arms up and down.

"Cold?"

Julia nodded, unable to stop the slight tremors raking her body.

Griffin stood and extended his hand. "Come, my lady. Your bath awaits."

He guided her over a slab of stone to the pool she had glimpsed when they arrived. Moonlight danced over the surface, a few tendrils of steam floating lazily. Julia had heard about these natural springs, but she'd never had the pleasure of entering one.

Quickly, she removed her breeches and vest. Not even Bernardo had seen her fully unclothed. Tiptoeing to the edge with only her cotton shirt, she glided inside, hissing as the water welcomed her with a fiery embrace, tickling the exposed skin of her thighs.

The pool reached her collarbone. Her muscles loosened with the heat, soothing the tiredness of her feet and her calves. A splash sounded behind her, and she braced her elbows on the rocky edge, resting her flaming cheeks on her palms. She closed her eyes, attuned to every movement, every stir, every shift in the liquid surrounding her.

One second, she was alone; the next, his chest was against her spine, and her skin tingled. He circled her with his arms, and she rested her hands over his. When he kissed her cheek, she sighed, enjoying the closeness and the silence.

Leaning her head over his collarbone, she inhaled, consuming the scent of his nape—musky, warm, and smoky from the campfire, a dizzying combination.

He nipped her earlobe. "Why do you believe wine is all you have to offer?"

She stiffened and tried to escape his hold. He clamped his left hand around her hip, turning her. They were chest to chest. He caged her face, his fingers tangling in her hair, his eyes delving into her soul, intent upon uncovering her secrets.

"Since Portuguese have no sense, take my word for it. As a trader, I understand the value of things. You are a remarkable woman. You raised a great urchin. You can weave a tale like no one I've ever known. You are a passable rider. And that ragtag army of yours? Those people believe in you." He seized her hand, tracing circles on her wrist. "I believe in you."

Julia took a shaky breath. "You do?"

"Yes." He licked her palm, and she felt the caress down to her toes. "In some extreme cases, I would even say your stubbornness can pass for perseverance. You have a not-terrible taste for food. And I can't say you are too hard on the eyes."

She sputtered. "What—"

He shushed her reply, kissing her with slow, deliberate strokes. "I won't allow you to repeat that nonsense."

Julia caressed his prickly beard, then sifted her fingertips through his glistening hair, marveling at the silky strands. His matter-of-fact words filled her heart with joy. No one had paid such close attention to her before. She glided her hands over Griffin's naked chest and circled his neck, bringing his face close. "Thank you." Boldly, she traced his lips with her tongue.

He pulled his head back. "Don't steal my moves."

Julia chuckled. "That night at Saint John's party... Did you like the *pastel*?"

"Not sure. I may have to sample it some more." He nipped her lips and trailed wet kisses down her chin and along her neck, lingering where her pulse throbbed.

"And the answer is?" Julia had difficulty speaking, her toes curling over the smooth rock underground.

"God, Julia, your taste ruined me for anything else," he said, his voice hoarse.

His body touched hers from feet to chest, her softness to his hardness. Her limbs became liquid and floated on his arms, dissolving in the warm water.

He mashed their lips together. This kiss differed from anything they had shared before—it was hungry, urgent. He pressed closer. The jagged rocks bit into Julia's back, but she welcomed the pressure, clinging to him. Nothing compared to finally being able to feel his body like this. Like he belonged to her.

"I can't keep away from you." He panted and buried his mouth on her nape. The bite was surprising, and a pang of desire shook her. "I tried, but I can't. Not anymore."

Before this trip, before this night, she would have run away to the farthest edge of the forest, preserving the distance, guarding her modesty and her heart. But tonight, with the crickets singing and all the stars as witnesses, she simply did not want to run. She wanted him with a desperation that rivaled the desire flashing in his eyes.

"Then don't."

Chapter 35

"All men by nature desire to know. An example of this is the delight we take in our senses. For even apart from their usefulness, they are loved for their own sake, and none more than the sense of sight." Aristotle

The words resounded in his head, the need to possess her storming inside his veins. He clasped her to his chest and pushed out of the rock pool like the conquerors of Portugal's golden age. Standing by the groove with Julia near his heart, nothing else mattered. Not the chill of the night, nor the absence of civilized comforts, nor the wolf howling in the distance. Just her and him, in the same place, at the same time. No obstacles in between.

Griffin laid her down on the blanket near the fire. She was a goddess, hair tangled around her like a raven cloak, the skin of her cheeks and limbs glowing the color of sunset. With deliberate movements, he lowered himself by her side.

When he reached for the fastenings of her blouse, her pupils dilated, the fathomless black pools pulling him in, and she nodded. She helped him release her arms from the tangled shirt, and when freed, she looped them around his neck.

"Do you want me to stop?"

"No."

For once, he found no fault in her monosyllabic reply and removed her cambric pantalettes. Finally, they were skin to skin. He pushed his weight away, sitting back on his haunches to better see her. She shielded her nakedness with her arms.

"Let me look at you."

She bit her lips. "Am I not too hard on your eyes?"

"The eyes? No, but on other body parts..." Griffin guided her hand to the place where all the blood in his head had pooled.

She smiled shyly but tugged her arm free.

"Julia, let me see all of you. I've been waiting ages for this." Perhaps all his life.

Slowly, she uncovered herself. Moonlight and the campfire's glow fought for possession of her naked skin. He was jealous of both. She was perfection, olive curves as sinuous as the terraces in the Douro, a body he longed to inhale, to savor, to discover all its secrets. The steam enveloped them in a sensual mist.

He reached out to fan her hair around her head in a shadowy halo, both sin and benediction. She stared at him with impenetrable eyes, perspiration dampening her brows. He shifted his regard to her breasts, teasing her with small bites and licks.

Unable to wait a moment longer, Griffin fumbled with his breeches, freeing himself. Nudging her legs apart, he mounted her, touching her entrance, wanting in with desperation. As he pushed an inch inside, she tensed. She feared lovemaking. With great self-control, he withdrew. He kissed the tip of her nose and shifted to his back, crossing his palms behind his head.

"It was a surprise." He masked his ragged breaths with a nonchalant tone.

She turned on her side, confusion written on her beautiful face. "Surprise?"

"I expected Portuguese women to be better riders. With the Lusitanian horses being centaurs and all that…"

She lay her chin on his chest. "What do you mean?"

He used his most bland expression. "You don't know how to gallop."

"Excuse me?" She rose on her haunches, collecting her hair at her nape. Griffin devoured the lines of her profile, proud breasts, and lean arms. "When you are galloping, you keep your body too forward, and your," he gestured toward her derriere, "stays above the saddle. Clearly, the wrong technique."

She looked at him askance. "And Englishmen have this proper technique?"

He grunted and kept perfectly still, like when he had fished in Repton all those years ago, bathing the hook in the brisk water. He treasured tonight's catch infinitely more than the famous brown bass of his homeland. When she shifted, an elbow pressed against his chest, he held his breath.

"Do you think I can learn this proper English technique?"

She had taken the bait, and his heart sped up.

He gazed at the stars, the silvery dots blurring together. "I don't think you are up to it."

"Show me."

Reeling her in before she could fight the hook, Griffin sat up and grabbed her hips, lifting her so she straddled his lap. She startled, bending away and keeping herself inches above him, far from where he needed her to be.

"See, too high. You must keep in contact at all times." He put his hands on either side of her hips, guiding her down. She kept her eyes glued to his. He penetrated her, gaining a few inches. He devoured her gasp, nipping her lips, delving his tongue inside. In the kiss's haze, he had to constrain the urge to surge over her tight passage. But he held fast, waiting for her to get used to him.

"Now you ride."

"I don't know how." With brows furrowed and chest hunched, she remained away from him, keeping her distance.

"Julia."

She opened her stormy eyes glazed by passion.

"Stay with me." Griffin could not permit any obstacles between them. He leaned closer and wrapped his right arm around her waist, arching her spine.

A fine sheen of perspiration dampened her skin. With his left hand, he followed the tiny drops, touching her cheeks, her collarbone, circling her breasts, bringing her closer until their chests touched. She grew even moister around him, her resistance crumbling. Griffin checked the impulse to shout at the stars. They joined to the hilt, no distance, no obstructions between them. It was heaven, like reaching destiny after a strenuous journey. Like being parched for years and then drinking to oblivion. She circled her arms around him, caressing his back, clinging to him. He lost himself in the absence of space between them, bridging their bodies, straining, hurling, blending.

With both hands cradling her waist, he showed her how to move. They rocked, her shyness evaporating like the vapors in their pool. She made love as she laughed and cried and did everything else—without restraint. As they galloped to completion, that elusive sensation burst inside him, of being precisely where he wanted to be. Still, it grounded and took shape for the first time, tangible as the pliable form he claimed.

Long after, they lay together, the soft glow of the campfire playing on her skin. The sky covered them in limpid black satin, the constellations twinkling. Scorpio pointed its claws north above their heads. A half-moon added enough light to discern her knees intertwined with his, the outlines of her breasts, and beyond them, the black shapes of the trees buffing them from the wind. Crickets sang, combining their soothing melody with the sounds of their breathing.

"Do you feel how the soil is warm? Even though the night is cool?"

Griffin grunted, still too exhausted to think clearly.

She moved on top of him and captured his hand, splaying it over the ground. "See?"

"Yes," he lied. To him, it was just crushed granite, good for vines but hard and damn uncomfortable for him.

She settled again over the crook of his arm, tracing circles on his chest. "This is the magic of the schist. It keeps the temperature."

Griffin chuckled. While he still reeled, Julia wanted to talk about wine. He was no novice, far from it. Back in Oporto, he kept mistresses, of course, but he'd never felt this joining of souls. Griffin shifted, accommodating her head so she would not have to touch the hard ground. "Why does it matter?"

The campfire faded to embers, and the smoke mingled with Julia's skin had to be the best perfume he'd ever smelled.

"Because grapes don't like sudden temperature changes."

"Do you mean those vain, impossible to please Portuguese fruits?"

"Yes." She bit his chin. "During hot summer days, the soil prevents them from getting burned, and through the chilly nights, the schist conserves some heat, keeping the grapes warm."

"Much like I did for you at the inn?"

She propped herself on her elbow, staring at him with those onyx eyes, her hair tangled between them. "The schist doesn't snore."

He chuckled, upsetting her position on top of his chest. She laughed too, her body shaking with the sound.

"Go to sleep now. Tomorrow we'll reach Braganza, and I won't tolerate your laziness."

She sighed. "I would not mind spending more time here with you."

Griffin opened his mouth, but no words came. Staying here was not an option. When they reached Penafiel's estate, these moments alone with her would end. They would face society as Mr. Maxwell and Mrs. Costa, nothing between them but a business association. The thought brought an ache to his chest, and Griffin closed his eyes, inhaling the scent of her hair and committing it to memory.

One of his mistresses had been a respectable widow. The relationship had been mutually beneficial for two years. They had been discreet, with no consequences for her reputation.

What if he and Julia found a way to be together? Being a mistress was beneath her, but what was the alternative? Marriage was not an option. Society would not overlook their differences because of a priest's blessing. And worse of all, Croft had started a bloody trousseau.

Julia didn't know of his betrothal. His stomach clenched. He must tell her the truth. In fact, he should have told her long ago. "Julia, I..."

"Hmm?" She turned her face, gazed at him with warmth and trust, both familiar and unexpected.

He must be the lowest cad, but he could not bring himself to ruin that look. "I promised Tony I would bring you back in one piece."

She yawned. "You are right, of course."

Her caresses stopped, and he noticed the exact moment she slept. The soft thuds of her heart were so near his that they shared the same beat.

The beauty of laying on the warm schist, joining with the elements, was better left to poets and fools. Pebbles poked his shoulder blades, and one pestered his lower back. But none of that mattered. Her head was pillowed on his heart, her torso touched his chest and not the temperature-keeping rocks, and she slept with a content smile on her lips.

Chapter 36

"Water separates the continents; wine brings them together." Portuguese saying

Griffin squeezed Julia's tiny hand in his, circling her knuckles, and watched the road's bend, waiting for the monstrosity that would take them to their last destination. The sky had a shallow casting of clouds, and the brisk wind reddened her cheeks. The courtyard of the posting inn filled up with passengers—a young couple clutching a toddler, two youths not older than eighteen, an old lady with a straw hat the size of a wheel of cheese, and some farmers and their produce.

Julia kissed his cheek. "Are you sure about this?"

"This is the faster way."

The sounds came first—shouting, groaning, laughter, and the rumble of hooves. Griffin gripped Julia's hands and closed his eyes as the diligence neared.

"You can change your mind, you know. You don't have to do this on my behalf." She bit her bottom lip, swollen from his kisses. "We can walk the rest of the way."

Because she had asked for his opinion, he was ready to make this sacrifice. He would ride the Portuguese mail coach. For her. His good intentions faltered when the mass of wood and hooves disturbed their line of vision with the delicacy of a blind ox in a crystal shop. When it stopped at the post, Griffin groaned. The diligence looked like the unsuccessful mating of a stage coat, a crate, and an omnibus. Three rows of disgruntled animals pulled at their bits and stomped their feet on the dusty ground. The lead horse, his front leg raised in the air, resembled a shaggy Irish Setter preparing for the hunt.

"All aboard," the coachman yelled.

As Griffin helped Julia climb to the outside bench, his ears burned as if his peers back at the English Factory were watching, shaking their heads, their mouths grim lines of disapproval. He seated her on the bench behind the driver's box and dropped by her side, shuffling to the left so he didn't touch the cheese-hat woman.

The coachman's whip flew precariously close to their heads and they took off, dissipating the smell of poultry and dust in the moving, blessedly fresh air. Julia squeezed his hand, giving him a lopsided smile. He meant to reassure her, but she yawned and rested her head on his shoulder. Griffin sighed, looping his arm around her instead.

The first ridge they climbed was so steep they risked falling backward to meet a crashing demise on the line of cork oaks lining the drive. When they arrived at the crest, it was worse. One second, the diligence stood suspended on top of the hill, looking down at a free-fall as the road fell dizzyingly to the valley below. Griffin gripped his seat and held Julia tightly. Before he could catch his breath, the coach plunged down the ramp, bouncing and jarring the passengers. His fingertips dug into Julia's shoulders, and she yelped.

"What's the matter?"

"We are going to die."

She wiggled her shoulder from his grasp. "Why? It's just a slope."

Griffin scanned the other faces then. The sole cognizant individual in the blasted coach was him. Either that or the other passengers belonged in the theater for how well they could mask their panic. By God, remind him to avoid playing cards with these farmers. Griffin swore at any moment, the omnibus/crate/stagecoach would run over its sad four-legged propellers.

When the slope ended, he nearly melted into the seat with his relief. His heart still pounded painfully close to his throat.

A mile or so after, the diligence stopped with a dull groaning sound. Not all the shouting from the passengers and the driver, nor the ominous flying whip, could make them move again. They were stuck, wheels deep in the mud.

One by one, the passengers alighted. Chickens, a pig, crates, valises, and even humans became the occupants of a road so rutted it looked like the back of a camel. Griffin leaned over a wooden fence, still reeling from their adventure down the hill, while Julia ambled close to the steeds. One mule snored.

Under the coachman's coaching, the lads and the young father applied their shoulders to the vehicle, their boots sliding in the mud, but the diligence scoffed at their efforts. The wheel wouldn't release this way. By the look of it, they had enough stamina to continue with the mindless pushing until nightfall. The British Factory members wouldn't stoop so low as to help unstuck the diligence.

Griffin caught Julia's gaze then, and she gave him a sweet smile. Well, those gentlemen wouldn't deign to familiarize themselves with this infuriating, alive, and charming side of Portugal, would they? Griffin peeled off his jacket and rolled up his shirtsleeves.

"Hold this, please." He extended the coat to Julia.

She brought it to her nose and then folded the cloth over her arm, a bewildered look on her face. "What are you going to do?"

"Help, of course."

First, he instructed the burly man to dig a hole around the wheel and sent two lads for rocks. Soon they had paved the way under the wheels and were ready to pull. He glanced at Julia, and she stopped talking with the young mother and beamed at him. He felt like a bloody king.

The coachman hurried to the front. Animals awake and baggage, pig, and ladies inside, they prepared to push.

"Whoa!" the driver yelled.

Griffin applied his shoulder to the carriage and pushed, the muscles of his spine straining, his boots making sulks in the mud. When they rolled free, the women cheered. Julia laughed and cupped her hands around her mouth, shouting for him to hurry. With a breathless chuckle, he raced in pursuit. The young father climbed atop the tail of the coach and extended a hand to him.

After he pushed his weight up, Griffin dropped by Julia's side, heaving. The passengers stretched their arms to shake hands with him, grins splitting their faces. The receiver of a round of cheers and hearty claps in the back, Griffin arrived at a bewildering conclusion. Indeed, the diligence was a collective sort of thing, but it was only embarrassing for those watching from outside. For those inside, it felt... well, it felt like being part of a collective sort of thing.

Chapter 37

"...an elegant little midge, or, better, a cicada in miniature, displaying four spread-out, transparent wings..." J.E. Planchon

Julia splayed her hands over her knees, panting. Her thighs burned, protesting the long walk from the center of Braganza. At least it was still broad daylight. Penafiel's estate was a grand, sprawling, medieval castle, the copper-colored stones a perfect counterpart to the green lawns and the cloudless sky. Two turrets flanked the square building and surrounding it all, a picturesque park with well-tended flower beds and hedges. The grass leading to the front drive stretched like emerald velvet, and Julia feared marring it in her unkempt, unwashed, bedraggled state.

"What do we do now?"

Griffin, his tan-colored trousers speckled with mud and grime, hair spiked at odd angles, his face half-wild, made a gallant gesture to the front door.

Julia pointed to their clothes. "Do you think they will receive us?"

A clanking noise and a low droning came from the right, and before she could utter a word, Griffin started toward a tall wooden shed to the side of the lawn. Inside, a sort of carriage hummed and vibrated on its own. It resembled her buggy, but without the long side poles used to hitch a horse, the thing was incomplete, like a cup with no saucer or a house with no ceiling.

A head appeared from the back of the coach, and Julia startled, taking a step back. With mustard-colored overalls and some odd-shaped glasses, the stranger looked like a giant housefly. His only human-like part was his close-cropped hair.

"Is this a steam-powered coach?" Griffin circled the contraption, looking awed.

"Yes, an original Rickett steam vehicle."

"I saw one from afar at the Oporto World Showcase. Can I see the engine?"

"Of course."

Griffin grinned at her, and then he disappeared inside what looked like an opened cupboard.

The stranger removed the leather upholstery covering the bench, exposing odd-shaped tubes and cylinders. "Here, the steam boiler is mounted under the seat. First, we need to check the water level in here." He clanked the tool somewhere out of Julia's sight. "The power comes from a two-cylinder engine connected by a chain to the rear axle."

"It's remarkable!"

"Indeed, it is."

"Julia, this is the future. Can you imagine these vehicles traveling up and down the roads?"

"I prefer the diligence," she mumbled, crossing her arms.

They were utterly lost in the conversation about mechanics and parts and speed and horses as if they had no other troubles in the world. Boys and their toys. If Tony was here, he would be atop the coach, demanding a ride.

She poked Griffin's ribs. "We have a mission, remember?"

"Oh, of course." He cleaned his hands on his trousers. "We are looking for the Viscount of Penafiel. Do you know him?"

The stranger shut the cupboard with a clank. "Who asks?"

"Griffin Maxwell from Oporto and Julia Costa from Quinta do Vesuvio."

Removing the odd-shaped goggles, he turned back to them. Without the housefly mask, he was a handsome man—coffee-colored eyes with laugh lines radiating from the corners, tanned skin, and a closed shaved beard. He gave Julia an accessing glance, as if only then noticing her presence, and the smile turned into a grin, flashing dimples in his cheeks.

He extended his hand. "Penafiel, at your service."

***

Griffin had to admit the viscount's laboratory was impressive, with sparkling marble, sky openings, and floor-to-ceiling shelves sporting various implements and books. Julia acted like a kid in a sweet shop, oblivious to the pungent smell, an odd mixture of burned matches and alcohol, her eyes absorbing everything at once. At least she seemed to be enchanted with the place and not the owner.

He curled his hand around her forearm and whispered in her ear, "You told me he was an old man."

She startled. "I said nothing of the sort."

"I particularly remember you describing him as a *fidalgo* with a scholar disposition."

She glanced at the viscount strutting in front of them and opening the wooden shutters. "I thought you had bonded with him outside. All that talking about steam pushed coaches. Unless..." She grinned. "Are you jealous?"

"It's a steam-powered coach, and no, I'm not jealous."

He had never felt an ounce of jealousy in his entire life and was about to explain so when she rose on tiptoe and kissed him on the lips. Griffin's eyes shot to the viscount, but he had his back to them, wrestling with a stuck window.

"After last night, you cannot doubt where my affections lie." She winked. "Now, behave."

She shook herself free of his hold and marched forward. Dropping his hand, he stared at her shapely back and the mass of hair he had tangled with over the schist. Her impudence knew no limits, but he had no complaints, none at all.

"Is this for grape maceration?" Julia admired a machine made of two dented cylinders like the cogs of a clock.

Penafiel touched the small of her back, and she skittered to the side. Griffin's fists tightened and he took a step forward, squaring his shoulders.

Pretending innocence, the viscount smiled. "Yes, how perceptive of you." Without taking his eyes from Julia, he operated a side hand crank. The cogs made it swirl in oiled efficiency.

Julia gasped. "This is amazing."

"True." Eyes twinkling, Penafiel fawned over her admiration. "Here, I developed this to facilitate adding sulfur to the grape must. You could—"

"Oh, I'm familiar with your work, Your Excellency. In fact, I apply the methods described in your book, *A Treatise on Winemaking*."

"Please, call me Henrique."

Griffin cleared his throat. "Can we focus on the primary reason we came?"

"Back to phylloxera, then. When did you say the malady first appeared on your property?"

Julia frowned. "Last week."

"How unfortunate. I knew of the plague at Viana do Castelo, but at least there, the sandy soil will make it less deadly."

"Tell us what you found." Griffin pushed himself between her and Penafiel.

"The French can't agree on the plague's cause. Part of the scientific community still believes in the physiology theory."

"Physiology?" Julia pursed her lips, a crease appearing on her forehead.

"Many scientists believe that, as with human diseases, the plague only attacks because there is a prior weakness."

"Nonsense. My vines were healthy. I saw the bugs attacking the roots."

"Aren't you a perceptive woman. I am of the same belief, as are many of the Pasteur disciples."

"How does it spread so fast?" Griffin asked.

"I'll show you."

They followed Penafiel to a long rectangular working table where three apparatuses stood side by side. Each looked like a musket barrel held upright by a metal arm, the whole thing pointing to a translucent square on the bottom.

"What's this?"

"Microscopes. They allow us to see the invisible." He adjusted the glass square below and pushed his head closer to the other extremity, rolling a wheel on the side. "What brings a lot of confusion about phylloxera is its life stages." At their blank faces, he pointed to the microscopes. "It will make more sense after you see the different shapes of the nasty bugs."

They took turns pressing their eyes to the metal tubes. A round larva with tiny antennas and a furry back appeared on the first. The second resembled a cockroach with a brown carapace and spindly legs. Griffin waited for Julia to free the third lens when Penafiel touched her face, adjusting her position.

Gritting his teeth, he stepped away from the table. They were kindred spirits. Not only did Penafiel love wine, but he also shared the same roots, the same culture. If Griffin was a true gentleman, he would not interfere. But rationality failed him when it came to Julia. Every time the other man touched her, he wanted to rip his hands off.

Julia finished with the third optical contraption. Flickering in the onyx depths, he glimpsed the same horror as when they had discovered the plague at Quinta da Felicidade.

She gripped the table. "This one has wings. Do you mean to say phylloxera flies?"

The viscount pursed his lips. "Yes, and that is how it spreads so quickly."

***

Thousands of bugs on a single root—if they could grow wings and fly, the vineyards were doomed. Nothing would stop the plague.

Breathless, Julia dropped into a chair, limbs too heavy to move. "But Your Excellency, is there nothing we can do?"

"Call me Henrique."

She took a deep breath. "Henrique. How are they fighting the plague in France?"

His eyes did that squinting thing and he nodded a few times, shuffling through a heap of papers on the nearest shelf. "There isn't a definite solution to this destroyer of vines. They've tried many things. One grower in Provence eliminated phylloxera by flooding his vineyards—for over a month. Also, reports show the louse can't survive in sandy soils."

Her heart sank. Flooding a hill? And sand in the Douro? Several miles from the ocean? The so-called solutions weighed a ton on her shoulders, and she dropped her head into her hands. Griffin touched her arm and she looked up, searching his eyes. His determination and understanding gave her strength.

She fisted her hands on the painted wood of the worktable. "There must be an alternative."

"Was there any viable experiment that could be replicated in the Douro's natural conditions?" Griffin's words resounded with authority.

The viscount brushed his jaw. "A few growers near Bordeaux had success stopping the spread—stopping it, not killing it—with sulfur pulverization."

She knew how to use the implement; she had several barrels from the latest mildew outbreak. "Do we pulverize the leaves—"

"Yes, but it also needs to be pushed inside the soil, close to the roots."

She nodded. "Thank you. We will."

Griffin stared at the scientific tomes disposed on the floor-to-ceiling shelves. "But why the appearance of this plague now? Vines are ancient. The Romans had wine, the Greeks. If the bug already existed, why have they waited all this time?"

"Good question, Mr. Maxwell. An American entomologist wrote an article affirming that phylloxera is native to his country and was, therefore, imported from the new world."

"But how did it get on the continent?"

"From imported American grapevines. The steamboats are partially to blame by reducing the voyage time, allowing the bugs to stay alive during the crossing."

Julia's stomach sank. "Oh my God. What have I done?"

Griffin came closer, cutting in front of the viscount. "What's wrong?"

Julia ignored the viscount's inquisitive look and focused on Griffin's blue eyes. "Do you remember the valley?"

"Yes, but why—"

"The rootstock I used to graft the vines was American, remember?"

If she was not sitting, the notion would have knocked her to the floor. She was to blame for the plague? Griffin was right. She acted impulsively, never asking for anyone's opinion or accepting advice. If she had assumed defeat graciously, the foreclosure of the contract, phylloxera would not have devastated her village, her neighbors. She took shallow breaths, the smell of chemicals making her stomach roll.

Aware the men were speaking but too dazed to pay attention, she shielded her face with her palms. The words *you are to blame* kept ringing inside her head.

"Mrs. Costa?"

Exhaling, she lifted her head. Instead of accusation in the viscount's eyes, she saw only curiosity.

"I'm to believe you succeeded in grafting a vine?"

"Yes, but—"

"And Mr. Maxwell here said you used American rootstock, implanting scions of port wine grape varieties?"

"I was just trying to—"

He laughed and raised his arms above his head. "All those scientists working themselves thin, and you may have well done it!"

"Done what? Speak clearly, please."

"Found the cure for phylloxera, of course!"

"But how?" Julia blinked several times, her heart speeding.

No doubt baffled as she, Griffin pulled a chair and sprawled by her side. They watched in silence while the viscount went to one shelf and collected a square book. He dropped into a chair facing them.

"Mr. C. Riley is a respected American entomologist." He shuffled the pages, his face scrunched. "Here."

Numerous drawings like the microscopes' images crowded the transparent pages, but the inscriptions were unreadable.

"In the United States, the bugs exist on the leaves of healthy vines without harming the plants, while here in Europe they became aggressive, attacking the roots. This entomologist believes American rootstock is resistant to phylloxera, while our European vines are not. If you combined the two, you could have created a plant that is both immune to the plague and able to produce high-quality wine. It's ingenious."

Lightheaded, Julia found Griffin's hand below the table. He intertwined their fingers, and warmth seeped from her hands all the way to her heart. They were together in this, and for the first time, she believed it.

Julia squeezed Griffin's hand. "But how can we be sure?"

"I must leave tomorrow for Lisbon, but on the return trip, with your consent, I will come to Vesuvio."

"It would be my pleasure."

Under the table, Griffin's fingers went lax, and he released her.

Chapter 38

"The great phylloxera paradox: the source of the disease and the cure for the disease are the same." George D. Gale Jr.

Griffin strode out of the laboratory, the sulfur and alcohol fumes embedded inside his lungs. Outside, he took shuddering breaths. The pungent scent stuck around him, a mist clouding his thoughts. Unable to stand still, he circled the mammoth building, his mood taking a nasty turn. The womanizer viscount would visit her, and Griffin would not be there. He had to return posthaste to salvage his partnership. Christ, the marriage with Beth. How could he deal with the betrothal?

Out of sight from the front door, he leaned against the castle wall, the rocks digging into his back. His secrets were like hooves trampling inside his chest. His relationship with Julia had careened down the hill, out of control, no different from the diligence.

Why couldn't he summon the iron self-restraint and cool emotional detachment that had steered his orderly life so far? He ached for her with staggering force, like the gravity pulling the carriage downhill to its demise. Now, seconds away from crashing, the coach inches away from jagged boulders, he glimpsed the pain separation would cost them. Griffin would chop a finger off before he hurt her, but he had obligations to his family. She understood responsibilities, right?

Rustling sounds to the left alerted him of the viscount's intrusion. Griffin shoved away from the wall and crossed his arms. The other man had shed the overalls and dressed in a tailored light gray suit and high neck cravat.

"There you are." The viscount neared, hands in his pockets, a crooked grin on his face. "Our lovely Mrs. Costa and I were wondering about your whereabouts."

Griffin raised his eyebrows. "I don't think she would approve of the familiarity."

The viscount flashed a smile full of teeth. "Walk with me?"

Griffin inclined his head, and they followed a path marked by manicured hedges. Braganza's landscape differed from the other places they had traveled with its high plateau and long stretches of maturing crops.

"No vineyards on the property?"

"Only corn and flax. I like it here, though. Dry climate, colder than back south, and the castle has been in my family for centuries. Filled with legends and history. Used to bring a lot of attention from the ladies. But nowadays, this pile of rocks does not feel like a home."

Aristocrats were all the same, here or back in London. Born in privilege, they transitioned from a gilded cradle to a gilded home, taking their fortunes for granted until all was ripped away from beneath their feet.

"I bet your guests get lost inside. The castle is huge."

Penafiel shrugged. "The housekeeper distributes crumbs at the front door."

Griffin rubbed the back of his neck. "Thank you for receiving us for the night and lending us one of your coaches for the return trip."

"My pleasure. I imagine you had an amazing journey. Carriage sabotage, getting lost, having to sleep outdoors." The viscount halted, studying his face.

Griffin cleared his throat. "Indeed, we faced many obstacles."

"Spending time with Mrs. Costa could not be a hardship, could it?"

Griffin tightened his fists. "Not at all. She is a remarkable woman. Why do you ask?"

"Do you see that tower?" He waved at a square monstrosity made of muck-colored rocks. Several feet taller than the castle, it had black wooden windows and what looked to be incongruous doors on every other floor. For the safety of his guests, Griffin hoped those were bolted.

"Hard not to."

"That is the *Torre da Princesa*, the Princess Tower."

"Don't tell me." Griffin rolled his eyes. "Another of Portugal's romantic tales?"

The viscount laughed and flung an arm around his shoulders. Griffin raised his brows at the offending limb until the other man reconsidered the familiarity, dropping the arm by his side. "It is not romantic at all. It's a gruesome legend. My ancestor locked his wife there because she made a fuss over his mistress."

"Your point is?"

The viscount glanced at the building, his face pensive. "I have a Princess Tower, but no princess. The emptiness used to suit me, but now? A man must consider the future."

Griffin frowned. "Do you take me for a matchmaking aunt? Your marital status does not concern me."

"God forbid, no. But before I decide, I wanted to understand the truth of your relationship with Mrs. Costa."

Griffin jammed his heels on the turf. "You must be insane."

The viscount raised a brow. "Last time I checked, my brain faculties were superb."

"Mrs. Costa suffered in her first marriage."

"I can make her forget." The viscount's voice turned dry.

If Griffin weren't a gentleman, he would plant his fist on that sneering face. "I doubt it." He turned to the house. How many hours until he could remove Julia from the property, including the ridiculous princess tower?

"You are a member of the British Factory, right? I attended one of your lofty affairs. A pretty exclusive event, I might say. I wonder how Mrs. Costa would fit in?"

Griffin gritted his teeth. "Stay away from her."

"Here in Portugal, we have a saying. If you don't intend to eat the meat, move away from the carcass." Penafiel winked. "Or the lady, so to speak."

Chapter 39

"He who loves not wine, women and song
remains a fool his whole life long."
Martin Luther

The tavern had a gothic flair, arched ceilings, rough wood planks on the floor, and the scent of wine and yeast permeating the sizable main room. A crimson tapestry hid the bare stone wall behind the counter. Griffin stared at the Braganza coat of arms in a feeble attempt to banish the viscount's incessant chattering. By now, the two puke-colored dragons were burned behind his eyelids.

The waitress had sentenced them to a tiny table, stuck between a family and a pair of matrons. Griffin had protested the location, but the salon was crowded. Their allotted space could barely admit two, and three were one too many. But he swallowed his irritation and suffered through the viscount's shallow attempts at captivating Julia, only a few unsuppressed snorts escaping his decision to behave.

"How are you enjoying Braganza, Julia?" Penafiel drawled her first name.

Griffin forced his hands to release the stem of the glass, less he fractured the crystal. He would not rise to the bait. He was not an emotional Portuguese, damn it.

"Very much, Your Excellency—I mean, Henrique. I especially liked the medieval castle."

The viscount gave Griffin a smug look. "Thank you, Julia. If we have time before our departure, I would like to show you my princess tower—"

"That won't be possible." Griffin drank from his glass at their questioning looks and set the wine back on the table, sloshing the liquid over the white linen. "We must leave before dawn."

The viscount leaned forward, no doubt to protest Griffin's statement, but a lad tapped his shoulder, delivering him a note.

"Trouble at my sister's house. Please eat your dinner without me. I'm sorry." He scowled at Griffin and pushed away from the table.

"I hope nothing is wrong, Henrique," Julia said.

"Thank you for the concern, dear. She is expecting, and her husband is out of town. I'm sure she is fine, only first-child jitters. Enjoy your meal."

Griffin studied Julia's expression, but she seemed neither pleased nor sad the viscount had left. He searched his mind for a witty thing to say, anything that did not ruin her content smile. "Interesting place, eh?"

"Hmm."

He twisted in the chair, following her gaze, and saw a wiry man adjusting the strap of a Portuguese guitar over his shoulder. A hush fell over the salon.

Julia came near, so close their shoulders brushed. "Have you ever been to a *fado* tavern?" Her breathed words teased his neck, and he wished her to breathe them all over his body.

"*Fado*?"

"The soul of Portuguese music." She whispered. "The *fado* sings about . . . I don't know the English term. Here, we call it *saudade*."

Her sibilant s and her open vowels created a magical vibration. Griffin knew at once what the word meant. "Longing."

"My earliest memories are of my father's bass voice, resounding around our Quinta. He was a devoted *fado* singer."

"Why the silence?"

"To show respect. Today, only amateurs will perform." Again, her breaths. Could she recite a longer text? The *Iliad*?

A lad rose from a table near the center. He had a bohemian air and far-away eyes. Griffin groaned, anticipating a session of silly sweet words, a poor reproduction of opera, like the *modinhas*.

An angry mother hen shushed him, and he glared back.

The young man sang rooted to his spot, face contorting, mimicking the lyrics' longing. His voice filled the stone walls with a robust tenor, both lilting and sad. Griffin's Portuguese was not great, but he supposed the *fado* mourned an unrequited love. Julia wiped a small tear and cleared her throat.

A round of applause rattled the low ceilings and went on for at least a minute, and the proceeding lull disoriented him, as in the aftermath of a gale. The tavern awakened with a start, kids laughing and poking at each other, people conversing, servers zigzagging around the tables—as if nothing had happened.

Julia, though, like the renewed lamps flickering on the stone wall, had lit up from within, her face glowing. When she gazed at him, an alluring smile playing on her lips, Griffin had to cross his arms to keep away.

The appearance of the waitress cooled his thoughts. She piled their table with plates and a jug of wine. The scent of codfish and warm bread made his stomach rumble. Griffin bypassed the main dish and took a crumbly piece of bread.

Julia served herself and ate a mouthful, sighing with pleasure. "This is amazing. You must have some."

"I'd rather not."

"You dislike codfish?"

Griffin coughed. "I've never tried it."

She raised her brows. "You've been living in Portugal for what? Fifteen years? Did you hear it's our most typical food?"

He had heard about codfish, all right—the buzz a constant distraction on his way to business meetings, having to dodge lounging Portuguese and tourists. Their flannel encased legs obstructed Gaia's wharf, filled the cafes and taverns, and they often ate the famous dish while enjoying the sunset on the river's mouth.

But the torment had not been limited to his hearing. No, he had scented it many times too, the smell of roasted onions and olive oil grabbing him on the way to the townhouse, impregnating his coat, the spiced wind stalking him as far as the last pontoon of the suspension bridge.

The sight had also pestered him over the years, the flaky white fish lording over its sea of vegetables, devoured by friends and his traitor sister, always accompanied by sighs of pedant bliss. Thank God he'd never touched the blasted fish, and he could say with a clear conscience he had positively, absolutely never craved a single taste.

He frowned at the people peeking into their conversation. "Twelve years."

She shook her head, strands of hair kissing her silk-clad shoulder. "Aren't you lucky. This codfish is *Bacalhau a Gomes de Sa*. The olives, onions, and cherry tomatoes are a delicious addition to the fish's flavor."

Griffin watched, transfixed, as she stabbed a hearty slab of potato and fish, extending the foreign food in his direction. Determined and playful, she would poke his eye out. Time slowed as the fish approached with taunting inexorability.

He grabbed her wrist. "I'll try it, but only if you sing."

She caught her breath and stilled, the arm he held turning lax. She moved to back away, and Griffin increased the pressure, raising his brows. The challenge had been impulsive, but now that he'd breathed fire to the words, he wanted them to burn.

She perked up again, her eyes flashing. "Fine."

He released her and the food came closer. Gripping the sides of the chair, Griffin controlled the impulse to stand. He closed his eyes and imagined tasting her delicate earlobe. The illusion worked, and he opened his mouth. She pushed the fish inside. Salty, but just so, the potato balanced it. Not overly seasoned as he'd feared; quite the contrary. When he opened his eyes, she was staring at his mouth. She brought another morsel, and he nodded. This time he caught her wrist, caressing the blue veins, the smooth skin, her delicate tendons teasing his fingertips. He gorged on the fish as if he'd hungered for a decade. Flickering light danced on her face—lips half-opened and eyes heavy-lidded. He took the fork from her hand and fed her, pushing the food between her plump lips. A thousand candles lit inside his chest, a warmth so compelling, a need for release so intense he wanted to burst out of his skin.

Someone cleared a throat, and she leaned back in the chair, chuckling. "What is your problem with food?"

He had no ready answer for that. The enjoyment he'd felt today at this tavern, in the company of a Portuguese woman, eating their food, listening to their music. He hadn't done this before, had always kept himself away from their way of life. The viscount was right. Griffin had stuck to the British community—played at their separate clubs, danced at separate ballrooms, read English authors, and attended English plays. How could he be enjoying this? A true British would have kept true to his origins, to his nature.

For so many years, he had resisted the peninsular call—the gentle sway of the sea, the flaunting of the rules, the balmy Mediterranean nights, the claim of emotions. But who could resist Julia, her stories, her passion and fire, her ebony eyes, so open and trusting?

"It's not about the food." He locked his jaw. "I'm no Portuguese, and you had best understand that."

The flames in her eyes banked, and she retrieved her hands, hiding them under the table. "If you love England so much, why did you leave?"

She looked up, hurt and confusion showing on her lovely face. She had shared with him all her secrets, and he had shared none of his. His gut tightened at the prospect of leaving her, of ending this trip. And then what? She would not be his mistress, and he was the worst sort of cad for considering the arrangement. But what kind of marriage could exist between a member of the British Factory and a Portuguese winemaker?

Griffin filled his lungs with the charged tavern air and exhaled in a burst. "What makes you think I had a choice?"

"You didn't?"

"My mother called me from Cambridge during winter term. I was eighteen. When I arrived at our estate, it was too late. The decision had been made. The house was taken from beneath our feet and the creditors reaped everything, including her beloved portrait collection."

"I imagine how you must have felt. I, too, had the choices removed from me when I was married. When they decided my future."

It wasn't the same. What did she know, this foreign princess? She did not have all the answers, and he would prove it. He drank the acid wine and studied the remains of codfish on her plate. "My father committed suicide."

Her itchy palms covered his hand and Griffin glanced back at her. Instead of shock, her expression was soft, tenderness pulsing from her ebony eyes. "I am so sorry," she murmured.

Chest hollow, he pulled his arm from her grasp. He had to remember now before it was too late.

Undaunted, her hand came up and reached for his face.

He recoiled, staring at the tapestry's clashing dragons, already mourning the distance when her hand traveled to her side of the table. He needed space between them to see things clearly. His future, his goals. He could not let them fade, choked by this peninsular haze.

The gas lamps dimmed again, and the table's single candle flickered on Julia's downcast face. Piercing their silent exchange, the Portuguese guitar released a few plaintive notes, sultry and magnetic.

Julia raised her chin then, and her eyes caught his, glistening with intent and unshed tears. She stood up defiantly.

The tavern hushed. Waiters stopped serving. A mother hurried away with a fussing infant. Every patron stood still.

She extended her arm and poised it, palm up, in the space between them.

The musician increased the tempo, twelve chords blurring beneath his fingers. Griffin sensed what would happen, imagined this scene with anticipation and dread—he balanced on the brink of a bottomless drop, knowing the rewards could be exquisite if he let go. But would he survive the fall?

Not all of him.

His pulse resonated in his throat and ears, and his vision blurred for everything that was not her, dressed in the loaned emerald silk, an exotic queen beckoning.

She sang.

Her eyes bewitched him and her hand summoned him, her hair a sable mantle around her face.

She sang.

Dark and musky, her voice filled the arched ceilings with velvet notes, often smooth, sometimes husky and gravelly, always glowing.

Heart swirling in the shadows, he vibrated with her low range and soared with her high notes, floating in her burgundy spell only to plummet as she pushed him closer and closer to the brink of an abyss.

She sang, and Griffin closed his eyes, the opalescent notes crumbling his defenses, curling around the hollowness inside his chest, penetrating deep inside his soul.

Chapter 40

"Like the best wine . . . that goeth down sweetly, causing the lips of those that are asleep to speak." The Song of Solomon, 7:9

Julia padded over the fluffy carpet on bare feet. The nightclothes provided by the housekeeper hadn't included slippers. A lonely lamp flickered at the end of the corridor, and she feared her loud breathing would wake the viscount's residents.

She counted the doors in the long hallway until she reached the fourth. Heart beating a crescendo faster than the Portuguese guitar, Julia rested her forehead on the heavy oak, the wood useless to cool her feverish skin.

She straightened her spine. If singing in front of strangers had not bolstered her courage, nothing else would. With one last fortifying breath, she knocked two times. Nothing.

She splayed her palms on the solid oak, listening. Had Griffin gone to sleep? She was about to give up and return to her room when the door swung inward on unexpectedly oiled hinges. Suppressing a yell, she was yanked into the room, darkness and a set of arms pressing her against the wall. Unable to see, the scent of his warm skin invaded her senses and her space was reduced to Griffin's bare-chested torso, his heavy breathing upsetting her loose hair.

"It's me," she panted.

"Julia?" Voice husky, he moved away to close the door.

The only light came from the hearth as it cast shifting golden patterns over the mosaic wallpaper. Like hers, Griffin's room was castle-large, a four-poster over a raised dais, the tousled covers and scattered pillows like a love nook carved out of a fairy tale dream.

Griffin paced to the window. "What are you doing here?"

Julia could not imagine he saw anything but blackness beyond the glass panes. If he preferred looking at a void while she offered herself to him, then she had made a terrible mistake.

Nose burning, she took a deep breath and a last look at the long-muscled ridges of his spine. "I wished to talk about our findings and the return trip, but it can wait until the morrow." Throat aching, she spun for the door. She reached for the doorknob when a firm hand closed around her forearm.

"Stay."

The word, spoken hoarsely, reduced her to a creature with no endings and no beginnings—no outlines—just feeling and cravings.

Griffin lit a candle, the flames loving his sharp profile and turning his skin golden. Julia moved to the liquor tray on a polished mahogany desk. With only a slight trembling in her hand, she opened one decanter. The ruby liquid burst out in a cloud of ripe berries and roses.

"The viscount is a connoisseur of great wine."

He raised his brows, his mouth a grim line. "You think?"

"You don't?"

He leaned his back over the bedpost and crossed his ankles. "I am skeptical, that is all."

"About what?"

"The whole," he waved in her general direction, "wine experience people are so fond of talking about, the bouquet and the terroir and all the French words. I think they are overrated."

Julia narrowed her eyes. "And so, your opinion of wine is that..."

"There is good wine and bad wine. People create an unnecessary fuss about it."

She sucked in a breath. Unbelievable. Griffin ignored the world of wine, all the delicious aromas, nuances, and flavors. "Bad or good? A shoe or a saddle can be described as such, but not wine. Wine is complex, rich, with myriad combinations of tastes and smells."

Aware of the frowning cobalt eyes following her gestures, Julia picked the black cravat he had worn to the tavern. Perfect; the opaque black silk would hold the light well.

He had yet to move. Wordlessly, Julia took the glass from his hand and led him to the velvet chair. He went without protest, his body radiating more heat than the fire in the hearth.

She brought the silk close to her nose and breathed in his scent. "May I?"

When she lifted the cloth to his face, he raised his palms.

"Trust me."

He dropped his arms and held tight to the chair wings as if anticipating torture. Unfazed, Julia leaned over his torso to smooth the silk on his face, covering his eyes. Her breasts brushed his shoulder when she tied the cloth behind his head. His breath caught, and he went unnaturally still. The temptation was too strong, and she sifted her fingers through his straight hair, curling at the ends.

"Julia."

***

"I will bring the first wine close to your nose. I want you to tell me what you feel." Julia's voice, husky and fruity, raised the hairs on his forearms.

She moved away, and Griffin sat still.

All black. The sound of liquid sloshing. Soft rustling on the carpet. Her presence again, nearer this time. Her scent, warm and better than any liquor she could blend. His heart thumped louder with each step that brought her closer. The faint whisper of her nightgown on his legs. His hands tingling, wanting to reach out. Press her to him.

Griffin was a blackguard. He should have sent Julia away the moment she'd stepped into his room. Any further intimacy would lead to more pain later. As if there wouldn't be enough of that already. Christ, their proper lives hovered near, waiting to ambush them with judging eyes, exposing their differences, ready to swallow them back into their routines and obligations.

Rationality eluded him—this desire was too powerful to fight. Perhaps that was why he allowed her to torture him. Forcing him to sit still in the darkness, the arms of the chair groaning under the grip of his hands. It was agony. He wanted to rip the cravat off and feast his eyes on her, devour her luscious curves, enjoy the moments they had left. But he would play her game, even if it killed him.

When he wrestled his breathing into a semblance of control, the sight deprivation ceased to feel so immediate. His senses expanded, taking in the musical creeping of the fire, the cool silk pressing loosely on his face, and her scent. The awareness he had of her. He felt her now and his mouth went dry.

"Here is the first."

The wine fumes invaded his nose. Breathing harshly, he wanted the game over to take full advantage of her closeness, of her willingness. "Alcohol and grapes."

"You are not making much of an effort, are you?"

"You have no idea," he replied sullenly.

She laughed, and Griffin placed the sound, sultry like melted caramel, just to his left. He tried to grab her, but she danced out of his reach.

She giggled. "I have an idea. If you guess it right, I will kiss you."

He gripped the armrest to keep from reaching out. "Yes."

She brought the wine back, and this time he let the scent invade his nostrils. He inhaled several times, but it was bewildering. The fragrance tickled his memory, but the name eluded him. Like trying to spear a fish in a lake, but the prey flirted out of reach.

"Violets." Her breath close to his ear made him shiver. "Can you tell me what else?"

As if she unraveled the first word of a ballad, it came to him then. The more subtle tones, diluted fragments of smoke, roasted nuts, wood.

"Is this a tawny?" The notes had faded, leaving just a footprint to be remembered. "Older than ten years?"

"Yes."

The moist heat of her lips brushed his mouth, and the jolt of desire caught him by surprise. Unwilling to let her escape, he groped for her in the dark, finding her nape and fusing their mouths again. He was thirsty, impossibly so—parched—and her lips were his oasis. She gasped and he pulled her closer, a hand on her nape, the other above her lower back. He kept tugging until she had no alternative but to climb on top of his lap, her knees on either side of his legs, straddling him. Weight had never felt so good. Her body molded to his, and when her heat pressed where he ached for her, he groaned. Like a vise, his arms closed around her, and he devoured her mouth.

The kiss got out of control, and she pulled away, panting, her forehead resting against his. Desperate to see her, he ripped off the cravat. She was flushed, her hair spread over them, her nightclothes straining under her heaving breaths. God, she was glorious.

"We haven't finished. There are more wines to taste."

"I've had enough."

The gown had climbed up, revealing her calves and the delicious bit of leg just above her knees. He trailed his palms over her smooth olive skin, gliding up and rolling the cambric in his path, displaying her thighs. He massaged her supple flesh with firm strokes and tickled the back of her knees. She squirmed on his lap, and Griffin clamped his teeth to keep from thrusting like a mindless beast. The cloth wouldn't budge further, so he pushed his hand inside her nightdress, inch by inch, until he splayed his palm under her buttocks. Her face glowed, and a sheen of perspiration covered her forehead. While he nipped and licked her lips, he trailed his caress higher, caging her waist and bringing her flush against his hardness. She gasped, and he dipped his thumbs lower until he found her apex.

"Griffin."

Hearing her moan his name was better than hearing her sing the *fado*. He increased the pressure. "I want to give you the same pleasure you gave me."

"But I didn't..."

"When you sang." He nipped her neck. "When you sang for me."

Without hurry, he drew circles lower, enjoying her soft mewling sounds, until he arrived at his destination—her entrance, moist, waiting for him. He pushed his thumb inside, and with a shudder, she rocked closer, undulating her hips. He touched her like this over and over until her eyes were rolling and she clung to his neck, her warm breath igniting his blood.

Their gazes met. Her pupils dilated, molten onyx taking over her irises.

Coherent thoughts vanished. Griffin couldn't wait. Without moving her from his lap, he rose from the chair. She buried her face in his nape, her ankles crossing over his lower back. If he pressed her against the wall, he could be inside her within seconds, but she deserved better.

Restraining his urge, Griffin lowered her to the bed, and she kneeled on the mattress facing him. Her hair tousled around her torso, the loose ends brushing the copper counterpane. Her skin radiated desire and the golden light of the fireplace.

Nothing else mattered.

He peeled away the borrowed nightgown. Below, only a thin chemise separated her from him. He opened the buttons, revealing a tantalizing glimpse of her collarbones and the tops of her breasts. As if unwrapping a delicate gift, he slid the gossamer tissue first over one shoulder and then the other. Transfixed, he stared at the perfect mounds as the golden light flickered over her naked skin. He was the luckiest blackguard in the world. He grazed his fingertips over her peaks, and she shivered.

"We should blow out the candles." She pulled her hands up to cover herself, but he intertwined their fingers.

"You are stunning."

He caressed her reverently, starting at her eyelashes. Everywhere his hand touched, he followed with a kiss. He reached her navel, and she moaned and tugged his head up, claiming his mouth. Their fingers tangled over the placket of his trousers. When he freed himself, they were both panting. She sprawled on the linen, hair fanning around her face like a halo, lips parted, arms reaching for him.

He fused their chests, and her legs opened to accommodate him in the cradle of her hips. Ravenous, he buried himself inside her. She moaned and arched her back, her intimate walls gripping him deliciously. Griffin quenched the instinct to move, allowing her to get used to him. Everywhere their skin touched was heaven, was right, was perfection. He brushed her hair out of her face, tracing her eyebrows and the hollows below her cheekbones.

The part of him inside her throbbed, mimicking the pulse beating on the column of her throat.

She skimmed her hands over his spine and rested her palms on his face. Their eyes locked. Hers had nothing to hide; no guilt, no sadness, just contagious joy and pure desire. The world around them faded into the sounds of their breaths mingling, their hearts beating as one. She sighed, and because they were connected on such a primal level, before she rose to kiss his chin, he knew what she was about to say.

"I love you."

The words resonated inside him like the bells of a cathedral. He felt the repercussions in the hollow chambers of his chest, in the recesses of his mind, in every nerve ending, filling him to the brim. He wanted to wrap the words around himself, to shelter inside them, to cultivate them and see them flourish, to blend them and return to them time and time again.

"Say it again."

"I love you."

Griffin thrust, agonizingly slow and deep, over and over. He filled her with everything he was, bad or good, different and the same, pushing her against the headboard until she moaned and thrashed her head from side to side. Still, it wasn't enough. He needed deeper, harder, frenzied.

"Again."

"I love you."

With each unrelenting thrust, Griffin forgot about what would happen at dawn.

***

Urgent and possessive, Griffin coaxed her to respond, to arch her back, to rise and meet his hips halfway. She allowed him to peel away her defenses, to lay her bare, crumbling the barriers between them with his relentless thrusts.

Julia was beyond resisting. She clasped him to her, accepting his intensity, greedy for all of him. His musky scent enveloped her senses and she licked the seam of his lips, catching the traces of wine he had tasted.

When he rose above her, their eyes locked. Julia infused her gaze with love. He stopped thrusting, and she stilled, holding her breath. How ironic that she had often rebuked declarations of love, and now her heart craved them.

But strained lines marred his forehead, and the emotion lurking in his eyes bewildered her.

Julia placed her palms on his cheeks and brought his face closer. Exhaling a ragged breath, he buried his face in her neck. "Please, don't stop."

With a shudder she felt all the way to her core, Griffin lunged forward. Pleasure raced through her veins in intoxicating waves, spiraling out of control. Her thoughts turned hazy, her skin tingled, and her breaths came in short bursts. She raced to completion and her inner muscles clamped around him when the climax overtook her.

Her limbs melted and her spirit soared. "*Eu te amo.*"

Griffin plunged inside her one more time and withdrew, his breathing resounding in the now silent room. He dropped by her side on the mattress, an arm shielding his eyes, their bodies not touching. Her skin cooled fast without his weight, as if sprinkled with shards of ice.

Julia watched him sleep, eyes restless behind closed lids, and rubbed her arms. Her skin was prickled and cold. Had she taken from him more than he wanted to give?

Where had that silly notion arrived? Griffin would die before he said romantic words. It meant nothing.

Clutching the sheets to her nakedness, she rose from the bed, collected the clothes scattered around the floor, and padded out of his room.

Chapter 41

"We are all mortal until the first kiss and the second glass of wine." Eduardo Galeano

The English vault offered a valiant fight, the avant-garde system of padlocks and tumblers believed impregnable, but in the end, Pedro emerged the victor.

He cleaned sweat from his brow and smirked at the duke's beady eyes following him across the room as he discarded the chisel and screw. Father's know-it-all smile, frozen for eternity in the study's portrait, gleamed diabolically in the light of lamps and candles lit to facilitate the stealth operation.

The iron-cast door clicked open, and Pedro's heart sped up. His father's vault would surely give him a hint of why the duke had come up from Lisbon to meet a bunch of nobodies from the Railroad Company. With a slightly shaking hand, he inspected his father's treasures. Ingots and diamonds from Africa, velvet boxes with Mother's jewels, and resting in the shadows of the vault—a sheaf of documents protected by yellowed vellum. Shuffling through the papers, Pedro sat behind the desk.

The first document of the pile was the deed for Quinta da Felicidade. Bought for $2,000 *Reis*, a property that only last year had produced $30,000 *Reis* in wine pipes sold to Oporto. The duke had bought three other wine properties for a fraction of their worth.

A bill selling a shipment of American vines to Vesuvio, signed by Julia's estate manager, came next. His father knew France had banned sales of the American grapevines, as the plant brought the plague to French vineyards.

The old man had induced phylloxera to their country. It went beyond his wild imaginings, an incredible feat for Pedro, who expected only the worse from the duke.

That was why his father wanted to avoid the railroad here. The old wolf intended to keep the prices low while he bought the land for the cost of sheep.

With a disgusted sigh, Pedro pushed the papers away. The plan was brilliant and possessed, a testament to his foresight and financial acumen. Money would change hands because of this plague, and his father would pick the lion's share. But to do this to his own country and countrymen? It was monstrous.

He should shed light on his father's sins, take these to the king right away, force the duke to pay for his crimes. Pedro traced the fading typography of the first deed. *Felicidade* meant happiness. Alone by the flickering glimmer of the gas lamps, Pedro stared at the lines until they blurred.

The voice of his conscience—muffled and half-dead after Mozambique—quieted. These documents were precious leverage against his father. With them, Pedro could keep him away from his affairs, from his promise of happiness.

The secret left a bitter taste in his mouth, and he fisted his hands over the table, restraining the urge to crumple the papers. Where the hell were Julia and his brother? She wouldn't permit him to become a monster like his father, would she? Upon returning from Braganza, Pedro would make her submit. Her will was stronger than the girl he'd met by the river, but even the most stubborn of women must see the vantages of being under his protection.

Flavio cleared his throat.

Pedro straightened. "Have you found Cristiano?"

"The riders came back. No signs of Mr. Queiroz. Should we send another search party, Your Excellency?"

Pedro rose and walked to the window. The air blowing from the river had a metallic tang, not different from the spark of powder. He loved storms and their sheer staggering power, but today the graying skies raised the hairs of his arms and nape. The Douro gushed violently, waves pushing against the bank, water pummeling the Roman bridge as if testing the mettle of the ancient stone construction.

Cris should've been back by now, unless...no. His father would not dare. The duke's devilish sneer flashed in his mind as the first lightning scratched the coal-black sky. An uneasiness gripped his chest. Long ago, on the dried plains of the Zambezi River, he had learned to heed these foreboding signs. Something portentous brewed outside, and Pedro must be a part of it.

"Flavio, have my horse saddled."

"But, my lord, the storm—"

"Now."

Chapter 42

"Be careful to trust a person who does not like wine." Karl Marx

A rumbling, low and thick, pulled Julia from sleep. She blinked and stretched her neck. They were still inside Griffin's brougham, but darkness crept inside the carriage. Could she have slept so long? They should have reached Vesuvio before nightfall.

Another thunder awakened Flor. Griffin examined the countryside, his face the same expressionless mask he'd been using since they reunited with the servants at Moncorvo. She should be grateful he'd stopped devouring her with his eyes and he didn't reach for her hand or tuck a stray strand of hair over her ear. He acted like this to protect her reputation. Yes, that was the only explanation.

After they arrived, they could be alone again and this dull ache in her chest, this coldness in the pit of her stomach, would disappear. Whatever troubled him, they could solve it together, right? Had they not succeeded in this incredible adventure?

Julia straightened and stared at the carriage's window. The sun had vanished, steel gray clouds consuming all the light. She blinked a few times, digging her fingers into the bench's burgundy leather. There were no signs of relief from the plague, no verdant hills or foliage ripping with the breeze. Instead, the vines contorted outside in various stages of the disease. Carts rested on the sides of the road, piled up with dead vines. The vineyard had turned into a graveyard. While this tragedy unfolded, she had been away, more preoccupied with her own heart than with the hearts of so many.

Julia splayed her palm on the frosty glass. "It is much worse."

Flor squeezed her hand. Griffin crossed his arms, his expression ominous. As if her sorrow had conjured the storm, the sky opened. Fat drops of rain pelted the carriage windows, the wind buffeting them from all sides. A flash of brilliance brought the light of a thousand sun rays, only to black out again. The following thunder shook the vehicle like a wooden toy.

Griffin rapped on the carriage's roof. "We cannot go on like this."

"But we are so close." If they crossed the Roman bridge, they would be home. Her heart ached to see Tony, to hug him. She had never been away from him for so long.

Their gazes locked. Griffin's eyes held a gentleness so bittersweet, her nose burned with repressed tears.

With a heavy sigh, she averted her face, lest she gave in and climbed onto his lap, begging him to hold her.

"It's not safe to continue with this storm. I'm sorry."

Griffin instructed the coachman to pull up at the roadside inn after Lamego. The gale whistled around the courtyard, stealing hats and parasols from the assembled travelers as if they were brown leaves at the end of fall. Julia bent her body forward, her coat flapping behind her. Jako shoved the double doors open, and they burst into the crowded inn. Families and gentlemen gathered close to the hearth, filling the tables and perching on the only couch.

With his usual authority, Griffin arranged for a private room and ushered her and Flor upstairs. With a warning to lock the door, he went back to the public room. Julia stared at his black greatcoat as it vanished out of her sight, choking on a plea for him to stay.

***

Smelly, small, and smudgy, the place was a miserable excuse for an inn. Griffin waited forever for wine and his legs cramped under the short table that would better suit a child than a grown man. Would this trip keep going forever? How long must he endure Julia's proximity and be forced to keep his distance? Her face, overflowing with emotion, invaded his thoughts without asking for permission. Her words of love still played in his ears, driving him mad.

Jako cleared his throat. "Sir, the blacks are stabled. I informed Roberto you wished to depart as soon as the storm lessens."

"Good. Have a seat."

Jako frowned, his bushy eyebrows meeting above his nose. "Are you sure, sir—"

"Why not? I ordered wine. As soon as they are done threading the grapes in the kitchen, it will be here."

Jako nodded several times and perched on the edge of the chair as if afraid he would sully the grimy furniture. Griffin feared the opposite, as the servant was perfectly groomed, including the signature pearl on his neckcloth. How he managed that after several days on the road was one of life's mysteries.

At last, the server placed a jug of wine and cups on their table. The way she collected the coins, pinching her nose, one would think they had an offensive smell. She moved away quickly enough, but not before Griffin caught how she pursed her lips at Jako. How could people be so ignorant? Just because his skin was different?

Julia's story about the sultan's son and the Portuguese girl made perfect sense. If the prince had survived the soldiers, they wouldn't find a place where differences didn't matter. Such a place did not exist.

Griffin had always known that, but now the reality rankled with awful unfairness. Even if he convinced Croft to take the partnership without the betrothal to his daughter, he could not marry Julia. The English community would never accept her, and he would be frowned upon by many Portuguese.

"How can you stand their prejudice?" Griffin swallowed the bitter red and slammed the earthenware cup on the scarred table. "Don't you hate Portugal? Wish you were back in your own country?"

Jako pushed his glass away. "Sir, when I was a boy in Goa, the Hindus avoided playing with my sister and me because my father was Portuguese. The matron who lived across from us seldom invited my mother to her house because we were Catholics. My father was begrudged a promotion because the head of the plantation was a Muslim. At least here, they agree on what to hate me for."

"I'm serious. This is no matter for play."

"I'm not playing, sir, I swear. I love Portugal. I love the food and the weather, and I love the terrific people who look at my skin and see nothing different." He sighed and twirled his pearl. "It feels like home now."

Feels like home. Unless he counted the moments shared with Julia, in the twelve years he had lived in Oporto, he'd never felt at home. How could Jako feel such here, suffering prejudice, when Griffin, who never had to endure any indignities, could not?

"Don't you fear wearing their clothes and eating their food will make you," Griffin exhaled and rubbed the back of his neck, "less Indian?"

"How so? I was born a Goan and will die a Goan. The fact I embrace this country, and enjoy all the good it offers, has nothing to do with it, sir."

Griffin's eyes widened, and he blinked several times. The patrons laughing and eating around him became a blur of watered colors, mixing in social disarray. Outside, thunder and lightning went on, but Griffin hardly heard them.

Jako was right. All this time, he'd held to the belief that to control his life, to retain his origins, he had to stay away from everything Portuguese. The music, the culture, the food, the people. But by avoiding making Portugal his true home, he had only hurt himself.

To marry Julia would not make him a Portuguese. He was British—not even marrying a chimp would change his origins. He and Julia were different, but while their differences would matter to the entire world, they shouldn't matter to him. Not if he truly loved her. And God, how he loved her. Not despite their differences, but because of them.

How could he have missed it? The truth had to smack him in the face. He needed to say it to her in this precise instant. They would wed, and they would enjoy their differences over and over for the rest of their lives.

Griffin slammed his cup on the table and bolted to his feet, knocking the chair backward. "Jako, I will find Mrs. Costa now."

He inhaled the greasy air of the tavern as if it was the sweet perfume of jessamines. The decision to secure Julia as his wife removed a Brougham-sized weight from his chest.

Jako flashed him a knowing grin. "About time, sir."

Griffin whirled, trying to spot the stairs to the second floor. Julia's room stretched farther than that Roman road back in Braganza. An ocean of wet and tired travelers blocked the way, hovering about the hearth as if it was the last bit of warmth in the world.

Heart straining against his ribcage, Griffin weaved between families and merchants, their wet wool coats smelling of mud and mold. When he saw Julia, he would shout the words to her, scream a bloody serenade, or better yet, a *fado*. She would enjoy a *fado* above all. Afterward, they would laugh, and he would kiss her senseless and bring her to Boa Vista, where he would make love to her and take immense pleasure in convincing her he loved her too.

He gripped the stair's oily railings and pushed his weight to the first step.

"Maxwell? You old dog! What are you doing here?"

***

Julia exited the stuffy room. She needed to find him. A terrible augur gripped her chest. If she didn't see him, he would vanish in the storm.

Heart pounding, she raced down the stairs. The last step was slippery, and she lost her balance, gripping the railing to stay upright. Because of her forward momentum, she only noticed the group when it was too late.

Their conversation died a sudden death as all five sets of eyes settled on her. Julia swallowed and, releasing the balustrade, straightened her skirts. The strangers were dignified, their clothes and carriage setting them apart from the rest of the storm-stranded travelers.

Griffin, his shoulders tense, took a step forward and steered her to the fringe of their circle. Julia searched his expression. His face was pale, and his spine was straight as a stake. He introduced her first to his mother, a tall woman in her fifties. Her gentle eyes, a shade lighter than Griffin's, met hers with warmth. He then presented Mrs. Croft, a middle-aged woman with amber hair streaked with gray, pulled so tight in a chignon that her cheeks were drawn up unnaturally. Julia ignored the obnoxious glance, the name Croft pushing the air from her lungs. What were they doing here?

Griffin raised his palm in the young lady's direction. "Mrs. Costa, this is Elisabeth Croft."

Julia greeted the beautiful girl. With a hat perched smartly on her red hair, and a fashionable traveling dress, she seemed fresh and accomplished, the type of woman who always looked her best. Julia fidgeted with a loose button on her wool coat, then straightened it with unsteady brushes. When it was time to address Croft himself, Julia's skin was clammy, her breathing unstable.

Lightning flashed outside. A gush of wind invaded the public room, extinguishing one of the gas lamps and plunging them into semidarkness. Julia hugged herself, the chill seeping into her very bones. Above her pounding heart, she listened as Griffin explained how they had met at the roadside inn by chance, looking for shelter.

Croft spoke over a blazing cigar. "It is certainly a coincidence to find you both here." His stare was assessing and lewd.

Julia's gut tightened. He looked like a cat who had cornered a helpless rat. Would he expose them somehow? Her throat locked, and she stifled the impulse to cover her burning cheeks.

Croft glanced at his daughter and sucked his cigar. "The coincidence is fortuitous. It was my intention to call on Vesuvio during this trip." He puffed obnoxious smoke in her face.

Julia coughed. How stupid of her to fear for her reputation while ignoring the genuine danger of his visit. If Croft had come all the way from Oporto, if he was here without giving her notice, he would execute the contract. Julia sought Griffin's gaze, but he shook his head enigmatically.

"Of course. It would be my pleasure." Julia raised her chin. "I trust you had a safe trip?"

"The roads could have been better, but Maxwell here forced us, eh?" Croft slapped Griffin on the shoulder, his eyes flashing. "Your bride was eager to see you. With you practically becoming a rustic here."

"Father!" the girl, Beth, gasped in dainty surprise.

The blow made Julia jerk away. For several heartbeats, she gazed at Beth's shoes. The ankle boots were soft and feminine, the caramel leather polished to a gleam—the kind of shoe Griffin's wife would wear. Croft said Julia's name. Over to the left, glasses clinked. Outside, the storm pelted the windows.

Chapter 43

"In victory, you deserve Champagne. In defeat you need it." Napoleon Bonaparte

Roaring and rain drowned her senses. Coat flapping, Julia kept her chin down, her torso leaning forward, each step a battle against the will to curl on the mud-splattered ground. Lightning flared, casting light on the Roman bridge's arches, only to vanish again, covered by pouring water. She was close.

The river thrashed against the embankment. Careening downstream, shattered pieces of a skiff, uprooted trees, and lonely pipes all hurtled toward the bridge, like her.

"Stop!" Griffin's cry came from behind, nearer than she expected.

Running now, she stumbled in the mud, hissing when her knee connected with the schist. Without looking back, she pushed to her feet. Under no circumstances could she gaze at him now. Her resolve would wash away like the dirt flowing underfoot.

When she stepped over the raised stone of the bridge's walkway, her boots sank. The river had flooded the ground level. Water, brown and foaming, gushed through the rail. She stilled, bracing herself. To turn would mean facing him. Hearing the painful truth from his own lips, or worse, more lies. But if she kept on, she risked being dragged into the Douro's current.

It was reckless, even for her. But the need to put distance between them, to blot out how naïve she'd been, believing a man like him was falling for her, spoke louder. The other side was so near. A few more steps and she would be on her way home to Vesuvio, where false hopes could not hurt her.

She pushed forward, her strides dragging over the slippery stones. When she crossed the Roman pillar marking the center, the bridge groaned, a low-pitched sound that lifted the hairs on her nape. The rocks beneath her feet quivered. A screeching pierced her eardrums, and her steps turned desperate. She grabbed the railing but kept her eyes ahead. The hills' terraces were barren, vines sticking out like drowned thorns, the gale forcing junipers to bend like tall grass.

When she stuck both feet on the mud-splashed hay at the other side, she whirled, gulping air, her side burning. The bridge's first arch had vanished. In its place was a four-foot gap. Julia stared as the current lashed out at its remains. The ancient construction she'd known all her life plunged into the Douro stone by stone.

Griffin broke from the blurred trees, galloping toward the bridge.

Julia's heart slammed against her ribcage. He meant to force the horse over the gap!

Remo reared. Once. Twice.

Julia's breath caught. Lightning flashed.

He whirled around and came again, faster. He would kill himself.

She heard screams. Hers? His?

Strength seeped out of her body, and she crumbled to her knees.

On the third failed attempt, he ceased. The broken bridge was a meager protection against his glare.

Julia squeezed her eyes shut. Moments passed; the wind stopped flapping her coat. She heard splashes nearby. Soft thuds. Then there was a presence near her side, and she pried her eyes open. Blond hair hung around a chiseled face, rain dripping from spiked eyelashes, and an unsmiling mouth.

"Pedro."

He offered a leather-covered hand. Julia took it.

The count helped her climb onto his white horse and mounted behind her. The storm had dwindled to a drizzle. Still, the cold found its way inside, seeping under her skin and puncturing her heart. She pushed the hair from her face and glanced at the other side.

Griffin sat still atop Remo. Behind him, vineyards painted the gray of rocks and the brown of naked earth.

Thunder sounded, this time further away, just an echo of what had been.

Pedro circled his arm around her waist, and Julia leaned her weight on his solid chest. They cantered away.

Then, blackness.

***

The bridge gave out in a vortex of crumbling mortar, turbid water, and shattered screams. Panting, Griffin pressed his fists to the side of his head, wanting out of his thoughts, more violent than the Douro's raging current. Julia had raced away from him, risking her safety without giving him a chance to explain. She left behind a chasm wider than Remo could jump, and any attempt to swim in the revolted waters would lead to certain death.

Griffin could only watch as the woman he loved crumbled to her knees on the other side of the riverbank. The obstacle that separated them grew larger by the second as the Douro erased the bridge stone by stone, as if it had never existed at all.

They faced each other, she vulnerable and out of reach, he unable to do aught, the sounds of his heartbeats thrashing inside his ears. He wore a raincoat, but she had nothing to protect her from the cold. Tremors wracked his body, either from him or from Remo's quivering legs. The horse lowered his neck, exhausted, the white plumes of his breaths vanishing under the pouring rain.

When the distinct shape of a horseman approached her, Griffin released a pent-up breath, squeezing his eyes shut. If the rider took her to Vesuvio, saving her from the elements, Griffin would have time to find a cursed way across the river and explain himself. He would make her understand, damn it. He had to.

Lightning crossed the sky, exposing the color of the horse's coat—glaring white against the charcoal hills.

The count's Lusitano mare.

A roar erupted from Griffin's chest. The bastard helped Julia atop the horse and mounted behind her, his arm coiling around her waist. It should be Griffin rescuing her, cradling her body, not that man. Griffin's eyes locked with the count's. He couldn't discern the bastard's expression, but he silently vowed to rip his guts out.

The count turned the mare south.

Powerless, impotent, Griffin watched as Almoster cantered his woman away.

It was the hardest thing he had ever done.

Griffin pressed his heels to Remo's flanks and turned him back to the inn. The innkeeper would know where to cross. The less than a mile distance passed in a blur.

If the count harmed her… if he forced her to—no. No matter what Griffin thought of the bastard, he would not hurt her.

As soon as he crossed the courtyard, he vaulted from the saddle, screaming for Roberto to take care of Remo. When he stumbled inside the deserted room, he halted his strides, disoriented. How could the day have turned out like this?

He rushed to the dining area, his boots leaving pools on the hard plank floor—no sign of the owner or a servant.

"Griffin?" His mother descended the stairs.

"Where is everybody?"

"The Crofts left for Boa Vista when the storm subsided. Where were you? I've been worried sick. You are soaking wet. You must change your—"

"I don't have time. I am leaving again."

"What? You'll catch a cold, or worse. Wait!"

"I can't." He pushed past her in the kitchen's direction. Where were the bloody servants? The absence of a soul to give him information squeezed his ribs, making it hard to breathe.

His mother followed, clutching her skirts. "Is it to do with that young Portuguese widow, Mrs. Costa?"

"Please, stay out of it." He raised his palms, and the innkeeper finally appeared. Griffin advanced toward the rotund man. "The bridge is out. I need to cross the river. Where is the nearest—"

The innkeeper stopped paying attention to him, looking beyond Griffin's shoulder. "*Senhora*, are you well?"

Griffin turned. His mother paled, gripping the edge of a chair. Griffin took her hand and cringed at how cold it felt. He barked to the innkeeper to summon a doctor. "I will carry you upstairs."

"No. Please, take me to your house. I can't stay on the road for a single minute more."

Her eyes fluttered shut.

Chapter 44

"A bottle of wine contains more philosophy than all the books in the world." Louis Pasteur

The thick carpet muffled Pedro's steps as he paced around the room. The lit hearth made a halo of copper light over Julia, intensifying the darkness everywhere else. Her shallow breathing rasped in the silent house, broken only by the pines' occasional bursts when captured by the flames.

Julia was here.

How many nights had Pedro spent offshore, sleeping in barracks, listening to strange languages? This had kept him going—the promise of her in his home.

His eyes lost focus, and he glanced at the prone figure beneath the merino wool covers. Still, she appeared impossibly out of reach. Pedro strode to the bed and kneeled on the floor, his face level with hers. Her breaths lacked strength, but she seemed so tranquil. With a slight tremble in his hand, he touched her forearm, hidden beneath the wool. He felt . . . nothing.

What had he expected? The same jolt of desire he experienced with whores? Julia was different, and besides, she was not his yet. Pedro would send for Father Cosme in the morning. It was time the Franciscan repaid the Almosters' generosity.

Her eyelids trembled, and a flush climbed from her neck to her cheeks. Pedro removed his glove and touched her forehead. She burned. He vaulted to his feet and opened the door. "Call the doctor!"

Flavio, still at his post outside the bedchamber, widened his eyes. "But, Your Excellency, it's way past midnight."

"Now."

The servant scurried away, and Pedro returned to her bedside, clenching his fists. She would have died out there, exposed to the cold for too long, or drowned. Removing the quilt, he bathed her face in cool water.

Why did you need to run, Julia? You trust that bastard better than me?

His father would say Pedro had failed to eliminate her options, that his strategy had been flawed. But he was nothing like the duke. Julia was not a toy to be manipulated, damn it! If it wasn't for that Englishman, she would have come to him of her own free will. Was it too much to wish for light back in his life? Must he live forever in the shadows?

Julia stirred, her eyes shifting behind closed eyelids, her lips moving silently, and Pedro soothed her feverish skin with the wet cloth.

Agitated, her head turned from side to side. Her hands, so still just a second ago, now gripped the covers, her knuckles white. Tears spilled over her cheeks—two rivulets of sorrow that tugged at his heart. "Griffin," she whispered.

"*Por que choras por ele*?" Pedro leaned over her prone body, held her shoulders, and shook until she focused on him. "What did he do to you? Answer me."

Her eyes were shining feverishly, and she rested her palm over her chest. "He broke my heart."

Pedro shot to his feet. No. Every fiber, every drop of blood, every organ rebelled. If she loved that man, there would be no redemption for him.

With shaking breaths, Pedro stumbled to the window, gripping the velvet curtains, searching the night through the glass panes. Only a black void and his twisted reflection stared back. He wanted to rip the curtains, the wallpaper, smash the cursed glass.

If she loved the Englishman, she wouldn't love Pedro, and all this had been for naught.

With heavy breaths, he bridled the destructive impulse, roping his emotions inside. He needed a strategy. A battle lost meant nothing.

His saber flashed from its perch on the wall, the Prussian steel solid and trustworthy. Sitting behind the desk, he carefully placed the whetstone and the oil flask atop the surface. With deliberate movements, he honed the blade back and forth, back and forth, matching his breathing with the slow-paced hissing sounds as the edge turned sharper, lethal.

Pedro had tried to remove this obstacle without violence. The appeal to Mr. Maxwell's greed had failed, and enlightening him of Pedro's impending marriage hadn't sent him away.

Pedro tested the blade with his thumb, letting the steel gleam against the coppery light. He traced the family motto etched on the handle. *Non Ducor, Duco.* Never the conquered, always the conqueror.

How many times had he killed before? Meaningless lives lost before their prime to petty conflicts in the colonies. Every single one nicked a chink in his soul. God knew there were few pieces left.

His gaze strayed to the bed. Julia slept, her breaths calmer, peaceful even.

Unlike the beliefs of his comrades, nothing justified death—not the church, not the government, not family nor king. Bloodlust hadn't consumed him in battle as it had the others. He had been staggering sober for each and could still see the cold realization in their eyes just before their lives had flickered out.

What about the souls he had sent to a fate worse than death in Mozambique? They still haunted him, their whines keeping him awake even when he was exhausted. What was another misdeed in his long row of sins? At least this time, it would have meaning. For him. The next time Julia gazed at a man with longing in her eyes, it would be at him.

Dressed all in black, Pedro approached the bed. The gentle light from the hearth played over the velvet curtains and made her white nightgown glow. Her sleep was peaceful; the fever had receded, her breaths much quieter than his own. He thrust his hand inside the gloves with decisive movements, covering each finger in supple black leather. He hardened his heart for another mortal sin, this one his last.

With the saber pointing to the floor, he strode out of his bedroom.

***

Not a soul haunted Pedro's private wing. Where was Flavio? He was supposed to be guarding the door. Steps echoing ahead—the servant rushed forward.

"Flavio. I rang for Francisca to sit with the future countess until the doctor arrives, but you should not move from your post."

"Sir, Cristiano is here."

"About time." Pedro tied his hair behind his neck. "Send him to the stables."

The former soldier avoided his eyes, his countenance grayer than his coat. "We put him in his bedroom, sir."

All air left his lungs. Pedro didn't wait to hear more, rushing to the other side of the house. Light spilled out from Cris's room as maids moved in and out. A few servants congregated near the open door, faces somber.

Pushing past the threshold, Pedro caught sight of the bed, where the sturdy frame of his brother lay lifeless.

Heart thrashing against his ribs, Pedro took a few steps closer, letting the saber clank to the floor. He dropped to his knees by the bedside and grabbed Cris's wrist. The pulse was there, low but steady. Pedro closed his eyes and inhaled. Thank God.

Cris's skin had a gray tinge. His hair was matted and dirty, lacking its usual luster, clothes torn and splashed with mud.

Pedro pushed away from the floor, cursing under his breath. This was not supposed to be happening, not with his younger brother. "Where did you find him?"

"Near Barca D'alva, sir." Flavio's gaze fell to the carpet. "He escaped from a ship bound to Macao. Dantas asked around. It transports prisoners. A one-way trip to the colonies for convicted men."

Pedro nodded, his gut tight. He would go after the ship and tear it down plank by plank.

Cris groaned, his forehead shining with perspiration.

Pedro shook his head, cleared his mind, focused on what needed to be done, on what his brother required now. "Francisca, we need to shed these soiled clothes. Fetch a knife. You there, bring carbolic soap, bandages, and my salve."

Pedro rolled his leaves and set to work. The shirt came off first, revealing black and purple bruises over Cris's chest and sides, the skin looking like a navigation map. Some had already turned green around the edges, probably older than a few days. The thought of his brother locked in a ship's fetid hull made Pedro's vision haze, but he shoved the emotions inside. Cris's trousers were stiff, and when they cut it, blood flew anew from a gash on his leg. Pedro had seen many men die with similar wounds. If the blood loss didn't kill him first, the infection would do the reaping later. But not his brother. He would not allow it.

Cris's eyes shot open while Pedro cleaned the wound with soap.

Pedro pressed his hand and moved to his brother's line of vision. When their eyes locked, his brother relaxed, falling back on the pillows. Pedro threaded a needle. "This will hurt like a devil."

Cris squeezed his hand weakly and nodded.

Two hours later, the wounds were bandaged. Pedro dismissed the servants and pulled a chair close to the bed. He needed to hear it from his brother's lips. "Who?"

Cris's green eyes were dull and defeated. He shook his head once.

Pedro seized his hand. "Who?"

"The duke."

***

Pedro stared at his father's portrait. The duke smirked at him from his perch on the wall, forehead gleaming like a lamp from hell. Pedro dislodged it from its lofty height and hurled it to the carpeted floor. The gilded frame splintered, but the canvas remained intact, more heinous and manipulative than ever. He rammed his feet on the salmon-colored forehead, and the oil-painted cloth ripped with a satisfying screech.

A black hole stood in the place where his father's face used to be.

The roar trapped inside his throat fought for release, and Pedro fisted his hands. He could scream until he was hoarse or he could punch all his father's portraits, but neither would change the reality. The duke still dominated his life.

Father had made him a boy again, living under his terror, his brutal teachings, always manipulating, always advocating he acted in Pedro's best interests. A lump of steel needed to be beaten to be shaped into a sharp sword. Emotional attachments were for the weak. If the duke believed Cris's influence was worthless, he would only stop after removing him from Pedro's life. Just like he had with Julia.

If Pedro retreated now, the duke would destroy Pedro's only family. No, the winning strategy would be to bring the war back to the duke's terrain.

Time to use his best weapon—the documents incriminating his father in the phylloxera scheme. This time he would outmaneuver the duke.

Pedro strode inside his bedroom and lit the gas lamp. The light hissed, chasing away the room's shadows.

Shallow breaths rasped in the otherwise silent room. Julia.

Pedro whirled, extinguishing the lamp before it could wake her. How could he have forgotten her presence? He approached the bed with silent steps and touched her forehead. Her fever had returned. Her skin, always so luminous, had dimmed to a gray pallor.

Pedro's chest felt hollow, and he sucked in a breath. She had left of her own volition, but who had driven her into risking herself? His inaction against phylloxera had forced her hand.

He sighed and brushed hair away from her forehead. "I thought you would bring light back to my life, but it was the other way around, was it not?"

Her breathing was painfully fast and restless. Curse the doctor. Pedro knew how to mend external wounds, but not this internal sickness. Her fever was low, and he gave her water. She mumbled and drank. Her tears had dried, but he could still see the translucent trails on her skin.

Before Cris arrived, he had intended to kill the man she loved. Unknowingly, she had kept him sane, healing him more than once. And he had almost made her bear his wrath.

If he killed Maxwell, what would separate him from his father?

Pedro dropped to his haunches, burying his face in the bed. Two horses raced inside his chest, stretching his sanity. Erebus screamed for him to think of himself, to conclude his plans; the other, Hemera, white mane flowing gently, urged him to consider what Julia needed.

How could he force her to marry him? It was so close he could taste it. All he'd ever wanted was to be with her, and now she was within his grasp. How could he let her go? But to kill her Englishman would make Pedro worse than his father. Could he do that?

Chapter 45

"Wine is like men: age sours the bad and improves the good." Cicero

Julia was kneeling on the schist, rain pelting her hair, her shoulders, her nose.

And then . . . she was not.

A soft mattress and downy pillows surrounded her in warmth. Velvet curtains shielded the bed from the rest of the room. She blinked, the milky light enough to sting her eyes.

A sharp pain invaded her head, and the memories came crashing back—the rain, the bridge, and worse, Griffin's betrayal. Her chest flooded with despair, oily and thick. Her nose burned and tears came to her eyes. She let them flow freely. Groaning, she tried to sit up, but a fit of coughing made her body spasm and hurt as if being raked by iron nails.

"You are awake."

Pedro? Julia startled and wiped away her tears. He walked the few paces to the giant bed. His skin was pale, and he had dark circles under his eyes.

"How did I get here?" she croaked.

"I found you next to the broken bridge. You were freezing."

Julia tried to smile. "So, you saved me just like in the dovecote when we were children."

"The doctor was here. Your fever is low, but you must rest." Pedro sat on the mattress facing her.

Too tired to move, Julia leaned back on the pillows.

He raised his hand as if intending to touch her cheek, but then dropped it and took a deep breath. "Why did you leave? Why not ask for my help instead of that Englishman?"

If only she had. How much heartache it would have spared her.

She shrugged. "I couldn't stay and watch my vineyards be devoured."

"But if you had waited, I would have set everything to rights. Had I not promised you?"

Julia bunched the sheets in her hands. "Yes, but then you did nothing, and I could not afford to wait."

"But if you married me—"

Julia grabbed his hand, splayed so close to her on the bed. His eyes were troubled, and his shoulders stiffened. How could she make him understand?

Holding his cold palms, she interlaced her fingers with his. "Pedro, I am not the girl you saved from the dovecote. I've changed." She took a shaky breath. "Too much."

They were silent for a long moment. What could he be thinking? His expression was impenetrable; not a glimpse of his feelings escaped his intense eyes.

He pulled away from her touch. "Do you remember that day by the river? My father had . . . I was bleeding, and you—" His voice, always so sure, faltered.

"How could I forget? He was horrible, was he not? I wanted to soothe your pain."

His lips raised a bit on the edges in the resemblance of a smile. "You did. More than you can imagine."

Her chest ached for the boy who had also grown and changed so much, perhaps more than her. "But not enough."

"No." He gazed at the coverlet, brows furrowed. His profile showed the aristocratic lines of his face, but the usual intensity had dimmed. "Do you love him, then?"

The tears returned and she dropped her gaze, unable to face him through her pain.

Tenderly, whisper soft, he brushed her tears away. His eyes were sad.

It came to her then—the truth. Pedro had genuine feelings for her, and they ran deeper than she could have imagined. How could she have been so blind?

She touched his cheek. "I am sorry to have hurt you, Pedro."

"The bastard does not deserve you."

Julia did not know how to reply. Griffin had made no promises. The belief of a future with him had been a dream. Her dream. She should have known better. But she still had her family, still had Vesuvio. And Pedro... she could never love him the way he needed, the way he deserved.

"I want . . . I need to go home. I miss my son."

Avoiding her gaze, Pedro left the bed, opened the curtains, and let in a sliver of sunshine. The light danced on the swirling patterns of the oriental rug.

All those times he had vowed to make her his bride. Would he force her now? She was in his bedroom and completely vulnerable.

He was silent for several heartbeats, and when he turned to her, his eyes were closed. With the sun shining behind him, he looked like a hallowed angel, powerful, implacable. When he opened his eyes, his gaze was solemn, soft even, and it reminded her of the boy he had once been.

"Rest and eat. I will order a carriage to take you home."

Chapter 46

"Man makes the wine, and the wine remakes the man." Portuguese saying

Griffin cantered along the cypress-lined road leading to Vesuvio. The extra miles to cross the bridge at Barca D'alva had been the longest of his life. Flashes of her running away, straight into the bastard's arms, pierced his mind.

What had the count done to her? Doubt poisoned him. Griffin would not allow Almoster to ruin their lives. He would convince Julia he loved her. She would understand the betrothal with Beth Croft had been a business arrangement.

The sight of the property made him suck in a breath. Yesterday's torrent had devastated the garden, shedding the leaves from the vines and the bougainvillea. The sun had already set, turning the light into a sickly gray, but no welcoming torches flickered on the walls or glinted through the glass panes. Apart from Thunder's crunching steps, the courtyard was silent.

Movement behind the palm trees—Almoster descended the steps from the front door. Gut churning, Griffin narrowed his eyes, his body shedding the exhaustion from several days on the road. Thunder, sensing his violent mood, pranced. His fists clenched over the reins. Why was the knave still here?

Vaulting from the saddle, Griffin advanced. This close, Almoster's face looked haggard, with deep purple lines under his eyes. Instead of smugness, he exuded aggression, his feral appearance no doubt mirroring Griffin's rage.

He grabbed the count by his lapel. "What did you do with her?"

Almoster's eyes glinted brutally. "Keep your filthy hands to yourself."

Griffin pulled him closer, uncaring the *fidalgo's* hand had moved to his scabbard. "Tell me."

"I ask you the same." The count advanced a step, bringing his face so close, the black lines of his half-wild eyes stood in sharp relief. "Was she not under your protection? Was it not you who took her from her home? She is sick, too weak to stand. Because of you."

Griffin staggered back, hands falling limply to his sides. This bastard had lied before, but this made sense. Julia had stayed in the freezing rain too long. An urge to see her gripped him, to the exclusion of everything else. He would go inside now. If he had to demolish the door, so be it. He moved to climb the stairs, but Almoster blocked his passage.

"Step out of my way." Griffin intoned each word, body humming with aggression.

"Not in this lifetime."

Griffin barraged forward, but the count stepped to the side, obstructing his path again. The *fidalgo* had interfered enough times with his life. Griffin needed to crush his flawless veneer, to smash it over the stones paving the ground. The urge hazed his vision and muddled his thoughts.

Staring into Almoster's eyes, he arrowed his elbows and shoved his chest.

"Is that all you've got, Englishman?" The bastard blocked his path again, planting his feet wide.

"Move, or I will break your face."

"What, have you lost your British restraint?" Almoster sneered. "You are welcome to try."

The count took his saber from the scabbard at his waist and dropped it on the ground. The sword clanked once and lay forgotten upon the white rocks.

Griffin removed his coat and rolled his shirtsleeves. Vesuvio remained deserted, the windows black as night. It was just the two of them. Perfect. As a gentleman, he had only brawled inside clubs, practicing the art of boxing as a manly sport. Now he felt capable of smashing the other man's face without the slightest compunction.

The violence of his thoughts should have acted as a deterrent, but it didn't. The desire to drive the man away from their lives was more primal than chivalry.

Fists up, Griffin circled Almoster, crunching the gravel underfoot. His adversary kept his arms down. If he thought Griffin could not fight, he was in for a nasty surprise. He would do a quick job of the bastard. Griffin advanced on him, but the other man sidestepped and attacked. The punch exploded in the right side of his face, pain radiating from his brow straight to his brain. Griffin shook his head and touched the bruised skin.

"Is that enough for you? Are you ready to go back to your own people?"

Griffin advanced toward the *fidalgo*. His left hook connected with the bastard's head. He welcomed the jarring impact on his arm and the pain in his knuckles. The count retreated a step, glowering, blood dripping from his lip. Griffin seized the advantage, intent on overthrowing him and pummeling him until no one recognized his obnoxious aristocratic face.

A sight on the second floor made him stop. Tony rested his hand on the glass, the foggy surface failing to hide the frown on his smooth brow. It was the hardest of blows, more potent than any punch the count could give. Over a week ago, Griffin had stood under these same palm trees, promising the boy he would take care of his mother. The hug he'd received still warmed his chest.

"Haven't you done enough?" Almoster asked.

Griffin looked at his hands. The knuckles oozed blood in two spots. His clothing was disheveled, and his left eye had swollen shut. The tight grip he kept on his emotions had slipped away completely, and he hardly recognized himself. The realization made all the fight drain from his body, and only shame remained in its place.

Griffin took a ragged breath. "She will never love you."

"Perhaps not. But I wouldn't hurt her."

Tony moved away from the window and vanished into the darkened room above. Almoster was right. Griffin had more than hurt her. Not only was he responsible for her sickness, but he had shredded the trust of a seven-year-old boy.

Dragging his feet, Griffin made his way back to Thunder. A last look at Vesuvio's facade revealed just black glass. No one was there, not anymore. As Griffin pushed himself on the saddle, a cold realization seeped into his chest.

Julia was better off without him.

Chapter 47

"Good is life, but better is the wine." Fernando Pessoa

Elizabeth Croft played the piano with the utmost grace, slender fingers cajoling the old instrument to a beautiful and proper Mozart composition, showing off her skill and talent.

Griffin shut his eyes. Why was it that a *fado* could make him burn while these perfect notes left him cold? He gripped the leather upholstery of his chair, forcing himself to stay in his parlor and not dwell on the past, the trip, or the way Julia and he had parted.

It would be so simple to marry the girl and be done with it. Curse that Portuguese woman to have wreaked havoc in his life. Before her, everything had been black and white. Now he didn't fit inside his skin, and it was all her fault.

It took him no longer than a dragging piece of music to realize this couldn't work. No matter what had happened between Julia and him, he could not marry Beth.

He had to speak with Croft. It would not be easy, but it was necessary.

Since Griffin had returned last evening with his right eye swollen and blue, the women had avoided looking at him, including his mother. It was as if he had crossed the limits of gentlemanly behavior by becoming a common brawler, and by doing such, he had become invisible. Not that he cared. Turning invisible was damn convenient right now. Croft, with his rude jokes and tactless remarks, was the only one making a valuable effort to keep the mood civil.

His mother's applause startled him, and he shook himself, clapping his hands morosely.

"Ahem. What a talent, eh, Maxwell?" Croft shifted in the armchair and winked.

"Of course. Congratulations."

Mrs. Croft, her nose at the haughty angle she enjoyed showing to the world, lowered her embroidery and rolled her eyes at Boa Vista's living room. "Only the best instructors for our lamb."

Griffin cleared his throat and was about to call Croft into his study when Jako entered the parlor and announced dinner. Groaning, he stood and offered his arm to Miss Croft. She rose gracefully from the piano, her fingers fluttering over his coat sleeves, and he controlled the impulse to shrink away from her lace-covered hand. The first time Julia had touched him like this, back at Saint John's party, she had gripped his arm with enough force to crumple his jacket. Even then, he'd known Julia wouldn't retreat from his teasing.

Beth gazed at him expectantly, and Griffin brought his mind to the present. The girl was innocent of his wrongdoings, and he owed her a minimum of courtesy.

"You played beautifully, Miss Croft."

She lowered her eyes, a blush covering her porcelain cheeks. While he steered her to the dining room, Croft escorted Griffin's mother and Mrs. Croft.

Picking up the napkin and covering her lap with surgeon's precision, Mrs. Croft eyed Jako's departure. "Foreigners. How difficult it is to find proper help these days."

Griffin stiffened. "Jako is extremely efficient—and a friend." He didn't stop to examine her displeased frown, but pulled a chair for Miss Croft and assumed his place at the head of the table.

"I see you decided not to decorate the house." Mrs. Croft sipped the wine, her bejeweled finger clinking on the crystal.

Griffin gritted his teeth and counted to ten. The decoration suited his tastes. The airy, neoclassical style was better than the cluttered feel of England's homes the community emulated in Oporto. No doubt it was the prospect of having him as a groom that had left her bitter as a pot of burned coffee.

The housekeeper entered the dining room. Griffin nodded with approval to her perfectly pressed uniform and dignified demeanor. She displayed several entrees, including freshly made cheese and warm bread, olives picked at Boa Vista, and the famous smoked *presunto*.

"Are we supposed to eat this?" Mrs. Croft eyed the food with pinched lips, her nose averted as if the smell was offensive.

"*Pois sim.*" The housekeeper bobbed her head and hurried away.

"How do you put up with their yes or no replies?" Mrs. Croft's voice was sharp enough to cut steel.

Griffin's hand closed around the carving knife. "You just have to learn to ask the right questions."

He chanced a look in his mother's direction and found her shrewd eyes darting from him to the Crofts.

"Humph!" Mrs. Croft glared at the pork leg. "What do you call this aberration, then?"

"This is *presunto*. You should try it. It is quite delicious."

Griffin tried and failed not to remember Julia's impudence while instructing him on the difference between wild boars and the pigs that roamed the cork forest.

"What a vulgar word." Croft's wife scrunched her beak of a nose.

Back at Oporto, he had learned to ignore the veiled superiority some of his community assumed against the Portuguese. Now it was too hard to swallow. The prospect of hearing their crude comments and opinions for the rest of the dinner was as pleasant as walking on lit coals.

"Beth, dear, how was France? Did you enjoy your summer?" Mother must have sensed his mood and shifted the group's attention.

"Why, yes, Mrs. Maxwell. I stayed near Marseilles with friends."

"With the Smiths. I can introduce them to you, of course. They earned a fortune with wine speculation." Croft winked and licked his greasy fingers. "Speaking of France, I think it is time to buy lands here. What with phylloxera driving the prices so low."

Griffin gritted his teeth. With the vineyards gone, people were desperate, losing their homes and abandoning the country. His mouth went dry. What about Julia? No, Julia would be all right. She had the grafted vines, the sulfur.

"Instead of buying their lands, have you considered helping them?" Griffin dropped his napkin on top of his plate and stood. It was a terrible breach in etiquette, but he'd had enough. "If you will excuse me."

He strode through the double doors to the veranda, immune to the bite of the late autumn day. The sun hadn't shone since the storm had taken Julia away from him, and the humidity was still present in the muddy ground, the dripping leaves, and the heavy air.

Griffin gripped the railing, his guts boiling in tune with the river. The Douro was on a hangover, the water a turbid brown, the current swollen, reaching to the floor's checkered tiles.

Steps behind him made him stiffen.

"Is everything all right, lad? I don't mean to intrude, but you seem a tad disturbed. The ladies have noticed." Croft cleared his throat and leaned against the railing.

Griffin shook his head without taking his eyes from the river. "The Portuguese will go hungry, John."

"You've been spending too much time here, eh? When we go back to Oporto, Beth can do charity work if you desire. The girl has the softest of hearts."

He could not live this lie anymore. Griffin's pulse surged, and he inhaled the Douro's scent. "I can't marry your daughter."

Croft's eyes widened, and he took a step back. "I beg your pardon?"

"I apologize, but my affections lay elsewhere."

Croft turned his face to the river. "Since when do affections have anything to do with marriage?"

The statement made his stomach tighten, but it would be pointless to argue. "For me, it does."

They were silent for long moments, watching as a mother duck tried to keep her yellow chicks from wandering too far. What a pointless endeavor. Every time she forced one to climb atop the log, another swam away.

Croft took an audible breath and faced him. He eyed the bruise on Griffin's face and then lit a cigar. "May I presume to inquire if this involves a Portuguese widow of both our acquaintances?"

"It's personal." Griffin crossed his arms. "If this will prove our partnership impossible, you are at liberty to say so."

The man looked at him with beady, assessing eyes. Griffin held his breath.

"Why, Maxwell, I wanted you as a son, but your qualities and business acumen will be much appreciated at Mess's, Croft and Maxwell Port Trading." Croft extended his arm.

Griffin eyed the chubby hand with its tufts of hair protruding in all directions. After a second, he clasped it.

Chapter 48

"One should always be drunk. That's all that matters...But with what? With wine, with poetry, or with virtue, as you chose. But get drunk."
Charles Baudelaire

Julia measured the passage of days by the doctor's punctual visits, Tony's hugs, and by Amelia's appearance to read her novels in the afternoons. Julia paid scant attention, but her soft, generous voice soothed her, and she craved any solace.

Aunt Rosario also helped with her constant fussing, admonishing her to drink broth, airing the bedroom, and making herbal teas for her breathing. A letter from her husband had increased Aunt's Rosario cheery disposition. He had asked Aunt Rosario and Amelia to join him. They didn't speak of it, and Julia avoided the subject, unable to consider their departure, but she knew they were afraid. No wonder. Though the trip on the newest steamships took less than fifteen days, they would have to leave everything they knew behind.

The doctor deemed Julia fit to leave the bed after the third day. She felt sick, but not with cold, more like an ache of the soul. If it wasn't for the family's constant care . . . she cleaned tears from her cheeks. She would not let her mind wander there.

Seated on the leather armchair of her study, Julia stared at the view from her glass panes. The scenery had a shattering beauty, as the leaves had turned orange and red, the colors of fall mingling with the colors of phylloxera. As the vines prepared for the winter sleep, Julia prayed their efforts would contain the disease and they would wake up next spring, promising a better future.

Pedro went to Lisbon for a few weeks. Before he left, he had delivered sulfur to the smaller producers from his own coffers and the whole Alto Douro was being pulverized with the noxious-smelling powder.

Griffin had never come. It was great that he hadn't, for she had decided not to love him. She did not love his treacherous voice, nor when he teased her, cajoling a smile out of her reluctant lips. She did not love his heinous hands and how the mere thought of them made her skin tingle. His scent wasn't dearer to her than the best of vintages, and his blue eyes had never moved her. She hated how his chin was at the perfect height to brush against her forehead and how he could take her breath away just by looking at her mouth. It disgusted her how he was gentle and caring in his gruff, arrogant way. She hoped he went away to be happy in Oporto.

She let her eyes wander over the gloomy day. A boat floated down the river. Its sails sported tears, the color a dull gray. Had it braved a storm in the river?

A soft rasp sounded at the door, and Wentworth entered the study.

Julia perked up. Could it be him? "Yes?"

"I'm sorry to disturb, but Mr. Croft insists he must see you."

"The spirit is changeable like the wind,
More stable is the body, and more discreet...
Your thoughts you changed many times,
But never your favorite wine."
Mario Quintana

Pedro armed himself with the documents. It was finally time. The man beyond this door did not deserve to breathe the same air as Cris.

Pulse throbbing inside his veins, he paced around his father's waiting chamber. On the wall, the duke's mementos of battles won for the country's glory—a portrait with the emperor and gleaming sables used in war—were calculated to awe the visitor before the poor soul gained entrance into the Prime Minister's office.

Pedro cleaned sweat from his brow and smoothed the creases from his coat. He held the power now, not the duke. With the deeds to Douro's Quintas, he could push the man away from their lives.

This was taking too long, even by his father's standards. Why couldn't the secretary just call him inside?

Pedro paced to the window and gazed at the light gray sky covering the capital.

Hooves clattered on the pavement as the king's guard crossed the square into the Ministry's front entrance. Civilians followed, an angry mass waving against each other. Pedro sucked in a breath—a coup.

Exiting the waiting room, he strode forcefully to his father's assistant.

The man cowered below his Georgian desk, a ridiculous wig askew on his head.

"What is happening?"

"It's his rival, the Duke of Loule. He must have convinced the king to oust your father." His voice trembled.

Pedro caught him by the neckcloth and forced him to stand. "Block the doors and summon the duke's guard."

He did not stop to hear excuses and entered the Prime Minister's office. The duke stared outside, tall frame leaning precariously to the side, a wiry arm the only anchor to his upright position. It reminded Pedro of a defeated galley, its mast listing broken. For the first time in his life, his father did not seem like a god among men. Quite the contrary—his face was haggard and his eyes stared unfocused, senile.

Pedro swallowed his discourse. He had meant to come here and accuse his father, to force him to make amends, to promise to stay away from his affairs, to leave Cris alone. But the duke was no more. His father had already been beaten.

Pedro's gut churned. He could simply end this. Deliver him to the angry mob outside. He wouldn't have to dirty his hands.

Shouting and angry utterances invaded the dark-paneled walls. Each second Pedro wasted staring at his father, they got closer.

Cursing under his breath, he grabbed the duke's arm. "Come. You need to get out of here."

His father turned and their eyes met. The haze of confusion lifted from his green eyes, and for a second, the usual malice returned. Then the spark went out as if he had turned his mind elsewhere, shutting himself out of Pedro's reach.

Knocks and shoves sounded on the front door. The wood strained against the invasion.

No more time to lose. Pedro guided the duke downstairs through the hidden stairwell and then into the glaring light of the palace's service courtyard. There was only one hope for his father. Exile. Making a quick decision, he supported his father's weight and turned to the docks.

They made slow progress through the Rossio neighborhood, keeping to the shadows of buildings, pulling up the flaps of their coats to avoid recognition. When they arrived at the Belem Marina, his father was out of breath, hair disheveled and skin pale.

A few hours and Pedro's yacht was ready to sail. He stood on the pier while the duke prepared to embark. His father gave him one last glance—his skin white as paper and nose reddened by the chill. "I will be back. Mark my words. The government will be mine again."

Pedro turned his face to a pair of gulls flying near the water, screeching loudly in the quiet morning. "No, Father. Your time is gone."

He watched for long moments as the boat drifted away, taking the duke from the shore. His vision blurred around the masts, piercing the mist over the Tagus. There was no joy, sadness, or remorse, just a numbing nothingness and a realization colder than the capital in December.

Pedro had believed he could shed his father's influence on his life, but he was wrong. The worst his father could have done to him had already been done. It was inside him.

A piece of iron beaten too hard, for too long, could not be melded again. Pedro gazed at the sails, now under the shadow of gray clouds. Nothing and no one could ever change that.

Chapter 50

"There were sins whose fascination was more in the memory than in the doing of them, strange triumphs that gratified the pride more than the passions, and gave to the intellect a quickened sense of joy, greater than any joy they brought, or could ever bring, to the senses."
Oscar Wilde

Mr. Croft was here. Julia closed her eyes and leaned back in the chair. It would be all right. He would listen to her arguments and grant them the accorded time to repay the loan.

Blocking out all thoughts of Griffin marrying the man's daughter, she bade him entry to the study. It was odd to have him inside her private place. She should have asked Wentworth to put him in the parlor.

Winter was fast approaching, and raindrops spattered over the glass panes, making shadows on the carpet. A gelid current whispered over her cheeks and nape. Perhaps there was a window open somewhere in the house.

After a polite greeting, Croft sat on the armchair facing her desk, the wooden frame straining to contain his rotund figure. Without asking her leave, he placed his briefcase on her table.

His appearance was amicable enough, his white mustache twitching under his smile. But his gray eyes shifted restlessly, as if constantly grasping the furniture and adornments around him, assessing their worth.

Julia had rehearsed this many times—how she would speak to him, how she would assure him of the production advances. But now, looking at the hint of condescension in his upturned lips, she felt like a ten-year-old wanting to impress a stranger with a silly trick. She took a deep breath. "How can I help you?"

"Mrs. Costa, it's dreadful news. Simply dreadful news."

"What do you mean?"

Shifting on the chair, he flattened the cravat over his belly. "With phylloxera, you cannot deliver the agreed production. I am so sorry."

Julia ignored the lump in her throat and sucked in a breath. "You are right. The plague is dreadful, but I still have time. Two years—"

"Yes, but the contract says that if at any point it is perceived that Vesuvio would not meet the requirements, the final clause would be executed. I am sorry, I truly am."

Julia fisted her hands on the table. "Mr. Croft, I'm certain any lawyer would back me up if I pleaded with the courts. The plague is completely out of my control."

He widened his eyes as if surprised she would dare threaten him.

Julia straightened her spine. If he thought she would give up, he was sorely mistaken.

He cleared his throat. "I would wait for the agreed time if I didn't suspect you wouldn't reach the quota accorded with your late husband, Mr. Bernardo Ferreira."

Julia caught a glimmer of hope. She had indeed increased the production. "Listen, Mr. Croft, you don't understand. I did all the plantings."

He sighed heavily, the movement upsetting the sides of his mustache. Then he turned and rummaged through his leather case. Julia followed his chubby hands, icy perspiration dampening her back.

"I could excuse your transgressions, Mrs. Costa, you being a woman and a widow, but as a businessman, I must consider the interests of my shareholders."

He unrolled a piece of paper atop her desk, and Julia craned her neck to see. A map. With a flick, he turned it in her direction.

"Mr. Maxwell advised me on this matter, Mrs. Costa. In short, I know you planted outside the demarcated area. I am so sorry."

"Griffin—Mr. Maxwell sent you this? I don't understand."

He puffed his chest, narrowing his eyes. "Why, yes, my future son-in-law is extremely practical. He agreed to postpone the marriage with my daughter just to come here and do me this favor, you see?"

"No, I don't."

Julia could not see because her vision blurred, and she had to grip the chair's arms to remain upright. Griffin had made this map. He had known all along, and he had done this to her. He could not have hurt her more if he had stabbed her.

Julia shook her head, lifting her palms. "No. No, you cannot mean that. I still have time."

His beady eyes glinted, and his lips tugged up in a small, cruel smile. Of course he had wanted this. Julia's throat ached, and she swallowed furiously, the tears threatening to choke her. But she had shown too many emotions to Croft and would be damned if she gave him a glimpse of how this betrayal shattered her.

He patted her hand. "Mrs. Costa, you were not meant for this kind of setback. You should have left this matter to men. It caused you unnecessary affliction. I am truly sorry."

Julia jerked her hand from his grasp. English bastard. He wasn't sorry, not for a single minute. She pushed up from the chair and looked straight at his face. "Vesuvio is mine. It is my son's birthright."

"You have until year-end to vacate it. I am so sorry."

With a pitying glance, he rose from the table and collected the briefcase, strutting to the door as if he already owned the place.

"Wait!" Her pride threatened to choke her, but she owed it to her people. "What about the workers, the tenants, and the house servants?"

"I think it is up to you, Mrs. Costa."

"I beg your pardon?"

"Their fate is in your hands. Should you vacate the house without causing me any disturbances, they can retain their positions. Otherwise..."

Chapter 51

"Wine brings to light the hidden secrets of the soul." Horace

Griffin ambled about Boa Vista's garden. The situation was unsustainable—Mrs. Croft's witticisms, the veiled criticisms, the flaunted superiority. When would they leave for Oporto? A week had passed since he had broken the engagement. Still, they remained under his roof.

Gut churning, he crossed to the orchard, searching for Julia's fragrance. His mother had tried to question him, but he could not share his intentions. After his decision to end the betrothal, she would undoubtedly compare him to his father. Think of him as unreliable, putting his own needs in front of the family's.

The sun peeked from behind wet clouds as he followed the path of limestones, his boots leaving brown prints on the white surface.

His feet brought him near Julia's tree. The blooms had fallen and, in their place, under-ripened fruits hung from the dark foliage. He inhaled deeply. But instead of her fragrance, he got the herbal scent of leaves.

"Sir, I found it." Jako approached him, a wobbly smile on his lips. The pearl was absent today, and oddly, it made him look sad.

The faithful servant produced a polished key from the pocket of his coat. Griffin tilted his head. The locked garden. He had forgotten about its existence.

"Thank you, my friend." He pressed the other man's shoulder and walked to the hidden door. The oak portal opened with a groan.

Griffin crossed into a different world—a world where shadows and foliage mixed in beautiful designs all made with grapevines. A trellised gazebo stood in the center, crisscrossed with the gnarled trunks and shooting languid lines of branches that intertwined at the top, forming a canopy of foliage. The sun, filtering through the translucent leaves, painted the pale marble on the floor in pools of bright orange and soft yellow and deep gold. The latter reminded him of Julia's eyes when touched by the same sun. In the center stood a delicate marble fountain with a girl treading vines, her traces both mischievous and sweet.

Griffin walked on dumb legs and dropped his weight on the cement bench built around the fountain. The water must come from the river through underground pipes. It was flowing; the sound was pure joy, like Julia's laughter.

She was wrong. Vines were not meant only for wine, needing to be pruned into submission. They were pliable and strong and beautiful and adaptable. She must see this place. The stubborn woman would not believe her eyes, giving him excuses or blaming it on a fanciful Englishman's design. But it would delight her. He could just picture her here laughing with him while Tony raced around the fountain, splashing the water. Afterward, they would sit on this bench and kiss while watching the boats floating down the river.

He brought a hand to his chest, rubbing the spot above his heart, but the pain was too deep.

God, he was alone. She wouldn't see this place as much as he would not hear her voice or her opinions.

The count was wrong. He had not done enough. Not nearly enough. It would only be enough after he had spoiled her into the happiest woman alive. Simple as red wine was purple and white wine was green. This would be their place, their fountain, not of sorrow like the one in Vila Nova, but of joy.

Chapter 52

"A poet, you see, is a light thing, and winged and holy, and cannot compose before he gets inspiration and loses control of his senses and his reason has deserted him." Plato

The greenhouse's glass roof failed to admit light today. As Julia tidied up the last of a lifetime's belongings, knickknacks, and memories, she had to stop to focus her vision. She should fetch a candle or kindle the hearth. Still, a weight had settled over her shoulders and the most menial of tasks didn't bother her.

At least she had not waited to deliver the bad news to the family. It was surprising how people united in moments of difficulty. There was a tired, heavy kind of relief to be had when the worst happened. After fighting against such lofty odds for so long, she had finally sank deep. But at least she had arrived at the bottom, and at any moment now, she would start kicking back up to the top. Eventually, she'd breathe again.

Amelia squeezed Julia's hands. Her eyes were gentle, and a tight smile appeared at the corner of her lips.

"You will love Bahia, cousin. We all will." She nodded forcefully, maybe as much for Julia as for herself.

"Of course, dear." Julia forced a smile.

"We need more crates. I'll ask Jose to bring a few from the stables."

"Thanks."

Most things would have to stay. The tickets Abelardo had bought only allowed personal belongings to be brought on the ship. Tony already adored the American monstrosity that would take them away from Vesuvio. He was excited about the six decks and amazed at how it transported over two thousand passengers. God, they had never seen this many people in the same place, not even a tenth. The thought made her stomach churn again, and she held tight to the desk. It would be better for him if he pretended this was a fantastic adventure.

Julia sighed and gazed at the room, committing it to memory—the joyful hours spent here, studying botany, creating perfumes, drying flowers and fruits, dreaming about the future and the vintages to come.

Picking up the last book on the shelf, she traced the drawings that had helped her graft the first vine. A lone tear traveled down her cheek. She didn't bother to clean it; they came and went at will, and she had lost the strength to control them.

"Hello, Julia."

She gasped, his voice hitting her like a punch. Her hands shook, and the book fell on the granite floor with a dull thud. Squeezing her eyes shut, she leaned on the bookcase for balance. Who had let Griffin in? Had he come to gloat? He would not witness her humiliation. It took all her will to turn instead of fleeing from his sight. He was here, the same man who had loved her so tenderly, a foreign stranger now.

"Vesuvio is closed for visitors." Her chin trembled, and she fought an overpowering need to race into his arms and weep into his chest. She gripped the shelf—she must not take comfort from her tormentor. How could he have done this to her? To them? She averted her eyes and looked instead at the lofty cravat adorning his neck. Focusing on his tailored clothes helped her view what he really was—the Englishman who had ruined them.

He shoved his hands inside his pockets. His expression lacked the usual arrogance, and his eyes were gentle. "Julia, please. I came to explain myself."

"You don't need to tell me anything."

"I made mistakes, but I am—"

"Mistakes?" Blood boiled in her veins, and she fisted her hands by her sides. Mistakes, indeed. "You lied to me—about everything. You were engaged to another woman, and worse, you...you betrayed me."

***

He exhaled and stepped forward. "I have broken the engagement."

She lifted a troubled gaze to him. Her eyes, the same ones that had challenged him, teased him, inflamed and loved him, were defeated. She had lost weight and deep purple shadows marred her cheeks. "I'm sure you will recover. Now I'm busy. If you could please leave."

The hoarseness of her voice pierced him, and Griffin had to look away. He had done this to her. Guilt burned inside his chest, an icy fire that left him gasping. Slowly, noticing his surroundings like one waking from a dream, Griffin blinked at the boxes piled where once there were a myriad of toys and vases. Where were the pots with fragrant spices and dried flowers? Without Julia's mishmash, the place had lost its enchantment—just a barren room.

He rubbed the back of his neck. "What happened? Why all the boxes?"

Arms crossed in front of her chest, she bent over as if pained by his words. "Are you going to pretend ignorance?"

"I don't know, damn it!"

"If you came here to take possession, you are too early. Croft gave us until the end of the month."

Griffin advanced another step. "Croft? What are you talking about?"

"Your precious partner explained all, including your invaluable participation. The map allowed him to execute the loan clause. Croft was so very sorry, but that was what you two wanted all along, wasn't it?"

"No." He felt like shoving the crates to the floor. "Julia, please look at me."

He came closer and extended his arm, reaching for her hand. She flinched away from his touch as if he meant to strike her.

His chest was so heavy it was difficult to breathe. "I love you."

"I have nothing else to give. My love, my trust, and now my home—you took it all." Her chest heaved with dry sobs.

Her home was being dismantled box by box. Julia was being evicted from Vesuvio. On a chilly afternoon, he too had stood powerless while they removed his mother's collection of portraits, carelessly stacking them on the floor. His mother had wept, each frame that left leaving a shadow on her soul. When it was all done, the wall would not let them forget, still showing the contours of where the frames used to be. He had hated his father then, and he hadn't forgiven him for causing them such pain.

"Mrs. Costa, is everything all right here?"

Julia covered her face with her palms, shutting him out. "Wentworth, please accompany Mr. Maxwell to the door."

Chapter 53

"Run from bad neighbors and wine excesses." Portuguese saying

Griffin raced to Boa Vista and strode into his study. Where were Vesuvio's ledgers? Julia had sent them to him before their trip to Braganza. Until he saw the books, he could not breathe. He scanned the romantic volumes displayed on the shelves, trailing his eyes over the titles written with golden letters until the black leather tome caught his attention. He grabbed it with unsteady hands. A sheet was lodged inside. His heart picked up speed—Vesuvio's contract.

Griffin settled behind his desk with both documents. He opened his top drawer and searched for Vesuvio's map. As he'd suspected, the rolled paper wasn't inside. Had Croft taken it behind his back? Saving that question for later, he went to the racks. Uncle had owned a Baron Forrester's cartography book. In under a minute, he had the green volume open.

The maps started near Oporto, each page depicting a land scale of one mile and a half. The only constant as the sheets turned north was the river, continuously drawn in the center. Griffin recognized many places, sweet memories to be treasured forever. He soon got to the Vila Nova section. The next one depicted Vesuvio in all its glory—the elegant house with the palm trees painted in the heart, the First Light ruins brought to life by clever use of shadows. The baron had left nothing out.

Griffin traced the sinuous lines of Vesuvio's hills as if he touched her curves—the proud cheekbones, the pert nose, her flaring hips, and arched feet. He had accepted her gift of passion and yet failed to protect her. A deep sigh escaped his chest, emptying him of strength.

For long seconds, he stared at the lines, his eyes searching for clues. It flirted beyond his grasp. Numbers were his expertise, damn it.

He rubbed his eyes and pinched the bridge of his nose, a headache lurking. Julia needed him. With renewed determination, he matched the contract with the ledgers, comparing the number of barrels promised with the past five years' production. Then he stared at the map. This one was in precise scale, and with a ruler, he measured the hills that weren't planted with grapes. Griffin released the instruments and leaned back in the chair. Even with Vesuvio's superb productivity, the property's demarcated area couldn't yield the increase in production demanded by Croft. Therefore, the contract was a trap. Could this be a mistake? Griffin shot to his feet. Only one way to find out. He had to confront Croft.

Griffin exited the study to a conspicuously empty house. He inspected the parlor and the veranda, but there was no sign of his unwelcomed visitors. Where the hell had they gone? The whole week they had bothered him, always underfoot. Now that he needed them, they had vanished.

Heart beating in his throat, he found Jako. "Where is Croft?"

"He left a few hours ago, sir."

"Where?"

"He went back to Oporto." His mother rose from the settee. "And took the ladies with him. He said he had some business that couldn't be delayed and sent his regrets."

Griffin imagined just what kind of business he had in the city. If he filed the petition at court, Julia's property would be lost forever. Griffin had to get there first and convince the man to spare her property.

"Jako, prepare my Brougham."

"But son, where are you going? I just got here, and I expected to spend more time. It feels like—"

He grabbed her hands. The unfamiliar touch startled her, but her eyes softened and she stepped closer.

Griffin exhaled. "Mother, this is a grave matter. Do you trust me?"

"Is this to do with that charming Portuguese woman?"

"She is in great danger."

Her face turned resolute, and she gave a firm nod. "I will pack my clothes."

He'd expected disdain or protest, but what he got filled him with warmth. "By helping Julia, I might have to give up Croft's partnership."

She rose on her tiptoes and kissed his cheek, then turned on her heels and walked away. Her approval and understanding were the last things he'd hoped for, but damn, it was good.

In less than two hours, they were on the road to Oporto, the steady clopping of the blacks much slower than the urgency he felt within. He must get there before Croft filed the contract. Julia's life depended on it. She would never accept him again, but he couldn't let her lose her home.

As the carriage moved away from Boa Vista, Griffin closed his eyes and rested his head against the leather bench, oblivious to the rutted road. Images flashed inside his mind, each bittersweet—aching and soothing. Amethysts in green baize. Ebony hair flying in the ruins of First Light. Breathed words near his skin. Intoxicating vintages. The scent of lemon flowers. Laughter like bells on the hills. Golden eyes veiled by black.

He would protect all that, even if he couldn't be a part of it. Saving it for her would be enough. As long as she had a home, there would always be one for him.

***

The squinting windows of the British Factory House had barely appeared in his line of vision when Griffin jumped from the carriage, wheels still in motion. He pushed the door open with enough force to wrestle it from its hinges and scanned the club's parlor.

The place was filled with patrons in their formal black and white suits, flocking about like contented sheep. Damn, it was Wednesday. After three days on the road, he had forgotten the day of the week. No matter; he would have his answers, even if the club was Dante's hell on judgment day.

His quarry stood near the bar, sipping champagne and laughing, surrounded by fawning members. Griffin advanced, his steps muffled by the red carpet, ignoring the greetings sent his way. He stopped so close to Croft he could see the wispy veins crisscrossing his nose. "I require a conversation."

The other man startled, widening his eyes, no doubt at Griffin's wrinkled and dusty traveling clothes. "Oh, Maxwell, you are back already. What a surprise. I will gladly receive you after lunch."

"Now." Griffin infused the word with only a fraction of his urgency.

In less than a minute, they were inside the treasurer's office, Croft with the customary cigar dangling from his lips.

"So." He smiled, brushing his mustache. "You thought better about the marriage?"

"What?"

Croft shrugged. "I figured with the latest developments in the Douro, you would be more than willing to reconsider your hasty decision."

Griffin deposited the briefcase on top of the Georgian desk. With slow, deliberate movements, he took the cartography book and placed it over the table.

"Forrester's maps? What is the meaning of this?" A sheen of perspiration appeared on Croft's forehead, and he leaned away as if Griffin had presented snakes on a platter.

Croft knew. Why else would he be this nervous?

For so long, this man, this most respected member of the British community, had held the key to Griffin's future. Croft disgusted him now.

Griffin produced his copy of the contract and flapped it over the desk. "Vesuvio's contract and a map of the property." He stared at Croft, schooling his expression. "My only question is, have you known from the start?"

"If you imply that—"

"I know what I am implying. I just want your confirmation. We are going to be partners, after all." Griffin swallowed bile to imply the words, but he needed this confession.

Croft flushed, and his hands trembled when he reached for his cigar. "Mr. Ferreira was so eager to have the money. Mr. Burns introduced us. Do you know him, the banker?"

"I've had the displeasure, yes." The weasel was the worst sort of man, preying on people who were already in tight spots.

"Well, Bernardo Ferreira wanted to invest in a cloth industry. Do you know the type? Discontent with their lot in life? Mr. Ferreira was such and, I have to confess, not overly bright."

Griffin shook his head. With a wife like Julia, a son like Tony, and living in paradise? How could the jerk throw all that in the wind? "Go on."

"The property was not in Mr. Ferreira's name. He was only the administrator. He grumbled about his father not trusting him with the precious Vesuvio. So he came to me. He signed the contract eagerly." Croft took a puff of the cigar, spitting foul-smelling smoke. "He would have consigned more of the production. It was so easy. You would have done the same in my place."

Would he? He had to believe not. For his soul, he was not like this. He was a staunch believer in free trade, but this was corruptive, and the thought that Croft has been doing this to Julia? It made him want to slam the cigar down the man's throat.

"But why give him the money if you knew this Bernardo could not increase production?"

"Why? To take the property, of course." Croft's eyes shone with intent. "You can have it if you reconsider the betrothal. I'll add it to Beth's dowry."

Nausea swept Griffin in waves. How could Croft be so heartless? "No."

"I beg your pardon?" Croft bounced his shoulders and stood up.

"I will not allow you to do this to Mrs. Costa."

"If you want the widow, by all means, have her! Nothing needs to change, eh?" He smiled cruelly and extended his hand.

Griffin stared at the offending appendage until the other man dropped it and smoothed his coat.

"Don't need to be shocked. If Mrs. Costa is destitute, she will be more pliant to become your mistress." Croft wiggled his brows. "Just put her in a house. She would be quite thankful to you for saving her."

Blood pulsed in Griffin's temples, and he fisted his hands. "You will write a letter to Mrs. Costa now, releasing her from the contract. And then you will burn the blasted paper, and you will seek no dealings with Vesuvio."

Croft widened his eyes and stepped back. "I will do nothing of the sort."

"Yes, you will, or your bad conduct will be in every newspaper and every mouth of the English community from here to the other side of the Atlantic."

"You do this, you can forget about the partnership, do you hear me? Forget about it!"

"I would not want to partner with a dishonest man like you for all the gold in the colonies."

Chapter 54

"And wine can of their wits the wise beguile, make the sage frolic, and the serious smile." Alexander Pope

Julia left the house, tripping over the last step. What was all this ruckus in the courtyard? The shouting had brought the others outside, too. Aunt Rosario and Amelia appeared at the front door. Tony pushed between them and raced to her side.

Abelardo's hair was flying about his head, and his glasses were beige with dust. He brandished a large envelope in his right hand, a package in his left, and a startled grin on his face.

Julia crossed her arms. "What is it?"

"This just arrived from Oporto. By private courier," he panted.

From Oporto? Her chest tightened. Worse news? What else could it be? Nothing good ever came from that quarter.

Flushed, Abelardo took a gulping breath. "It's from Mr. Maxwell."

A vise gripped her heart. From Griffin? What could he have to say? And addressed to Abelardo?

"Tell us at once, boy." Aunt Rosario raised her voice.

"He discovered Croft made the contract in bad faith and confronted the man. It is all explained here in the letter." He tapped the volume, a lopsided grin on his face.

Ears ringing, Julia gripped Abelardo's arm to steady herself. She breathed in measured bursts, forcing the dizziness to subside. She brought the vellum to her face, searching for his bergamot smell but finding only paper and ink.

With unsteady movements, she pulled the sheet of paper from the envelope and scanned his large handwriting. So like him, bold without unnecessary flourish. He had addressed Abelardo, trusting her estate manager to deliver the news to Vesuvio's inhabitants. Her heart sank at the formality of his words. She squinted her eyes at the last lines, a little blurred by her tears.

They were free from Croft.

She was involved in a hug, and they jostled her back and forth as Flor and Amelia grabbed her arms and formed a circle, dancing and swaying from side to side. A startled laugh escaped her chest. Others came, no doubt attracted by the merriment and cheers. Jose carried a table from the kitchen, and wine and food flowed freely. Carlo started the accordion, and the lively tune infused the celebration with gaiety and relief.

Julia took the package from Abelardo and brought it close to her chest, moving to the front door. She looked at the revelers one more time. Nobody noticed her absence. Vesuvio's inhabitants, as he had put it, were twirling and laughing.

She entered the study and sat behind her desk, hands trembling around the brown paper of the package. Her Englishman had not betrayed her.

The parcel weighed only two pounds. She let it sit on the surface, staring at it for long seconds, then she unwrapped the sides, careful not to rip them. It was just a book—*Camões Sonnets.*

What had she expected, really? He must have felt honor-bound to help them, that was all. He could be with another woman already, even if it wasn't Croft's daughter.

The thought made her throat ache. She rubbed her nose, but the tears came anyway. She must find contentment. Without the contract, fighting phylloxera and rebuilding the vineyards would be her goal. It was all she'd ever wanted, was it not? It had to be enough.

Chapter 55

"Love is the poetry of the senses."
Honore de Balzac

"It is here, Henrique."

Julia halted the buggy at the valley's center. The viscount alighted first and offered his hand. She stared at it for a heartbeat before placing her palm over his leather gloves.

"I expected to find Mr. Maxwell here." He looked above her shoulders as if counting on his appearance. "Where is our English friend?"

Julia's heart twisted painfully. Where indeed? A question she had asked so many times. Just yesterday, at the First Light ruins, her neck had prickled as if he would climb the stairs and berate her for her imprudence.

"Probably back in Oporto."

He whistled, his eyes flashing. "I can't say I miss him."

His grin had an inquisitive quality, and she thought it prudent to take a step closer to Abelardo, who joined them after tying the reins. If the viscount had any designs in coming here other than checking the grafted vines, he would be disappointed.

She cleared her throat. "This way."

They walked along the staked lines. The rich red soil was so different from the schist of the hills. The vines were already three feet high, jutting out from the earth, occupying their places over the stakes, the branches decorated by delicate green buds.

Penafiel strolled around without uttering a word. Julia and Abelardo followed a few steps behind. Every time he saw a leaf through his magnifying glass, she held her breath, her stomach tied in knots. He kneeled on the ground and smelled the leaves of the sprouted vines. He collected a branch, inspecting it with his lenses. When he pulled a scrawny vine exposing the roots, Julia had to glance away.

After what felt like ages, he whirled around. Julia had to take a step back so as not to collide with him.

"And?" She wrung her hands.

He tilted his head to the side and squinted his eyes. "American vines, you say?"

She shuffled her weight back and forth. "What have you found?"

"Phylloxera lice are present both in the leaves and the roots of your grafted vines."

She sucked in a breath. "Do you mean they will die, like all the others?"

"All evidence points in the amazing direction that your grafted vines are immune to phylloxera."

"How?"

"The lice are on both roots and leaves, but they are not feeding on the plant, just like their behavior on the immune American rootstock." Laughing, the viscount rushed at her. He wrapped both hands around her waist and threw her in the air.

She grabbed his shoulders to steady herself and backed away. "Thank you for coming, Your Excellency."

By his pursed lips and crossed arms, he understood her unwillingness. Julia sighed. Even now, faced with this excellent news, the celebration without Griffin lacked flavor, tasteless like coarse wine.

She turned in a slow circle. The valley was an oasis of emerald sprouts budding in all directions. In sharp contrast, the terraced hills stared at them like an ancient amphitheater, gray and brown, as if locked forever in winter.

The viscount touched her shoulder, and she stifled the impulse to shrink away. "What is it?"

She pointed with her chin. "The terraces—"

"It will take at least two years to rebuild." He looked up from a branch he had collected. His head tilted sideways. "Are you up to it?"

Was she? Her shoulders slumped, and she crossed her arms over her chest. More than her body, her mind was tired, as if weighted down by all the dead vines.

"We will help her, Your Excellency." Abelardo caught her eye and nodded.

Chapter 56

"Wine is bottled poetry."
Robert Louis Stevenson

Through the floor-to-ceiling windows of Julia's study, the vineyards presented a picture of rebirth. She had chosen the school vineyard, the oldest in Vesuvio, to be the first to receive grafted vines. It would take time, but they would prevail. The vineyards would be safe, the contract was gone, and she could start selling wine with Vesuvio's mark soon.

But when her heart pulsed inside her chest, it clenched over emptiness.

Mechanically, she ambled to the book gathering dust on top of her desk. For the winter months, she had steered clear of it, refraining from walking too close or watching it for more than a few heartbeats. She knew most of Camões poems, and she had squelched her curiosity for so long.

Biting her lip, she stretched her hand to the tome. The first page was bare. No dedication and no sprawling arrogant handwriting letters. Her heart sank and tears blurred her vision.

She pushed the offending book aside, and it dropped to the floor with a thud. An envelope peeked out from between the pages. It must have slipped.

Brushing the tears away, she kneeled near the table's foot and ripped it open.

Julia,

I don't need Camões to tell me love burns,
I feel it consuming me every waking hour.
I don't need him saying it hurts,
I feel it in this place the poets call a heart.
I don't want him professing it is lonely,
I feel like the loneliest man alive.
If love wants to stay locked,
I confess I want to stay locked forever,
With you.

Ever since I left England, I have been drifting like a stray ship without port. You showed me the meaning of the word home.

Ever yours,
Griffin

All the emptiness left her as his words filled her with warmth. Griffin Maxwell had written her a poem. She laughed, tasting the salt of her tears. Who would have thought? Her Englishman was a romantic. Could he be waiting for her? Her heart latched on to hope like a vine to the stakes, wanting nothing more but to believe it. To embrace it. To flourish and nurture it.

Still, what guarantees could she have that he would love her?

The clock tolled the hours, and Wentworth brought the daily tray of port-filled glasses.

She swirled the liquid against the last sun rays. The color was rich, but a gravelly substance clung to the crystal, drawing designs on the glass. The wine hadn't been filtered. A vintage, then. She looked closer, trying to guess the year the producer had called it. Maybe 1843 or 1858. She brought it to her nose and smelled the roses and violet so clearly, as if she raced through a meadow surrounded by flowers. She brought it to her lips. The taste was so dark and intense it made her head swim. The body was heavy, coating her mouth with red fruit and nuts and vanilla and smoke and a hint of citrus? She let the divine liquid spread over her taste buds and swallowed it. Still, the wine lingered on her palate, the fig, the berries, the violets, ever-changing and moving.

She opened her eyes. Wentworth watched her intently.

"This is it. You found it. This is..." She closed her eyes. The flavors persisted, touching her very heart. "This is a soul wine." Julia drank more. Was the finishing real? It was there still, delicious and persistent.

She peeked at her faithful butler. She wanted to embrace the man, to cheer his promise fulfilled. But before she could say a word, he stood and straightened his coat.

Julia tilted her head. "How long have you known?"

"Long enough. What about you? Have you found yours?"

She stared at the view. The sky still showed all shades of blue, from pastel to indigo, but the hills and the forest were already in shadows. Just then, the sun vanished behind looming clouds above the horizon—orange and yellow hidden behind dark gray.

Julia glanced away, heart heavy. Could she risk everything? Would she survive losing him again or discover he had forgotten her and moved on?

"I don't know, Wentworth. I thought I did, but I'm—" Her voice faltered, and she tucked her face in her palms. "I am afraid."

The study was silent but for the muffled calling of birds getting ready for the night. A door creaked open somewhere in the house.

He touched her shoulder, and she stilled.

"The sun sets every day, regardless of what we do. It is up to us to glimpse this flashing moment and to register its beauty. Make it worthy and to elevate our souls. So I ask you, dear Julia, will you turn your face away? Or will you permit yourself to look?"

She dropped her hands, facing the expanse beyond, eyes wide. The sun had conquered the gray clouds, spraying golden spears of light upon the silvery water, the glorious rays exploding in all directions, the river reflecting the heavens above.

Julia allowed the sun's brilliance to burn away her doubts, her fears. Love was all that remained.

Chapter 57

"How much better is thy love than wine!" The Song of Solomon, 4:10

"The partnership is lost, but I will find another way to buy the house you deserve." Griffin glanced away from his mother's all-knowing eyes and gripped the ornamental railing.

The galleries atop the British Factory House's ballroom afforded an adequate view of the revelers, with the added advantage of staying away from the crust of guests. Gentlemen spun around with pastel-colored ladies on their arms—the black and white of their clothes contrasting with the tulles of the tulip-shaped gowns. Anne danced on Boyd's arm. Griffin raised a warning brow at his friend. Implied was the demand the Scotsman bring his sister back here after the waltz.

"Forget about it." She waved a silk-clad hand. "Don't you think it's time to go to your Portuguese lady? Why keep suffering like this?"

He closed his eyes. "I cannot expect Julia to forgive me."

"Forgive you? You saved her home."

"She thinks I betrayed her. She believes I caused her eviction from Vesuvio. How can she forget that? God knows you couldn't."

"Griffin, do us both a favor. Let us speak from our hearts. What are you implying?"

He closed his hands on the railing until his knuckles were white. "The portraits. I know you never hung another because you couldn't forgive Father for uprooting us from our home, from losing everything."

"That is why you want to buy me a bigger house?"

"When you feel proud of your home, you will want to start anew." His voice lost strength. Now that he had voiced his reasons, they rang overly simplistic and childish.

"Don't you see?" Her voice was ragged. "I never bought another portrait because your father and I collected them together. After . . . I could not bear to look at them. I loved your father so much."

"Even after what he did?"

"People make mistakes, Griffin. I never stopped loving him because of what he did. I only blamed him for not trusting me enough to help him." Her eyes shone with tears.

It was not his mother who had not forgiven his father. It was him—not only for the bankruptcy but for leaving them behind.

Griffin gazed at the couples below, the pastel shades blurring behind his watering vision.

His mother peeled his hand from the balustrade and kissed his palm. "Don't let her go, Griffin."

"I don't think she wants me anymore." His voice wavered, but a small flame ignited inside his chest. If his father's deeds could be forgiven, perhaps there was hope for him.

"I cannot believe that."

"She has Vesuvio, free from Croft, and now she can pursue her dreams. Apart from me."

Eyes twinkling, she smiled. "If that is so, why is she here?"

Griffin scanned the crowd. His mother must be mistaken. Of all the places, this would be the last she would come. He saw a flash of burgundy on the stairway. His vision hazed, and he had to lean over the railing for support. She wore wine red, her raven hair flowing like the wings of a black swan. She descended the steps to the ballroom—an exotic princess in a world of bland ladies. Everywhere she walked, people parted for her, whispering behind fans and cupped hands. Oblivious to their scrutiny, she moved regally, her hands trailing over the stair's railing, the elbow-length silk gloves so tempting he wanted to remove them with his teeth.

His heart threatened to cease pumping. His legs were rooted to the spot, deeper than a grapevine's.

"What are you waiting for? Go to her!"

His mother's words startled him, and he moved. Slowly at first, as if underwater, but then his strides gained intention. He needed to assure himself she was here and that she would not vanish back to the Douro.

They met in the center of the ballroom. A waltz involved them in poignant notes, but his eyes could only focus on her, on his Julia.

"Griffin." She breathed his name, and his heart took flight. "I came to—"

"Shh. Allow me this dance. I need to feel your body close to mine."

She poised her hand over his, and he circled her waist. He breathed, filling his lungs with her lemony scent, his first real breath since the bridge had broken them apart. Julia sighed, a deep, shuddering sigh, and he wondered if she too had lacked air without him.

Soft and sultry, the violins lifted them with soaring sounds. They whirled around and around, higher and higher, the sensuous notes suspending them above the floor. Griffin moved then, pressing her closer, cherishing her nearness, inhaling the flowers in her hair. God, how he had missed her scent.

The coda spiraled to a stop, and they drifted to the ground. She broke away and wandered to the window. Unable to stay apart, Griffin followed. They stood side by side in silence, gazing at the moonlit night where golden lamplight pooled on the sidewalk, illuminating the way for night strollers. A lucky few had their better halves hanging on their arms.

After a heavy sigh, she turned to him, wringing her hands, mouth pressed in a sad line. He stepped closer, but she placed cold fingertips over his lips.

"I came here to say you were wrong." Her voice was husky, as if she hadn't spoken for a long time.

Griffin caressed her cheek with the back of his hand. "How so?"

"You once told me soul wines were a silly romantic notion." She gave him a wobbly smile. "But you were mistaken. They are real."

"Are you sure?" To him, she was real in a way nothing else was, but if she needed to speak, he would listen.

"Yes." She sighed. "I found one."

His heart leaped against his ribs. "You did?"

"Yes. But you see..." Her eyes turned liquid, trembling in the candlelight. "I let him go. I shouldn't have sent him away."

His heart ached at the pain in her voice. "Julia, I—"

She cradled his face and gazed deep into his eyes. "You are my *Vinho d'Alma*, Griffin Maxwell. Will you let me keep you?"

Griffin groaned and embraced her. Nothing was between them, not anymore. Warmth invaded him in a rush. The tension ebbed from her shoulders, and she nuzzled into his chest, her hands intertwined at his neck. He wished they weren't in a crowded ballroom but standing high in the First Light ruins, alone and surrounded by her vines.

He forced himself to pull away and held her at arm's length. "You are not my soul wine."

"Oh, I hoped—"

Griffin nudged her chin until her ebony eyes met his. "Christ, Julia, I'm not sure what you are. You must be my mind wine, as you have ruled my thoughts since you fell from that megalith straight into my life. I'm positive you are my air wine because when you aren't with me, I can't breathe. You are my heart wine, for obvious reasons, and above all, Julia Costa, you are my home wine. All my life, I've searched for a place to call my own, and then I found you—my home." He released her shoulders and kissed the back of her hand. "Will you marry me?"

Because she was Julia, she laughed and cried and nodded all at once. "Yes."

For once, he was absurdly pleased with the monosyllabic reply and kissed her, right in the middle of the Factory House, conscious of many gasping females and curious gentlemen peering at them, but he didn't care. All that mattered to him was cradled in his arms, and he had no intention of ever letting her go.

Chapter 58

"Wine brings to light the hidden secrets of the soul, gives being to our hopes, bids the coward flight, drives dull care away, and teaches new means for the accomplishment of our wishes." Horace

Port wine and *Vinho Verde* flowed freely. After the wedding mass, they had come to Boa Vista, and Portuguese and English were mingling just fine. Summer hydrangeas decorated every corner. The soft notes of a *fado* floated from the music room.

Julia swayed in Griffin's arms, her feet floating above the ground as she let the dream became a reality in her heart.

"We should retire," Griffin said near her ear, his voice husky.

"But won't people talk?"

"Do you think I care? Any man with eyes in their heads would understand."

She chuckled and pressed closer, not minding there was no distance between them during the slow dance.

The brilliant summer day had turned into a fragrant evening, with the sky keeping the last rays of the sun, the clouds painted a beautiful orange and pink.

They danced, sharing the floor with friends and family, both Portuguese and English. Baron Forrester chatted with Griffin's Scottish friend and Mr. Edmond Blackwood. She caught the cartographer's eyes, and he raised his glass at her, his dark eyes twinkling. With Croft retiring from the British Factory, he was accepted again. Still, more often than not, he preferred to live at his Quinta.

Tony played with the other kids on the veranda and Julia caught his eyes, sending him a silent plea to keep away from the river.

"Let the boy have fun."

Julia sighed, tears coming to her eyes. Tony had brought the wedding rings to the altar, and after proudly delivering his treasure, had asked Griffin to take care of his *mamã*. Griffin had dropped to his knees and, after a tight hug, had pledged to take care of both forever.

Griffin's mother and sister sat with Mrs. Albuquerque and her daughter, their faces close together. Her new in-laws laughed and dabbed at their eyes with a linen kerchief from time to time.

"You did this."

She didn't need to ask what he meant. She knew—the British and the Portuguese together. "We did it."

When the waltz stopped, Griffin placed his hand on her lower back, steering her away from the parlor and into the garden. They strolled along the marbled stones covering the grass, their steps bringing them to a door covered by ivy.

"What is it?"

"Patience, Mrs. Maxwell."

It would take time to get used to her new name, but she would make the adjustment. It was important to Griffin, and he had already made many concessions, including being married by a Catholic priest.

He took her hand, bringing it to his warm lips. "Close your eyes."

When he guided her over the threshold, the scent of grapes caressed her cheeks, cool and fresh with the river breeze. Sounds of water murmuring nearby and the chirping of birds enveloped her with a lovely feeling of peace. A sweet melody rose in swirling cadence, no doubt a canary's song.

His voice tickled her ear. "You can look now."

Julia blinked her eyes open, turning in a slow circle. Grapevines were everywhere, decorating the iron arches and forming intricate designs. Clusters hung from the trellised ceiling like magical paper lanterns. The afternoon sun filtered through the grapes and painted the floor in pools of bright green and deep mauve. Julia touched the translucent leaves, marveling at the fantastic place hidden behind the covered walls of Quinta da Boa Vista.

"Do you like it?"

At the husky words spoken behind her, Julia shivered. "I don't know. I'll have to think about it."

He caught her by the waist and brought their mouths swiftly together. He tasted like port and Griffin. She would taste him and feel his strength and rely on his wisdom for the rest of her life.

"You once told me the only purpose of vines was to make wine." He released her and turned her around, his hands crossing over her middle. They looked at the vines spreading lazily, making beautiful designs, growing unfettered. "This is the true purpose of vines."

Epilogue

"Wine is life." Petronius

They escaped the work at the vineyards and climbed the First Light ruins. Julia was breathless but persisted on the stairs, reaching the crenelation. Griffin enveloped her in a warm embrace, hands clasped over her tummy, chin resting atop her head.

The view was one of change. Ox carts filled with grafted vine cuttings brought new life to the empty terraces. Most of the dead grapevines had been uprooted, and rebuilding the vineyards would take a long time.

Griffin had started growing American grapevines in Boa Vista. Soon they would help other farmers restore their lands.

"Baron Maxwell?"

"Hm?"

He was still uncomfortable with the title. His eyes would shift downward when a visitor called him that, but he deserved it. After the news of their assistance with phylloxera had traveled to Lisbon, the king had granted him the title.

"Why don't we invite your sister Anne to live here? She prefers going to hell than finishing school."

"You are right, of course." He nuzzled her neck. "Portuguese women are very wise."

Julia laughed. "You only say that because you have wicked intentions, Englishman."

He gasped and placed his hands over his heart. "With you?" He smiled crookedly. "Always."

He pulled her to their alcove. She feigned reluctance, planting her legs and yanking back. Gone were the days she came here by herself to escape the loneliness of her cold bedroom. Instead, this had become their own paradise with a view. In the corner, there were colorful plush pillows and sweet-smelling candles and soft coverlets. The jessamine, planted in a terracotta vase, was the perfect excuse to come here at night when the flowers bloomed. As if they needed any...

She let go of all restrictions and went eagerly. Griffin made quick work of her shirt and took his sweet time with her breeches.

"I love these."

Soon they were sated, and he propped a few pillows under his back as she rested her face over his heart. With her fingertips, she drew tiny leaves on the planes of his chest. It still surprised her to caress him at will, and she feared this happiness would somehow disappear.

As if sensing her sudden insecurity, he brought her closer. His hand sifted through her hair, massaging her scalp. “Tell me one of your stories.”

She wracked her brain for one she hadn’t told him. “Do you know our most accomplished prince descended from English royalty?”

“No.” He stilled the caresses.

“Philippa of Lancaster married the first king of Aviz. She had Plantagenet blood, the daughter of John of Gaunt.”

The muscles of his chest tensed. “And did they have children?”

“One of them, Prince Henry the Navigator, started Portugal’s age of discoveries.”

“Tell me more.”

“Hmm. He conquered Ceuta and founded the first university in Lisbon.”

“I want to know about the offspring.”

“Oh. I may be mistaken, but at least six survived infancy.”

He breathed a long sigh. “So Portuguese and English do mix.”

“What?”

“Never mind.”

She turned in his arms, facing him. “What are you talking about?”

He shrugged. “There are some notions that pervade the public mind that, you know....”

“Spill it, Englishman.”

He rolled his eyes. "It all started with King Charles and that Catarina de Braganza woman."

"What of it?"

He lifted his hands. "All right, all right. Border implied that Portuguese and English don't mix. The king died without issue, with no sons and especially no daughters to continue his line. I was worried. There, I said it."

"Why, Mr. Maxwell, you are worrying in vain."

"I beg your pardon?"

She took his hand and brought it to her midsection. It spanned the small mound easily. When she lifted her face, their eyes met, hers unwavering, his bewildered.

"Are you sure?" His other arm reached behind her, bringing her close.

"Yes."

The End

Please review The True Purpose of Vines. I will love to know your opinion, and you will help other readers decide if the novel is the right story for them. Thank you so much!

Join my Wine and Love Club for updates
on The Winemaker's series.
https://giovannasiniscalchi.com

Click here to claim my Gift for you, The Wedding
Surprise, book two in the Winemaker Series:
https://dl.bookfunnel.com/khuba4lsda

The winemaker series: Passionate and headstrong, the Portuguese will capture your heart in these sun-drenched novels set in the Douro Valley, Portugal.

Book 1: The True Purpose of Vines - Fly across the Atlantic for a sun-drenched adventure in the Douro Valley. A headstrong winemaker meets her match in an arrogant Englishman who threatens her lands. When the wine plague strikes her vineyards, they put differences aside to find a cure, blind tasting their way into an intoxicating passion.

Book 2: The Wedding Surprise - Be a part of Portugal's celebration of the year in this delightful novella packed with laughter and charm.

Edmond Blackwood, an overly rational Englishman, has to attend his superior's wedding. When a meddling godfather risks the ceremony, he must ally with Elise Rocha, a passionate Portuguese, to save the day. Can he put logic aside to embrace love?

Book 3: Shattered Innocence (coming soon): Don't miss the story of The True Purpose of Vines' beloved villain. The Count of Almoster, a cynical aristocrat, is enjoying a life of dissipation when Anne Maxwell, the naive sister of his rival, appears on his doorstep. Before he can recover from the dazzling vision, an accusation of regicide turns both into fugitives. To prove his innocence, Pedro leads the girl to a world of glamour and intrigue. When a conspiracy is revealed, he must find worth within himself before his true love is lost forever.

Dear reader, I hope you enjoyed *The True Purpose of Vines*. I absolutely love the Douro's scenery, people, and of course, port wine, and I hope you tasted a little of this amazing region through my scenes. The inspiration for the novel was a B&W photograph of a British gentleman and his Portuguese wife gracing the private museum of a beautiful wine property.

This romance between different cultures marked me, but research indicated my couple was the exception. These marriages were rare back in the nineteenth century and imagining the obstacles they faced helped shape the characters and the novel's plot.

Phylloxera was very real, and every piece of information about the "Nouvelle Maladie" is authentic. Nonetheless, the plague was not solved by Julia and Griffin but by French winemakers. I mentioned its impacts in Portugal and France, but it devastated every European producer, from Italy to Sweden to Spain. For the sake of the plot, the plague attacked vineyards between the years 1869 and 1870. The blitzkrieg invasion I showed was not how it happened. In reality, it was more protracted, extending from 1860 until 1890. Nowadays, except for a very few, all vineyards in Europe are grafted with American rootstock.

Julia Costa is inspired by Antonia Ferreira, the Ferreirinha, a prevalent figure in the region. She was the owner of Quinta do Vesuvio and several other Quintas. She worked hard to relieve workers' and winemakers' conditions during the plague, including constructing the stone wall around her lands.

Griffin Maxwell is inspired by John Fladgate, an associate at Taylor's. He traveled to France to understand more about the plague and later used his Quinta to conduct experiments on killing phylloxera. For his efforts, the King granted him a barony.

Quinta do Vesuvio is a real place, now owned by the Symington Family. Most settings in the novel are inspired by this magnificent property, open to the public for visitation. Whenever in Portugal, don't miss this excellent outing.

All wine information is accurate.

If you have never tried it, I recommend a chalice of port as the perfect accompaniment for chocolate desserts. Drink it iced! It is even better.

About Me

Stories are the very fabric of life. I want to transport readers to exotic settings, where they can find romance and happy endings and hopefully bring some back to their daily lives. Portugal brims with beauty and passion, and I research every tiny detail of my novels, hoping to make the reader treasure my grandparents' country as I do. I have a loving husband who still is my hero and two amazing kids. When it's cold and rainy, I run inside to read and watch movies under blankets, sipping wine. You can find me on the beach during summer, surfing with my family.

Made in the USA
Coppell, TX
02 August 2022